A Walk in a Darker Wood

An Oxygen Man Books production

A Walk in a Darker Wood
An Anthology of Folk Horror

Published by Oxygen Man Books

Edited by Duane Pesice, Sarah Walker, & Gordon B. White
Cover Art by Dan Sauer
Interior Art by Alan Sessler, Sarah Walker, & Kai Bryan
Interior Layout by Michael Adams

Special thanks to:
Typographer Mediengestaltung; creator of **Germania**, & ANRT; creator of **Fust & Schoeffer**, custom fonts used in this volume

Project Coordinated by Sarah Walker

ISBN: 978-1-7326839-7-6
ISBN 10: 1-7326839-7-2

All contents © 2020 the original authors

Table of Contents

Introduction by Sarah Walker, Scott Couturier, & Shayne Keen 7

Who Maketh Fertile the Fields by David Barker....15

Observations of a Black Toad by Phil Breach 33

The Silhouettes by D.L. Myers......................................39

Towards A Place Where Everything's Better by S.L. Edwards..43

Moonville by John H. Howard 55

Therein Lies a Tail by Duane Pesice 83

Rosaire, Master of Wolves by Manuel Arenas 89

Putting Down Roots by Russell Smeaton..................95

There Came the Sun by Ivan Zoric 103

Spring Leanings by Alan Sessler 121

Daughters of the Hare by K.A. Opperman 139

Morton's Woods by Jill Hand......................................143

The Scarlet Room by Adam Bolivar 155

Jack and the Magic Ham by Adam Bolivar............161

The Fork in the Road by Ashley Dioses................177

Table of Contents

Cat-o'-Lantern by K.A. Opperman 179

The King of Mudlings by Shayne Keen 183

The Willow Stand by Scott J. Couturier 193

GreenFingers by Sarah Walker 217

The Blackdamp by William Tea 229

The Untold History of the Grimorium by Maxwell I. Gold 267

The Mill District by Maquel A. Jacob 273

Fine and Fancy Arms by Gordon B. White 283

Her Dark Hymn by Hayley Arrington 301

Hyenas by Michael S. Walker 303

King O' the Wood by Can Wiggins 315

Jenny Green-teeth by Chelsea Arrington 339

Of Blood and Flowers by Chelsea Arrington 341

A Slow Remembered Tide by John Linwood Grant ... 351

Witch Woman by Hayley Arrington 365

Logan Mill Ranch　　　　　　Illustration by Sarah Walker

Come, Take a Walk in a Darker Wood with Me...

Introduction by Sarah Walker, Scott Couturier, & Shayne Keen

October 2020

The house I grew up in was an old silver mill from the 1800s. Smack in the middle of the Rocky Mountains forest and surrounded by pine tree's sweet scent, it was not unusual for my parents to tell me not to go to a certain area as a bear or cougar had been sighted, slinking around the area. We even had a party line phone which was a source of never-ending amusement to me as a child as I would stay on the line and join in my neighbor's conversation much to their annoyance.

Because the house had been the sorting place for a mine, there was an old one in our front yard. In fact, all around my father's property these old mines were scattered. Carved into the red and rocky soil, their black tunnel throats called me with a breath of cold wind rushing up from unknown depths. Their hidden lungs were secret and soiled.

I loved those dark places, and the stories my father and mother told me about their troll inhabitants. As I grew older, my love for the terrible grew. And grew. I found myself consuming everything that involved Horror from books to films to Crypt Keeper comic books bought from the local comic store for ten bucks a garbage bag full. These cheap bags of comics were a boon for a child of 10.

Luckily for me, they had gone out of style in the 80s and 90s, and no one else wanted that stuff anymore, instead vying for the new graphic novel template. I collected Halloween masks and candles, wore black clothes, and held seances, and despite this, no demon came to whisk me

Introduction

away. Soon I was an adult. And I began to wonder.

Why do humans enjoy scaring themselves? Where did the first horror story originate? So, I began to dig.

Humans, it would seem, have told scary stories since we crawled out of the muck or were plopped here by whatever humorless god that really controls this show.

From the first ghost story told by Pliny the Younger, a well-known Roman writer and Quaestor, to campfire tales reportedly invented sometime in the 1800s by North American homesteaders in order to keep the people watching over their camps awake, humans have loved to scare each other and themselves. The ancient Mesopotamians told even scarier tales, for to them, these ghosts were very real entities that could affect one's life negatively. In fact, the Mesopotamians had a belief that sickness could be caused by an unhappy spirit, normally a relative of the person who was sick.

In Mexico and Latin America, we see a similar set of ideas in the concept of Soul Sickness. One must step back a moment from the Eurocentric worldview many of us were raised with and understand that to the Native peoples of these locales, one's soul often has more than one part. These parts could even live outside the body and if one of those parts was lost or hurt, it could make you extremely sick. Usually, this soul loss is connected to a trickster spirit who has taken something of yours, a part of you. A 'shaman" is necessary to get that part back and bring back balance. To heal your illness, they would travel into the spirit realm for you and bring back your missing piece.

So, what have these ancient ideas to do with modern Horror, you ask? And Folk Horror in particular?

Well, to understand that we must understand why humans started this in the first place.

As a species we are not very tough. We do not have long retractable claws like cats, we do not have strong and sharp teeth like dogs. We are small, soft, and full of fat. We are like lost children in an Arctic night.

How in the hell did we survive the sometimes-vicious environment around us?

Our social nature, our ability to create culture, and our brainpower giving us the ability to pass on information is undoubtably what has saved us from extinction. In other words, teaching each other saved us.

Imagine living in the wild, a small band of humans around you. Food is not plentiful, nor entirely scarce, but one certainly cannot eat all day or be selfish if the group is to survive.

How can an adult possibly teach a child this? What does one tell a child who does not understand that we must save the last of food, ration it out, when they don't understand why they can't have the last of the apples, or acorns, or dried fish, because they are hungry. Oh, so very hungry.

You tell them a story instead.

You tell them about the Wendigo, a story told by the Algonquin, an Indigenous people of the American East Coast. In this tale, there is a tribe. One of the tribal members is a glutton. Each day when everyone goes out foraging and hunting, he does, too. And although he successfully hunts and finds food, he cannot help himself and always eats all of it, arriving back at the camp empty handed, lying to all the other members that he had no luck.

Over time the others in the tribe start to notice. Why doesn't this person lose weight when everyone else is on the verge of starvation? They are all thin as rails while he is getting fatter and fatter.

One day they secretly confer and agree something must be done. The leader says they should just leave him. Who wants to be in a tribe with someone who is so selfish? They shared their food with him, but he clearly did not do the same. So, one day while the glutton is out foraging, the rest of the camp picks up and leaves, abandoning him to the brutality of an East Coast's winter.

Introduction

When he finds himself alone, he is a bit nervous but after a moment, he shrugs. Screw those guys, I will take care of myself, he thinks as only an egocentric child would.

But he cannot. The days grow colder, darker. He hears things in the bushes following him, sniffing. Slowly, he becomes more and more desperate.

One day he is out trying to find *something, anything* to eat, and he cuts himself. He licks the wound to take away the burn. He realizes it tastes good as his stomach rumbles. He takes another lick. It is good.

Salty. And then something awakens inside him. He takes a little nibble, and another. Soon he has eaten his whole arm down to the bone.

But still, he remains hungry.

So, he eats his other arm, his own intestines, his own legs, and even his face.

But he can never get enough.

He begins to look for others to eat.

He has become a Wendigo.

Hearing that as a child would certainly have an effect. Don't be greedy, don't be a glutton, or you will end up like ol' boney in the tale.

Horror stories, it seems, were necessary for the survival of the human species.

We have never abandoned this knowledge. The folk horror of the 1960s and especially the 1970s warned people who became too "sure of themselves" and their absolute righteousness—rich, academic, intelligent people who "knew better" were bested by the rural practitioners of a form of nature worship that honors and appeases those spirits and forces that live in the old growth forest, that help bring the crops fruit, and always demand certain sacrifices…

Fast forward to the 21st century and we see a resurgence of Folk Horror in popular media. We have the movies *Midsomer*, *Hereditary*, and *The VVITCH*. All quite different takes on horror and what it might have to do with us, what lies beyond the thin sheen of "normal reality."

We are looking back to the old ways for guidance it would seem.

In *Midsomer*, we see a call back to films like *The Wicker Man*, what egocentrism, selfishness and greed do. These behaviors will not work for our social species. We must have team players amongst us, not liars, greedy people, or thieves.

In *Hereditary* again we are warned against selfish actions, of ignoring a child, of keeping secrets from the familial group.

These tales are warnings against behavior that is outside the group, behaviors detrimental to the group.

But you ask, what about Folk Horror where the forest is the monster? Where the people are killed, or harried, by supernatural forces or by nature itself? In Folk Horror, the supernatural is usually a very uncommon facet of nature that most people don't get to see.

There is a lesson hidden there, too. Despite our houses, our cars, and our sophistication, we are still at the mercy of nature. Despite our belief that we are above it, we are not. I just learned that when the Pacific Northwest had one of the worst fire seasons on record. It is strange to watch buildings, human creations that are supposed to keep us safe from it, devoured so readily by nature itself.

The most horrifying aspect of Folk Horror is the "folk." People being people, zealous and unafraid, sure of their authority over all they survey, who lead others to either a demise or crisis. These are people who disregard the rules of nature and of those who live with it and instead choose to conquer it, destroy, or live with it in a way that is out of sync with its desires and needs.

To me, the movie *The VVITCH* is a clear and direct warning, a reminder of what nature can and will do. It reminds us why so many are afraid of the natural world unbound, but so, too, why so many are willingly drawn into that wildness, a place closer to a home and cathedral than any square building, no matter how well adorned, could ever be. If Hell is, after all, other people, well we've probably always known that in one form or another.

Introduction

In many of these Folk Horror films we also see a deep fear of the feminine, the darkness of our fluctuating moods is evident in the way the Moon and the night is often tied to women in many cultures. There is a power in that Dark Mother, in Kali, the mother that gives life, but also destroys and tears and rends it apart without even a small nod to the suffering of her own children being trod underfoot. Because in that destruction lies the truth of existence—eat and you shall be eaten.

These scary tales show us that there are things beyond the scope of human control. There are still mysteries and secret hollows. There are animals whose eyes glitter in the dark of a forest night, creatures hidden in the waters where we swim unawares, and we best be sure that even if we do not see them, they most certainly can see us. So, be wary. Take care.

We are but children on this green planet that is millions of years old.

And somehow, we know this.

Somewhere deep in our collective unconscious we know…

Illustration by Sarah Walker

Who Maketh Fertile the Fields
by David Barker

Of all the jobs he had been assigned so far at Meshkent Abbey in Western Oregon, the one Brother Philip liked best was toiling in the vineyard. It was hard physical labor, no doubt about it, but he loved being outside, breathing the fresh air, smelling the rich aroma of the ripening grapes, and taking in the spectacular view of the Willamette Valley below. Fortunately, he worked in the fields mornings before it became too hot and spent his afternoons in the air-conditioned monastery library, performing routine clerical tasks. The library work was less invigorating, but it had its share of intellectual charms. He particularly enjoyed handling the more ancient volumes among the books that needed to be reshelved, noting the serious, sometimes cryptic titles imprinted on their spines, and—if his supervisor wasn't around— reading their title pages.

On that particular morning, Philip had been working alongside another novitiate, Brother Thomas, thinning out grape clusters on the lower terrace of the vineyard bordering the woods between the monastery land and the farmlands below. Part of the time they talked about day-to-day matters at the Abbey while other times they worked in silence, each lost in his own thoughts. Toward the end of their shift, apropos of nothing, Brother Thomas suddenly stopped what he was doing and asked, "Do you think there's any truth to what they say about the nunnery?"

Brother Philip drew a complete blank. He hadn't heard anything about a nunnery in the area. "What nunnery might that be, Brother Thomas?"

"Why, the ruins in the woods, right over there," Thomas answered, pointing at a nearby thicket of trees. "Surely you've seen it?"

Who Maketh Fertile the Fields

Brother Philip, in fact, had never noticed the derelict building standing in a state of near collapse not far from where they stood. It was buried just deeply enough in the woods to be largely obscured by the intervening trees, but now that he was staring at it, he was surprised that he hadn't previously seen the three-story structure.

"Well, I'll be. What do they say about it?"

A solemn expression came over Brother Thomas's face and his eyes grew wide. "All sorts of terrible things!"

"Such as what?"

"Well, for starters, that it's haunted! Allegedly there was a terrible murder committed there many years ago. It wasn't a regular nunnery, mind you. Rather, it was where they sent nuns from all over who had gotten themselves into trouble so to speak, to keep them in seclusion while they waited out their time, until they were ready to return to the monastic community."

"You mean *pregnant* nuns?" asked Brother Philip with a tone of skepticism that he soon realized Brother Thomas did not detect.

"Yes…*with child*." Brother Thomas whispered, blushing at the words.

"Well, it certainly happens, although I suspect it's a rare event."

"Well, they were from all over the country, after all. Anyway, rumor has it that one of the nuns didn't want to give up her infant for adoption after it was born, as was required. She ran off into the woods with it and hid. She managed to elude the search party that went out looking for her for five days. But by the time they finally found her, the baby had died from exposure, and she was mad with fear and starvation. They dragged her back to the nunnery and forced her to do acts of penance for a while, but in her heart she didn't repent. Instead, one night she brutally slaughtered Mother Superior, who she blamed for her child's death. Slit the woman's throat from ear to ear as she slept in her bed. Then she set fire to the nunnery, and all the sisters perished in the blaze. The nunnery was a total loss. Only the charred shell of the building remains."

David Barker

"That's quite a tale. And supposedly now the place is haunted as a result of this tragedy? But whose spirit is it that has not moved on? Is it Mother Superior, or the wicked nun, or her unfortunate child?"

"That part's not at all clear," said Brother Thomas. "Brethren who explored the ruins over the years claimed to have experienced unusual things: unexplained gusts of cold air, strange sounds like moans of pain or agonized weeping, fleeting shadows in empty rooms."

"Do you believe them, Thomas?"

"I don't know, Brother Philip."

"We could go inside and have a look for ourselves."

"Oh no! That would be courting trouble. There's no good that can come from stirring up unwholesome spirits. Best to mind one's own business and leave such things alone."

"True," agreed Brother Philip. "I suppose you're right." But glancing over at the abandoned structure, he felt an urge to not let the matter rest. Sooner or later, he expected he might enter the ruin and see for himself if it felt haunted.

⌘⌘⌘

Evenings after Compline, the monks retired to their individual cells. Brother Philip normally read for enjoyment or studied the scriptures for an hour before going to sleep, but that night his mind was unusually restless. Brother Thomas's story about the nunnery had captured his imagination. Questions flooded his thoughts. When did this tragedy occur? What was the name of the homicidal nun? What was the spiritual fate of her poor, innocent baby? It had died before it could be baptized; did that really mean its immortal soul was condemned to the eternal fires of Hell? Was the poor thing forever denied forgiveness for original sin, forever banished from Heaven or even Purgatory? What a terrible situation. That harsh judgment alone may have been enough to push the unfortunate sister over the edge into madness. Mother Superior telling the nun that her dead baby was already burning in Hell may have unleashed a bloodthirsty rage for revenge against the Church and its

Who Maketh Fertile the Fields

presiding authority figure, the Abbess. He had to find out the facts of the situation. He would do some furtive research in the monastery library during his next shift there. Perhaps some historical record of what had transpired at the nunnery survived within the extensive archives.

From the lone window of his small cell, Brother Philip could see the nearest edge of the vineyard, but not far enough down the hill to glimpse the woods containing the nunnery. He stood at the open window, his palms resting on the sill, inhaling the rich night breeze that flowed in from the hillside. It was pungent with the fragrance of many organic things: blossoming plants and flowers, the insect-teeming soil, still warm from the day's sun, the faint scents of animals of all sizes, from the smallest of rodents to the wild, predatory beasts of the night. And beyond all the natural smells, he distinctly detected something more elusive and fantastical: the essence of some spiritual entity that roamed the dark, devil-haunted land, searching for innocent souls to devour.

⌘⌘⌘

At the end of the chapter meeting, his workmaster, Brother Paul, told Brother Philip that he was needed in the bakery that morning to fill in for Brother Charles, who was in bed with a cold. Later that afternoon, he would work in the library, as usual.

"I'm happy to help out, but I'm afraid I know nothing about baking," warned Brother Philip.

"Not a problem," said Charles. "You'll be mixing and pouring batter. It's very repetitive work. No special skills are required. Brother Michael will instruct you on what to do."

Brother Philip quickly discovered that the bakery was a relaxed work environment, and Brother Michael was easy going and friendly.

"We're making fruitcakes today," said Brother Michael drolly. "Hundreds and hundreds of them. They're our bestsellers, after the wine." He wrote down a list of ingredients and the amounts for each and pinned it up above the table where Philip would be doing his mixing. "It's a foolproof system, really. Just use these amounts, dump them into a bowl, mix vigorously, and pour the batter into one of these trays and place it over there. Then it goes into the oven and *voilà*—fruitcake!"

Philip found Brother Michael quite approachable and gathered he'd been at the monastery a long time. If anyone there might know the truth about the rumored murder at the nunnery, it would be him. Taking a chance that he would not land in trouble for expressing interest in what could be viewed as a scandalous topic by his superiors, Philip asked Michael if he knew anything about the alleged killing.

"Oh, it's quite true. Happened in the early 1950s, if I recall. What was it you heard?"

Brother Philip repeated what Brother Thomas had told him.

"Yes. That pretty well sums it up. And did he tell you about the associated haunting?"

"Well, he mentioned it, but he didn't give it much credence. I think the occult aspects of a spirit or spirits haunting the ruins makes him very uneasy. I suggested we poke around in there, but he wanted nothing to do with it."

Brother Michael scanned the room to make sure none of the other monks were within earshot, then continued in a near whisper. "Probably wise, especially if he's overly sensitive to such things. But it doesn't seem to scare you any. If you're truly curious, and don't mind taking a certain risk, you can witness a most remarkable event that's scheduled to happen this weekend, by coincidence."

Brother Philip's ears perked up. "Pray tell," he uttered softly, looking around to make sure they were still alone in that part of the bakery.

"Saturday night, at midnight, a small group of monks are holding a secret gathering at the ruins of the nunnery, where they will perform an ancient chant that's been used every year at this time since the murder to call forth the spirit of Sister Angelina—the distraught nun who slew Reverend Mother for refusing to give her infant a Christian burial. They pay homage to her in the belief that she alone decides whether the vineyard's annual crop is a success or failure. It's a kind of fertility rite, if

Who Maketh Fertile the Fields

you can believe such a thing still exists in this modern age. You can conceal yourself in the woods a short distance from the nunnery and observe the ritual, but you must be extremely careful not to be detected. This band of heretics are highly jealous of keeping their forbidden pagan practices a secret from the elders, especially the Abbott. I don't even want to imagine to what extreme lengths they will go to protect the private nature of this heathen ritual. If you're caught, don't tell them I told you about it! I'll deny everything." Then, to end the conversation on a lighter note, Brother Michael winked as he plopped a large wooden mixing spoon into one of the batter-filled bowls.

⌘ ⌘ ⌘

During his afternoon work shift, Brother Philip spent a few minutes searching the library's card catalog for books about the history of the monastery. He found entries for three such volumes, and conveniently they were all located in a section where he happened to be doing some shelving anyway. A check of the indexes in these books produced no references to a murder at the nunnery. One book did have a few paragraphs on the nunnery's history, including the intriguing claim that it was "abandoned by the nuns after a devastating blaze in 1952," but there was no mention about these nuns having been sent there because they were pregnant, nor that a Sister Angelina's baby had died before it could be adopted, let alone the murder of a Mother Superior. He was about to write off both the killing story and the subsequent haunting as groundless hearsay when a slip of age-browned paper fell out of the back of the book. It was a letter-sized sheet with mimeographed lecture notes on one side. Printed at the top of the notes was the date "Spring semester, 1961." There was no indication of the professor's name, nor at what college the course was taught. He was about to drop it in the nearest waste basket when, on a whim, he flipped he it over and saw that the back of the sheet was covered with hand-written notes. The notes were unsigned, but apparently whoever wrote them had been doing research along the same lines that he was. There were several lines

David Barker

comprising a timeline of the nunnery, with entries such as "1890 ground floor built...1900 2nd and 3rd floors added...1920 first arrivals of sisters with child...1921 infant burial ground established," and below that a cryptic paragraph dealing with the formation of a group calling itself "The Sons of Angelina." Following that was a series of questions including, "Newspaper accounts of killing?" and "Are reported ghost sightings related to murder legend?" At the bottom of the sheet the final line read: "See Fr Moore booklet in Rare Book Room (Uncatalogued.)" "Fr" of course was an abbreviation for Father, a title for a priest. Brother Philip remembered having seen a small stack of books in the library office that had been placed there for eventual reshelving in the Rare Book Room. He went and fetched them, along with the keys to the glass cases, thinking as he walked to the Rare Book Room that he would be looking for a thin book by an author named Moore.

The Rare Book Room was separated from the open stacks of the main floor by a plate glass window, but its door was never locked, allowing patrons to enter and examine the books on display, all of which were kept under lock and key. The volumes stored there included incunabula (early printed works dating back to the 1450s), as well as medieval manuscripts. Had the booklet he was looking for been cataloged, he could have quickly retrieved it using its call number, for all the volumes in the glass-fronted shelves lining the walls were kept in call number order, but it wasn't, so instead he used a process of elimination to find it. First, he ruled out everything in the display cases occupying the center of the room, where the books lay face up and open. Those were all antiquarian items; a 1980s pamphlet would be completely out of place there. Size and thickness made it easy to rule out most of the other volumes lining the walls. The vast majority of these were large quarto or folio volumes bound in leather or vellum, invariably thicker than any pamphlet would be. That left only a handful of thinner books grouped at the end of a row of larger volumes dealing with Cults, Paganism, and Witchcraft. He unlocked the case containing these smaller items and began sorting through them. A minute later, he had the book he wanted.

Who Maketh Fertile the Fields

Titled *A Modest Oblation*, it was a 60-page tract published by a small press in 1987, housed in a protective pressboard binder, its author and title typewritten on a label glued to the cover. The moment he saw that the author was Father Moore, he knew he had found the object of his search.

Given their irreplaceable nature, the volumes in this room were not available for borrowing by the public, but monks were allowed to check them out using a sign-out sheet in the office. This policy allowed the monks to study these materials at their leisure. When he finished shelving the books he had brought, Brother Philip took the pamphlet and checked it out while returning the keys to the office.

⌘⌘⌘

The rest of the day dragged by slowly as Brother Philip anticipated studying the pamphlet in the privacy of his cell after the last antiphon to Our Lady had been sung at Compline. He had not looked at the text in the Rare Book Room, having only glanced at the title page. Once he dug into it, the booklet was not at all what he had expected. He had been picturing a standard nonfiction work—local history or journalism—but after reading a few pages, he realized it was some sort of imaginative literary work, perhaps an allegory. The style was more prose poetry than narrative exposition, with an abundance of lush language, evocative images, and complex symbolism, but no real factual information being revealed. Here and there interspersed among the prose pieces were short poems. He read one of them out loud, softly so as not to disturb his brethren in the neighboring cells.

"Oh Mesenet, goddess of childbirth, we beseech thy intercession; may the seed of Man produce the bounty of the Gods.

"Oh Renenutet, goddess of the harvest, who maketh fertile the fields, we implore thy intervention; may the vengeance of the Gods fall upon the Barren Mistress who condemned the cherished infant to the merciless pyre.

"Oh Sopdet, goddess of the life-bearing soil, we invoke thy visitation; may the spoiled fruit of the tomb nourish a flourishing vintage."

David Barker

He puzzled over this poem for several minutes, struggling to extract its meaning. He recognized the names from his readings in mythology; Mesenet, Renenutet, and Sopdet were ancient Egyptian fertility goddesses. Here they were apparently being called upon to produce a bountiful crop—presumably for the vineyard. But why would monks in a Christian monastery in the American Northwest, even rogue ones, be summoning ancient Egyptian deities of all things? Was this the work of some unorthodox friar who had traveled in Western Asia before coming to the monastery?

Furthermore, he began to see that each of the lines seemed to relate to one or another aspect of the rumor of a pregnant nun having murdered the Mother Superior. The line about Mesenet could be about Sister Angelina becoming pregnant, and the spiritual value of the resulting child. The Renenutet verse likely had to do with Sister Angelina seeking retribution for her deceased baby being denied burial in consecrated ground, if "Barren Mistress" could be interpreted as representing the virginal Mother Superior. Lastly, the line about Sopdet implied that the corpse of the infant buried behind the nunnery somehow provided sustenance for the vines that he and other monks had been tending all season, and every season since the tragedy occurred. After all these years, that nourishment must have been more symbolic or metaphysical than physical, the remains of the poor infant having long since fully decayed and dissipated.

⌘⌘⌘

The next morning Brother Philip and Brother Thomas spent a couple of hours repairing trellises in the vineyard's lower field. It was already a warm day when they started, the sun growing increasingly hotter as it climbed in the sky, and soon they were both drenched in sweat.

"Time for a break," groaned Thomas, rubbing the small of his back in an exaggerated display of exhaustion. Philip took a swallow of water from the bottle he had been carrying and handed it to Thomas. They

Who Maketh Fertile the Fields

had worked their way to the end of a row. The shady woods stood a short distance away.

"What do you say we go sit down on those rocks by the nunnery?" suggested Brother Philip. "It looks nice and cool in the shade over there."

An expression of abject terror swept over Thomas' face. "Absolutely not!"

"Why not? Still worried about those ghosts?"

"It's not that—well, yes, I do indeed fear unholy spirits—but aside from that, lately, I've had the most unsettling thoughts about those woods —they're so *dark*—and the…well, the abandoned nunnery. It's creepy!"

"Unsettling thoughts? What kind of thoughts?"

"Oh, I don't know," mumbled Thomas. "Nothing very specific. Just an uncanny feeling whenever I think about that building and the terrible things they say happened there. That perhaps *still* happen there."

"Hmmm," grunted Brother Philip. "You think maybe something bad will happen if you enter the ruins?"

"That's how it feels."

"Well, what if we were to stay outside the nunnery, just sit on the rocks in the shade?"

"No. That's still too close. I don't want to be anywhere near that place."

Brother Philip had a fleeting impulse to tell Brother Thomas about the secret gathering that was scheduled to be held there on Saturday night, which was tomorrow, then thought better of it. Why torment the poor guy? There was no way Thomas could muster up the courage to observe the ceremony as Philip planned to do, hidden in the woods.

"Okay, suit yourself, Tom. Now if you'll excuse me, I'm going to go sit in the shade for fifteen minutes. It's too damned hot out here for me."

"I'll be fine right here," assured Thomas, trying his best to sound confident.

David Barker

Brother Philip walked through the fringe of unplanted soil separating the vines from the edge of the woods with the odd feeling as he did so that he was leaving the known, familiar world of the monastery and its tightknit community and entering a strange, isolated realm of mysterious natural forces, nonhuman consciousnesses, and unfathomable otherworldly concepts where he felt very much alone. Approaching the weathered structure, he saw it was in rougher condition than he expected. Any trace of paint that had survived the fire had long ago been eroded from the blackened boards by decades of wind and rain. The majority of the window frames lacked their glass panes. The front door stood open, its knob missing. Peering inside, the staircase occupying the center of the parlor was in the process of collapsing. He found a wide flat spot on the boulders by the door and sat down. Looking back to where he had just come from, Brother Thomas was crouching in a row of vines, staring at Philip with obvious envy at his daring and courage. Philip was struck with how timid and vulnerable Thomas looked. Thomas was several years younger than Philip, as well as being shorter and with a slighter build. If a group of monks were picking players for a game of football, Thomas would be the last one chosen—no doubt about that. He looked like a guy who was bullied a lot as a kid. Always looking over his shoulder to see who might be coming for him. Seeing Thomas from this perspective—alone, ill at ease, fearful—Brother Philip was genuinely concerned for him.

⌘⌘⌘

Saturday was a typical day for the monks, with two work sessions and several periods of prayer, chanting, and singing. At dinner that day each monk was allowed a second glass of wine. Normally they were limited to a single glass, but in anticipation of this season's coming harvest, which was beginning to look like a promising one, the Abbott ordered several bottles of their finest vintage to be opened. Brother Philip quickly consumed his first glass and then slowed down so as to fully savor the second glass one sip at a time between bites of the delicious pot roast that

Who Maketh Fertile the Fields

Brother Timothy had prepared. Holding the rich fluid in his mouth for a long moment allowed him to appreciate all its charms and character. He pictured the Sun radiating down life-giving rays upon the leaves of the grape plant, perceived the minerals in the soil surrounding the vines' roots, tasted remnants of the gentle spring rain that had fallen and slowly dried upon the grape skins. There was something truly holy about the wine they made at the monastery, a life-sustaining energy that mystically connected the natural world with its plants and creatures to the astronomical bodies that moved in concert with the Earth: the Sun, Moon, and stars.

And, perhaps, mused Brother Philip, one other presence could be detected in the wine, which, when he considered it, was more like holy blood than profane water. There was an essence there, a remnant. The remains of something. Or was it a *revenant*—the ghost of someone who had once lived on the land where the grapes had grown? Was the wine itself haunted?

⌘⌘⌘

From his desk by the window Brother Philip had kept watch all evening for signs of activity in the field behind the monastery. Had he seen anyone walking away from the dorms in the direction of the nunnery, he would have given up his plan of positioning himself in the woods where he could observe the secret ceremony unnoticed, but there had been no one out there. The crickets began chirping a little before 9 o'clock, and by 10 their collective song was a powerful, rhythmic chorus resonating under the bright wash of the full moon. He decided that if no one had appeared in the field by 11 o'clock he would go downstairs and make his way across the hilltop to the edge of the vineyard and then down to the lower field and into the woods. He didn't want to leave his cell any later than that, fearing the chances of being seen by one or more of the participants was too great during the last hour before the event was scheduled to begin. Standing at the open window as he made ready to leave, Brother Philip felt a thrill of danger mixed with excitement as the cool night wind flowed under his shirt and across his ribs. Thinking he might need it in an emergency, he took a small battery-powered flashlight from his desk and placed it in his pocket. At 10:55 he quietly opened the door to his cell and went down the hallway past the doors of several other monks until he reached the stairwell at the end of the hall. Exiting the dormitory on the ground floor, he was surprised to see the silhouette of Brother Charles, who was standing in a dark courtyard about twenty feet to his left, enjoying a cigarette with his back turned to Philip. While the unexpected presence of another monk outside the dorm at that hour momentarily alarmed Philip, he decided it really wasn't a problem because he was able to walk quietly all the way to the extremity of the lower field without being noticed by Charles, who never did turn around to face him. Once Charles was out of sight, Philip breathed more easily. He saw nobody else and, as far as he knew, entered the dark woods unseen by anyone.

The spot Brother Philip chose to hide in was a particularly dense cluster of trees located twenty feet from the ruins of the nunnery, to the left of the front door. From there he had a view of both the nunnery entrance and the infant burial ground behind the building where row after row of tiny headstones receded into the woods: graves representing the final resting place of the myriad infants who had perished before they could be baptized and cleansed of their original sin.

Brother Philip had expected that his wait for the secret ceremony to begin would be a long and tedious one, but in actuality, it was worse than he had imagined. After what seemed like ten minutes, he looked at his wristwatch and was dismayed to see that only five minutes had elapsed. Another long while passed and it became ten minutes. The walk there from the dorms had taken him about five minutes, so he still had three quarters of an hour until midnight. He mulled over the possible reasons why Brother Michael had informed him of the event earlier that week. Was it simply because Michael wanted to brag about being privy to clandestine doings at the monastery, or was it a more calculated move on his part, a ploy to lure Brother Philip into joining the band of heretical

Who Maketh Fertile the Fields

monks? He also wondered if Brother Michael himself would show up that night, as a member of the group. As Brother Philip mentally worked through the complexities of such a manipulative maneuver by Brother Michael, his thoughts were interrupted by a sudden awareness of a low, musical sound approaching from the direction of the dormitory. After a few seconds he identified it as being many human voices, all chanting the same psalm or hymn. That could mean only one thing; the monks were arriving. A few seconds later a black shape appeared at the crest of the hill: the cowl-obscured head of the lead monk. The dark form soon grew to become a head and torso, with other black-clad heads and torsos lined up and moving behind it, following the lead monk. Just as suddenly they became complete figures, solemnly marching in a column toward the nunnery. The black robes worn by these men were unfamiliar to Philip, being considerably darker than the brown cassocks normally worn by the brethren. As the monks came closer, their chanting became clearer, but it was in Latin, and Philip only understood a few of the words, his knowledge of that ancient language being quite rudimentary. Reaching the nunnery, the still-chanting monks fanned out in a semi-circle until they were all positioned in an orderly fashion around the open door. When the last monk took his place on one end of the semi-circle, the chanting abruptly stopped, resulting in sudden near silence, with the sole remaining sound being the steady, rhythmic singing of the unseen crickets—the only witnesses to the ceremony besides Brother Philip.

⌘⌘⌘

Days later, still shaken by the terror and madness that characterized that night, Brother Philip's memories of the last few moments of the ritual were extremely chaotic and fragmentary. The assembled monks had stood silently for no more than a minute before one of them, the presumptive leader, stepped forward and turned to address his brothers. Unlike the chant which they had performed during their march there, the leader's address was in English, and although it may have been his imagination playing tricks on him, Brother Philip thought that some of what the man said sounded familiar. Upon deeper reflection, he realized the leader had quoted some lines of verse from Father Moore's esoteric pamphlet, those being the first lines Philip had read on the day he borrowed the pamphlet, which were an invocation to three fertility goddesses who had been worshipped in ancient Egypt. He couldn't be sure at that distance, but the leader looked and sounded like Brother Michael, confirming Philip's suspicion that he had been intentionally lured there. That much formed a clear, continuous scene in his memory. But then things so bizarre and unexpected occurred that in retrospect Philip was never sure if some of them had actually happened or if he had fantasized them. As the leader continued his speech dealing with sacrificial death and magical rebirth, an eerie luminosity formed above one of the headstones in the infant graveyard off to the speaker's side. At first this vaporous cloud of light was faint and amorphous, but with the passing moments it began to glow more brightly and to take on a definite shape: that of a naked, newborn infant. The infant was suspended in mid-air above the tombstone, head up, with its arms extended to either side. A crown of thorns ringed the child's head. Then, from nowhere, a shower of fresh flowers rained down upon the floating baby until the grave below was buried in white blossoms. This apparition was so startling that Brother Philip remembered being entirely mesmerized by it and unable to look away. Was this phenomenon real, he later asked himself, or was it a waking dream, a weird hallucination induced by the suggestive furtiveness of the secret ritual?

When he was finally able to turn and face the speaker again, a second shocking sight met his eyes: two previously unseen monks who had been lurking inside the abandoned nunnery—apparently since before Philip had arrived—now stepped out of the shadowy interior of the ruins and entered the moonlight behind the speaker. Brother Philip instantly comprehended that they might have seen him entering the woods; he wasn't as safe there as he had thought. Each of these newly revealed monks clutched a guttering candle in one hand and with his other hand dragged along a third monk who was held between them as

Who Maketh Fertile the Fields

their unwilling prisoner. That he was, in fact, a prisoner was abundantly clear to Philip; the man's hands were tied behind him and his eyes were tightly blindfolded. The captive was dressed in the standard brown cassock of a novice. The horror of this third monk's perilous situation was rendered all the more shocking by the fact that Brother Philip immediately recognized the unfortunate man despite his eyes being covered. He was none other than Philip's only real friend at the monastery, the timid Brother Thomas. At that point Brother Michael ended his recitation and stepped aside, making way for the two monks to drag Brother Thomas over to the cluster of small boulders where Philip had rested on that hot morning earlier in the week. Although he had been oblivious to it before, Philip now realized that the grouping of stones was not a random outcropping of rock, but in fact formed a primitive altar, such as would be used to perform a ritual sacrifice of an animal or person. The ruddy coloration of the stones' upper surfaces was nothing less than the weathered residue of dried blood from victims who had been put to death there in rituals past. An awful sound reached Brother Philip's ears: the muffled screams of Brother Thomas as he futilely struggled against his would-be killers. Using ropes, they tied Brother Thomas in a supine position to the altar, then stepped away. Without delay a new, more somber chant arose from the assembled monks. This song, Brother Philip instinctively knew, was an invocation to the goddess.

As if summonsed by the chanting, a crimson glow arose within the ruins of the nunnery, faint at first but rapidly growing in intensity. Then Philip saw the uncanny figure of a beautiful woman draped in white, not walking but floating out of the center of the mysterious luminescence. Her blue eyes shined like Lapis Lazuli, and her open hands were raised to the full Moon as the two monks from the ruins pulled out their silvery knives and fell upon Brother Thomas like ravenous jackals.

The only thing Brother Philip clearly remembered following that awful vision of his friend being slaughtered was his own frenzied escape into the depths of the dark woods, certain that he was being pursued by several of the attending heretical monks. In stark terror for his own survival, Brother Philip frantically fought his way through the dense foliage, certain that his only hope of not being captured was if he could reach the open farmlands below before the monks could catch him. The further downhill he went, the better his chances of escape. At one point, sensing that he had probably succeeded in outrunning them, Philip used his flashlight to make his way through a patch of particularly dense undergrowth. Finally, after what seemed like a dreadfully prolonged period of extreme danger, he emerged from the woods, stumbling exhaustedly into a field of corn stalks where he felt relatively safe from capture. From there, Brother Philip reached a two-lane country road which he followed to the nearby small town of Tusk, where he ultimately found sanctuary.

Brother Philip never returned to the monastery, never contacted the Abbott to explain his sudden departure. Nor did the Abbott ever suspect what had happened to Brother Thomas or Brother Philip, both of whom had suddenly left the monastery that night; they had been such promising novices, thought the Abbott. It was reported that the monastery enjoyed an abundant grape harvest that year; some saying it excelled that of any other year in recent memory.

Illustration by Sarah Walker

Observations of a Black Toad
by Phil Breach

At my will, my warty hide expresses
a milk-pale toxin precious to my master,
who picks me up and licks me, front to back,
tongue tip a-tease at every noxious sac.
Nightshade-faced, his straining heart beats faster,
as the leafy dell about us effloresces.

Perched now 'pon a rock, I watch him spree,
slicked with slimes and naked in the glade.
These nymphs he dallies with, leaf-green and lithe,
dilate their lobed stomata as they writhe,
and spray their saps o'er leaf and twig and blade.
My master, 'midst their tendrils, giggles glee.

Think not, to make mere lusting play he swives.
There is a keener purpose to this fling;
to lure a scamp of base, unwholesome stripe.
To enter it, and strip it of its tripe,
leaving wrack and wreck inside the thing,
then to carve a cruel departure with his knives.

Observations of a Black Toad

The very matter of the dell begins to waver
'neath the gimlet of my stern, batrachian eye.
Planes churn and warp, and angles fold and flutter.
Reality's lineaments melt like butter.
I sling my tongue and snag a passing fly,
then settle down, for there is much to savour.

I watch as, in a corner of the dell,
the Real crimps to a sphincter, dense and knotted.
It forthwith begins to spasm, then dilates;
with pus and ichor welling, gurgitates
a flood of rank corruption, sweet and rotted,
and births a caul-wrapped imp heaved up from Hell.

Baited by the stink of sap and seed,
the scamp within the caul begins to squirm,
then bucks and jerks until the membrane tears
with a gush of filth and foul, mephitic airs.
From the ruptured sac, a wriggling worm
swims out amidst the muck to slake its greed.

My master, Myles Marchpane; cunning fellow,
herbalist, and mage of fell renown,
swift dresses, takes up his tools-of-trade
- his speculum, and shears, and lancet blade -
then embarks to bring the hapless demon down,
and cause the thing to scream and yelp and bellow.

Phil Breach

Along the worm clawed, spindle limbs burst free.
From vermic rind erupts a hornéd head,
its single eye a green, acidic pool.
It spreads a maw all strung with sizzling drool.
Master Myles, he'll drop this demon dead.
He spell-spits, shrinking down to less than flea.

No. Not shrinks. There is no diminution.
He treads instead upon concealed directions
that lead him down the whenth and width of Time.
Through tortured angles fouled with fractal slime,
he stalks the imp to make his vivisections,
then to duly make a puissant execution.

I know his ways; he casts the Gate of Janus
to open up a tesseractic gate.
He enters from the low Etheric Plane,
and thus, from penetralia to brain
he'll harvest; pluck and excise and eviscerate,
then make a harsh egression through the anus.

Wherefore this toil? This enteric travail?
Because a cleric, unholy of profession,
hunts my master with a hatesome zeal.
Many witches have been broken 'pon his wheel,
have met his pincers prior to confession.
And so, Myles needs must milk this demon's chyle.

Observations of a Black Toad

And with its chyle, and lengths of tract, and tripes,
an homunculus he'll make, in his own guise;
a living trap to draw the churchman in.
To capture him, relieve him of his skin,
and set fires in the pits of both his eyes.
This is why he creeps the demon's pipes.

My master's at his work; the howling starts.
Poor scamp. Forsooth, its torture shall be long.
Then, at its screeching peak of ruination,
'pon a sudden, in its throes there comes cessation.
Methinks, mayhap, my toxin was too strong.
Methinks my master's failing in his arts.

O woe. How tragic. Something's gone awry.
He's lost; precisely where cannot be gleaned.
Poor Myles strayed Beyond the Bowels We Know,
unto a place this toad cares not to go.
A hazard, 'tis, when one invades a fiend.
I regard the broken imp and gulp a fly.

Illustration by Sarah Walker

The Silhouettes
by D.L. Myers

It was on a lonely ramble through unfamiliar tracts that I came upon the tangled path between two steep, conifer-crowded hills. The trees arched crookedly above the trail casting deep shadows that swallowed the way forward in a gloom my eyes could not fathom. A faint breeze, on which the salt tang of the sea rode, issued from the tenebrous path, and I was drawn to that distant water and the mystery of where that path might lead. I approached the darkness and stepped into that vast umbra. What seemed impenetrable blackness under the midmorning sun became a deep, moss-green world under the trees. The path stretched narrowly into the distance dodging its way round gnarled roots and clumps of dark brush that swayed in a languid dance. The thickly forested hills rose sharply to either side until they were lost in mist and shadow, and it seemed to me perhaps something other than the mist swirled in that dimness. When my gaze returned to the path, I saw that ahead the light was brightening, and soon the hills parted to reveal a muddy beach that sloped down to fog-bound water.

How long it was before I fled that place, I cannot say. I stood upon that beach and watched the fog lift to reveal a small island high and green and then the sun emerged, and the blue sky returned. Next moment, a gelid wind assaulted me that seemed to come from all directions as I turned trying to avoid its icy breath, and when again I faced the island it had changed utterly. Where before it had been covered by a dark, green verdure, now all was black silhouette, as if the sun had fled and twilight had descended. Yet the sun still blazed in a bright, blue sky.

The Silhouettes

A cold terror froze me to the spot, as I saw the blackness spread to the water and then the beach. I believe it followed me as I ran up that trail, but I cannot be sure. I only remember flashes before I found myself back at the inn by the mill.

It is the silhouettes. The silhouettes haunt me still.

Illustration by Alan Sessler

Towards A Place Where Everything's Better
by S.L. Edwards

When you first come home you think mom is having a panic attack. Her canvases are scattered across the white floor, her heavy, almost-screaming breathing bouncing off walls which seem to contract and expand as if part of her own heaving lungs. Her trembling fingers are in her hair, furiously twisting like meaty spider legs through a dark, thick web.

You came with mom to White Rock Lake because she needs you, because when you offered to go with dad, he told you, maybe coldly and maybe bitterly, "*Your mother needs you more.*"

This will be mom's third panic attack this month. You left the house in Richardson three weeks ago, because it reminded you and everyone else of the explosive fights, the permeating misery that worked its way from the framework of your parents' miscarried marriage and into the sinking architecture of the settling house. Dad went north, back towards Sherman and closer to his rural roots. Mom went south, towards the pulsing, sleek heart of Downtown Dallas.

Mom thought that White Rock Lake would be calming. The whole world was green in the summer. There were neatly paved trails to hike, a dock not far from the two-bedroom apartment where you could fish alone. A slice of isolation and rural life resting close enough to see Downtown Dallas across the other side of the Lake. And you both thought at the time, mom would have all the time in the world to work on her art.

Now she is *surrounded* by it. Watercolors of pink-red sunsets, swirling brown-and-blues of waiting winter forests, crumbled around and underneath her.

Towards A Place Where Everything's Better

You move your hands towards her spasmodic fingers. They're so rigid, so hard, thin muscles locked as if they're made of solid bone. Mom yelps, but you tell her you're there. You hum, the same song she once hummed for you during your nightmares.

Her breathing slows. Her crying stops. The song reaches her, wherever she is. Soon she's leaning against you, letting you rock her in your arms.

"I saw something."

Her voice is tired, listless.

"What'd you see?" you ask her, as calmly as you would ask her if she were your own frightened child.

"I don't know," she responds, somehow farther away now in her calm than in her panic. "But it had horns."

At night you call dad.

You don't want to admit it, maybe he doesn't either, but he *hurt* you. You miss him, you want to see him, but he's right. Mom needs you more.

"Hey, baby girl," he says when he picks up. You smile, because his accent is coming back.

"You sound like grandpa," you joke, making your own attempt at an East Texas drawl.

Dad laughs. He tells you that he spent most of the day with grandpa, on his farm in Dennison. Lifting hay, feeding cows. You used to love going to grandpa's farm, but you're fourteen now. You don't want to be away too long from Wi-Fi, from your friends and any small opportunity to grow up. Puberty hurts. They told you it would hurt, but you didn't know how much.

Sometimes you wonder if you're the reason they split up. When you started growing and hurting, the rotting thing in the foundation of your parents' marriage began spreading. You don't know exactly why they split, but you believe whatever was ruining your parents' marriage was born years before you were. You try to find comfort in that, but somehow can't.

S.L. Edwards

"How are you?" he asks.

You tell him about the lake, how calm it is in the summer. You tell him that you're taking the DART down to Deep Ellum, that you've found a good bookstore tucked between the brown-bricked barbecues and bars.

"How's Mark?" he asks, teasingly.

You growl. Mark sucks, you tell him. He went on vacation without telling you and is probably spending all his time on the beach.

"Dump his ass."

You laugh. You might, you tell dad. You might.

For a moment, the levity lingers, but you know dad can't help himself.

"How's your mother?"

What do you tell him? What's he entitled to know? If he cared, why couldn't he stay?

"Sara?" he asks.

"She's *mom*, okay?"

"What does that mean, honey?"

It means that she saw a monster in the woods today. It means that she's hallucinating now. That soon she'll start seeing faces in the mirrors that aren't her own. It means more night terrors, more of you being the parent and her the child. It means you won't be fourteen much longer or ever again.

"It means she's *fine*!" you hiss.

For a long time, dad doesn't say anything back.

"You know you can call me any time. Right?"

"Yeah."

"I can come get you if you need me to."

"Mom 'needs me more than you do,'" you hurl back at him.

You feel his hurt in his silence. You revel in it.

"I love you, honey."

Towards A Place Where Everything's Better

"You, too."

⌘⌘⌘

Your phone jostles heavily in your pocket. Mark hasn't called you all day, hasn't responded to your texts. Brittany texted you should be worried because all the girls in Miami are 'easy' and your stomach has been upset ever since.

You left the apartment early when the sun was just starting to come up. You don't want to play a sport, too much drama and too much ego bound up in it, but you like running. The floaty way the endorphins make you feel after you cross the fifth or sixth mile, breaking your limits and letting your legs hum and buzz the day after.

The summer morning breeze is cool and humid, carrying the leaves and heat along in blue-purple currents. The birds start singing early, calling and whooping above the soft sound of your soles slapping the ground. Somewhere a boat motor whirrs, and you briefly think about fish smell and the taste of battered fries.

You come to a long pedestrian bridge, steel and concrete neatly crossing the water. You've crossed this long bridge plenty of times before, never with any thought or concern. But today you cross, and it feels colder. You think of inexplicably vaulting over the handrails, of falling to the water and being dragged down by some iron-wristed monster below.

There's a shadow at the end of the bridge. Waiting for you. It's tall and it's broad, vaguely man shaped.

You don't scream before it's gone, taking your sense of fear with it.

You stop.

Around you, the world is quiet. The birds still singing. The sun still rising.

There's no shadow at the end of the bridge. No danger of falling over the safety rails.

You start again, running away as long as you can.

⌘⌘⌘

S.L. Edwards

Mom's up when you get home.

She flits around the apartment kitchen, furiously chopping potatoes and onions while oil sizzles in the pan. Sunlight starts setting in through the window blinds, a calm yellow orange of the world before noon.

"How are you feeling?" she tenderly asks.

This was mom. Mom, who you know who would do anything for you, who would work to where you were as safe and happy as you could be.

When she could.

"I'm good. Went seven miles today."

"*Goodness*, honey."

This was mom, who put emphasis on simple words to inject a sense of profundity and humor into them. Who cut up potatoes, onions, ham and tomatoes before adding eggs to the pan.

Mom has a habit of making normal things better, or at least trying to. Beginning somewhere familiar and ending somewhere unexpected. "Denver Breakfast Tacos," "Orange-Lemonade Popsicles."

She slides a plate in front of you because this is mom. Who only talks about her hurt when she is hurting.

"How are you?" you ask, though you know it's in vain.

She doesn't even spare a second of silence before she responds.

"Oh, I'm fine."

And that's it.

Over breakfast she asks you what you are going to do today. If you have any plans. You're gonna nap, that comes first. But all your friends are gone, so maybe some fishing.

What about her?

Here she struggles, unable to effortlessly shrug off the question like she did before. You know mom has several commissions, some from private collectors and other from small businesses who need artwork for

47

Towards A Place Where Everything's Better

their logos or lobbies. You know she has two gears, which you've started privately thinking to yourself of as "furious" and "fatalist."

It would be hard, difficult to push forward by yourselves if her summer commissions dried up because she found it too hard to get out of bed.

"Work, I guess," she replies with the first draft of depression breezing into her voice.

You don't push any further. You don't have the energy.

But mom doesn't work, not on her commissions.

When you come back from Deep Ellum you find her furious, paint brushes moving so quickly across the canvas that she seems to have eight arms, not two. The newspaper on the floor is splattered with blacks, reds and blues and the window blinds are drawn so that the whole world seems dim. You open your mouth to ask mom how she can see when you see the canvas.

The face she's painting isn't human. It's long and narrow like a vertical oval with slit nostrils and a wide grin full of flat yellow teeth. Eyes impossibly large, black hair on all sides like a lion's mane.

Mom's face is contorted and strained, but in the dark, you can't tell if it's in fear or rage. She slashes, grunting and heaving her shoulders with each stroke.

You whisper for her, but she is far away. Too far for you now.

You leave the apartment for an evening walk.

You can't stand to be around her when she's like this.

The sky is purple blue again, but now the color only makes you sadder. You go along the trails and reach for your phone. Mark hasn't responded to any of your texts and you can't help but be angry at how unkind he is. You burn in rage, and finally send him a text:

"You're inconsiderate. Find someone who will deal with it. Goodbye."

S.L. Edwards

The phone feels lighter when you thrust it in your pocket, but it immediately begins buzzing. You scream.

And something in the woods screams back.

Was it a bird? A cat? No, because whatever it was it almost sounded like it was *laughing*.

You're alone. You're alone and now all the trees are black. The stars are coming out and the moon is beginning to shine. You wait for the sound again.

But there's nothing. Only the buzzing of your phone.

You give up on the quiet, give up on the peace because no one is ever going to let you have it.

You storm back into the apartment, now lit up.

Mom sits on a chair in front of her completed canvas, even worse when it's clear.

"That's what I saw."

"Mom," you start, already tired, "Is it possible that you're too stressed? Do you think you need to take a break?"

"It doesn't matter if I was tired. It doesn't matter if it was real or not. I saw it. That's what matters."

You try not to run to your bedroom. You try not to slam your door. But you're hugging your pillow, throwing your phone against the wall and biting into the soft fabric in the narrow hope that Mom won't hear you cry.

⌘⌘⌘

There's a story in Denton, about a bunch of college kids who opened a portal to hell. There's a story around Lake Worth, about a monster with hooves. And there's a story here, in White Rock Lake, about a horned man.

You know all the stories now because they're all mom talks about. The summer goes on and she starts every day by reciting her "research"

Towards A Place Where Everything's Better

to you. About how the Greek god Pan lent itself to Christian depictions of the devil, about gateways to other worlds that exist in lonely places.

She smiles wildly, promising that this is proof that she isn't crazy. That what she saw is real because other people saw it too. She tells you she feels "lucky" to have been "blessed" with her encounter with the unknown.

But you've seen her throw herself into bleak obsessions before. You know how this story ends. At least, you think you do.

Mark wants you back because he doesn't have you. He's not purposefully mean, just forgetful. Is that any better, or does the fact that he could go so long without thinking about you hurt more than it would if he hated you? You're standing firm, because he's not here to dissuade you. He's thoughtless, but he's pretty and has the best smile. You remember the smell of his deodorant and the touch of his hands and you hate yourself for missing him.

Breaking up with him eats at you, but you keep trying to distract yourself. August in Texas is oppressively hot, with thick air that seems like water when you walk through it. You run earlier now, when the stars are still out and the whole world silent.

Before you leave, you catch a look at Mom's latest "project." Mom had been trained, once, as a makeup artist, and it's evident in the horrible thing looming in the living room like the centerpiece of some haunted shrine. The mask is large, with a long face and leering smile. Its horns are crude and incomplete, paper mâché cones in the process of yellowing under corpse-hue paint.

You curse and leave the apartment, beginning a dark jog through grim, painful thoughts.

You stopped calling Dad a while ago. You're tired of him, his vague half-commitments to helping you towards a better place. While dad deals in empty promises, you see the facts: He hasn't come down, hasn't visited once. He hasn't met you for a milkshake, anything. And he could. He has a car, he has weekends. He *could* visit you and he won't. He just calls and says everything will be better.

But he has no control over this. Over mom.

And like mom said, it didn't matter if what she saw was real or not. What mattered is she *saw* it.

Dad said, 'mom needs you more.' Does she? You're here and mom's not getting better. The goat thing, whatever bullshit name she finds for it, has made her worse than ever. You're nothing but a bystander, a spectator in watching her wither and crumble.

Dad said, 'mom needs you more.' Does he need you *at all?* Or is he just Mark, wanting you now just because you're gone, thoughtless and accidentally hurtful.

You run further into the woods, along the dimly lit trails beneath wilting tree branches. A park bench comes up and for a moment you rest, bringing a cold plastic water bottle to your mouth as you desperately wait for the endorphins to make you happy.

You stop breathing when you see the man under the streetlight.

You only see his outline, tall and hairy in the orange light.

You can't make out his face, but his eyes are on you. On your shoulders, on every part of your body.

And he crouches. The way he runs. Shambling, and thrashing on all fours towards you.

You scream. High pitched, terrified. Weeping.

You run. You run and run and run.

⌘⌘⌘

You call the police.

You were chased. Fucking *chased*. There's a weird man in White Rock Lake stalking teenage girls.

The officers, for their part, seem concerned. For good reason. You've seen true crime shows. You know how they escalate, start with peeping and end with a basement full of bodies.

Towards A Place Where Everything's Better

That's what you thought of when you ran, being an open cold body beneath the dirt. A tally mark in some FBI report. You saw your face, pale and bloodied, over and over again in your screams.

They ask you where your mother is. You tell them she's working, that they can reach her on her cell. You pray, though it's only a 50-50 chance that they reach her on her cellphone.

"Yes, ma'am," one officer says from some distant shore.

You're tired. More tired with mom than you've ever been before.

You don't know what would have happened to you if she didn't answer, but you also don't know where she is. Don't care. Mom may need you; dad may need you. But you don't need *them*.

And this man, this sick fucking pervert, even though he didn't catch you, even though he didn't touch you, he took something from you. No more running outside, no more enjoying the quiet places because there's just no telling what's *in them*.

The officers eventually leave, promising to patrol the area more regularly. For a while you are still, but you feel the Goatman's eyes on you. From paintings. From sculptures. Poring every part of you.

And you strike back at him.

The paintings crack under your fist, the notes rip in your hands. You destroy this thing, the monster you've been made to compete with because your mother is incapable of being a full person. The art breaks under you, swirling into a whirlwind world of white, red and black.

When mom comes through the door, she drops the art supplies at her side.

From your distant place you expect her to ask you what happened. You expect her to ask why the police aren't still there. If you are okay.

But she doesn't. Her eyes don't even meet yours, but rest quivering on her ruined work.

"Why'd...why'd you do this?"

S.L. Edwards

You tell her, in the same far-away voice that she uses with you, about the man who chased you through the woods. About talking with the cops. About being afraid for your life. About the nightmare way he moved his body. About how you're not sure why you're still alive.

Mom's expression doesn't change. Her eyes don't go off the ruins of her paintings.

"A mean thing to do," she mutters.

She buckles to her knees.

"A mean, *mean* thing to do!"

And you tell her.

Tell her what you've both known for as long as she's been alive.

She's no mother. She's a burden.

⌘⌘⌘

You wait for her crying to stop. And then you wait for three hours more.

Her bedroom door is open. Her nightlight bright enough to just illuminate your body.

You wait for her in the corner, watching her sleep in unearned and selfish peace.

When she wakes, you'll show her. Show her your mangled hair, your leering smile. The mask is heavy and awkward, but it's the only face she deserves.

She rises slowly and looks around the room.

When she sees you, she freezes.

Under the mask, you smile, too.

And you're after her. Out of the apartment down the staircase, out into the woods.

Shambling after her like an animal in the night.

Illustration by Sarah Walker

Moonville
by John H. Howard

"You are entering an area with incomplete route guidance. Please drive safely and obey all local traffic laws."

"Welp," said Dan. "No more GPS."

"No more cell phone signal, either" Erik said, and put his cell phone to sleep, tucking it away. In the back seat next to him, his younger sister, Jennifer, shut hers down, too. At the same time, the satellite radio signal turned to static and NO SIGNAL appeared on the display.

"That's okay," Laura replied. "We're almost there. Just a few more miles."

"Ugh." Seventeen-year-old Erik made his discontent plain. Bad enough his parents dragged him along for an eight-hundred-mile road trip to attend the memorial service for one of his father's uncles whom none of them really knew—and more than two years after he had disappeared—but he was tired of all the sightseeing. "Why couldn't I have just stayed at the house? I'm tired of seeing caves and coal furnaces and Indian mounds."

"He means he'd rather be checking out the hot neighbor chick," replied Jennifer, his fourteen-year-old sister.

"Shut up, Jen!"

"You're only mad 'cause you know it's true." Jen stuck out her tongue at her brother.

Swatting her on the shoulder with the back of his hand, Erik said, "I'd rather be doing anything other than this. We're a hundred miles from nowhere, in Bumfuck, Egypt, and still driving."

"Erik!" cried Laura. "Language!"

"Bumfuck, *Ohio*, you mean," said Jen.

Moonville

"Jennifer!" Their mother's tone was horrified.

"She's right, though, Mom. Have you seen how these people live down here? I've never seen so many mobile homes on blocks in my life. And it seems like everyone down here just throws all their shit out in the yard. You'd think it was Appalachia, for fuck's sake."

"Erik," in her exasperation, Laura was close to yelling now, "we did not raise you to use that kind of language!"

"Watch your language, you two," said a very distracted Dan in a bored voice.

"Sorry," Erik and Jen replied in unison.

"Here!" Laura said excitedly as the car bounced over a narrow, rutted bridge, her annoyance at her children's choice language completely forgotten. "Pull over, Dan. Pull over!"

He slowed down but did not stop. "Where? There's nowhere to park."

"Just pull over on the side of the road."

"No, seriously. Where am I supposed to pull over?"

"Right! Here!"

"The road is barely wide enough for two cars as it is. And you want me to pull over on the side of it?"

"Yes, goddammit! Pull over!" Laura was bouncing in her seat. Dan slammed on the brakes and the seatbelts locked. He pulled over at a slight widening in the road and stopped.

"Jesus, Dad!" Erik complained. "Thanks for the whiplash. My day wasn't quite bad enough already."

"That's enough," Dan said, turning to face his children. "Your mother has been looking forward to this all week. We are not going to ruin this for her. Understood? Erik? Jennifer?"

"Yes, Dad," Jennifer said. Erik let his silence speak for him.

"Let's go see a ghost town!" Laura said. She unbuckled and got out of the car, followed a moment later by Dan.

John H. Howard

"Yes, let's," muttered Erik. He and Jen followed their parents out of the car. Then stood there, waiting for instruction.

"So where are we going?" Dan asked.

Laura looked around intently, searching for some sign of where they were supposed to go. None was readily apparent. The narrow road they had been driving on was overhung by green-leafed trees on both sides. On the right was a steep incline covered with thick underbrush. They couldn't go that way. The road itself wandered lazily out of sight in both directions, disappearing under the canopy. Laura took out the crumpled notepaper on which Grandpa Coe had scribbled directions earlier that day. "There should be a path around here somewhere." Referring to the crude map, she tentatively headed back up the gravel road in the direction they had come from, the rest trailing like awkward ducklings. As he walked over the bridge, Erik spit over the rusted steel guardrail into the fast-moving creek below. Reaching the other side, Laura spotted what she was looking for: a well-worn path just off the road, flanked by tall grass and thorny bushes.

Barely fifty feet in, they realized they hadn't dressed properly for hiking in these woods, that wearing shorts was a bad idea. Insects swarmed and bit. Brambles tore at their feet and ankles. Erik quickly regretted wearing sandals and cargo shorts. Jennifer complained loudly that no one had told her not to wear her favorite white sundress. It was continually getting caught on the underbrush and she had to keep tugging it loose. The hem quickly became frayed. Dan muttered under his breath as his legs quickly became scratched and bit. Laura bore her discomfort from the heat, insects, and brambly underbrush in silence.

The path was just wide enough for one person at a time, although it opened up in a few places. They carefully picked their way over fallen trees and avoided the muddy sections as best they could. To their right, the stream that they had crossed on the bridge flowed briskly. A sheer rock face rose on their left, sporting graffiti by local teens with nothing better to do. After spending the last week in the area, Erik wasn't

Moonville

surprised the locals would consider defacing a cliff a dozen miles from the nearest paved road a good time.

Erik and Jennifer had enough after about ten minutes of hiking and said so, complaining about the mud, the thorns, the insects, the heat, and just generally being outdoors. Laura was having none of it. "I don't know what you two are complaining about," she said over her shoulder. "This is all natural, beautiful country."

"Yeah," Erik muttered. "Until you hear the banjos." Jennifer giggled.

The trail angled back toward the creek and rose sharply. For about ten feet, it zigzagged up a nearly vertical incline. Dan pulled himself up by grabbing onto jutting rocks and small trees, nearly losing his footing once or twice. Upon reaching the top, he helped Laura and Jen up while holding onto a small tree trunk for leverage. Erik made his own way up, declining any help.

With everyone at the top, Dan brushed himself off and ran his fingers through his short-cropped, salt-and-pepper hair to get any leaves out. Laura noticed neither the leaves in her hair nor the burrs in her socks and shoelaces; she was already following the path the only way she could, since the creek was to the right and now far below, down a steep bank.

Laura spotted what she came for and left the rest of her family behind, her curly blonde hair bobbing above her shoulders as she walked briskly down the trail. Just ahead lay one of the few remaining pieces of evidence that there had ever been a town here—an enormous train tunnel with "Moonville" inscribed over it in bricks, many of which were broken.

The town vandals had found this place as well, graffiti marring the tunnel façade, the bright spray paint ruining the experience of being in a long-abandoned, forgotten place. The tunnel had been cut through a small mountain. The entrance was flanked by step-like stone retaining walls.

John H. Howard

"Southern Ohio's worst-kept secret" was what Grandpa Coe said, describing how there had once been a small town here of about a hundred people. It had been founded around the prosperous coal mines of the area, but died out decades ago, the last family leaving in the forties, after the coal mines dried up. The trains kept running well into the eighties, he said, but to look at the place, Erik would have guessed Moonville had been abandoned a hundred years before that. All the tracks were gone, the bare trestle supports across the creek (or "crick," as Grandpa Coe pronounced it) sad, lonely monuments to the small but thriving civilization that had once been.

Laura had her camera out and was snapping pictures of everything in sight—the woods—the leaning telegraph poles—the tunnel entrance. Even the graffiti. Everyone again trailed behind her, with less enthusiasm.

A self-proclaimed "sensitive," Laura insisted that they come here as soon as she heard about the place from one of the local relatives attending Uncle William's service. Apparently, he told some friends he was planning on coming out here himself the day before he disappeared. His car was eventually found down the road, but no other evidence was ever found that he came. Laura wanted to retrace his steps to see if she could get an idea of where he might have gone, as well as to "feel the energy" of the historic place, especially when she found out that it was reputed to be haunted. Grandpa Coe confirmed this, saying it was considered one of the most haunted places in Ohio. He told them about Baldie Keeton, who was murdered right outside the train tunnel by two men he'd angered in a bar earlier in the evening and whose ghost now liked to drop pebbles on the heads of passersby. He talked about the lavender woman, to which Laura responded enthusiastically, "Ooh! I love lavender," which was such common knowledge among the family that it had become a running joke. Grandpa Coe talked about the girl in the white flowing dress who walked the tunnel. Lastly, he told them about the mysterious ghost with a lantern, presumed to be one of the townspeople, who seemed to be trying to warn people away.

Moonville

The entire time, Grandma Coe shook her head and rolled her eyes behind Grandpa. But at the mention of the ghost with the lantern, she piped up and explained that the town had been suffering from some sort of plague and was short on supplies, and the man with the lantern was probably a townsperson trying to get the train to stop at Moonville. Grandma also made it very clear that she didn't believe in ghosts, and that Grandpa's stories were just that—stories.

No matter. Laura was hooked as she begged and cajoled her family to go with her the next day to see the area.

Now, Laura stood in front of the tunnel entrance, which dwarfed the short, stocky woman. She raised her arms, palms upward. The tunnel beyond was lost in darkness. The opening at other end was a small spot of bright light that could easily be blocked out by Erik's fist held at arm's length.

"Can you feel it?" The excitement in Laura's voice was clear.

"Feel what?" Dan asked in a bored tone.

"The energy! It's so…vibrant! It's like the ground is humming. I can practically feel the trains passing by us, the spirits of the people who used to live here. It's amazing!"

"Mm-hmm," Dan said.

"So much energy here," Laura said to no one in particular. Then she stepped forward. As she passed through the entrance, a shower of pebbles fell around her. Laura jumped and gasped, then turned excitedly to her family. "Did you see that?" she said. "That was Baldie Keeton! Baldie Keeton just dropped stones on me!"

Dan shook his head. "Laura," he said. "It's an old train tunnel in the woods. It was probably an animal or maybe the ground settling."

"Oh," Laura replied. "Yes, I'm sure that's it. Still, though. The timing was odd. It was just as I entered the tunnel."

"Yes, Dear. That was odd."

"Hey!" Laura exclaimed. "Stay here, you guys! I want to try something." Dan, Erik, and Jennifer all exchanged puzzled glances as

John D. Howard

Laura made her way to the other end of the tunnel, but they did what she asked and waited. Once at the other end, Laura, a small, dark silhouette against the bright daylight beyond, spoke. And the others heard her clearly, just as if she were standing right next to them.

"Can you hear me?"

"Yes!" Dan shouted.

Laura shouted back, "You don't have to yell! Just talk in a normal tone!"

"Okay," Dan yelled. Then he dropped his voice. "Can you hear me?"

"I heard you!" Laura exclaimed. "That is so cool!" Erik had to admit it was a neat trick being able to talk to one another from better than fifty yards away without raising their voices. They each tried it. Once they got bored with that, they made their way to the center of the tunnel. As their eyes adjusted, they discovered that it wasn't as dark as it looked from outside. Again, vandals had tagged the brick walls. There was also evidence of at least one campfire. A pentagram had been spray-painted on the ground in the middle of the tunnel with arcane symbols around it. Melted candles suggested a séance, or perhaps something more nefarious had been attempted in this spot. Erik wondered aloud if whoever was responsible had actually made contact with the other side. They four of them then moved on toward the other end of the tunnel, pointedly ignoring the more explicit graffiti.

At one point, Laura, Dan, and Jennifer all jumped and brushed off their faces and shoulders, saying something about walking through a spider web. Looking for it, though, they were unable to see it. Erik felt it, too, as he walked forward, a sensation of tiny fibers catching on his skin and clothes. He likewise brushed at his face and shoulders, but he couldn't find the spider web either.

Suddenly, Laura stopped, her curly hair bobbing as she did so. "Did you hear that?" she asked. The others listened.

"Hear what?" Dan asked.

Moonville

"Shhh! Listen!" They did. And then they heard it, too—a far off train whistle. "There! That! Did you hear it?"

Dan replied, "It was just a train."

"But there aren't any trains within miles of here," Laura said, frowning.

"The way the acoustics are around here," Dan said, "it could be echoing off the hills, for all we know. There certainly aren't any trains out *here*, though, that's for sure."

"But then why can I hear it running on the tracks?" Laura asked.

Dan frowned, listening. Then his eyes widened. At that moment, Erik and Jennifer heard it, too—the distinct sound of a train running on rails. The whistle sounded again, louder this time.

"Uh, guys?" Jennifer said, her voice quiet.

"What, Jennifer?" Dan replied, the annoyance plain in his voice. "We're listening to something."

"I hear it, too," she said. "And it sounds like it's getting closer."

"Yeah," Erik said softly, starting to freak out a little. "It does. It really does."

"And were these tracks here before?" Jennifer asked.

Startled, they all looked down. At their feet was a set of train tracks that Erik was certain hadn't been there a moment before.

"Okayyyy," Erik said, stepping away from the rails. "Those definitely weren't there a second ago. I'm getting pretty freaked out here."

"No," Dan said in a quiet voice. "No, they weren't. However, I'm sure there's a rational explanation for this. There has to be. But it doesn't matter, because we're leaving." And he started walking back the way they had come. The others followed.

But they didn't get very far when they heard the train again. And this time it was close. Very close. In fact, it was coming toward them.

Just beyond the entrance of the tunnel, on the very same tracks they were standing on, an enormous black steam locomotive was bearing

John H. Howard

down on them, a great black cloud of smoke belching from the smokestack. The cowcatcher on the front grinned malevolently. The whistle screamed again. Carried to them by the perfect acoustics of the tunnel, the sound was deafening.

Erik shouted "*Run!*"

They did.

Everyone scrambled along the tracks. Jennifer tripped and nearly went down at one point, but Dan snatched her under the arm as he passed, barely slowing to do so.

They were still twenty or so feet from the end of the tunnel when the train entered it from the other end. Erik took a moment to look behind him. The huge locomotive took up the entire tunnel; there was no room to even squeeze against the walls. The whistle blasted again, drowning out the sounds of their own shouts. Erik shouted anyway: "*Faster*! It's nearly on top of us!"

Somehow, they managed to run faster—even short and stocky Laura, who hadn't run since her softball days in college.

The four of them reached the end of the tunnel at the same time and dove, Erik to one side, and Dan, Laura, and Jennifer to the other. Erik landed in a tangle of brambles and horse shit. Still, it was better than ending up a greasy smear on the front of a train. The locomotive blasted out of the tunnel and thundered past them, the earth itself shuddering as it passed. Several cars were attached to the engine, but Erik wasn't of a mindset just then to count them as he had when he was a child.

A few moments later, the train had disappeared around a bend in the tracks. They could still hear it, though, clacking its way into the mountains, its whistle shrieking every few moments. Erik stared at his parents and his sister on the other side of the tracks. Sitting there for a minute or two, they took their time catching their breath while marveling at the fact that they were all still alive. Finally, Erik got up and stepped over the rails to help his mother and sister to their feet. They all had leaves and burrs in their hair and mud spattered on their clothes, but they were all too much in shock to notice or care. Laura's face was the whitest Erik had ever seen it. *Like she's seen a ghost*, he thought, then had to stifle a laugh.

"What the *fuck!*" Dan shouted. Then he shouted it again. Then once more for good measure. He grabbed Laura by the arm and turned her sharply to face him. In stark contrast to Laura's paleness, Dan's face was a deep shade of red, bordering on purple. For a split second, Erik thought he was going to hit his mother. But he didn't. Dan just continued shouting. "What is going on?" Spit flew from his lips. "What is this place? And what have you gotten us into?"

Laura's lips trembled. She tried to speak, but only a whimper came out. Then she burst into tears. Dan let go of her and she sank to the ground, bawling loudly into her hands. "Useless," Erik heard his father say under his breath. This shocked Erik. He had never seen his father act this way before. He had never treated any of them like this. But Erik had to admit that he was pretty angry at his mother, too, for dragging them all out here into the middle of nowhere for a stupid old ghost town that no one cared about when he could be back at his grandparents' house sleeping or playing videogames on his laptop. But, thanks to his "sensitive" ghost-chasing mother, they were nearly run over by a train. A train that shouldn't even exist. And now the sun was setting, and they still had a long hike back to the car and then a longer drive back to civilization—or what passed for civilization around here. Erik stood and brushed off his shorts. He had lost one of his sandals running from the train.

Great.

He turned toward the tunnel, intending to look for it and then hike back to the car, his family be damned. But at that moment, Erik heard footsteps behind him. Someone was running. Turning back around, he saw a man wearing period-style clothes—brown leather shoes, dirt-stained brown trousers, and a long-sleeved shirt that probably used to be white. One of his arms was in the sleeve of a brown woolen jacket, but the rest of the jacket was flapping wildly behind him. The man's thin dark hair was plastered to his head with sweat. He approached Erik's family at a dead run, but it was evident something was very wrong with him—he seemed barely able to keep his balance, his lower body seemingly having trouble keeping under his torso, which flailed in every direction. Drunk, Erik guessed. But what was the man was running from?

A moment later, that question was answered as two more men, dressed just as oddly as the first, burst out of the woods. They were shouting something. The first man tripped and went down. The man with curly blond hair tackled him and started pounding him with his fists. The older gentleman struggled to get away but was too impaired to make much of an effort. A moment later, the third man—younger than the other two and with long, dark, greasy hair—caught up. Still at nearly a full run, he landed a vicious kick in the gut of the man on the ground, who grunted at the blow and curled up around his stomach. "Teach you to cheat at cards!" he shouted. "Rotten son of a bitch!"

The blond man was punching and kicking, aiming for the prostrate man's face, head, stomach, kidneys—anything that wasn't protected. Meanwhile, the darker-haired man kept kicking him, punctuating each blow with a word: "Baldie! Fucking! Keeton! Baldie! Fucking! Keeton!" over and over.

Finally, Dan realized what was happening and called out to them. "Hey! You! Stop that! Get away from him!" The two men stopped and looked up from the man they were brutally beating. They exchanged glances, blinked, then looked down at the man on the ground lying in a pool of his own blood. Their expressions changed to ones of fear. Then, seeing Dan coming toward them, the two men bolted back the way they had come.

Dan chased them for a few steps but stopped at the bleeding man on the ground. He wasn't moving. Dan bent down and turned him over on his back as Erik, Laura, and Jennifer ran over. Jennifer let out a small cry and hugged Laura at the sight of the ruined man on the ground. His face was bashed to a pulp, one eye socket smashed. Some of his teeth lay in

Moonville

the mud, both lips were split, and blood was everywhere. Dan hesitated to touch the man, but he finally put two fingers to the man's neck. Laura gasped. "Ohmygod!" she said. "That's…that's Baldie Keeton! But…but…it can't be…"

At Dan's touch, Baldie coughed, spraying blood everywhere. He gasped for breath. One eye opened; the other was too swollen. He gripped Dan's arm. "Sam?" He said. His voice sounded like he had swallowed gravel. "What're you doing here?" Dan floundered, not sure how to reply, but before he could say anything, Baldie grabbed him by the arm and pulled him close. "Sam," he whispered, then coughed again. Erik saw flecks of blood fly onto his father's face and shirt. Dan flinched away, but Baldie had a firm grip on his arm. "Sam, you fucked up, you stupid ass. You fucked up bad lettin' that train come through here." He coughed again. More blood flew.

Dan struggled to make sense of what Baldie was saying. "What…what are you talking about?"

"The train. The train!" Boulders grinding together would have sounded less dry than this man's voice. "You let somethin' out, Sam. Drillin' through that goddamn mountain. And now it's angry. And it's killin' us all."

"I don't…I don't understand," Dan stammered.

"Git out!" A hacking cough racked the man's body and he screamed with pain. When it had subsided, he gripped Dan harder. "You…have…to get…out. Or it will…kill…you, too."

"What!?" Dan shouted, spittle flying in Baldie's ruined face. "What will kill me? What are you talking about?"

"Sam…Listen, Sam." Baldie's voice was fading.

"What, man? What is it?"

"I didn't cheat."

Dan blinked. "What?" But there was no response. Baldie's eyes had gone distant and Erik suspected he was no longer in residence of his body. He had never seen a man die before. It was surprisingly peaceful, especially considering the brutality surrounding his death. It was as if his soul had slipped out the back door while they were looking in the front windows.

He was just…gone.

That didn't make it any easier for Erik to stomach, however. The man's shattered face and the pooled blood made his stomach churn. It apparently had a similar effect on his sister, who was heaving up her guts in between sobs in the weeds at the side of the trail. His mother went ashen and still, just stared at the body as if willing the man not to be dead. Tears snaked down her face. Dan still knelt by the man. No one moved, everyone waiting for someone else to do or say something.

Finally, Dan broke the silence. "We should probably find someone and tell them what happened here," he said.

Just as Dan regained his feet, they heard shouting in the direction the two killers had run. Whoever it was, they were coming toward Erik and his family. The angry tone of the shouting raised the hair on the back of Erik's neck. He looked back at the tunnel, wondering if they should just leave and let these people sort it all out. But before he could say anything, the two men who had beaten Baldie to death rounded the corner in the path with a half-dozen others, all large, burly men. And they all looked angry.

"There they are!" the blond man shouted. "They're the ones who done Baldie!" He was pointing in their direction. The greasy-haired man was shouting and pointing, too. Erik actually turned around to see who he was pointing at. Seeing no one behind him, he realized—too late—what had happened.

They were being framed for Baldie's murder.

"You sure 'bout that, Jim?" asked the man in front, a tall, broad shouldered, bald man. His work shirt sleeves were rolled up to above his elbows, revealing heavily muscled forearms. His hands and wrists were stained black. Erik recalled his grandfather saying something about coal mines in this area. Was it possible that this man was one of the coal miners? But that couldn't be—there were no coal mines in this area anymore. Not since Moonville was still a town and not an all-but-forgotten footnote in the history of Southern Ohio.

"Positive, Jacob," said Jim. "Like I says, Dunn and I were taking a little walk in the woods here when we heard shouting. So, we run up the trail and saw these folks beatin' poor Baldie. They was just a-hittin' and a-kickin' him. He was beggin' for mercy, but they just ignored him. That'n—" he pointed at Erik, "that'n was holdin' him down while the others did their worst. When me and Dunn saw what they was doin', we shouted at 'em to stop, but they told us that they'd do the same t'us if we din't mind our own damn b'ness. And look! They done kilt him!"

All eyes, including Erik's, turned to the body lying in the tracks. Erik thought, *we're royally fucked.*

Then the men's eyes turned back to Erik, Dan, Laura, and Jennifer in turn. The anger burning in the backs of the men's eyes was obvious. It burned so hotly, in fact, that Erik could see it; their eyes—Jim's and Dunn's included—burned with a coppery red glow like the moon in partial eclipse. "Ya shouldn't-a kilt Baldie," Jacob's voice rumbled forth from his throat like thunder rolling before a summer storm. "He was a mean ol' fuck, but he was our'n. An' nobody fucks with our'n." The men started moving closer, seemingly of a single mind.

"Now just wait one goddamn minute!" Dan said, holding up his hand, palm out. "We didn't kill this man! They did!" He pointed at Jim and Dunn. "We were innocent bystanders."

"If yer so innocent," Jacob rumbled. "Then why're ya covered in Baldie's blood?" He was standing right in front of Dan by then, towering over him. Erik had to give his dad credit for not backing down when his own knees felt wobbly. Erik's instincts were telling him to run, but he wasn't confident in his ability to do so right then. Two more very large men were making their way toward him, that same coppery glow in the backs of their eyes.

John H. Howard

Dan looked down at his blood-spattered shirt. "He was coughing up blood before he died," Dan said.

"Judging from the beatin' ya gave him, I'm sure he was," Jacob said. Then he smashed Dan on the side of the head with his fist. Dan crumpled to the ground. Laura and Jennifer screamed. Erik shouted something. Then a ham-sized fist hit Erik square in the face. His world turned red before it turned black.

⌘⌘⌘

Erik awoke, choking. He struggled to rise to consciousness, struggled to open his eyes, struggled to remember why his world was full of pain. He successfully managed to drag one eyelid open. The other only opened a crack. A tickle in his throat and then the sensation of something wet in the back of it caused him to choke again, which sent fiery pain through his entire face. He spit and a large gob of blood splattered the dirt in front of him. His entire head felt swollen and sore. He touched his nose and winced. It was broken.

He tried to sit up, but he couldn't move his arms, belatedly realizing that his hands were tied behind his back. Then he remembered Jim and Dunn and Jacob and the two men who had put his lights out. Groaning, Erik tried to look around, but it was difficult with one eye swollen shut and the other half-closed. It was dark, wherever he was.

Trying again to sit up, the pain in the center of Erik's face flared up at the change in position. He called out at the surge of fiery pain but pushed through it until he was upright and leaning against the wall, panting heavily.

Flickering light barely illuminated the room he was in, which was tiny and bare. It looked like a log cabin. The source of the light was on the other side of a wooden door to Erik's left, which had a small window toward the top. In the opposite wall was a small window, this one covered in what looked like tar paper. Erik remembered that it had been about sunset when he and his family had been attacked but had no idea what time of day it was now.

Moonville

"Was that Erik?" Jennifer's voice came from behind him. She must be in the next room.

Then his mother's voice chimed in. "I think so." Louder. "Erik? Erik is that you? Are you okay?"

"I'm fine," he lied. His throat felt as if someone had been pouring sand down it. "Just a little banged up."

"That man hit you so hard. I thought he'd killed you."

"Unfortunately for him, I'm still very much alive," Erik replied. His attempt at humor fell flat.

"What about Daddy?" Jennifer asked.

Erik looked around. His father was lying still on the dirt floor a few feet away. "He's here." At that moment, his father groaned and started to move, groaned some more, and stopped.

"How is he?" Laura asked.

"I can't tell," Erik said. "I'm all tied up. But I think he's hurt."

"We need to get out of here!" Laura said. Erik could hear the panic in her voice. *No shit, Sherlock*, he thought. He was verging on panic himself. He didn't understand what was happening here, but these people were clearly out of their minds. It was blatantly obvious that Erik and his family hadn't killed that man, but Jacob and the others didn't seem to care. They were out for blood and they were going to have it. He recalled the reddish glow in their eyes and shuddered. Then he heard again what Baldie Keeton had said as he died: *You let somethin' out, Sam. You let somethin' out drillin' through that mountain and now it's killin' us all.* Is that what was going on? Was it some sort of disease infecting these people, causing them to lose all sense and kill each other? Was this the plague Grandma Coe had talked about? Or was it something else? Something with a mind and intent? Is that how Moonville met its end? Grandpa Coe said that the official story was that the town gradually died out as the mining dried up, but he also said there were hints that what really happened to the town was much darker but might never actually be

John H. Howard

known. Otherwise, he pointed out, why would there be fewer than a dozen graves in a cemetery for a town of over one hundred?

There was clearly something very wrong here, and somehow, they had found themselves right in the middle of it. Erik started to vow to himself that he would get to the bottom of it, but then decided that all he really wanted was to get his family out of here and go home and never come back.

He opened his mouth to say something to his mother and sister, but at that moment, a solid wooden bang came from the outer room and loud voices broke the silence. A moment later, his door was being opened and several large men entered, filling the small space with their bulk. Erik looked in their eyes and saw the same reddish hue in each of them. This close, it looked like the reflected light from a wild animal's retinas, except the light seemed to originate from within.

Two of the men hauled Dan to his feet. He groaned at the rough handling. Two more men grabbed Erik under his arms and lifted him up. The sudden jerking motion and change in elevation made him feel like he had been struck in the face again. He nearly passed out from the pain.

The men hauled Erik and Dan, and behind them, Laura and Jennifer, through the outer room, through the open door, and through a small town consisting mostly of wooden shacks. The building Erik and his family had been in was one of only a few larger cabins.

Erik tried to keep his feet under him—not surprisingly, he had lost his other sandal somewhere along the way—but he was still groggy from having been knocked unconscious, so most of the time, the men ended up dragging him. It didn't seem to matter to them either way.

They were taken to the center of town. When Erik saw what they were being led to, his bowels turned to water.

Dominating the town square was a large oak tree with four nooses dangling from one branch. Torches on long poles had been planted in the muddy ground around the area, the flickering light causing nightmarish shadows to dance in the trees. Apparently, the entire town

Moonville

had come out to witness the execution. The mob was shouting, calling them killers, murderers, saying they needed to be put down like the dogs they were.

Erik started to struggle then, tried to get away. The man on his right swiveled and hit Erik in the stomach with a fist like a hammer, knocking Erik's breath out of him. He didn't give them any more problems after that.

As they were dragged up underneath the oak branch, the crowd closed in around them. They were made to step up on overturned washtubs, one underneath each noose. Erik heard Laura and Jennifer screaming and crying. A rough voice told them to shut up. Then he heard a series of loud fleshy smacks. Erik winced. The women quieted, but Erik could hear them stifling their sobs. His father made almost no sound other than an occasional groan. Only when the noose was around his neck did Dan seem to realize what was going on and try to struggle. It took two men to hold him still.

As the noose slipped over Erik's head and tightened around his neck, he felt something wet on his cheeks and realized that he was crying. The men below him leered at him. Looking around, Erik noticed that every single person in the crowd had those same blood-moon eyes.

And then Erik noticed something that he hadn't before, something that chilled him to the bone. Behind the mob, deep in the woods and high enough that Erik had to look up to see, even from his position on top of the washtub, were more sets of glowing red eyes. Four pairs of glowing crimson slits. The trees were shrouded in mist, but Erik had the sense that something huge and powerful lurked amongst the trees. Anger radiated from it, permeating the forest, soaking them all in its wrath. Erik felt it soaking into him through his skin, his hair, his pores. For a moment, the clearing in front of him became red-tinged, and all he wanted to do was kill everything that moved, destroy every tiny creature that had woken him from his slumber under the mountain…

John B. Howard

Erik shook his head and the red faded from his vision. That was when Erik understood he was looking in the eyes of the thing that had been sleeping under the mountain, the thing that had been awoken by carving the tunnel. Somehow, its rage at being disturbed had reached through time to drag him and his family back here, to this time, to this place, in order to be punished. But what he didn't understand was why. Why them?

Then he realized that Jacob was speaking to them: "…that you have been adjudged guilty by the citizens of Moonville, Ohio of the crime of the heinous murder of David 'Baldie' Keeton, and the punishment that will be bestowed upon you is hangin' by the neck until dead. Do you have anythin' to say for yourselves?"

"We didn't do it, asshole!" screamed Dan. "We told you that those other two fucks—" Dan's yelling was cut off when one of the men holding him kicked the washtub out from under him. The gurgling, choking noises as their husband and father kicked and flailed, jerking the tree branch overhead, was all too much for Laura and Jen, who started screaming and crying anew. Erik found himself screaming, too.

It took a long time for Dan to stop kicking. When he finally did, Jacob addressed them again. "Your judgment is absolute," he said. "Your sentence has been decided. There's no arguin' against it. Now, I will ask you one more time. Do you have anythin' to say for yourselves?"

Suddenly, something that Baldie had said in his final moments came back to Erik in a flash of sudden clarity in what he believed to be his own final moments. "Who is Sam?" he asked of Jacob.

"'Scuse me?" Jacob's low, gravelly voice seemed to have a hard time rising up to where Erik stood atop his washtub.

"Who is Sam?" Erik asked again. "Baldie called my dad Sam. And I want to know who Sam is before I die."

Jacob seemed genuinely confused. "Now why would he call him Sam?" he wondered aloud. "That don't make no sense at all."

"Who is he?" Erik asked again.

Moonville

"He musta meant Sam Coe," Jacob said. "The man who owns this land, Moonville, the mines, everything 'round here. He's the one talked the trains into comin' through here. He's the one authorized the diggin' of that tunnel. But he hardly ever comes 'round these parts, doesn't like to mingle with us common folks, 'less he has to, to check on the mines and whatnot. Baldie knew him, though. Baldie knew him, but he shoulda knowed better that that wasn't Sam. Odd, thing, though. Odd that he shore do look like Ol' Sam a bit. Ain't seen him in the better part of a year, though."

Erik's world swam. Coe. That explained it. Whatever had been stirred up by cutting that tunnel harbored a grudge against Moonville's residents and, he guessed, Sam Coe in particular. And now, it was seeking revenge on Sam's family.

Jacob approached Erik. "Now that you've wasted your final words…"

"No!" Erik shouted, desperate for more time. "Wait! I want to speak to the thing in the woods!" Jacob stopped as if frozen. The red moons in his eyes seemed to flicker. The entire town went quiet.

"What'd you say, boy?"

"You heard me. I want to speak to the thing in the woods." His voice sounded more confident than he felt. "You know," he nodded in the direction of the eyes. "That thing over there that's killing you all." General muttering met his statement. Outside the circle, four pairs of red, glowing eyes narrowed.

"I dunno whatcher talkin' about, boy, but——"

"Or is it too scared to come out and look us in the eye?" Erik raised his voice to make sure it carried the fifty or so feet to the woods, to where the creature's eyes gleamed like crescent moons in the dark. "Is it too much of a coward to come kill us itself? Can't it do its own dirty work?"

"Erik!" Jennifer's hoarse voice sounded horrified. "What are you doing!?"

I don't know, Erik thought. *Something. Whatever I can.*

John H. Howard

Erik continued to taunt the creature in the forest, and he could sense through the townsfolk that it was getting agitated. Their behavior was becoming angrier, their shouting louder. They came right up to where Erik, Jennifer, and Laura stood on top of their washtubs and called for their deaths. Erik could see that the red copper moons in the townspeople's eyes had deepened to a blood red, as had the creature's. Except Erik noticed that Jacob was looking confused. He was staring at Dan's swinging body, the bulging eyes in his purple face. The red glow in Jacob's eyes flickered. Erik wondered if that meant that the creature was losing its hold over him. Meanwhile, Erik continued to taunt the creature while his mother and sister implored him to stop.

As the mob's cries grew louder, Erik glanced down at Jacob. He couldn't hear him over the crowd's noise but was able to read his lips: *What have I done.*

Erik took a chance. "Jacob! Jacob!" When the bald man looked up, Erik saw that his eyes were clear. In fact, a single tear streaked his face. "Jacob! Please! Get us down!" Jacob blinked as if waking from a dream. He looked around and saw the mob as if for the first time. Looking up at Erik, he nodded. Then he turned back to the crowd. He pushed back those closest to him in order to gain some room.

"Everyone! Everyone listen to me!" The mob quieted at Jacob's commanding voice. "We've made a mistake here," he yelled to them. "These people are innocent. We need to let them go!" The townspeople's angry cries rose to a deafening level. The crowd surged forward again, threatening with lanterns and torches, hatchets, and pickaxes. Jacob seemed to realize the danger they were all in. He moved quickly, moving behind Erik to untie his hands, then removed the noose from around his neck. The crowd shouted in anger. Then Jacob quickly moved to Laura while Erik helped Jennifer.

The thing in the woods screamed then, a thousand tormented voices rising from an inferno. Nearly a hundred pairs of red-hot eyes were trained on them. Erik saw that Jacob's eyes were flickering again. "Run!"

Moonville

Jacob shouted at them, just as Laura and Jennifer were freed. Then his eyes blazed crimson.

At that moment, a young man with a two-handed scythe ran out from the crowd and swung it at Jacob. Jacob grabbed it from the boy's hands as if he were a toddler, then lopped the man's head off with one powerful swing. As the head hit the ground, the fire in the boy's eyes died out.

The creature screamed again and the crowd swarmed Jacob.

Erik bowled over the nearest townsman, on a whim snatching the lantern from his hand, and ran. He hoped his mother and sister were behind him.

From what Erik could tell, they were just north of the tunnel. He thought if they could get back there, they might be able to get back home. Behind them, though, they heard the mob shouting and pounding its way through the forest. Either Jacob had joined them again or he was dead. But it didn't matter because Erik saw the tunnel ahead. Chancing a look back to make sure his mother and sister were behind him, he urged them to go faster. He tried to ignore the stabs of pain from stepping on sharp rocks and sticks with bare feet. Still, that pain was nothing compared to the jabs of fire in the center of his face with each step.

The townspeople weren't far behind them as they approached the tunnel. Erik ushered his mother in first. But just as she crossed the threshold, a train materialized.

Laura didn't stand a chance.

The train thundered through the tunnel, striking Laura at full speed. The cowcatcher at the front of two hundred tons of steel engine flipped her into the air like a ragdoll. She caromed off the brick wall of the tunnel with such force that when she landed, she rolled right into the path of the locomotive.

She seemed to explode as the train ran over her. Parts of her flew every which way. Blood and gore splattered the walls of the tunnel. What was left of her body rolled toward them as the train ran over her again and again. One arm came off and flew past Erik. It landed with a sloppy wet thud somewhere behind him.

As the last of the cars passed, their mother's mangled torso rolled to a stop in front of them. One arm hung loose but had far too many angles in it. Her hair was matted with soot and mud and blood, the iron scent of which mingled grotesquely with her lavender perfume. Erik couldn't help but look into her face—and his mother's eyes looked back. Her mouth worked. It looked like she was trying to say something, but nothing came out.

Then she was gone.

He became suddenly aware that Jennifer was screaming hysterically. She started to run to their mother, but Erik grabbed her by the arm and pulled her in the other direction. Not only was the mob moments away from recapturing them—and probably tearing them apart—but he also felt as if they had been sent a message—there would not escape through the tunnel. And why would there be? That was the domain of the creature. Erik realized belatedly that they had been heading right for it the whole time.

With nowhere else to go, Erik pulled his sister up the mountain beside the tunnel. He held the lantern out to light the way. They scraped and crashed through the woods as there was no trail here. After a time, Erik realized that the mob sounded further away. When they reached a clear space, he took a chance and looked back. The angry townspeople had stopped at the base of the mountain. Apparently, they wouldn't—or couldn't—follow them. Erik kept going, practically having to pull Jennifer along. She was clearly in shock. Erik decided he'd allow himself to go into shock later, when it was safe.

Besides, Erik thought. *Mom and her bullshit "sensitivity," she just had to go messing around with things she didn't understand, to go prying into things that were none of her business.*

As they reached the top of the mountain, Erik's rage blossomed into a terrible thing. *And Dad, that weak sonofabitch. If he stood up for us, fought back,*

Moonville

told Mom no, we wouldn't be here. If he just stood up for himself one time, this never…would…have…happened. He got exactly what he deserved.

The sky started to lighten with the coming of dawn. Erik was hot, sweaty, bleeding, out of breath, had been stung by countless insects, and was full of anger, yet he knew they couldn't stop. Not yet. Not with that thing out in the woods, hunting them with its blood-moon eyes.

His thoughts turned to Jennifer as they crested the mountain and started down. Carefully, because it was dark on this side. And also, because the slope was steep.

And then there's Jen. If only she had spoken up, said something, not been such a pushover, fought back, anything, Mom and Dad would still be alive, we'd never have come out here, wouldn't have a mob behind us trying to kill us. Useless little bitch, more worried about herself than her own family. Why the hell should I risk myself for her?

Erik suddenly became aware of a gurgling noise. He blinked his eyes and looked down. And saw Jennifer, lying on the ground, covered in blood. Her face had been smashed in, her blonde hair torn out, her skull shattered. Erik's hands were around her neck. A bubble of blood formed on her lips with her dying breath. Then it popped and dribbled down her chin.

Erik released his sister's throat. It took some effort, as his fingers had been clamped so hard that they were stiff. He looked at his blood-soaked hands in horror.

He had killed his sister. And he had no memory of it.

He screamed then. Loud and long. He cradled Jennifer's ruined head in his arms and cried, not caring who heard him: the mob below, the creature haunting these woods. Bring them on! He would kill them all!

Yes, kill them all. The thought rose to the surface of his mind like a bloated white body rising to the surface of a lake. He managed to push his anger aside long enough to realize that the thought wasn't his. This was the effect of that creature. This was the source of the plague that had destroyed the entire town.

John H. Howard

Finally, a long time later, his emotion spent, he laid his sister's corpse back on the ground. Her beautiful white flowing sundress was now soaked with blood, ripped to tatters, and full of thorns and burrs. It was ruined. She would have been upset at that. He gave a hollow laugh at the absurd thought.

She was dead.

What did it matter?

The lantern had fallen several feet away. Somehow, it was still lit. He picked it up, although he didn't know why. Then he trudged the rest of the way down to the tunnel entrance, the same side he had entered with his family only yesterday, which now seemed like a year ago.

He stopped at a flat, bare place above the tunnel and took measure of his situation. No one had followed him. Nothing was on the path before him.

Erik started to make his way down toward the trail when he became aware that the rage was once again building inside him.

The creature must be near. He moved back up to the place above the tunnel. His anger abated.

He was trapped. With a mob behind and the creature ahead, there was nowhere else to go. So, there he stayed.

⌘⌘⌘

Sometime much later, a family appeared down the trail, hiking up from the same place where Erik and his family had. Erik no longer knew how long ago that had been. They looked wrong, somehow, as if all the color had been bleached out of them. He tried shouting, but they didn't seem to hear him. As they drew closer, he grabbed up a handful of rocks and pebbles and threw it at them. They looked up, startled, but didn't appear to see him.

He stood and shouted and waved the lantern in his hand. The little girl, who was maybe six or seven, saw him and pointed. He heard her say something, although her high-pitched voice sounded distant and muted.

Moonville

Her parents looked to where she pointed, shook their heads. The mother said something, then brought out her camera out and started taking pictures. Then they wandered into the tunnel.

⌘⌘⌘

"I don't see anything, Sweetie," Jack said. Although for a second, he thought he had seen the glimmer of a lantern just there, above the tunnel. But he didn't see it now.

"I promise I saw it, Daddy," Annie said. "I saw a man with a lantern."

"I believe you," Jack hugged his daughter and stood from where he had crouched next to her to better see where she was pointing. "These woods are full of ghosts."

"Don't scare her, Jack," said Rhonda.

"Me?" Jack replied. "She's the one who saw something."

Rhonda pulled her camera out of her purse and snapped a few pictures of the tunnel entrance. "Well, let's just see if we can get anything on film," she said.

Then they wandered into the tunnel, where they exclaimed over the perfect acoustics. Jack explained how the arch of the tunnel and the precisely aligned bricks carried the sound from one end to the other. Annie was the last to get tired of the trick.

As they made their way to the opposite end, Rhonda suddenly stopped and sniffed. "Do you smell that?" she asked. "It smells like lavender right here."

"I don't smell a thing," Jack replied. "Hey, did you know there's supposed to be the ghost of a girl in a white dress here?"

Illustration by Sarah Walker

Therein Lies a Tail
by Duane Pesice

Those of you who come often to these F.E.D. talks have come to expect nothing but the best in feline entertainment, and I tell you that tonight's featurette is nothing but the best in running jokes and will likely curl your hair even if you're a sphinx.

We cats of course do not write, largely due to us not having hands, but we tell our tales orally, and nowadays we record them and have them transcribed.

I note that the idea of transcription was initially practiced during the reign of the great Kuranes, may he rest in fields of clover, that worthy cat-friend. Several moon-beasts were deployed in this manner. Zoogs were indentured for this but proved unsuitable.

This is the bulk, as you no doubt know, of the contents of the Library at Ulthar.

And a cat with its ears to the ground is also cognizant that the rat-fiend Jenkin has burgled that facility, making off with the very Pnakotic Manuscripts at the behest of archfiend Nyarlathotep.

The Pharaoh of Pharaohs bade Brown Jenkin to drop the parcel off with the King of the Zoogs, may they dwell in rotten logs.

Mind you, it isn't very likely that he had peaceful intentions. Those Who Dwell in the Skies seldom do. It did occur to us that we could broker a peace and we offered to let the King of the Zoogs steward the precious manuscripts if folk of all footednesses could view them as in previous time they did, in our Library, with the proper measures taken.

How the rat-fiend got in we will not go over at this time, save to say that we know how it was caused and it will not happen again.

Therein Lies a Tail

No, this is the story of the chase. Because of course we gave chase, we guardians of the Library, when we learned what had happened, and we nearly caught the miscreant, his ability to move sidewise through dimensions uncertain in the areas we ventured into, the lands of men.

We chased him past the border of the Enchanted Wood, unfortunately encountering him after he had made the drop-off, and up through the Valley of the Gugs into the foothills of the Great Mountains.

He was gnashing his teeth and cursing in a dozen languages, but he was fleet and tricksy and we were only able to keep up until he dashed down a concrete path and through a small door in the side of a featureless stone building.

A heartbeat later, we were down the path and into the room, where to our horror we found that we had entered the room just as the Roombas entered.

Naturally here was panic. We're CATS. We abhor vacuums. Spooky shrieked and batted at the machine. Moe slapped it hard.

It went about its business unperturbed.

Of course, the door has sealed behind it. Of course.

And of course, the fiend had managed to describe the right angle while we were recovering and lit out for unknown pastures.

Of course.

The Roomba stopped and was borne out by a descending floor tile.

We couldn't follow. It was over too fast.

Spooky howled and jumped into the air.

And then, and then…the showers commenced. Great gouts of water from the ceiling, washing over the floor in waves, and soap following, gushing from spouts in the walls, and another wave of water, and gratings swallowed it all and suddenly I understood.

"Hold your breath, guys," I said.

They gulped and held their breath, and all of the air was sucked out of the room with the remaining water.

Duane Pesice

Clean air was piped in.

The floor bore a small blue-and-yellow sign, with some human writing I couldn't read until I went around, and then I saw.

IKEA

I Howled.

"LOOK OUT!"

The robots came out and withdrew the hidden equipment and the media began issuing forth and the room was filled with activity, robot arms cutting wood, hammering nails, fashioning connections.

We were kept busy dodging, mindful of what had happened on the Isle of Man, so long ago, and also mindful of who else probably came from the Isle, the talking mongoose his own self.

The rat-fiend.

"I bet he had something to do with that, too," I yelled at nobody in particular, leaping over a hammer blow.

I got high enough to see what was going on.

"You guys," I yelled. "It's going to get worse."

"How can it?" They both asked.

"They're assembling rocking chairs."

We had no choice except to try to get to the ceiling, which was far overhead but did have a series of metal beams to cling to.

Moe managed it by actually climbing one of the long robot arms and he took a spot near enough its root that he felt safe-ish.

Spooky literally ran up the wall.

I did it in two jumps, angled off the wall.

Eventually the assembly stopped, and we were able to drop to the floor and escape when the Roomba entered from outside.

But by then the fiend was gone and so were the Pnakotic Manuscripts.

"We need the consult the Sponsor."

"Kibble! Kabble! Koom!"

Therein Lies a Tail

Before us appeared the Sponsor, a big giant human head.

"Talk...to...me," it said.

Moe explained.

"I...see," said the head. "All right. This, calls, for, ritual."

"Tell us, oh Sponsor."

"You're...not, going, to like, it."

"Regardless."

"Thank, you...for...not, saying, regardless. Ask...Bast."

We gasped.

"It's...it's the, only way," he explained, and winked out.

Asking Bast, as you know, is fraught with danger. She seldom recommends any course that does not involve bloodshed, and lots of it. And if you don't follow her advice, she does what she told you to, and then takes out her anger on you.

It isn't pretty.

We performed the proper ritual for summoning, the dance of the linoleum and the moon, in the kitchen at midnight.

"Yesssss."

"Lady of the Tooth and Claw," I began.

"I know what you want." She hissed. "And I am in a position to advissse."

We all knew better than to speak.

"Yesss. Do nothing. Wait."

"Wait?"

"Wait. The Zoogs will try to call up that which they can't put down. Be wary."

And she winked out.

"This intrigue is too much for me," I said.

And so, here we are, my feline friends, waiting for we know not what.

Illustration by Sarah Walker

Rosaire, Master of Wolves
by Manuel Arenas

1

There was once a young man who sometimes was not, and in these instances the ambit of his *maleficia* encroached way beyond the pale. His mother was a soothsayer-healer who lived on the outskirts of the village of Les Hiboux, in the French region of Averoigne, at the dawn of the *Century of Lights*, during which epoch Darkness still found a way to periodically rear its caliginous head. His father was a priest who called upon the cunning woman to bring her the Word of God. It is not known how well the Word was received, but idle prattle wending its way to the Abbey of Perigon was that the man of God was heard to call out His name several times during the protracted visit. To forestall any scandal, the *Abbé* Donadieu besought the diocesan bishop to send the priest to New France to get him out of the public eye then quashed all residual strains of gossip at the source with threats of excommunication. Despite all the ado, the Lord of Hosts must have countenanced the hospitality the young woman showed His humble servant upon his mission, because she was soon blessed with a prima facie healthy child just in time for the proximate *Noël*. Howbeit the midwife, a village slattern who owed the young mother a favor, was a bit ill at ease with the breech birth and crossed herself after handing the rubicund newborn to his mother.

In honor of the devotional contrivance which lead to the conception of her beloved babe, the woman named her son Rosaire. He was a beautiful boy with a full head of lush auburn hair, ruddy cheeks, and amber colored eyes. She loved her little cub and proudly sang his praises to whomever brought her custom. In time, he grew into a handsome and

Rosaire, Master of Wolves

clever stripling to whom his doting mother inculcated the métier of her craft as well as what little she knew of *faierie* and the shadow world.

Motherly love notwithstanding, Rosaire grew to be of a saturnine humor which caused his mother some concern, so she suggested he divert himself with some playmates from the village but the village hens would not allow their chicks to play with the by-blow of the priest, and told them to steer clear of the witch's urchin with his furry brow and toothy smile. Taking their aspersions to heart, she pondered whether her boy was not truly marked for unpropitious fortune and so one night, as he lay dormant before the hearth, she took it upon herself to look into his heart, with the aid of an obsidian palm ball, to divine what sort of man he was destined to be. Peering into its inky depths, she focused her thoughts on her slumbering cub but, to her dismay, found her efforts stymied by a tutelary spirit; a shadowy warden with fiery eyes, that guarded his latent nature like a Cerberus. As she pulled away from his redoubtable gaze, she envisaged an image of a funeral pyre, but dismissed it as a phantasm playing on a reflection from the hearth. Soon after, business began to drop as many of her former clientele became fearful of being seen at the "cursed hovel on the edge of the wood," so consequently, she was forced to take on some unsavory patronage which she would have formerly declined: skulking malefactors, calling under cover of night, requiring noxious philters and baneful charms.

During these calls Rosaire's mother would send him around the back of the hut to keep him hidden from esurient eyes. Ever and anon, upon conclusion of the nefarious dealings, the cunning woman would go to fetch her precious lad but would find him to have strayed, like as not to chase the prodigious toads which proliferated in the region, often not returning till the following morn. At first light she would find him curled up on his palliasse before the hearth, with his copper hair full of leaves and twigs, his pale face smudged with berries from the nearby brush, and his long nails encrusted with soil, like some wild child of the forest. On one raw November morning, however, she awoke to find her precious

Manuel Arenas

Rosaire with his erstwhile ruddy cheeks besmirched with gore and lamb's wool.

Fearing the windfall of woe following his discovery by some angry shepherd she grabbed her son by his rufous scalp and dragged him to the wash basin where she scrubbed him of the incarnadine muck from head to toe. During the ablution she discovered a supernumerary nipple on his torso, which hitherto had not been present on his wiry frame. She blanched and recoiled at its shivery touch, for she knew it to be the dread devil's mark, an ominous emblem of her son's befoulment by the unhallowed touch of the Archfiend. Again, she grasped him by his hair and demanded he tell her from whence he came by the noxious nevus. Rosaire then recounted the tale to his *Maman* of his misadventures in the phantom-haunted forest.

He told her of the swart Lord of the Forest, whose sooty chill hand he was bidden to kiss. He told her of daubing salves and donning skins, of rutting at revels and running with wolves. He told her how the Lord of the Forest saw how he was cunning and said that if he served him unwaveringly for seven years, he would grant him authority over his own pack and they would rule the forest roads by night. His mother, dumbfounded, stared at her beloved cub, smacked him across the face, then held him to her breast as she bewailed the loss of his immortal soul.

Knowing that their time was limited before the aggrieved shepherd would be coming around with a *posse comitatus* to stir up trouble, Rosaire's mother adjured him to leave forthwith. She offered to pack him provisions but he declined, saying that the Lord of the Forest promised that with his new coat he would always be warm and he would never want for victuals as long as he ran with the pack, under his auspices. Embracing her son once more, Rosaire's *Maman* kissed her son goodbye and sent him on his way, after which she prepared for the direful upshot which was yet to come.

And come it did; first as the imprecations of an irate shepherd; then, as Rosaire's infamy grew, as the obloquy of the harried villagers. As

Rosaire, Master of Wolves

Rosaire was under the protection of the Dark Lord, they could not requite their wrath on him, so they took the next to best option.

II

Rosaire spent the ensuing perennial heptad terrorizing the woodland of Averoigne by night; riving bantlings, ravishing maidens, and ravaging graves in the service of the Dark Lord, during which time he was also instructed by his umbral lordship in the dark art of nigromancy. In those years he grew tall and brawny, and his chin lost its boyish smoothness as he became more than a youth, or a man for that matter. Upon the conclusion of his atramentous apprenticeship, he returned to his former abode beyond the woods to look in on his loving mother, only to find a razed ruin. Sifting and sniffing through the vestiges of his boyhood home, Rosaire found his mother's charred remains, which he carefully removed and inhumed with the pertinent obsequies. Determined to discover the transgressors, he used the forest lore his mother had taught him and lit upon an aggrieved hamadryad, whose sister had been lost in the ensuing conflagration, who provided the desired identifications. Grabbing what few keepsakes he could salvage from the debris, he returned to his sylvan lair where he gathered the appropriate ingredients for the shape-shifting ointment.

From his vile cache he pulled black henbane and deadly nightshade, mandrake root and the fat of an unbaptized babe, which he ground into a paste with his mortar and pestle. Then, stripping down to his natural state, he anointed himself with the resultant balm, donned the pilose coat of a black wolf and intoned the lycanthropic litany which consummated his transmogrification into a bloodthirsty beast, although when he turned, his coat was black but his muzzle, like his beard, was red, as if stained with the blood of his prey. He then summoned his lupine horde with a howl that resonated with equal measures of dolor and furor. Emerging from the dark recesses of their woody bowers, the bloodthirsty pack responded, snarling, their slavering jaws snapping with anticipation of the hunt. Whereupon their doyen, their *Meneur de loups*, lead them on a sortie of the village of Les Hiboux visiting bloody death upon the households of all those who partook in the harrowing death of his beloved *Maman*. They swarmed their abodes; dashing down their doors, crashing through their latticed windows, rending their thatch roofs; no crevice was left unexplored, no creature was left entire. No man, woman, child, or beast was spared from the wrath of the werewolves and their rancorous, ruddy ringleader: Rosaire.

Unseen by the slaughterous brutes and their shrieking quarry, a dark figure surveyed the carnage from a vantage point in the nearby boscage; his rufescent eyes glowed in the darkness like smoldering embers which threatened to catch flame on the contiguous branches. The canny shade's frore desiccate heart vellicated with an aberrant warmth to see Rosaire weaned from mother's milk with the blood of his enemies and so, in a fleeting moment of mentorial gratification, he accepted his protégé's blood-soaked oblation and smiled.

Illustration by Alan Sessler

Putting Down Roots
by Russell Smeaton

It is said that in England, seeing a mushroom ring in the morning is a sign of magic. For others, they just see food.

Chris definitely fell into the latter. He loved walking in the countryside, foraging as he went. Feeling like a modern-day poacher, stealing food from the land, Chris liked to go when the woods were empty. In truth, no one really cared. Well known in the village, Woody Chris (as he was called) was considered a harmless eccentric. Children sniggered behind his back as he tramped up the high street with his battered backpack, overflowing with branches and other green things.

On this particular morning, the woods were busy with walkers, cyclists, and laughing families. The rains of the previous days had stopped and whilst the paths were still muddy, the air felt clean and washed, buzzing with life. The hordes of people bothered Chris, fixing iron bands of stress around his chest and squeezing tight. When he thought no one was looking, he ducked off the main path and into the bushes. Jeans instantly soaked to the knees, he pushed on, bent low to avoid detection. After a minute of hunched-over shuffling, Chris straightened up, back cracking, looking around to make sure he wasn't being watched. This deep into the woods, the noise of people was but a distant memory, and Chris felt the bands of iron relax. He walked on, taking in the bird song and fresh breeze.

Before long, he came to a clearing in the woods. In the middle, a tree grew tall and proud. All around the base grew an abundance of mushrooms. He crouched down to examine them closer. They looked like Honey Fungus, common in the north of England. But there was something different about them Chris couldn't quite place. They looked darker, with thick veins of red running from the center to the edges.

Putting Down Roots

Chris was no fool. Mushrooms could be very dangerous in the wrong hands. And yet, there was something about these mushrooms that he couldn't resist. He plucked one close to him and after one last sniff, pinched off a piece and popped it into his mouth. He let it rest on his tongue a moment, savoring the flavor before chewing it. The taste was the best he'd ever had. It had that earthy taste he associated with mushrooms, but with an aftertaste so sweet it was like dessert.

Greedily, he scooped up a handful of the velvety mushrooms and plunged back into the overgrowth in what he hoped was the way he'd come. It didn't take him long to find the path, and he stood for a moment to take in some reference points, meaning to return later. He rushed home, oblivious to the crowds. All he could think of was frying up his bag of mushrooms, maybe treating himself to a glass of red wine. It was the weekend after all.

People taking their Sunday stroll saw him zooming by, pointed and smirked to themselves. There goes Woody Chris, they whispered to each other. He didn't care. He had his mushrooms, and they didn't. He got home in record time, desperate to try out his find. Wasting no time, he started frying up the 'shrooms in butter. The smell was divine. So heavenly, his neighbor Eileen noticed. Giving her the excuse that she needed, she knocked on his door. When he opened it, hot air wafted out, caressing Elaine with the heavenly scent of those sizzling 'shrooms.

"Hi Chris! I didn't see you come home," she lied. "Been anywhere nice?"

"Oh, hi Eileen," he replied, wanting nothing to do with this conversation. "Just up the woods."

"Oooh, it's a lovely day for walk, isn't it?" she continued, trying to peer behind him.

Chris sighed. He knew this endless back and forth would continue unless he invited her in.

"Yeah, it's beautiful up there. Managed to pick some mushies. Want to come in?"

Russell Smeaton

She didn't need asking twice and darted into his small but immaculate kitchen. Chris got back to cooking while Eileen gave a running dialogue of the past week. He decided not to break out the wine. That seemed too intimate. And yet, looking over at Eileen, he felt the briefest of flutters in his stomach. She was a good-looking lady, and he was, after all, a single bloke. Maybe this was a place for him to put down roots, settle down. For her part, Eileen liked Chris well enough. Her husband had passed almost six years ago, and she was only human. As she checked out his behind, she would happily feed Chris up a bit—he looked far too skinny for her liking.

They both went quiet, a not uncomfortable feeling. There was a moment as they locked eyes. To hell with it, thought Chris, and cracked open the wine. They giggled like school children, and before long both had flushed cheeks. Chris busied himself with the cooking and put down two steaming plates of freshly fried mushrooms. The taste was even better than before, and they both had second helpings. Any romantic notions disappeared as they both ate and ate, becoming oh so slightly uncomfortably full. Eileen offered to help with the dishes, but Chris shushed her, promising it was no bother.

"Eeee, did we eat all of those mushrooms?" she giggled, absently wiping her buttery lips.

"Oh!" said Chris, surprised to see his bag empty. "Looks like we did! I'd better go tomorrow and get some more."

"Can I come with you?" she asked, head bent slightly, peering up at him through her eyelashes. "I don't have much to do these days, and a little walk would do me good—especially after all that food!"

And so, they arranged to go the next day. As Chris closed the door, he wondered if they had arranged a date. Eileen went back to her home and picked up the phone as soon as the door was closed.

"Ooooh, you'll never guess where I've just had lunch," she babbled to her friend Nora and, as is the way of small towns, the knowledge of the

Putting Down Roots

blossoming relationship and those delicious mushrooms spread like wildfire.

The next day, the two of them went back to the woods. Chris found the tree without hesitation. The sun was shining, and the ground was littered with mushrooms, glistening in the sun and morning dew. They looked so beautiful; it seemed a shame to pick them. Chris spread out his jacket, and they say down next to the tree, enjoying the peace of the woods.

The sun felt good, and they chatted like old friends. It was only when an embarrassing grumble of their stomachs told them time was moving on. They both picked a large crop of mushrooms and headed for home. On the way home, Eileen phoned Nora on her mobile. Chris didn't say anything, but he had hoped to share the mushrooms with just Eileen. She was looking very beautiful today it seemed to him, more so than yesterday. He didn't want to share her or the mushrooms, but he also didn't want her to go home and so he kept quiet.

When they arrived home, Eileen followed Chris into his kitchen like old friends. It wasn't long before Nora was knocking at his door, and he grudgingly invited her in. However, as soon as the mushrooms were cooked and eaten, all bad feelings were gone, replaced by the warm afterglow of a good meal.

The next day, their little party of two was doubled as Nora and her friend Jade joined them. Eileen chatted to Chris all the way, Nora and Jade watching them both closely, grinning to each other at the unlikely couple. Chris wondered if there would be any mushrooms left so soon after their last harvest, but he needn't have worried. The ground was once more covered in mushrooms, and all four of them made short work of collecting a bumper crop.

On the third day, they headed back to get yet more shrooms. It was only Chris and Eileen this time. Nora and Jade had work, but both had made their own plans to get more mushrooms. The large tree was easy to spot, and they told their friends who told their friends. On this morning, both Chris and Eileen were quiet, neither having slept well the night before. Chris put it down to simply overeating an unbalanced diet and maybe a touch of nerves at their blossoming relationship. Nothing to worry about. Maybe add some other veg to the mushrooms, maybe some bacon. He didn't think too much about it. The sun was shining, the birds were singing, and he was happy to see he was holding Eileen's hand.

It came as no surprise to see the ground covered with a healthy spread of the velvet mushrooms, complete with their red veins. They both stood, shading their eyes from the sun, looking up at the tree. As they stood there, both of their stomachs started gurgling louder than ever. Chris thought he was going to either vomit or worse and doubled over in pain. Eileen was no better off, and she could feel the contents of her stomach churn into water. Simultaneously, they both fell on all fours, vomiting violently. Red fluid sprayed out, splattering the ground and their hands as it did so. Roots sprang out from the earth, waving in the air like the tentacles of an octopus. The vomit soaked away rapidly, leaving Chris and Eileen reeling and lightheaded as they stood up, wiping their mouths. They didn't notice the roots closing around their boots. They didn't notice the roots curling up around their legs, stretching higher and higher. They didn't even notice when the roots had found their way to their still dripping mouths and worm their way inside and down, down to stomachs that were now prepared to supply nourishment to the tree.

Chris and Eileen stood with blank eyes, staring up at the tree. As the roots started pumping vitals from their bodies into the tree, the two of them felt more connected than ever before. They were at one with the tree, and with each other. It was a beautiful feeling. They didn't mind when their now-lifeless bodies were pulled down into the welcoming earth. Both felt the wind gently caress the leaves at the top of the tree, gently caress their hair. A bird settled down on the branches and Eileen giggled at the tickling the little feet gave her. She tried to tell Chris, but discovered she no longer had a mouth, no longer had a body that was her own. But she didn't mind. She could feel Chris next to her, and that

Putting Down Roots

was good enough. Chris reached out and found he didn't need to. He was with Eileen, and they would be together forever.

⌘⌘⌘

Nora called for Eileen but found no one home. She knocked on Chris's door but there was no answer. She frowned. It wasn't like Eileen. Still, no matter. She had seen the two of them exchange glances like teenagers. Good for them, she thought. Better late than never. Her stomach gave a grumble, and she felt a craving for more mushrooms, so decided to go for a walk and see if she could find the spot where they had gone before.

The woods were alive that day. The wind made the trees sigh as they swished back and forth. Birds sang as they jostled for places to rest and things shuffled unseen in the undergrowth. Nora breathed deep, enjoying the fresh air. She soon found the spot where they had been before and felt a jolt of excitement when she saw ground littered with mushrooms. The tree looked radiant and green in the bright sun. As Nora looked up, she wondered just how big the tree was. Standing alone amongst a field of mushrooms, it looked huge—surely the biggest in the woods. So, thinking, she got busy, picking handfuls of mushrooms. Her stomach growled at the thought of those delicious mushrooms. Jade said Mike and Rich were coming around. She was sure they would all love her mushroom stew.

⌘⌘⌘

It is said that in England, you used to be able to walk from one end to the other under the cover of trees. It is said that in those days the trees spoke to each other. Those days are long gone. The once green land has been overrun with people and their pollution. And yet, the trees still speak to each other. And they are not happy. The time has come for them reclaim their land. It is now time for them to put down their roots, once and for all.

Illustration by Sarah Walker

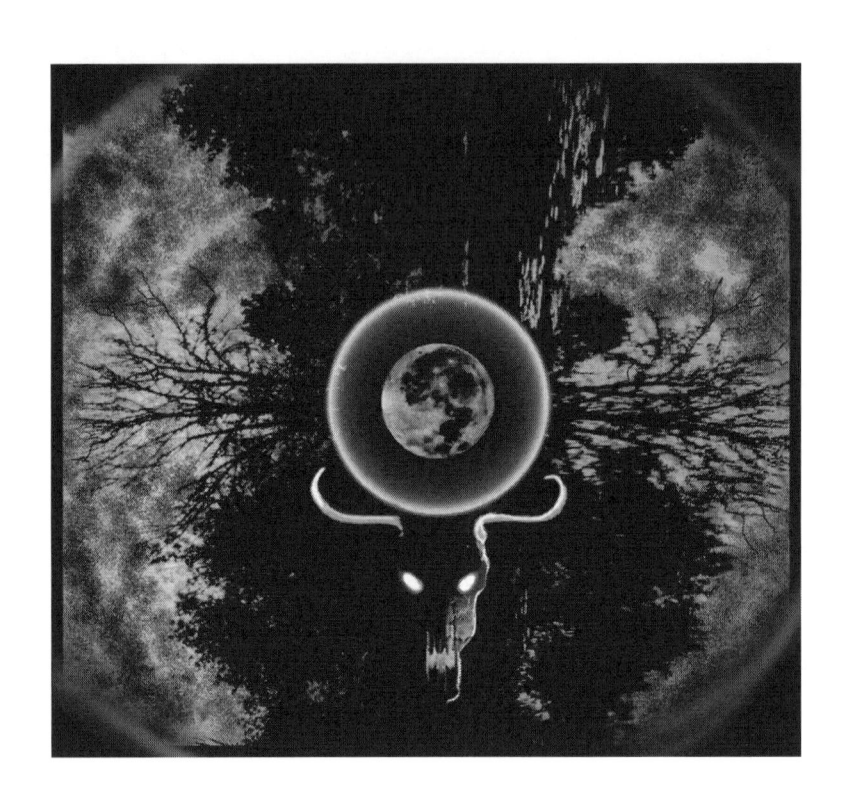

There Came the Sun
by Ivan Zoric

Five weeks after her bride to be passed away, Mikel finally washed the pillowcase Jelena had drooled on the night before the accident. She sat in front of the washer, set the spin cycle on high and cried as the last pieces of her fiancé's DNA centrifuged out of her life.

Thirty-eight days and just as many nights of barely existing. There is no torture quite like trying to sleep after you lose a loved one. She had spent so many nights listening to Jelena's heartbeat that now, suddenly, her own sounded alien. She would breathe in and breathe out and all that she could smell were her own lungs, chock full of ash. Her own skin a diary of loss. She read defeat all over it. It was hard to sleep when every single one of the senses screamed there was a stranger in her bed.

Her phone rang upstairs, on the charger in the kitchen. She got up, back aching in pain, and walked past the half-finished basement bathroom, now doomed to the eternity of incompletion. Projects were Jelena's thing; Mikel was just a hired muscle in that relationship. She did not have a mechanical brain, at all, but what she lacked in common sense she made up in eagerness to help. Every summer they would take on one room in the house and remake it into something new. Something of theirs.

"This house is us," Jelena would say, hammer in hand. "It was meant to be so much more than what they built her for." Mikel would just smile and move the bangs from Jelena's sweaty forehead. Determination and heat made her beautiful every time.

The name flashing on the screen was Johnny. She let it go to voicemail, as she changed into shorts and a t-shirt. It was probably more advices and rules about their trip to Serbia, and she did not feel like going over it. He meant well, of course. He had been there for her, ever since the night of the accident, a rock she could lean on even when she couldn't recognize she needed to. Funny how that works. Johnny was never her friend, but Jelena loved him to death. Now that they had both lost her, they found out they got along just fine. Grief is a spiderweb, holding a weight of loss on a single silky thread.

She walked outside into a blistering hot Portland day. Their front yard smelled of half-turned plums, scattered all over the ground, rotting. Normally, they would pick them while still in the tree and make jam for the winter. Normally they would do a lot of things. Normal was not who she was anymore. Mikel was something else now, a shell driven by pain and anger. So much anger.

She did not even get to see the body. Somehow, Jelena's family got ahold of it and arranged transportation back to Serbia before anyone could even tell Mikel what was going on. She should have been surprised. She should have, but she wasn't.

"I am Vlajna. We make things happen. The world does not want us pissed," Jelena used to say on rare occasions when she actually talked about her family. She loved them, especially her grandma, but kept them at a distance, behind a wall of silence. Jelena had many walls, a whole palace of them, which is why Mikel felt drawn to her. She was a place Mikel could lose herself in.

So, no, she was not surprised. Mad, yes, but only until they sent her an email with an already purchased ticket to Serbia and an invitation to stay at Jelena's home village for the Ceremony of the Sun, forty days after the passing.

"You are family. Jelena was bride. She still bride. We do Ceremony of Sun. You come, we burry her as family," was all it said. It was signed as Baba Mara. The grandma Jelena spoke of sometimes, the one she butted heads all her life, but respected. Strength recognizes strength.

Johnny got one, too. His was missing the bride part but was acknowledged as best man to be and as such, invited over. He was excited, of course. As a Serbian language and literature major, the opportunity to immerse himself in the culture he adored was all that he ever dreamed of. Gentle soul that he was, he really tried to hide it and focus on being supportive. Mikel did not deserve him. That was a part of Jelena's gift, she was the light to all of them lost souls. She would absorb their traumas, their pain, and spin it into something new and wonderful. Just like their house. She was a builder, no matter the material. In her hands all was clay.

Johnny called again as she got into her Pilot. This time she answered, as she pulled out into the traffic.

"Hey Johnny boy, what's up?"

"Hey precious, how are you? Where are you?"

She cussed under breath as an asshole in oversized truck with an American flag cut her off in the intersection.

"Johnny, why you gotta ask when you know the answer. It's almost noon, I have my daily appointment to make," she said.

He was silent.

"You know I can hear you frown, right." she said.

"Yeah, yeah, but it's only because I'm worried, okay? You'll push him over the edge one of these days," he said.

"Johnny dear, that's exactly what I'm hoping for," she said and meant it. Pushing assholes was her favorite pastime and this one? This one was personal.

"Well, make sure you get home on time and get some good sleep. We must be at the airport early in the morning. Just in case."

Johnny was a Just in Case type of a guy. Anxiety was the wave he surfed on often, not looking behind. World was full of sharks and his boat was never big enough.

"Yah, yah, yah, I hear you. I'll behave, I promise. Sleep, though, that's a different story," she said.

"Still having troubles?"

There Came the Sun

"If by troubles you mean crying and insomnia until the first light, then yeah. Troubles, Johnny," she said.

"I'm sorry, hun. It hurts still, I know. Just try, OK? That's all you can do," his voice was deep with worry.

"See you in the morning, kid. Love ya!" she said and hung up. She had a visit to make and Johnny would just try to make her behave. And she was all out of nice.

⌘⌘⌘

Jelena's murderer worked in Koin Tower, a huge brick building in downtown Portland, rising from the surrounding parks like a castle. It was a huge building with a mix of business offices and private condos at the top. Army of crows patrolled the skies around it, completing the look. Here, there be monsters.

His name was Charlie Morrison, and his office window overlooked the bench Mikel sat on every day at noon and ate lunch. She'd wave at him occasionally, when she caught him looking. He'd just hunker down and hide, the coward that he was. This was the same man who hit the love of her life, driving twenty miles over the speed limit, and pinned her against the wall. All the light extinguished with a flip of a switch. He was drunk, according to Johnny, who witnessed it, the poor soul. The official report conveniently missed out on that detail, largely due to the fact Charlie's father golfed with police chief every Sunday. Men who play with balls never have any. It's a brotherhood of danglers.

They made sure to show Jelena was high, in the same report. Under the influence and jaywalking. Charlie got away clean as a whistle. Or at least he thought so.

Mikel was there every day to remind him she knew. He did not get to just continue living like nothing happened. Making his life miserable gave her strength to get up in the morning.

She popped earbuds in, unwrapped her sandwich and bit into it with an appetite. It was egg salad, which she hated but it was Jelena's favorite.

Ivan Zoric

Anything else would feel like cheating. She spent the last few years pretending to like it and wasn't going to stop now.

The Beatles came on, singing about the sun. Another of Jelena's favorites, a song she sang every dawn, almost a ritual.

"Hey, you!" a voice behind her came loud enough to startle her.

Michael, a security guide for the building, stood next to her, hands in pockets. He smiled as she took out earbuds and nodded. They never shook hands, not with Charlie and others watching, but they were on good terms. He was Greek and knew Jelena from the art circles they both belonged to. Without his beanie and in a suit, he looked uncomfortable in more ways than one.

"You're wasting your time today," he said. "Fucker's on vacation."

"I figured something's up. Do you know how long?" she asked.

He shrugged and kicked an empty can of Red Bull off the sidewalk.

"No idea. He's in Greece. Couple of weeks, at least."

"No shit, Greece, huh?" she said.

Michael looked annoyed. He made an absentminded attempt to adjust the beanie that wasn't there and rubbed his forehead instead.

"Yeah, he even asked me if I can hook him up with someone who sells good pot there. Like, what the hell, man, I haven't been back home since the Athens protests. And even if I did know someone, fuck that noise," he said.

Mikel really liked the kid and not just because they shared the name. He was a genuinely good person, just trying to get by. She recognized her young self in him. All defiance and gangly limbs.

"Well, I better head home then," she said. "Got a big trip to go on myself. Heading to Serbia tomorrow. Meeting Jelena's family. Burying her according to tradition."

A shadow crossed his face. She could not tell what the look was. Fear, for sure, but something else, as well. A reverie of sort. Finally, he said: "Watch yourself out there. Vlajnas have reputation across Balkan. You don't want to piss them off."

There Came the Sun

"People keep telling me that," she said, leaving.

People did keep saying it. Men mostly. You would think by now they'd figure out it's not just village witches they should be afraid of.

⌘⌘⌘

There's no magic capable of reanimating moments lost. The touch of nostalgia is always a cold one. It's cruel, the game of remembrance. The more Mikel looked, the more dead she felt.

By the time their plane landed at Belgrade airport, she was a zombie, feeding on memories. They'd spent so many nights talking about Mikel's first trip to Serbia; talking about places they would visit. Jelena had a list of all the important places in her life she was going to show to Mikel, a roadmap of how she became the amazing woman Mikel fell in love with.

And now? Now she gets to visit one place Jelena felt happy to escape and lay her in the cold ground. She hated herself for being part of it, but she had to see Jelena one last time. She needed closure and she came half-across the world for it.

Johnny was in the element here. Not only did he completely take over the logistics of the trip, but he managed to somehow get enough food to last them a month. It was damn tasty, too. Jelena rarely ate meat in US, but she kept telling Mikel she would love Serbian street food. Turns out she was right all along. It was simple stuff, bread and meat and onions and some paste that tasted like roasted peppers, but it all worked so well together, Mikel could not stop shoving it in her mouth. She was making up for weeks of barely eating.

"Slow down, you'll choke," Johnny said, sitting behind the wheel of their rented car, something named Skoda, a brand they'd never heard of.

"I'm hungry and this stuff's good," she mumbled between bites.

"Oh yeah? It's called cevapi. Minced pork and beef. Ratio varies depending on which part of ex-Yugoslavia you're from. It's a matter of local pride and each city claims their recipe is the original one," he said.

"So, kind of like BBQ wars in US?"

Ivan Zoric

"Exactly like BBQ wars in US. No sauce, though. They'll kill you if you put sugar on meat here." He laughed and she smiled, and they were off into the unknown.

Serbia was a beautiful country. As soon as they were out of Belgrade, some half an hour into the drive, the gray of the old communist architecture gave way to open fields of wheat and sunflowers, colors exploding all around them. It was all so green and bright and full of life. Sky was crystal clear, clouds but a promise on the horizon. She rolled down the window and took in the smells and sounds of the countryside. Birds' song fighting over the noise of tractors and big harvesters; freshly mowed fields filling her nostrils with the rich aroma of fertility. This was a place of vitality, something she did not expect to find. She was so busy thinking of death, life caught her by surprise. No wonder Jelena loved to sing "*Here comes the Sun.*" This place was full of it.

Two hours later they started climbing up in elevation, road leading past the valley town of Zajecar and into the Balkan Mountains that extended past the Serbian-Bulgarian border, all the way to the Black Sea. All around them, the landscape was filled with pastures, rivers and meadows. She saw more sheep than she ever thought possible in one spot. Flocks ran across the road often, slowing the car to a crawl at times. Not that they minded at all. It gave them time to take in the beauty of the land and to talk.

"So, how much do you know about Vlahs and Vlajnas?" Johnny asked her, as another never-ending flock crossed their path. Mikel thought about it for a minute, trying to recall all the stories Jelena had told her over the years.

"Not as much as I would like, I guess," she said. "I know they are famous around the region for their customs and magic traditions. Feared almost."

"Very good. That's pretty spot on," he said. "Did you know they function as matriarchy?"

There Came the Sun

"No shit, really?" she asked. Jelena never mentioned that in any of her stories.

Johnny nodded, eyes still on the road, waiting for a break to start the car again.

"Yes. They are Christian only on paper, but most of their traditions are old pagan customs that snuck their way through backdoor of Christianity." He snickered at that, unapologetically gay as he was. "Every village has an elder who not only acts as a shaman and healer, but also a therapist of sort. People come to them for advice, help and often a favor. Also, they do not believe in written word. To write their ways down is to water them and make them easier to steal. Talk about homogenous and isolated, huh?"

It all made sense now. For all her artistic talent, Jelena absolutely hated writing things down. All their house projects, all the plans, everything was always in her head only. She was a genius when it came to creativity, but that genius was hers and hers alone.

"So, what is this Ceremony of the Sun we're a part of?" she asked.

Johnny started the car again, inching through the sheep. He waved to the shepherd, an elderly man in big wool cap and clothes that belonged to ages past. Man waved back, sporting a toothless grin.

"There are two main cults they worship in these parts. Death and Sun. There is a strong belief that life continues past death in another form and that the deceased must be prepared for the afterlife. At the same time Sun and light are considered as a way of rebirth, and if a person dies in the dark or an accident, it is believed that they can't find their way to the other side. They are doomed to wander lost in dark and cold until a light is provided by family. Women of the village craft a Paradise Candle, which helps them pass on. At forty-day mark, the casket is dug back out and opened so that the loved one can see the morning sun and travel to beyond reborn in its image."

Mikel shivered at the thought of Jelena roaming in the dark, like a lost soul. She was always the one lighting the way to others, guiding them

Ivan Zoric

to safety. It was such a cruel thought, that she teared up. Life was not fair, death even less so.

Johnny placed a hand on her shoulder, in support. She reached for it and held it for a while, their grief an unspoken bond.

"Do you think we will be welcome there?" she asked.

"Mikel, my dear, we will be welcomed like the queens we are," he said.

Above them, the mountain loomed motherly over the landscape.

⌘⌘⌘

As it turns out, Johnny was only partially right.

They pulled into the village late in the afternoon, as dusk worked its way up the mountain like a phantom Sisyphus. It was a group of some twenty houses or so, scattered around without any semblance of plan or reason. They stood two stories high, walls bumpy and uneven, all of them painted white with brown outlines around windows. Roofs were all clay tile, once orange but now covered in moss and dirt. A couple of large dogs patrolled around, eyeing them suspiciously.

They were still getting suitcases out of the trunk when the welcome committee showed up. The first thing that struck Mikel was how old they all looked. There was not a soul in that group younger than sixty. Some of them downright ancient looking, their faces an arabesque of experience and hardship. And yet, their eyes shone with such vigor and energy, Mikel found herself loving them before any words were spoken. These were Jelena's people. There were all the hands that raised and fed her once. This was home.

Mikel expected to see a woman in front, based on what Johnny told her earlier, but it was a man, holding a whole loaf of bread and a bowl of salt who approached them first. He extended his offer to Johnny and said in broken English: "Welcome, Mikel!"

Johnny shot her a confused look.

There Came the Sun

Oh shit, she thought. *She never told them.* The sting of pain rose but she stifled it quickly. This was not the time for that kind of hurt. She could only handle one at a time.

She moved past Johnny who was still just standing there dumbfounded, grabbed the loaf, tore a piece out and dipped it in salt. She lifted it to her eyes, nodded, smiled and ate it, hoping it was the right show of gratitude.

"Hvala!" she said, remembering the lessons in Serbian Jelena taught her. "I am Mikel. Bolje vas nasla!"

To their credit, they recovered faster than Johnny. If she expected judgement, she did not find it here. Growing up in rural Oregon she had to mask who she was until she was old enough to leave. It was hell hidden behind the cross and righteous sermons. But here, where some of the fences looked older than any church in US? Here, she got a quick second of wide-eyed confusion, followed by a kind smile.

"Of course," their host said. "Hungry? Dinner ready!" He pointed to the largest house in the village. Flickers of candlelight danced in the windows and even from where they were standing Mikel could smell food being prepared. Her stomach rumbled, like she did not just eat a ton a few hours ago.

"Yes, please!" she said and grabbed her things. She hip checked Johnny to snap him out of stupor. "You're supposed to be the expert here, you know?"

He smirked in shame and followed her and the villagers to the house.

They entered through a small hallway with pantry on one side into a large, well-lit room filled up to the brim with tables and chairs formed into a U formation. In one corner, a man sat on a three-legged chair, holding an instrument Mikel never saw before. It had a long neck, carved out of reddish wood, one string connecting it to a round, smallish body. The sound coming out of it was a wail, deep and full of sorrow, same as the song accompanying it. It was no Danny Boy, but you could not deny its sincerity. She was not the only one in pain inside these walls.

Ivan Zoric

There was so much food. Mikel remembered a saying Jelena would bring up every time they had people over for dinner.

"Wedding or funeral, you make enough food for three days. For every guest you invite three more will show up," she used to say, hunched over a boiling pot of cabbage rolls.

Mikel pushed the tears down. There will be time for that later, in the dark, when she's alone. So fucking alone.

The food was amazing. There was fresh baked bread, some sort of puff pastry filled with sharp and sour sheep cheese; there were cabbage rolls or sarma as they called it here; bowls of tomato and cucumber salad with feta cheese on top; and finally a whole lamb roast on a spit, centered in the middle of the table. Everyone was carving into it with vigor, taking platefuls.

"Now, this is what I call a rack of lamb," Johnny said as he raised a shot glass of plum brandy that was served around the table. "Ziveli!" he belted out, drank up and slammed the glass on the table.

"Ziveli!!!" the word went around the table, each time followed by a slam and a nod of approval. They might have been strangers here, but grief chose its own family.

At one point, in between the songs that got progressively louder and drunk-sounding, Mikel heard a car horn. She looked out the window and saw beam of headlight passing by the house. Another out of town guest, perhaps? Either way, the car did not stop but went by the house towards the other end of the village and was soon swallowed by the dark.

The dark was different here. Thicker, more complete. She stepped outside to smoke and calm her nerves and was taken back by the absence of the night glow she was so used to in Portland. There were always city lights bouncing off low cloud cover like an orange glow. Not here, in the mountains of Serbia. She could see the entire Milky Way above her, but it was a cold shine. Obituary to millions of dead stars. She shivered at the thought and lit a cigarette.

There Came the Sun

Someone sat in the dark, watching her. Mikel just about pissed her pants when the lighter flame revealed a woman on a bench next to the house, eyes locked on her, unwavering.

If the rest of the village was old, she was ancient. Tall, but hunched over, shoulders moved inward, like she was shielding herself from something. From time.

Her hands lay in the lap, wrapped around a small box. She motioned Mikel to come and sit by her and Mikel did it without protest. This was not someone you dare question.

The old woman made another motion with her hand, rubbing her thumb against other fingers.

"Can I help you with something?" Mikel asked.

Thumb again, this time more vigorous, moving the hand up and down.

"Wait, a lighter? You need a lighter?" she said and then remembering the word in Serbian: "Vatra?"

The old woman smiled and nodded.

Mikel pulled the lighter out of pocket and flicked it on. Woman lifted an oil lamp and Mikel helped her get the flame going. Shadows ran away from them, past the house and into the forest surrounding the village.

It was a treasure box, carved out of the same wood as the instrument she saw earlier. There was a red, silky shine to it. Cherry wood, maybe?

She opened it slow, with a tiny creak of rusted hinges. Inside of it, a lock of hair and a couple of photographs. Mikel recognized it immediately. There was only one person she knew with hair so auburn. She had spent many a night running fingers through it, happy and loved.

"Baba Mara?" she asked, and the old woman nodded. Then she pulled a photo out of the box.

Mikel knew the photo, knew where it was taken and when.

Maui, summer of 2016. Their engagement photo, Mikel in a suit and a vest, on one knee, proposing, and Jelena hiding her face with fists, trying not to scream. She loved that photo. A larger copy of it still hung in their empty house, back in Portland.

"You knew," she said. "Oh god, you knew!"

Tears came, then. She held them for so long, refusing to accept the truth. Her whole life she had to be strong, a rock, unflinching in the face of hate and prejudice that she forgot how liberating it felt to just let go. And let go she did, heavy sobs escaping her. She turned to Mara and saw tears rolling down the old woman's face, too. Grief is a universal language and they spoke in it, hidden from the world, strength supporting strength.

Hours or centuries later, they got up and walked back into the house.

Men were singing now, Johnny among them, as the women worked on something in the smaller room next to them. A Paradise Candle. They all wore white dresses and worked on a white sheet spread across the floor. Mara handed them the lock of hair and they weaved it in with the wick. It was a massive candle, a good two feet tall and thick as an arm. As they worked, they chanted, one at a time, verses that felt hypnotic and calming.

Finally, they all stood up and presented the candle to Mara, who shook her head and pointed at Mikel. With a lump in her throat the size of a meatball, she accepted it. For so long Jelena had been her light and look at them now. She was not ready for this, but is anyone ever ready? Death does not deal in permissions.

"Come, come," Mara helped her out the door. Behind them, villagers formed a line, two wide, with women in front and men following. All the way in the back, Johnny stumbled, holding on to the musician.

The cemetery was on the opposite side of the village, some half a mile down the road. If the houses were scattered and all over the place, the graves were in perfect order. Whatever the property lines quarrel they had during life, in death they all made good neighbors.

A massive oak tree grew there, on the eastern side of the cemetery, its treetop looming over the tombstones. The trunk alone was wider than

There Came the Sun

any tree Mikel has ever seen, and she'd been to redwood forests in California.

There was something tied to it, a bag or a sack, halfway ready to spill out on the ground.

Women started chanting again.

"It's not a song," said Johnny. "They are listing all the things Jelena will be able to do in the afterlife, now that she has a light."

Four men with shovels dug, silent as the voices of the women echoed across the mountain, like a bell. The air was crisp and cool, the heat of the day still hours away.

When the metal scrapped against the wood in the ground, Mikel gasped. The last time she saw Jelena, she was curled up in a ball asleep on the couch. And now she gets to see the work of worm and decay and the thought terrified her. She grabbed Johnny's hand. It was warm and sweaty and comforting.

"Hang in there, hun," he said.

Men raised the coffin out of the hole and planted it facing the tree. Women went around and cleaned it with white linens. It was all slow and methodical. Dead are always patient.

Two things happened the moment they took off the lid. The candle flame finally reached the lock of hair and shot up, filling the air with a stench strong enough to mask whatever was coming out of the casket.

Whatever was in the sack, tied to the tree screamed.

"What the fuck?" she said and turned to Johnny. His eyes were wide open, in shock.

Another scream pierced the night.

Mara walked over to the tree. She produced a long knife from somewhere in her dress and cut the rope used to hold the sack together. It fell to the ground, revealing what was hidden.

"Holly fuckin' hell, it's him," said Johnny.

Ivan Zoric

Charlie Morrison starred at them, in shock. His face was covered in bruises and there was dried, crusty blood in that country golf club blond hair of his Mikel hated so much. Big, dark stain spread across his pants, starting at the crotch.

"Pissed himself, just like that night," Johnny's voice trembled.

Before Mikel had the chance to react, Mara slapped Charlie back to reality. Three times, tat-tat-tat, like machine gun. He came to, shook his head and then recognizing who was in front of him screamed: "You will pay for this, you fucking dyke! You are done. You are so fuckin' done!"

"I'm not the one tied to a tree," Mikel said. "You know what they say around these parts?"

"What?" he snarled.

"Never piss of a Vlajna!"

Mara returned and motioned everyone to stand behind the casket. She then waved at someone, *something*, in the dark. The rumble of hooves filled the night. The biggest ram Mikel had ever seen trotted out of the shadows and into the clearing. The horns on it were the size of a car wheel and just as wide. It approached Mara, head bowed and let her scratch its head. She bent down slightly and whispered a single word.

"What the fuck is going on here?" Charlie was still going on. "You'll pay for this! You'll all pay!"

The ram slammed into him without warning, crushing the ribs with a wet sound. Blood burst out of Charlie's mouth and sprayed the wool on ram's back as it thrashed about. It dislodged from Charlie's torso and made another circle around the graveyard. Charlie whimpered, spit and dark red blood oozing from his lips and nose. Pieces of bone protruded from the shirt, glistening. He was finally out of words to throw at them.

The ram slammed again. Chest cavity exploded to the sides, sending bone shrapnel all around the tree. What was left of Charlie Morrison hung off the rope that went around the trunk, as the gravity slowly worked on pulling it down, like spilled jam.

There Came the Sun

The animal came back to Mara for another head scratch. It bleated and rubbed against the hand, looking for reassurance.

Moments later it trotted back into the dark from where it came.

Everyone fell silent. Mikel and Johnny were still processing what just happened when Mara spoke: "Oko za oko."

"Eye for an eye," whispered Johnny. "Eye for a damn eye, Mikel."

She heard him, but she did not care. The angry Mikel, the Mikel who, not even a week ago, would have given everything she owned to see this justice done, was gone. Rage does not bring the dead back. And another thing, something she understood even without speaking the language. This was not vengeance, no. This was the old way of the world, before the movies made it cool, before the books glorifying vendetta. Before the words. This was cause and effect, a way to bring balance to the world, without the need for cheap posturing of men. Tears were shed that night, and that was the true healing. That was love.

Strength recognizes strength.

As the first rays of dawn inched towards them across the glade, she faced the casket, opened the eye of the woman she will always love, and she sang.

Here comes the sun, and I say

It's all right

Little darling, the smile's returning to their faces

Little darling, it seems like years since it's been here

In her eternal bed, eyes opened to greet the afterlife, Jelena was smiling.

Illustration by Alan Sessler

Spring Leanings
by Alan Sessler

Ayden dragged the tines of his fork idly through the piece of birthday cake like a farmer breaking fallow ground. With his cheek propped upon his other hand, elbow on the table, he glared at the four narrow streaks of black crumbs following behind in a malaise he had only begun to know that Spring.

Carson sat to his left with a wide, clownish smile painted on his face with chocolate icing. He leaned over and pointed with his spoon. "You're letting your ice cream melt."

"I don't want any more," Ayden said and stood from the long picnic table where most of his friends sat.

He walked half in a daze past others caught up in games, barely fazed by the two-hundred-dollar mime dispensing balloon animals to kids he only knew by name. Several parents attended to their children or carried on in conversation with clear plastic cups of iced soda most of them wished was alcohol.

Ayden approached the wooded area bordering his back yard, where two of his friends challenged one another with their botanical knowledge.

"That's oak," said Alex.

"Wrong," said Jimmy, waving the leaf as if it were his head shaking no.

"No, I'm not," argued Alex.

"It's sycamore."

"No, it's not."

"Bet you a dollar."

"Yeah, and who's gonna say who's right?"

Spring Leanings

They noticed Ayden standing, silently.

"Ayden will," said Jimmy.

Ayden didn't answer.

"He's not a Scout," said Alex.

"So, he knows. Don't you, Ayden? Tell him this is a sycamore," Jimmy said, displaying the leaf for Ayden's examination.

Ayden looked at the hanging vines of ivy. His gaze followed them to the treetops until the noon day sun made him squint. He reached for a vine.

"Yeah, right. He can't even tell that's poison ivy," said Alex.

"Poison oak," Jimmy argued.

⌘⌘⌘

"Do you think Ayden's been acting strange?" Jane asked her husband as she poured him a cup of Sprite.

Bryce shrugged. "Not really. Kid's a kid," he said and took the drink.

Her back bowed beneath the weight of her worry. "He hasn't been eating right."

Bryce took a sip. "I have noticed that. Barely touched his hot dogs and macaroni last night. You think he's bulimic?" he said and stuck a finger in his mouth with mock retching.

She didn't laugh. "Don't act the maggot."

The kitchen door to the backyard opened. Alex dared not track garden dirt on the floor. "Mrs. Patton! Come quick!" he shouted, and behind him Jimmy's expression echoed the urgency without a word.

Bryce and Jane hurried out the door, nearly trampling the boys.

"Where is he?" Bryce yelled.

"Over there," Alex pointed. "By the poison ivy."

"Poison oak!" said Jimmy.

Alex smacked Jimmy's arm.

"Hey!"

"We tried to stop him," said Alex. "But we couldn't take it from him. It's poisonous."

Ahead stood Ayden, reaching for another vine.

"Ayden! Don't touch it!" Jane shouted.

He turned to face them, the vine in his left hand. He tore a leaf off with his right hand.

When Bryce saw Ayden handling the vine he was both relieved and mad at the boys for scaring the hell out of he and his wife, enough so he slowed to a walk and let the others run until they caught up with him.

"Put it down," said Jane. "It'll make you itch all over."

Bryce waved an arm. "It's alright. Let him learn the hard way."

Ayden popped the leaf and his mouth and began chewing.

Bryce's eyes grew wide. "Ayden! Spit it out!" he yelled and ran to his son.

He snatched Ayden up and reached into his mouth to pull the leaf out just as Ayden swallowed half of it. He pulled out a spittle-covered bit and threw it aside then reached into his son's mouth again. "Oh God, no, Ayden! Spit it out. Come on, son. Spit it out, right now. It's poisonous!"

Ayden's eyes were glassy. He looked right through his father.

"Sorry, son. Daddy loves you," Bryce said and shoved a finger down his son's throat, triggering his reflex to vomit up a stomach full of chewed leaves, birthday cake, half-digested hot dog bites and macaroni noodles.

⌘⌘⌘

Ayden lay in the emergency room bed, a number of lines and solution-filled bags surrounding him. A nurse tended to him while the doctor spoke to Jane and Bryce outside the room, their long, worried faces awaiting his judgment.

"The good news is he'll be alright," said Dr. Maitland, gripping his clipboard in both hands. "It appears your son possesses an amazing immunity to poison ivy. Most kids his age would…well …"

Spring Leanings

Jane turned away and choked on a sob, unable to face the doctor's grim expression.

"And" Bryce said, afraid to know. "The bad news?"

"The x-rays reveal he's been eating other non-food items as well."

Jane wrapped her arms tight around her husband.

"Like what?" asked Bryce.

"Mostly small pieces of metal or plastic, or possibly even rubber. It's difficult to tell, of course, from an x-ray, but definitely something solid, something inorganic."

"Why would he do that?"

Dr. Maitland sighed. "It would appear your son has what we call *pica*."

Bryce shook his head. He fell back to his trusted defense mechanism of attempting humor. "Is he going to turn into a fish?"

"Don't be daft," Jane said with a whimper and slapped his chest.

Dr. Maitland ignored the joke. "Pica is an eating disorder. Ayden's body recognizes its need for certain nutrients that his diet is lacking. Something he thought the leaves could supply. As for the other items, I can't say."

Jane was afraid of the insinuation. "You don't think we starve our son, do you?"

"Of course not, Mrs. Patton, and that's why pica is classified as a *disorder*. Ayden may reject normal food for something a subconscious part of him perceives to have the nutritional value he needs."

"You're starting to sound like a psychiatrist," said Bryce.

Dr. Maitland chuckled. "Well, of course I'm not. It's just common knowledge."

"You see this often?" asked Jane.

Dr. Maitland offered an assuring smile. "Often enough to know what it is."

"What's going to happen? Aren't all those things going to pile up in his stomach?" asked Bryce.

"The pieces are small enough that they should pass right through," said Dr. Maitland.

"They *should*. And if they don't?"

"Then we may have a problem. If something were to get caught in his intestine it could cause a blockage, but for now we'll concentrate on running some tests to check for anemia, malnutrition, mineral deficiencies. Our next step would be to recommend a behavioral specialist. And you do need to prepare yourself for the possibility your son may have autism."

"But he's perfectly normal," said Bryce, then faced Jane. "Or, has been, until now."

She ran a hand along his back to comfort him.

Dr. Maitland held his peace with a frozen ear-to-ear smile. "Again, let's run some tests before we jump to conclusions."

Jane and Bryce faced one another, both fearful and hopeful at the same time. "You mean right now?" asked Bryce.

Dr. Maitland nodded with the same smile, then let it crumble. "I'll put an order in for those and be back with your shortly."

"Shortly," he'd said, but he meant some 16 hours later.

⌘⌘⌘

"All done," Ayden said and sat up from the toilet, then pulled up his pants.

The bathroom door pushed open and both Jane and Bryce stepped in.

"Alright, let's get those hands washed, mister," Jane said and led Ayden to the sink, where she promptly turned on the water and lathered his hands from the liquid soap dispenser.

Bryce stooped over the toilet with a small hand net and went fishing. He caught two small brown trout—or finless browns as they're called in

Spring Leanings

some regions—and left the room to begin his thoroughly unpleasant examination.

Jane and Bryce had closely observed Ayden over the last several weeks, in particular his bathroom time. The boy was strictly ordered not to flush without letting his parents observe the contents of the toilet. Unfortunately, it was Bryce who had the difficult task of playing scatologist, which he considered his fair share of clock-punching for all the diaper changes he had missed out on due to his work schedule.

"How do you feel?" Jane asked.

"Okay," Ayden nodded.

"Your belly doesn't hurt?"

He shook his head.

"Are you sure? You have to tell us if anything hurts, even a little, okay?"

He nodded again. "Yes, ma'am."

Bryce peeked in the door. When Jane faced him, he shook his head slowly, another confirmation that none of the inorganic bits x-rays had shown were coming out.

Her eyes grew red at the diagnosis.

"Don't cry, Mam," Ayden said and hugged his mother.

She embraced him twice as hard. "I'm sorry. I can't help it."

"Neither can I," he whispered in her ear.

Her arms went weak and he pulled away. "May I be excused?" he asked and faced his father.

"Sure, son. Thanks for helping. You did good," Bryce said and patted him on the head as he left the room.

Bryce approached Jane and knelt down to hold her. "It's gonna be alright, baby," he said, looking past her to the unopened box of chocolate laxatives on the counter. "We'll just try something stronger. Those things can't stay in there forever."

⌘⌘⌘

Alan Sessler

With things somewhat back to normal, Bryce was pulling half-days at the office, leaving Jane to care for Ayden by herself most mornings. Jane and her friend Brenda were enjoying a cup of coffee in the dining room, and Jane the much-needed comfort of a friendly ear. They watched Ayden walk in the backyard through the bay window.

"Do you think it's good for him to play outside, considering?" Brenda asked.

Jane gave a half shrug. "If he's inside too long he eats the stuff that could really harm him."

Ayden stooped over the poison ivy bed bordering the woods, plucked a leaf off the sprawling vine and ate it.

Brenda's gaze set on the faux Tiffany lamp suspended from a hook in the living room. Where a chain had once ran through the two ceiling hooks now only a naked power cord ran to the outlet.

Jane observed the direction of her glare. "We had to throw it away. It was at least a foot shorter than it had been. We replaced the shower curtain, too. Half the rings were missing so we got one with those huge hoops. God forbid Ayden manages to swallow one of those."

Brenda reached across the table and patted her hand. "I'm so sorry, Jane."

The kitchen door opened, and Ayden came into the dining room. Brenda withdrew the moment Ayden's eyes settled upon their hands.

"Mam?" he said.

"Yes, Ayden?"

"I have to use the jacks."

Brenda's eyes flashed to Jane.

"Toilet," Jane explained.

"That's a new one on me," said Brenda.

Jane pushed her chair back and stood. "Go ahead. I'll be right there," she said and waited till he left. "Bryce thought a laxative would help him pass some of the 'foreign' objects. So far it hasn't worked."

Spring Leanings

"That makes sense," Brenda said. Her arched brow and exaggerated nodding hinted at her doubt.

"Be right back," Jane said and went to the guest bathroom down the hall.

Brenda patiently sipped at her coffee. She managed to check her watch, the microwave, and the wall clock twice before she found herself looking into the bottom of an empty ceramic mug. She went to the kitchen coffee maker and poured herself a second cup, determined she would leave if she finished before her hostess returned. She could always make up with a phone call and lunch on her.

She was halfway finished when Ayden passed by, followed by Jane, who resumed her place at the table.

"You want me to top it off for you?" Jane asked, reaching for her mug.

"I'm fine," Brenda said and refrained from mentioning it was her second cup.

"Well, I definitely need a second cup to wake up," Jane said and went to the kitchen, while at the same time Ayden returned and sat at the table.

He sipped something green from a tall glass.

"What you got there, Ayd?" asked Brenda.

He sipped silently, his eyes not leaving Brenda.

"Oh, that's kale juice," Jane said from the kitchen. "He never touched the stuff before. Now he seems to love it."

"Well, they say your taste buds change with age. Didn't you just have a birthday?" Brenda teased.

Ayden nodded. "It's almost finished."

She smiled awkwardly. His stare was becoming uncomfortable. She played with her hair, tucked a tawny lock behind her ear. "What's almost finished?"

He took another sip and stood up. "It only needs one more piece."

She snickered, still confused. He circled the round table until he stood before her, staring face to face.

He stepped closer.

"Yes?" she said.

He raised his hands toward her.

"Oh," she said, blushing with embarrassment, and opened her arms to accept the sweet offer.

Jane returned with a steaming cup in her hand.

His tiny fingertips brushed Brenda's ear.

"Ayden?" said Jane. "What are—"

He yanked the small silver hoop from Brenda's earlobe, tearing it straight from her ear, earning a scream and a hairline spray of blood than ran diagonal across his face.

Jane's hand went limp and the cup fell, smashing on the floor and spilling fresh coffee on her canvas shoes. Her feet were soaked in blistering heat.

Ayden tucked the earring into his mouth and swallowed. When the two women screamed, he took his cue to flee outside and hide.

⌘⌘⌘

Ayden sat naked in the dirty tub, the water an impenetrable gray from his romp in the woods. Bryce plunged his arms into the water to find the sponge and ran it over Ayden's back, gritting his teeth to ignore the bloody, stinging cuts he'd gained from the thorns and devil's walking sticks he had trudged through that afternoon to find his son. Ayden, for his part, seemed to have no fear of ticks or spiders or any number of creeping things one might encounter, instead lying fetal on the forest floor.

That evening, Jane told Bryce how upset Brenda was, inconsolable really. She even confessed her fear Brenda might call Child Protective Services. One thing was sure, the woman was never coming over for coffee and gossip ever again.

Spring Leanings

After putting Ayden to bed, Bryce made sure to put a fresh application of salve on Jane's feet. The blisters were small and, though unbroken, an angry shade of red that professed her pain.

⌘⌘⌘

4:30 am. Ayden stood in the door, a dark shape with only the foot lights of the hall to illuminate him from behind. "Mam, Dad," he announced his presence.

Jane rolled over, barely awake, eyes squinting to make out the shape of her son. The burning sensation atop her feet that sleep had numbed soon returned. "Ayden? What are you doing up?"

"I think I'm sick," he said.

She reached for the lamp on the nightstand and pinched the remaining stub of the beaded chain, a reminder of the lengths Ayden's unusual craving drove him to. "Come here so Mam can see you."

Ayden stepped from the shadow.

Her gasp woke Bryce, who rolled over and witnessed the same horror as his wife. Ayden's stomach hung below his crotch, swollen, distended. His face was a ghastly green hue, and something hung from his mouth.

"Oh God, Ayden," Bryce said, tugging on his wife's arm. "Jane, call an ambulance!"

"I am," she said with trembling voice

Bryce hurried from the bed to his son.

"Norville," Jane said to the operator. "It's my son. He's sick…I mean, really sick…his stomach is swollen and…yes…he's ten…he has pica…he eats things he shouldn't…leaves, bits of metal…I think he has a blockage …"

"Honey, go to the hall," Bryce said. "I can't hear what he's saying."

"Okay," she said and stepped out of the room and pulled the door closed. "I was just speaking to my husband…he's looking at my son…" Her voice faded, allowing Bryce to speak.

"Ayden, can you breathe?" he asked.

Ayden nodded. "But it hurts."

"What hurts? Breathing? When you breathe? It hurts to breathe?"

Ayden nodded. "But mostly my stomach. It feels like I'm going potty, but I can't."

Bryce stood straight and gently nudged his son to follow. "Let's go to the bathroom and see if you can go."

"I can't. It hurts," Ayden whined.

"You don't have to push. Just sit on the toilet, okay?"

Ayden nodded.

"That a boy. Come on," Bryce said and led him to the master bath door. "Pull your pajamas down, son."

Ayden obeyed and found himself picked up and placed on the toilet.

"There you go. If you feel like anything's coming out, just let it, okay?"

"It hurts, Daddy."

The only comfort Bryce could offer was to kiss his son's forehead. "I know, son. Just relax. The doctors will be here soon."

⌘⌘⌘

"I want you to remain on the line until help comes," said the 9-1-1 dispatcher.

"I will," Jane said, only slightly calmer now.

She wiped the tears from her eyes with the butt of her palm. It was only then that she looked down at her silhouetted form. She looked out the entryway window at the empty yard and decided to change before the ambulance arrived. She hurried up the stairs and down the hall to the master bedroom, light spilling from beneath the bathroom door. She put the phone on the nightstand and set it to SPEAKER. "Bryce, the ambulance is on the way. I'm going to get dressed real quick before they arrive," she said and opened a dresser drawer to grab a pair of jeans.

The dispatcher chimed in. "Ma'am, I need you to remain on the line —"

Spring Leanings

"You're on speaker. I'm just getting dressed before they arrive."

"Alright, ma'am. Let me know if your son's condition changes."

"I will." She found a faded gray tee-shirt and pulled it over her head and arms. "Bryce, how is Ayden?"

There was a violent heaving from behind the bathroom door. "Bryce?"

She stepped toward the bathroom when another heave gave her pause. Shadows danced in the light beneath the threshold.

"Ayden?"

A retching sound, then a sound like a drawer full of silverware spilling falling on the floor. "Honey, it's Mammy," she said and took another step. "Are you okay?"

"Ma'am? Is everything alright?" the dispatcher asked, but Jane ignored her.

A great tearing sound. The shaft of light was submerged beneath a growing spill of red.

Jane gasped and ran to the bathroom door. She threw it open, and immediately her eyes were drawn to Bryce's bare legs and bloody soles jutting out from the bathtub, and a length of chain assembled from metal beads and links, shower rings and gumball machine jewelry, running from the tub and across the floor to a disgusting, bloody mess she would not have recognized as her son could she not see the tiny legs beneath the heart of gore.

She screamed.

The chain writhed on the floor like a snake, clinking as it went taut and leaving a white swath of exposed tile in its wake. She followed the chain to what had been Ayden's face, more specifically his mouth, although now torn so wide in either direction it looked more like a dilated cervix. His broken lower jaw dangled over his heart.

A bloody hand emerged from impossibly deep within the grue, clinging to the chain. It pulled tighter and sent Bryce's body shifting in the tub. Jane stepped forward, the warm blood filling the spaces between her toes. She looked into the tub. The makeshift chain was wound about Bryce's neck three times, his face purple, eyes bulging.

The chain went loose, then taut again. Another hand emerged from Ayden's demolished mouth. Bryce's body was merely an anchor for some monstrous being to leave her poor son's body.

She stepped backward into the puddle of blood and lost her footing. She fell back across the threshold and into the bedroom, spinning counterclockwise half-way down to land on the meat of her arm. The crack of her arm then head connecting with the hardwood floor nearly knocked her unconscious.

"Ma'am," the dispatcher's voice came from the nightstand. "The medics are at the door. I need you to let them in. The police are on the way."

Jane moaned.

"Ma'am, are you able to get to the door?"

The clinking and tearing continued inside the bathroom, diverting her attention from the front door. Blood spread across the floor beneath her legs and back. She raised her arm to find it covered in blood, although hers or her son's, she wasn't sure.

Breathing came from the bathroom. Footsteps. Slow and lumbering. The distinct sound of toes sinking into blood, then the heel, then toes and heel again, until a large shape filled the doorway. She screamed at the sight of it.

"Ma'am. The police are at the door. They're coming in. Just hold on!" the dispatcher pleaded.

The figure stepped into the light. Beneath the glistening blood she caught glimpses of green. Shapes became clearer, the crisp edge of ivy leaves everywhere, covering its body—if its body were anything more than the leaves themselves. Lengths of vine weaved in and out of the foliage from head to neck to torso to the end of each limb as if a circulatory system of chlorophyll-carrying veins.

A crash came from downstairs.

Spring Leanings

The thing turned its attention to the hall. Jane wanted to look but she couldn't tear her eyes away from the thing. It spun back and toward the bedroom window to the left of the bathroom. Thudding footsteps came rushing up the stairs.

Jane finally looked toward the hall. "Help! I'm in the bedroom!" she screamed.

There was a grunt, drawing her attention back to the leaf man. The window was open, and the thing was climbing through to the pitched roof that terminated just above the first story of the house.

The police burst into the bedroom.

"It went out the window!" she yelled.

Seeing the pool of blood, one officer rushed to the bathroom, the other to the blood-smeared windowsill to peer down. "Who went out the window, ma'am?" asked the latter.

"I don't know," she cried. "It was a green man."

The first officer came out of the bathroom. "Good God, it's a massacre!"

The second shone his flashlight out onto the roof, revealing the bloody footprints. "Somebody get to the back of the house! Check out the yard. Call the K9 unit and search the woods!"

He pressed his chin to his lapel radio. "Dispatch, we need a bird in the air and K9. We have a perp on the run who may have escaped into the heavily wooded area surrounding the southern side of the house. Over."

"Copy that," said a woman's voice.

Another officer knelt at Jane's side. "Ma'am, can you move?"

She shook her head, tears streaming down her temples, her lips moving, her voice speaking, but nothing that sounded like speech.

⌘⌘⌘

Alan Sessler

It was April 30th. A bright Spring day. The sun was warm on Jane's bare arms, though her left arm ached with the dull throb of still-healing bones that often predicted the coming of rain.

She sat at the round wrought iron table in her backyard. Alone. She thought of Bryce and Ayden, but not of their horrible deaths. She had spent months learning how to block those images from her mind. She chose only to remember their lives, but she was still hopelessly alone.

Ever since that day she had sensed a presence, but never on the couch when she watched TV. Never in Ayden's room which she hardly visited anyway, and certainly never in the bed she lay in most nights beside the empty place her husband had lain. Not when she burned to make love just once again, and that feeling was in the air more and more as the days grew warmer.

Outside, however, she felt it all the time. Near the hedges along the border of her house. The flowerbed by the road. The herb and vegetable garden in the back yard. But mostly by the trees.

There she swore she could see it. The leaf man. Green man. Perhaps it was a trick of light, or maybe her brutalized mind struggling to cope with reality and the traumatic memories buried beneath the superficial soil of pleasant, happy thoughts. But it was there. No denying.

Sometimes, it smiled at her. Inviting. She would run her hand along the ivy, and she was sure it caressed her back. She ached for touch. Any. Such appetites should seem strange, but why? The metal pins holding the bones in her arm together didn't seem so out of place. Maybe it was normal to have the strange, the foreign, the alien come enter your body. To want it. She traced the scar that buried the metal bone. The thought of its perfect hardness aroused her.

But today was Ayden's birthday. A time for celebration. She stared at the cake before her. She imagined streamers hanging over the picnic table like it had before. A dozen multi-colored pointed hats and blowers, plates and matching napkins at every setting.

Spring Leanings

This year there were only three: one for her, one for Bryce, and one for the guest of honor, little Ayden.

She didn't feel like cake. It was chocolate, too, her favorite, just like it had been Ayden's. Beside it sat an open carton of Neapolitan ice cream, getting softer by the moment. Soon it would melt, and she didn't care one bit.

A breeze stirred in the air, blowing through her hair. She faced the wall of ivy and trees behind her. She rose and approached the forest. Her hand ran along the vines and plucked a single leaf.

She stared at it, how its veins spread out from the spine in the middle, like branches spread out from the trunk of a tree. She imagined her own spine, how it connected to all her nerves, much like the veins in the leaf. She tore it in two and placed half on her tongue.

She closed her eyes and her mouth, chewed the leaf and swallowed. She imagined the leaf a fertile seed, going down into her belly, the very place she had carried her only child for some long nine months.

She opened her eyes and smiled. "Happy birthday, baby."

Illustration by Sarah Walker

Daughters of the Hare
by K.A. Opperman

With pointed ears atop their hair,
And baskets in their hands,
The wanton daughters of the hare
Parade through daisied lands.

They walk in gowns of virgin white,
Bare feet upon the green;
They hold the great Ostara rite
In honor of their queen.

Eostre, Goddess of the Dawn,
Of Spring, and green new growth!
They frolic on her flowered lawn;
To her they pledge the oath.

Eostre, on her wooden plinth,
Hare-eared, with springing leg!
They pet her belly's labyrinth,
The spiral-painted egg.

With ash-drawn whiskers, blushing cheeks,
They hide their offered gifts;
They hide the eggs, though no one seeks—
Until the full moon lifts.

Daughters of the Hare

And then they make their rampant search—
They hop, but cannot run;
Who brings the most to Eastre's perch
Will be the chosen one

Illustration by Sarah Walker

Morton's Woods
by Jill Hand

Paige had always loved trees. One of her earliest memories was of falling asleep to the gentle sound of wind soughing through the branches of the Norway maple outside her bedroom window.

To Paige, the maple was a friend, with its own personality and varied moods. In the spring it was joyous, exuberantly sprouting greenish-yellow flowers. In summer it sent out flat, green, papery fruit with two wings. Paige thought of them as "helicopters." She liked to toss them in the air and watch as they whirled down. In autumn the maple was a majestic queen cloaked in gold. In winter it was solemn, a Chinese brush painting, pared down to its essence of black trunk and bare fanlike branches.

It would have been better for Paige—much better—if she hadn't loved trees so much.

Her love of trees eventually led her to defy her parents, who wanted her to choose a college major which would lead to her obtaining what they called "a good-paying job."

When she showed them her letter of acceptance to the State University of New York's College of Environmental Science and Forestry they read it with expressions of dismay on their faces.

"This forestry thing doesn't pay well," her father said.

"Not too well, no," Paige admitted. "But there's more to life than money."

Her parents stared at her, aghast.

"Your sister's going to be a lawyer," her mother said.

"That's great," said Paige. "I'm happy for her."

"And your brother's majoring in computers," her mother continued.

Morton's Woods

Her father chimed in. "It's called IT. It pays good money. Everything's computers now."

"What's your point?" Paige felt resentful. Couldn't they at least try and be a little bit proud of her?

The two vertical lines between her mother's eyebrows deepened, as they always did when she was angry or upset. "Our point, Paige, is that we don't want you to have to live under a bridge with drug addicts and crazy people because you threw away your chance to make something of yourself."

"Don't be silly, Mom. That's not going to happen," Paige told her.

She was right. That didn't happen. Something worse did.

Four years later, Paige graduated from SUNY at Syracuse with a degree in Environmental Science and Forestry. Her parents attended her graduation, as did her sister and brother. Her sister and brother brought a bunch of balloons with CONGRATULATIONS GRADUATE on them. They stood up and cheered when she accepted her diploma in the Carrier Dome. Her parents just sat there in their metal folding chairs, strained smiles on their faces.

"Bunch of hippies," her father muttered, meaning the forestry graduates.

The next step was finding a job. Paige had an unpaid internship at an arboretum during her senior year, which led to her supervisor emailing her with the following:

'Hi, Paige. Hope you're doing well. Would this be of interest to you? I'll be glad to write a letter of recommendation. – James Harris'

Attached was a PDF which said:

'Morton's Woods, a privately owned corporation in Crawley, PA, seeks a conservation and resource forester to survey and assess the health and status of our historic woodlands. Must have appropriate degree. Must have the ability to develop conservation and land-use management strategies. Must be able to address problems such as soil erosion, invasive species, and pests that threaten tree health. Must be able to determine how much timber can be harvested annually without endangering the sustainability of our forest ecosystem. Starting salary $86,400. To schedule an interview, call or email Nicole Beneducci, director of human services.'

There was an email address and a phone number.

Paige read it through twice, noting the daunting number of "musts." She also noted the salary. It was high for a field with a reputation for being less than lavish when it came to pay.

"I can do that," she murmured.

Crawley was in Bucks County, Pennsylvania, north of Philadelphia. It had horse farms, quaint stone houses and little towns that could have come straight out of a Norman Rockwell painting. To the southeast was the Delaware River. Paige was currently staying with parents, who lived across the river in a suburb of Trenton, NJ. She was back in her old room, the one with her old friend the Norway maple outside the window. If she got the job at Morton's Woods, she could afford her own apartment. She could afford a lot of things.

She consulted the TravLBuddy app on her phone and found it would take an hour to drive to Crawley. Easy-peasy.

Paige sent Ms. Beneducci an email with her resume attached, as well as a copy of her college transcript. Her GPA was 4.0, which she hoped made up for her lack of work experience. Beside her unpaid internship she'd worked for one year as a crew member at Fun Jumpers Adventure Zone, an indoor trampoline and rock-climbing venue. She'd also worked for nine months as a waitress at Rootin' Tootin' Buckaroos. That was a western-themed steak house where they made her wear a cowboy hat and call customers "pardner." She had to greet them by saying, "Howdy, pardners. What you fixin' to eat from the old chuck wagon? I bet you're hankerin' for a nice, juicy steak and a heap of our spicy bandito onion rings."

Two days after she sent the email, she got a reply arranging for an interview at 2 p.m. the following Wednesday.

Morton's Woods

The interview was weird, even to Paige, who didn't have much experience with job interviews. Something about it felt *wrong*, although she couldn't quite put her finger on why. It took place in a bland, unremarkable building made of tan-colored bricks, one of dozens of identical buildings in a sprawling office park off of I-295. Inside the lobby recessed lighting cast a harsh glare on the terrazzo floor tiles, making it hard to read the glass-enclosed sign listing the building's tenants.

Squinting in the glare, Paige made out the name of a physical therapist, a podiatrist, and a law firm. All the other spaces were blank. Paige knew from the email Ms. Beneducci sent that the interview was to be in Suite 319. She took the elevator upstairs and found a laminated sign taped to a door. The sign said **MORTON'S WOODS.**

Paige knew immediately what kind of place this was. It was an office space that could be rented by the month or the day or who knows? Maybe even by the hour. That was the first indication that something was hinky, as her father would say. Wouldn't a corporation with enough money to pay someone a starting salary of $86,400 be able to afford a permanent office? But perhaps they had a good reason for holding interviews here. Perhaps their offices were being exterminated or redecorated or something. Paige opened the door and went in.

Three people were seated in chairs upholstered in nubby, dark blue fabric. They were exactly like the chairs in the waiting room in Paige's dentist's office. The magazines spread out on a table were the same as the ones in Paige's dentist's office. There was the *New Yorker*, *Condé Nast Traveler*, *Men's Health*, and *Golf Digest*. Paige noted with dismay that the three people all had briefcases. She wished she'd thought to bring a briefcase. It looked more professional than showing up empty-handed.

A door opened to an inner office and a woman who appeared to be in her mid-thirties and who wore her brown hair in a French twist came out. "Olivia Parmenti?" she said. Her gaze swung between Paige and the other woman in the waiting room, unsure which of them was Olivia Parmenti.

Jill Hand

The other woman rose to her feet. She was at least six feet tall, blonde and sturdy as a Valkyrie. She picked up her briefcase and strode into the inner office. Three minutes later the door opened, and she emerged. "Thanks again," she called over her shoulder. "It was a pleasure meeting you."

The French-twist woman came out again. "Edward Renz?" she said. A big, broad-shouldered man with a shaved head and a face like a bull followed her into the inner office. That left only Paige and a man with foxy red hair and a sharp-featured face.

The red-haired man jerked his chin at the door to the inner office as it closed behind Edward Renz. "Giants," he said.

Paige said, "Huh?"

"Those guys? The woman? Parmenti? And that guy, Renz? They're really tall. All the other people that were here for interviews were tall. They were in and out in, like, super-quick-double-time. Slam, bam, thank you, ma'am. Nice to meet ya, now get lost. I got here early so I saw it happen. I wasn't sure how long it would take to drive from Harrisburg, so, I thought I'd better err on the side of caution. The traffic in Harrisburg's a bitch. Sam Nordby."

He stuck out his hand and Paige shook it. It took her a moment to realize that Sam Nordby was his name and not an exclamation intended to emphasize how much of a bitch the traffic in Harrisburg was.

"I'm Paige Carlisle," she said. "If they're hiring giants, I guess I'm out of luck." Paige was four feet, eleven inches tall. Not officially a little person, but close.

Sam nodded. "I hear you. I'm exactly as tall as Peter Lorre. He was five-three."

Paige said, "I never heard of him."

Sam's eyes widened in amazement. "Never heard of Peter Lorre? He was an actor, a good one. He was in *The Maltese Falcon* and *Casablanca* with Humphrey Bogart. Bogie was five feet, eight inches tall."

Morton's Woods

Just then the door to the inner office was flung open. Edward Renz backed out, shouting. Paige and Sam flinched.

"I don't know what your game is, but you people are screwed up," he yelled. "I have a master's degree in forestry. I worked at Breezeways, for Christ's sake, and at Lorimer Gardens. I was in charge of a crew of twenty! You wanted me to stand on a scale and I stood on a scale. Then you measured me. Then you went, 'Thanks for coming we'll be in touch.' Just like that. I drove all the way from Richmond. Damn you to hell."

Paige and Sam looked at each other, stunned.

"Hey," Renz said, turning to them. "Hey, you guys had better leave right now. These people are up to something. I think they've got some kind of sex fetish."

The French-twist woman came to the door. "You need to leave now, Mr. Renz, or I'll have to summon security."

He stuck out his middle finger at her. "Summon *this*," he snarled. He stomped through the waiting room, swinging his briefcase like a club. He grabbed the handle of the outer door and tried to slam it, but it resisted his efforts. He tugged on it, his face red, before giving up. His angry footsteps pounded down the hall as the door whooshed shut behind him.

"Holy crap," said Paige.

The French-twist woman shook her head apologetically. "Sorry about that," she said.

"That's okay," Sam said.

"We'll be with you in a moment," the woman told them before going back inside and closing the door.

Paige was shook up. She hated scenes. To hide her anxiety, she neatened the magazines on the table. She was of two minds. Part of her wanted to leave, just skedaddle on out of them. Another part wanted to stay and see what happened. Maybe the job was real. Maybe it wasn't. Maybe they—there must be a 'they' because the French-twist woman had said 'we'll see you in a moment,' not 'I'll see you in a moment'—

Jill Band

maybe they had some kind of ulterior motive. Maybe not. With the possibility of $86,400 dancing in front of her Paige decided to stay.

The French-twist woman was Nicole Beneducci, human services director for Morton's Woods. Two days after Paige's interview with her and two men whose names she didn't catch, Ronald or Richard Somebody, and Paul or Peter Somebody, she got a letter offering her the job.

That was in May. Eleven months later Paige stood on a ladder at Morton's Woods, finishing up pruning a Persian lime tree which was growing against a wall. Espalier, the technique was called. It trained woody trees or shrubs to grow against a two-dimensional surface. In this case the wall was south facing, allowing the lime tree to flourish and bear fruit in a region farther north than it normally would. They grew other kinds of citrus fruit outdoors at Morton's Woods: Meyer lemons and oranges and even grapefruit. It was like magic.

It was April 22, a special day at Morton's Woods. There would be what Nicole Beneducci had called "a small, informal celebration" shortly in The Lodge. That was the administration building. She had been vague about what it was about, other than it had something to do with trees.

Sam Nordby helped Paige fold the ladder and stow it in the back of one of the company pickup trucks. Sam had been hired, too. He and Paige were dating. Nights were usually spent either at Paige's apartment or at his. Sam had turned out to be great boyfriend, meticulously neat, considerate, funny, and good in bed. "I'm flexible, like a Slinky. They call me the Slinky of Love," he'd told her, cracking her up.

"The party could be in honor of Arbor Day," Sam said. "Isn't that in April?"

Page got into the driver's seat and buckled up. "I think so. Let's go mingle. I hope there's food. I'm starving."

"Wonderful! You're here," Nicole greeted them as Paige and Sam entered The Lodge. "Look everyone, it's our very own Keebler elves! Aren't they adorable?" A group of well-dressed people were standing

149

around, holding flutes of champagne. Paige recognized her boss, a gruff, middle-aged man named Mitch, and several others who were executives at Morton's Woods. The rest were strangers.

There was laughter and murmurs of approval.

"They're absolutely darling," cried an old woman who wore a boxy wool bouclé suit and a string of black pearls.

"Join the party, kids. Have a drink," said Mitch.

"Here, we have a special drink for you," said Nicole. Her high heels clicked across the slate floor as she fetched two glasses. She poured Paige and Sam something red from a cut-glass decanter.

"To trees!" she cried, raising her glass of champagne. "The lungs of the world!"

"To trees," chorused the well-dressed people.

"To trees," echoed Paige and Sam, raising their glasses and drinking.

⌘⌘⌘

Paige woke up some indeterminate time later. The slate floor was marvelously soft, like sleeping on a billowy cloud. Who would have thought stone would be so comfortable? Paige closed her eyes and tried to drift back to sleep.

"Time to wake up," said a voice.

Oh god, it was her boss, Mitch. He'd caught her sleeping. How embarrassing.

Paige struggled to her feet. She recognized where she was. It was the meeting room at The Lodge. There had been a party. Sam had been there, and some other people. Now everyone was gone, except for her and Mitch.

"Where's Sam?' she asked. Her tongue felt thick. It came out sounding like, "Wha's Sa?"

"He's outside. Come on, it's time to go," Mitch said.

A black SUV was parked at the curb, its motor running. A rear door slid open, revealing Nicole in the back seat. "Climb in, dear," she said.

Jill Hand

Paige hung back, unsure of what was happening. Were they taking her home? Did they think she'd had too much to drink and shouldn't drive? But she'd only had one glass of sweet red wine. Maybe not even a whole glass. She couldn't recall finishing it.

She asked, "Where are we going? Where's Sam?"

"He's with some of the men. They're looking at a tree," said Mitch. "Now in you go."

He took her by the arm and hoisted her into the back seat. He climbed in next to her, so she was flanked on one side by Nicole and the other by Mitch. In front were two men Paige didn't recognize. "Let's go," Mitch told the driver.

They drove around the circular drive before turning left on a narrow service road. It was pitch dark, the only illumination coming from the SUV's headlights. To the right and left were ranks of trees, tall, silent sentinels, their leaves rustling in the night breeze.

The road curved. Up ahead, Paige could see flickering light. Torches. Somebody had stuck torches in the ground, the kind with metal baskets on top. In the torchlight Paige could see Sam, his red hair gleaming. He was surrounded by a group of men.

"Stop," Paige cried. "There's Sam."

"Don't worry about him," said Nicole.

"He's getting his tree. Nothing to worry about," said Mitch.

"An ash tree. Quite an honor," said Nicole.

"Yggdrasil, the cosmic world tree. That was an ash," said Mitch. He turned to Paige. "You okay? You look like you're going to hurl."

Paige watched in horror as one of the men grabbed Sam, pinioning his arms behind his back. Another man threw a cord around his neck and was strangling him. Sam rocked back and forth, frantically struggling.

"Nooo! Stop it! Stop it! They're killing him," Paige screamed.

Morton's Woods

"Simmer down. If you won't be quiet, I'll gag you with my scarf. It's an Hermès. I hate to waste a good scarf, but I'll do it if you don't shut up," Nicole told her.

"Relax. Let her holler. Nobody can hear her way out here," said Mitch.

Nicole pursed her lips. "It hurts my ears, Mitchell."

They drove on. Paige covered her eyes with her hands and wept. She had hoped, for a desperate moment, that it wasn't really happening, that it was a bad dream. Wrong. It clearly wasn't a dream. She could smell Nicole's perfume and feel the SUV bounce on its springs as it went over bumps in the road.

"Here we are!" Nicole trilled. "Here at last."

The SUV rolled to a stop. Mitch opened the door. Torches were burning among the trees. Two men stood in front of a huge Norway maple. It was identical to Paige's old friend, the maple outside her bedroom window at her parents' house.

"No!" she screamed. She punched Nicole in the stomach.

Nicole sucked in her breath and raised a hand to slap Paige.

"Don't! Leave her unmarked. It ruins the sacrifice if you mark them," Mitch said. "Come on out," he told Paige. "Don't try to resist. There's nothing you can do. Submit and it'll all be over soon."

"You're not getting away with it. Somebody's going to find out and then you're going to jail," Paige said.

Nicole laughed. "That's unlikely. They've been offering people to the trees for a long time at Morton's Woods. Every twenty years, like clockwork, for over a century. Nobody ever knew what happened to them; they just disappeared. Poof! Gone! People disappear all the time, Paige."

Smiling viciously, Nicole went on, "They'll strangle you and put your body in a hole in the tree, like mailing a letter. It's hollow inside. You were hired because you're small, so you'll fit. Squirrels will make nests out of your hair. Insects will have a feast. They'll eat you, starting with your eyes. Squirrels will eat you, too. Between the insects and the squirrels, they'll pick your bones clean. Squirrels are omnivores in case you didn't know."

Mitch took Paige by the arm. "Come on," he said, his voice gentle. "It'll be over soon. You told me you love trees. What could be better than becoming part of a tree?"

Paige looked to where the men stood in the torchlight, silently waiting. The maple's branches waved in the breeze, as if welcoming her. She thought about running but realized it would be no good. They'd catch her. No one would hear her scream, but she screamed anyway, screamed, and screamed until she could scream no more. It made no difference.

Illustration by Sarah Walker

The Scarlet Room
by Adam Bolivar

There was a man named Mister Fox,
Whose house was grand and old;
He kept a room of bloody frocks
Quite ghastly to behold.

He courted Lady Mary Drake,
This charming gallant squire,
A handsome suitor did he make,
Whom any would admire.

A wedding day was set of course
That coming Eve of May,
Upon the moor amongst the gorse
Picked for the bride's bouquet.

The House of Fox lay in the wood,
Though she had seen it not,
And for as long as it had stood,
Black rumours had it brought.

The Scarlet Room

When her betrothed had gone away,
She ventured to the wood
To learn if what she'd heard folk say
Had been misunderstood.

The House of Fox at length she found,
A mansion very old,
Which ancient forest did surround,
And legendry enfold.

Above the gate were writ the words:
'Be bold, my dear, be bold.'
And on the walls were bloodstained swords,
A horror to behold.

She went into this beastly lair
And struggled to be bold,
For what she saw inside of there
Would make her blood run cold.

A scarlet chamber lay within
With piles of bones a-filled,
A place the Foxes hid their sin,
The many they had killed.

Adam Bolívar

Now Mary heard a piercing shriek,
And hid behind a cask;
She raised her head to take a peek,
And trembled from the task.

The gallant man betrothed to her
Held captive here a maid,
Who flailed and made a frightful stir,
Recoiling from his blade.

The blackguard cut a hand from her
To steal a ruby ring;
In Mary's lap it landed, sir,
A most abhorrent thing!

Quick Mary fled that wicked room
And on her frock a stain;
She fled him who would be her groom,
His deed etched in her brain.

Then at the breakfast feast she said
Last night she'd had a dream
That she had found a room of red
Where blood flowed in a stream.

The Scarlet Room

'Alas, it is not so, my dear,'
Quoth Mister Fox, her groom.
'It was a dream, so have no fear
Of any scarlet room.'

'Into that room you dragged a maid,
A ruby ring she had;
To have it you withdrew your blade
And cropped her hand, you cad!'

'A dream, a dream, that's all it was,'
The skittish Fox demurred.
'To spread such tales there is no cause;
I say they are absurd!'

'And here's the ring, the ruby ring,
And here's that poor maid's hand;
The House of Fox must surely bring
A blight upon our land.'

Then Lady Mary's kindred all
The wicked Fox struck down;
That Eve of May his house would fall,
And burned was Mary's gown

Illustration by Sarah Walker

Jack and the Magic Ham
by Adam Bolivar

Things had gone from bad to worse. I knew it had been a mistake accepting a ride from a scowling hillbilly in a beat-up old pickup truck. But when you have been standing by the side of the road for hours and the sun is sinking low, discrimination is no longer an option. My driver and I exchanged few words, and when I realized that we were progressing further and further away from the highway and deeper and deeper into a morass of backwoods trails and mountain passes, I think he was as relieved as I was when I asked him to let me off at the next turnoff.

But now, as the twilight was rapidly fading into paler and paler shades of pink and I felt the first few tentative drops of rain splatter against the brim of my hat, I began to wonder if I had made a mistake. The road stretched interminably in either direction and had not been traversed by a single car in all the time I had been standing there. The rain was picking up and I started looking towards the forbidding expanse of forest that bordered the road to one side. Perhaps it was the unlikely possibility of finding shelter under a tree, or else I was possessed by some animal instinct that asserts itself in times of desperation, but whatever the motive, I found myself making my way into the dark forest's depths. My ears were assailed by the sound of the rain playing on the canopy of leaves overhead and of twigs cracking underfoot. Before long, I was soaked to the skin and in an ever-increasing state of panic as it dawned on me that I was thoroughly lost and could not even find my way back to the road now. In the darkness, the trees looked alive, evil and gnarled, laughing to each other at my plight. A mean-spirited root caught hold of my foot and sent me sprawling face first into the now muddy forest floor.

Jack and the Magic Dam

I was nearly out of hope and resigned to spending the night in this humiliating position that fate had maneuvered me into, when I spied a flickering light in the distance ahead of me. Clutching my backpack close to my body in a vain attempt to keep it dry, I broke into a run towards the source of the light, beckoning me onward like a beacon.

To my wonderment, I came to a log cabin, of the sort that did not belong to this century, but was apparently still inhabited, owing to the light in the window and the thick gray smoke billowing up from the chimney. For a moment I hesitated, my mind filled with fantasies of murderous, inbred hill-folk who preyed on hapless strangers. But, seeing no other possible course, I knocked on the door somewhat more loudly than was necessary. The door opened, and what I saw I could not have concocted in my most fevered imaginings. It was an impossibly old man, with eyes like glowing coals set under eyebrows that fanned out from his forehead like a pair of white wings. But the most fantastic of all was his beard, spilling out from his chin in waves, and tangled in knots so intricate a sailor could not have fashioned them, so long it reached almost to the floor. He looked me up and down, appraising me with his burning eyes and then chortled mirthfully to himself.

"Well now young feller, you look like you've been a-swimmin' in the crick with all yer clothes on!" I was at a loss for words, but to my infinite relief he motioned for me to come inside.

"I was just fixing myself a mess of vittles," he volunteered. "It ain't much, but you're welcome to 'em."

I felt in a dream as he helped me off with my hat and coat and hung them up by the fire that blazed in the hearth and filled the little cabin with a heavenly warmth. As I sat by the fire in a daze, the chill and dampness were driven from my bones until I felt human again, and no longer a hunted animal. My host brought me a bowl full of steaming hot stew and a sizable hunk of cornbread, which I devoured ravenously. It was the best meal I had ever eaten. The finest dish at the most expensive gourmet restaurant I had ever dined at couldn't hold a candle to this old man's stew. He watched me intently as I sopped up the last bit of stew with my hunk of cornbread, until that too disappeared into my gullet. Then he took a stick of wood from the fireplace and used the burning end of it to light a long-stemmed wooden pipe.

The old man blew out a cloud of fragrant tobacco smoke and said, "You sure don't talk much, boy. What's the matter, cat got your tongue?" I apologized profusely and began in a haphazard way to recount my travels. I told him that I was an aspiring writer, hitchhiking across the country from Boston to the West Coast to gather material for stories. On the way I had stopped to pay a visit to some relatives in Virginia before heading west.

"Boston?" he snorted. "Well, at least you got some Southern blood in you." He looked into the fire introspectively for a moment as if he were deliberating some matter in his mind. Finally, he turned and fixed me with his terrifying stare.

"So, you're looking for stories, you say? You ever hear tell of Jack?" Gulping nervously, and briefly considering lying, or even bolting from the house altogether, I was forced to concede that I hadn't. He chuckled at my obvious dread.

"No reason why you should, young feller from *Boston*." He pronounced the word with obvious distaste. "But there ain't nary a soul alive in these mountains that can't tell at a tale about Jack. Nary a soul alive." Needless to say, I didn't need to press my host to tell his. He settled back into his rocking chair, and taking a long reflective draw on his pipe, began to spin a tale.

⌘⌘⌘

This happened a while back. It don't differ how long. Jack was a young man back then. But I reckon he was always young and always will be. He was lost in this very wood, which is right easy to get lost in, on account of this is no ordinary wood, and much bigger than it looks. After wandering around all day, he came to a pond all covered with lily-pads. He was plumb tuckered by then and rested under an old willow tree that

Jack and the Magic Dam

grew by the bank. Not having had a thing to eat since breakfast, his stomach commenced to rumbling so loud you could hear it a mile off.

"I'm huuungry," he moaned. "I'm so hungry I could eat up all of them lily-pads!"

A deep voice croaked from nearby. "Please don't! If you do, I'll nary have a place to stand."

Jack jumped to his feet. "Who's there?" he demanded.

There was a splash and a pair of teensy eyes peeped up from under the water, followed by a scaly green toad's head. "Errrr… R-r-ribbit! It's only old Mr. Gulpworthy."

"I ain't a-fixing to eat up your lily-pads, Mr. Gulpworthy," Jack said. "Why don't you come on out of there and set a spell with me? I could use the comp'ny."

Slowly, the rest of Mr. Gulpworthy's body rose up out of the water and climbed up on a lily-pad. The toad was all dressed up in a weskit and breeches like an old-time dandy. His throat swole up real big.

Then another voice squeaked, "What in heaven's name is all the racket down there?"

Jack looked up and saw a mouse wearing bonnet on her head, peeking out from a tiny hole in the tree.

"Evening Miss Nibble," said Mr. Gulpworthy. "I've come to court you. Yup. A-courtin' I come. R-r-ribbit!"

"Percival T. Gulpworthy," the mouse said with enough vinegar in her voice to wilt a garden. "How many times do I have to tell you? I'm a mouse and you're a *toad*." She spat out the word out like a wad of chewing tobacco. "It simply won't *do* for us to marry." Mr. Gulpworthy sat on his lily-pad and stared up at Miss Nibble.

"Don't you give me them sad eyes," said Miss Nibble. "Go on, get going now. Shoo!"

Mr. Gulpworthy shuffled to the edge of the lily-pad and then hopped into the water. *Gloop!* He was gone.

Adam Bolivar

Then the mouse fixed her tiny little eyes on Jack. "And who might you be, young man?"

Jack swooped off his old hat and bowed like a gentleman. "I'm Jack. I'd be much obliged if you could tell me where I might find me some supper."

Miss Nibble thought for a minute. "Well, I'd invite you up. But I don't reckon you'd fit inside my tree. 'Sides, all I've got's a few nibbles of cheese. It's barely enough for a little mouse like me. You should head on over to Mr. Longtooth's house. He'll fix you up with a supper fit for big folk. Maybe even give you a place to stay the night."

"That sounds right neighborly," Jack said. "Where does Mr. Longtooth live?"

"'Bout a mile to the west of this pond."

Jack saw which way the sun was setting and nodded.

"One more thing," Miss Nibble said. "Don't mistake Ol' Threetoes for Mr. Longtooth. They're twins and look just alike. But Mr. Longtooth is a good wizard and Ol' Threetoes is a right mean one. The only way to tell 'em apart is by their feet. Ol' Threetoes has three toes on his left foot and Mr. Longtooth has all five on his."

Jack tipped his hat to Miss Nibble. "Much obliged for the warning. I reckon I'd better head out for Mr. Longtooth's house afore it gets too dark to find my way."

Miss Nibble wished him good luck and then closed her shutters. Jack followed the last light from setting sun as long as he could. But he wasn't sure if he was heading the right way after that. In the dark, all the trees looked the same.

"Blame it!" he spat. "I'm a-going 'round in circles. Maybe I ought to head on back to that pond. I reckon Miss Nibble won't mind none if I slept under her tree."

Jack tried to backtrack, but he wasn't sure where the pond was now. The more he looked for it, the more he got turned around. It was like the trees were conspiring to lead him someplace else. He crossed an old stone

Jack and the Magic Dam

wall at the border of a clearing. In the middle of the clearing was a single-pen cabin. Outside the cabin a herd of pigs was busy feeding at a trough.

Jack jumped for joy. "That must be Mr. Longtooth's house," he said to himself, and gave the door a knock loud enough to wake the dead. After a minute, the door opened up. Inside was a grizzled old man with a long gray beard that went clear down to his stomach.

"Howdy do!" Jack said. "You must be Mr. Longtooth."

The old man looked confounded for a heartbeat. Then a wide grin spread across his leathery face, showing sharp teeth like a wolf's.

"That's right," he said in a voice as dry as old leaves. "And who might you be, stranger?"

Jack took off his hat. "You can call me Jack," he said. "On account of that's my name. I heard that you might have lodgings for a poor boy lost in the woods."

"Why don't you come in?" the old man said, opening the door up wide.

"Don't mind if I do," Jack said. "But first I have to ask you one question. How many toes do you have on your left foot?"

The old man laughed. "Don't you fret none, Jack. I've got five on each foot. You can take my word for it."

"If you say so," Jack said. "Then it must be true." He stepped through the door and put his hat on a peg. The inside of the cabin was near about empty. There was not much in there besides a potbelly stove, a table, some shelves and a rough cot in the corner. A heap of upturned jugs lay on the floor. On the table was a big old book. It caught Jack's eye right off.

"I'll go fetch some straw for you to sleep on," the old man said. "Maybe you wouldn't mind helping out with some chores later on?"

"Happy to oblige," Jack said. The old man grunted and stepped out the door, leaving Jack all alone in the house. He sat down at the table and opened up the book's cover. It fell right open to one page that looked like it'd been read a mess of times before. Here's what it said:

To turn a mortal man into a swine there are three methods the magician can employ:

The first method is to kill the subject with a sharp blade such as a knife or axe and recite the following words:

Whick! Whack! Whig!

A man and a pig.

One is small

And one is big.

Whick! Whack! Whig!

The second method is to drown the subject in deep water such as a sea or a well, and recite the following words:

Bacon pork and ham

Taste better than a man.

Pick a pig,

Poke a pig,

Eat it when you can.

The third method is the most extreme and should only be used as a last resort. Feed the subject on the flesh of another pig, even as little as one bite and recite the following words:

You are

What you eat,

A jar

Of pickled cloven feet.

Jack flipped through the pages, but then the old man came back in, carrying a bundle of straw under his arm and a great double-headed axe in his hand. Jack snapped the book shut.

"You ain't been reading none of that nonsense in that old book, have ye?" the old man thundered.

"No sir," Jack said. "Just skimming it."

Jack and the Magic Bam

"Good," the old man said. "No sense filling up your head with all them fairy stories and old wives' tales." He took the book away and put it up on a high shelf. Then he handed Jack the axe. Jack almost dropped it, it was so heavy. "I've got a couple of chores I want you to do. Against you doing 'em well, we'll have ourselves some supper afterwards."

"Whatever you say, daddy," Jack said. "I sure am raring to eat."

"The first thing I want you to do is go out back and chop me up some firewood out of them old logs you'll find there."

"I reckon I can do that," Jack said, swinging the axe around to get a feel for it.

"Careful with the axe, Jack. Careful with it now."

Jack took the axe out in back of the cabin and found a pile of felled pine trees. Raised the axe over his head and was fixing to swing it down when he heard someone croaking behind him. "R-r-ribbit. Ribbit. I wouldn't do that if I was you. Or else you'll split your head in two."

Jack turned around and there was Mr. Gulpworthy.

"Well howdy do, Mr. Gulpworthy," Jack said. "What're you doing here?"

"I've come to give you some advice," the toad said.

"Heck. I don't need no advice," Jack said. "I've been chopping wood since I was knee-high to a...well, knee-high to a toad."

"That's as may be," the toad said. "But I'll bet you ain't never chopped wood with a backwards axe before."

"A backwards axe?"

"That's right, Jack. It's a backwards axe on account of it does the backwards of what you want it to. If you tried to chop that wood, it'd rear back on you and chop your head clean off."

"Bedads!" Jack said. "Then how in tarnation am I going to get this axe to chop the wood and not chop my head off?"

"You've got to aim for your head and the axe'll chop the wood instead."

Adam Bolívar

"Aim for my head?" Jack said. "Are you sure about that?"

"Sure as the heavens are high," the toad said. "Sure as the ocean is deep."

"Well, that sounds mighty sure," Jack said. "Thanks for the advice." The toad croaked farewell and hopped away.

Jack took a deep breath. "I sure hope he's right about that." He gripped the axe's handle and swung the blade right towards his own face. Sure enough, the axe reared back in the other direction and chopped one of the logs right in two.

"Well I'll be!" Jack said. With a few more licks, he'd cut himself a nice pile of firewood. He hauled it back to the cabin.

The old man looked like the moon had fallen out of the sky when Jack carried in the pile of firewood. "Err…Eh…Finished already?"

"Yes sir," Jack said.

"You chopped all that wood with the axe I gave you?"

"That's right."

"Well, uh, good job, son. Good job." He took the pile of wood from Jack and stoked the stove with it. Then he started it kindling. All of a sudden, the old man was his old grinning self again. "Since you did such a good job chopping wood, Jack, I've got another chore for you."

"Whatever you say, daddy. I'm raring to eat anytime."

"Go to the well out back and raise me up a bucket of water."

"I reckon I can do that," Jack said.

Jack went out in back of the cabin and found the well. He grabbed hold of the crank-handle and was fixing to turn it when he heard a croaking in the darkness. "R-r-ribbit. R-r-ribbit. Listen Jack to what I tell. Or else you'll fall into that well."

"Well howdy do, Mr. Gulpworthy," Jack said. "What're you doing here?"

"I've come to give you some advice."

Jack and the Magic Dam

"Aw heck. I don't need no advice. I've been drawing up water from wells since I was a glint in my daddy's eye."

"Maybe so. But I'll bet you've never drawn water from a backwards well."

"A backwards well?"

"That's right, Jack. It's backwards on account of if you try to draw water up from this well, it's you who'll fall down it."

"Mercy!" Jack said. "Then how do I get the water up from the well and keep from falling down it?"

"Turn the crank the other way, and the water'll come up to you."

"The water'll come up to me? Are you sure?"

"Sure as the stars are far away," the toad said. "Sure as a goose has a secret name."

"That sounds mighty sure," Jack said. "Thanks for the advice." Spitting on his hands, Jack grabbed hold of the crank-handle and turned it towards him. Sure enough, the water rose right up to the top of the well. Jack filled up the bucket.

"Let me give you some more advice, Jack," the toad said. "That ain't Mr. Longtooth in that house. That's his brother Threetoes, and he means to do you ill. He plans to witch you into a pig and eat you up for supper!"

"But I don't want to be witched into a pig and et up for supper!" Jack said.

"Then don't eat any ham that Threetoes tries to give you," the toad said. "Don't swallow a single bite."

"Thank you, Mr. Gulpworthy," Jack said. "You've just saved me a whole mess of botheration."

"One more thing." The toad put his head over the top of the bucket and spat into the water. "If you can get Ol' Threetoes to drink this water, I don't reckon he'll be bothering you no more. Only don't you drink none of it yourself. Y'hear?"

Adam Bolivar

Jack thanked Mr. Gulpworthy and hauled the bucket back with him to the cabin. If Jack had dug up his dead grandmother, brought her back to life and came in dancing a Virginia reel with her, Threetoes couldn't have been more surprised.

"Finished already, Jack?" he said.

"Yes sir," Jack said.

"You got all that water out of my well? The one in back of my house?"

"That's right."

"Well, good job, son. Good job." Threetoes took the bucket from Jack and set it on the floor. "Why don't you go 'round to the smokehouse in back of my cabin and fetch us a couple of hams for supper?"

Jack went around to the smokehouse in back of the cabin and found it full of smoke-cured hams. He picked out a couple of choice slabs and brought them back inside. Threetoes told Jack to cook up the hams on the stove in a cast-iron skillet, so he did. He served them up, piping hot. Threetoes sat down and commenced to wolfing down his ham. Jack just played with his, turning it over and over with his fork.

"What's the matter, boy?" Threetoes said. "Don't you like ham?"

"I like it just fine," Jack said. "Only back where I come from, we wouldn't touch a ham 'less it was salted first."

"Well, why didn't you say so?" Threetoes got down a saltshaker from one of his shelves and shook some salt on Jack's ham.

Jack laughed. "That's no way to salt a ham!" He grabbed the saltshaker and poured out the whole thing on Threetoes's ham and on his own. "That's the way to do it!" Then he cut himself a slice of ham and popped it in his mouth. Threetoes smiled so wide he could barely keep it on his face. He ate up the rest of his own ham and smacked his lips.

The old man started sweating. "I've got me a powerful thirst!" he said. He filled himself a cup of water from the bucket Jack had brought in before. While his back was turned, Jack spit out the bite of ham he'd

Jack and the Magic Dam

taken, and put it in his overall pocket. Threetoes drank down the cup of water and poured himself another. And another. And another. Then something mighty strange happened to him. His eyes got to staring so wide they nearly popped out of his head.

"I can't work in these clothes!" he said. Then he commenced to stripping out of his overalls and union suit till he was naked as a jaybird, nary a stitch on him. The old man turned all his clothes inside out and put them back on, hopping around on one foot. He looked like a scarecrow come to life. Drool poured out of his mouth and he hollered, *"Whick whack whig! A man and a pig! Whick whack whig!"*

He knocked over the table, plates and all, and turned somersaults all around the cabin. There was something funny in that water all right. The old man ran out of the cabin and came back with a pile of hams in one hand and a hammer on the other. "I need some pictures on these walls!" he said. "Lots and lots of pictures!"

Jack commenced to laughing. Threetoes was crazy as a loon. Whatever that toad had spit in the water had left the old man plumb addled. Jack was glad he hadn't drunk any of that water himself.

"That's a good place for one," Jack said, pointing to a space on the wall.

"Much obliged, son," the old man said. "I can see you're one of us." Then he nailed one of the hams right to the wall. He pounded the nail real hard. It wasn't till he stopped that Jack heard a knocking on the door.

"I wonder who could that be at this hour of the night?" Jack said. He opened the door and saw another old man with a long gray beard standing there. He looked just exactly like Threetoes. And standing beside the old man's foot was Mr. Gulpworthy, the toad.

"Howdy do," the old man said. "You must be Jack. Mr. Gulpworthy told me you might be having a spot of botheration."

"This here's Mr. Longtooth, Jack," Mr. Gulpworthy said.

Adam Bolívar

"Well howdy do, Mr. Longtooth," Jack said, pumping his hand. "I sure hope you've got something to eat and drink at your house that won't witch me into a pig or turn me into a ham-nailing fool."

Mr. Longtooth smiled. "I reckon I can scare something up."

Threetoes meanwhile didn't take a lick of notice of his company. He was already nailing another ham to the wall right next to the first, only this time it was a little lower.

"Looks like my brother got what was coming to him," Mr. Longtooth said. "Can't say I'm sorry about it."

Mr. Longtooth took the old book down from the shelf and put it under his arm. "I'd better hold on to this for safekeeping."

The three of them left Threetoes back in his cabin, but the sound of his hammering followed them a long way.

"Will you join us for supper, Mr. Gulpworthy?" Mr. Longtooth asked. "It's the least I can do for you after warning Jack about my brother."

"No, I'm going home to get some shuteye," the toad said. "Want to get up bright and early to get to courting Miss Nildh. Though I don't reckon I'll have no luck."

"Hold ever'thin'!" Jack said, snatching the book out from under Mr. Longtooth's arm. He flipped through the pages. "I saw something in here when I was rifling through it last time...Here it is!" Jack cleared his throat and read aloud slowly what the book said, sounding out some of the bigger words:

To have the lady you love unrequitedly fall in love with you, present her with a bouquet of four-leafed clovers picked under the light of the full moon and recite the following words:

Ana kata, one two three.

I love you, now you love me.

Well, it just so happened that very night was a full moon. And Mr. Gulpworthy picked himself a bouquet of four-leafed clovers on his way home.

Jack and the Magic Dam

⌘⌘⌘

The old mountain man finished his tale and settled back in his chair, refilling the long-stemmed pipe with tobacco from a leather pouch, which he fished out of his pocket. All was silent in the cabin except for the crackling of the fire and the rain clattering on the tin roof like buckshot. I let my eyes wander about the cabin's walls and noticed a large leather-bound volume tucked away up on a high shelf. A chill ran down my spine, and the hairs on the back of my neck began to stand on end. The old man chuckled quietly to himself. "Don't even think it, boy. Don't even think it."

⌘⌘⌘

The next morning the rain had abated, and it was with much relief that I took my leave of that impossible log cabin. The old man gave me a few landmarks to help me find the road again and wished me farewell.

"Don't forget about that story, now," he called after me as I was walking away. "Tell folks up in *Boston* about Jack!"

Later on, after I had returned home, I pored over numerous maps of that region of the Appalachian Mountains which I found in the library. But I could never find that forest that I had inadvertently stumbled into. Like the book on the mountain man's shelf, I decided that some secrets were best left kept.

Illustration by Sarah Walker

The Fork in the Road
by Ashley Dioses

Through darkest pitch,
The shadows fall.
Blind as a witch,
Deranged, they crawl.

There are two trails
Before your feet;
One crosses veils,
One hints defeat.

Which will you choose?
Left could be right.
Or will you lose,
With taint in sight?

Illustration by Alan Sessler

Cat-o'-Lantern
by K.A. Opperman

I carved my pumpkin like a cat,
With whiskers, nose, and perky ears;
I set it on my welcome mat,
As people do when twilight nears.

It wasn't long—the doorbell rang—
And who should stand upon my stair
But thirteen cats, a green-eyed gang
As black as pitch, or witches' hair.

I poured them out a pan of milk,
And happily, they lapped it up—
But mirrored there, with skin like silk,
Were pretty witches crouched to sup.

'October ghosts and autumn dreams,'
I whispered as they slipped away—
But in the cat-o'-lantern's gleams,
My mind more tricks began to play.

I thought I saw them stand on twos,
In pointed crimson caps encrowned—
I surely had begun to snooze,
The way those sneaky felines clowned.

Cat-o'-Lantern

A grinning, fanged, grimalkin moon
Soon rose, invoked by feline's cry,
And like a draping crepe festoon—
A chain of witches crossed the sky.

Illustration by Sarah Walker

The King of Mudlings
by Shayne Keen

The last time any human saw Jeff Rowe he was in the woods beyond the house where he lived with his mothers Nan and Grace, sister Shelby and her twin brother Dominic. Jeff, being the eldest at six, still needed tending but less so than the twins, who were four years younger and sickly. Since he was a good boy, and since his mothers believed in free-range children, they let him run unsupervised in the woods beyond the house as long as he stayed within earshot.

"Jeff!" Nan called from the back porch.

"Yes, mum!" Jeff yelled.

"Let me see you!"

Jeff grumbled and stood, wiped off the dirt from his pants and went to the edge of the wood. He waved at his dark-haired mother, who waved back and smiled.

She said, "Supper's in a half-hour, so wrap up your play."

Jeff didn't want to wrap up his play. He scuffed his shoes through the duff, broke off a handful of low, thin limbs and threw them at tree trunks.

His annoyed, dramatic stride led him to a jagged, broken-off and rotten stump with clumps of grass growing around it. Jeff liked to squat before the old stump and look down the hole in the middle, which seemed to lead all the way into what was surely a massive cave under the forest. He'd found the stump weeks ago, almost as soon as he was allowed to play in the woods by himself, and began hanging out around it almost constantly. When he put his ear to the rotting wood or over the hole he could hear the low, hissy voices of the people who lived down there in the dark. They called themselves Mudlings, or something like it. Often, he reached his hand into the hole, but could only get his arm in a little way

The King of Mudlings

– after all, he was still very small and his arms were short. Once, he took a long stick and poked down as far as he could, then let it go and listened. After nineteen alligators-worth of counting it hit bottom with a clatter and a splash, surely a very long way down.

Jeff wished he could fit through the hole and join the Mudlings. Their life under the stump seemed a sort of heaven to him, with no over-protective mothers interrupting his explorations every half-hour, and no whiny, crying, always-sick twins to take up all the good attention. In fact, the Mudlings had already told him in their sharp lispy whispers that if he ever wanted to go down there, they would let him be their king. Jeff imagined their realm as a huge shadowy vault that somehow let in the light from above. Surely there would be a tall throne for him, made from living roots of trees that grew together in an ornate tangle. All the food, the Mudlings said, would be what he most liked. They would honor and cherish him singularly, with the reverence a true king deserved. More, he believed, than his mothers did, at least since the annoying twins were born.

Jeff put his hand in the hole in the stump, then pulled it out. He put his mouth over the hole and shouted (with an assurance lacking in most boys his age): "I'm ready for you to bring me down, to leave this silly life with my mothers and the twins! I'm ready to become the King of Mudlings!"

He fell silent and listened. At first there was a deep quiet, as the Mudlings pondered his request, then a rush of hissing voices as they palavered over whether or not they should bring the boy down for real.

He did ask, after all.

Jeff listened to their sibilant back-and-forth for some time. When they finally fell silent, apparently having reached a decision, he still didn't know his fate. So, he lay there for a moment.

Hearing the shrill call of Grace, his light-haired mom, he bent and whispered sharply down the hole: "If you want me, you should come get me, because I have to go in for supper."

Shayne Keen

As the last word fell from his lips the ground churned and rolled in on itself, right under where he lay. It folded him into itself, making a complete rotation that left the tufts of grass in their original positions as Jeff plummeted down a long, mud-slicked slide into complete darkness. He screamed more shrilly than his mother had as he realized this was actually happening, and not just his imagination. He became terrified at the thought of forever living underground. As he slid, he sobbed between screaming fits, already sure that he would never see his family again, and he loved them no matter how much they annoyed him.

Finally, Jeff came to rest on something soft and mostly dry. He felt hands on his arms and legs, felt them strip off his clothing and drape a garment over his nakedness, a shift made of soft, tender, loosely woven roots. He felt hands, wet and slimy, upon his arms, and stood at their behest. He wanted to wipe off the mud, but knew there was no reason to try to stay clean down here. At first he thought it was completely dark in the cavern, but soon bits of glow appeared here and there, and before long he could see at least outlines of those down in the ground with him.

The Mudlings were slightly smaller than the boy, with big round bellies and huge, out-bugging eyes. He supposed they had no trouble seeing in the dark. Their long, phallic noses hung over wide mouths frozen into perpetual grins, from which protruded pointed teeth at haphazard angles. They seemed to have slick skin, but it could've been just the moisture and the mud. Their language was a mixture of hisses, grunts, guttural discharges of sound that made no sense, and word-image combinations that appeared in his head but not before his eyes.

"You are our king, great one!" said a Mudling, the largest one, as it took from its own head a crown of thick roots, stripped and polished. The Mudling set this on Jeff's brow, then placed a beautifully woven mantle over his shoulders. It was soft and warm, lined with what seemed like fur. A quick flash in his head showed him it was made of moles and voles, little mice and even a few careless rabbits. The boy was then led to the ornately grown throne and helped up to the seat, ridiculously tall,

The King of Mudlings

stitched of the finest tendrils of living root threaded through with rodent fur.

"Oh great King of the Mudlings, you have forsaken the world of light and wind and rain to be with us in the damp unchanging darkness: For this we worship you. You have our promise of utter love and obedience – we shall do anything you wish, save return you to the world you have forsaken. Now we will feast and drink, and you shall know what it feels like to be King!"

The cave brightened as Mudlings uncovered fungi that glowed shades of green, blue, yellow, orange, and red. There were no purples or pinks, but the light was much nicer – warmer – than King Jeff would've guessed. He saw his subjects clearly now, perceiving them as lovely beings with fine lines. Though their noses were big and their eyes and bellies huge, their limbs were lithe – the women were beautiful and supple, with long mossy hair, while the men were sinewy and well-muscled. He felt satisfied with them, and as they looked upon him, he in turn became the most beautiful being any of them had ever seen. The last king was not a shining angel from above, but just another Mudling; it was long before the memory of any living dweller of the cavern that the Mudlings had a new Overworld king or queen.

All night long they brought him tribute. They fed him mushrooms that tasted of every glorious meat Jeff could imagine, special fungi that excreted a juice when squeezed that was exactly like fresh, raw sheep's milk, and another beverage that was strong and tangy and made him feel light-headed, but brave. He drank much of the beverage, and before long stood on his throne and danced in the now-much-brighter cavern. He felt like a new form of being, nothing like whatever he was before, either upon the earth or below it. He felt himself growing larger, and realized that was why the seat was so high, the throne so huge: He was supposed to grow. He became a man, then grew beyond the pathetic boundaries of man.

After a while his subjects lined up. One-by-one they pressed their noses to his forehead and bowed deeply, implanting him with an ardent,

Shayne Keen

obsessive love for each of them. He grew as they touched him, and they, in turn, lay prostrate in rows before him, not daring to look up at the glorious new shining King who radiated back their love like a sun, filling the caverns with his light, dispelling all those shadows that dwell underground.

⌘⌘⌘

Long times passed. Sometimes, he heard one of his mothers calling his name in the woods. There was suffering in their cries, and he wanted to comfort and assure them that he was much better off now, occasionally yearning to show them he was no longer the young boy they loved. But, such thoughts were fleeting, and soon left him entirely.

Jeff grew and changed rapidly. Soon, though it might have really been months or years above, he became a different thing, inhuman and primeval, that saw clearly in the pitch-dark of caverns. His eyes were so sensitive even the merest thought of sunlight made his face twitch from imagined pain so sharp that he clutched his hands – were they still hands? – over them, longing to block it out. Memories of that pain made him anxious and disturbed, so he stopped thinking of sunlight and soon forgot about it.

Each wake cycle he feasted on fungi his subjects brought to him, and each sleep cycle he grew more and more until finally his legs – if they could still be called such – touched the rocky bottom of the cave. He towered over the Mudlings.

"The change is almost complete!" the big one hissed. They never talked to him anymore, and if things like that still mattered, Jeff would have been lonely or felt used. But his change extended far past his eyes and body. His entire mind was mutating, and he didn't feel things like "lonely" or "upset" anymore. He beamed with pride as the little men and women danced sacral pirouettes around his throne each black hour. He thanked them with all his soul as they fed him a near-constant stream of mushrooms, lichens, and molds, all tasting strange but pleasant, familiar after the first bite. When his hunger abated he left mounds of

The King of Mudlings

the fungi uneaten save a bite or two from each, for he still had the drive to learn each taste.

Jeff forgot about the concept of time. He was conscious when he was awake, semi-conscious when he slept – the groggy near-sleep of the underground dweller, the slug and ant, the earthworm and weevil. If he dreamed he wasn't aware that he did.

Eventually, as he sat on the throne very fat and warm, dozing contentedly from the previous celebration in his name, the Mudlings stirred him awake and, for the first time since he became King, demanded he slide off his throne and follow them.

King Jeff had some concept of what his new body was like. He looked at it as well as possible, considering he had no neck to swivel, and felt what he could. His skin gleamed a brilliant white, body composed of thick segments with a pair of legs protruding from each, shorter than his old limbs and without the complex appendages at the ends. He didn't know how many he had, as he could no longer count or think in numbers.

They led him down from the throne and he lashed out with his pincers, pulling a Mudling into his maw. Sharp, gnashing mandibles made quick work of the succulent flesh, but even as it slid down his incredibly long gullet, somewhere in the back of what little brain he had left Jeff understood he was not supposed to eat the beings that surrounded him. He regurgitated the flesh, a group of Mudlings hastening to clean it up, carrying the remains to a burial hole.

Jeff felt the Mudlings poke and prod him, but there was no pain, just the slightest pressure. They led him to a hole in the far wall revealed by the removal of a large, round, flattish boulder. He scuttled through the hole and down the twisting tunnel beyond it, becoming aware of a long, low rumble, followed by hisses and scratches against the tunnel's wall. What had been Jeff continued forward, feeling increasingly aggressive. If he still had hair it would have stood on end.

Shayne Keen

The thing that was Jeff rounded the corner and stopped for a moment, its legs wriggling, its segments forming a new shape as it lurched upward, taller than it had ever reached in the throne room.

Before him a giant, white, segmented worm, like a monstrous grub, reared up on its hind parts. Its mandibles opened, then clicked shut as it waited for the challenge. The thing – once Jeff – rushed toward the larger, older worm, grasping it firmly with clutching, crushing limbs. It was pleased to discover that the old worm, though much bigger, was weak and worn out. Immediately the Jeff-worm bit a wide gash in the fatty flesh of the older worm.

The pale maggot rallied as it tried to vie for a better position, grappling with its short limbs and making slashing motions with its jaw. Sometimes it struck home, but its force was spent, the worm barely strong enough to scratch a furrow in Jeff's pliant, youthful flesh. The Jeff-worm made a long keening noise that took the place of victorious, maniacal laughter. As the weaker worm writhed, the Jeff-worm grappled tightly with its limbs and reached for the space just on the other side of the mandible, where the back of its neck would be if it had one, and began to chew.

It was short work cutting off the thrashing worm's head. After it fell off, but before the body stopped twitching, the Jeff-worm began to devour the old worm's carcass.

The Mudlings heard the Jeff-worm's cry of victory and shouted in ecstasy. They cheered and caroused, then fell into an orgiastic debauchery, allowing themselves all the depravities known beneath the ground, which are as many and varied as those above it.

For the first time in above-ground centuries a new worm ruled! They would have food and drink, they would have all they needed to live, for the fungi of strange tastes and colors all emanated from the great Worm. The King of Mudlings, possessing the ability to manifest multifarious shapes and flavors of matter, would ensure the fungi grew. The Mudlings would be well-fed again for a very long, almost-infinite, time. In the dark

The King of Mudlings

cave behind the stone that rolled, the Jeff-worm assumed its place at the back wall of the cavern, chewing at the elder maggot's remains. It would take several Mudling lifespans for the Jeff-worm to eat all of it, but beginning tomorrow it would secrete spores, and sow them into the mud, forming new nutriment. Tomorrow there would be fungus that tasted like the food Jeff loved – Ceaser salad, lemonade, pumpkin pie and vanilla ice cream, like everything he'd tasted before and since he took the throne. The Jeff-worm, now really just the Worm, the King of Mudlings, settled into the existence of one eternal night, experiencing anew all the foods it had ever savored.

Somewhere above, Nan, Jeff's dark-haired mother, stumbled through the woods one last time before the move to a new place – far away from the hated forest – and called out for her lost child.

Illustration by Sarah Walker

The Willow Stand
by Scott J. Couturier

It was clear early on the water would be high that year.

Higher, in fact, than in living memory. Old records were consulted, revealing parallel lake-levels had been reached only once, in 1918. Then, pestilences of plague and war beset the world. Now…. Paul bit his lip as he stared out over Lake Clearwater, placid but dark and hungry-seeming, lapping at the shore just feet from their cabin's tiny front porch. All his life he'd been coming here, ever since his father built the place when he was still in swaddling. The fresh, crisp scent of pine needles underfoot, the soothing whisper of wind in the trees…this year these nostalgic, eternal-seeming tokens of summer all took on a ghoulish cast. The weather never really warmed up – spring lingered in muddy bank and pothole well into June. Behind their cabin Diana's tomato plants withered in their cages, done in by a combination of chilly nights and lack of care. The clouds were already turning into scudding dishrags, heavy with chill rain, and it wasn't even September yet. Paul sighed, reached down and picked up an oblate stone. He tried to skip it across the lake; it sank with a sloshing *plunk*.

He turned and looked to their cabin. Made of logs his father cut from the land, coated with gleaming golden varnish. Some cracks were starting to show in the chinking, but otherwise the place still looked homey, almost new-built. Smoke streamed from the fieldstone chimney like the scraps of ghosts, coiling off through a dense rood-screen of maple leaves. Beyond lay the forest – unbroken for miles in all directions, notwithstanding the occasional cabin or rustic weekend getaway. Just by the woods' edge stood Diana's studio. It looked like a spacious garden shed, as indeed it once was, but she had spruced it up and festooned it with hanging plants, painting a wondrous outer space mural on one side.

The Willow Stand

She spent hours in there every day, and most nights, alone with her canvas.

Paul nodded to himself. Reaching down, he hoisted his axe. He'd been splitting logs before reflection on that season's truly remarkable water levels overtook him – was it any wonder? For five years the table had risen steadily, but this summer there was an abrupt gain. Never mind that practically every basement in northern Michigan was flooded, lily pads popping up in back yards, toadstools creeping unctuously into gardens. Here, on Lake Clearwater, a host of new growth thronged on the redefined bank. Heavy rains had eroded away the sand, exposing feelers of maple, oak, and elm roots that snaked into the deep water. Paul shuddered as he thought about one of those slimy roots tangling about a swimmer's ankle – to him they resembled avid tentacles, writhing *out* of the lake.

At any rate, the water was no good for swimming this year. Pond scum flourished, algal blooms coating fully half the surface. Certainly this was without precedent. Paul even checked with his old neighbor, Mrs. Crenthorn, who'd been fishing Lake Clearwater since before he was born. The woman just squinted and shook her withered head, saying, "Nothing good in the water this year." She confided the lake was greasy-feeling on the skin. "And dead things – little rodents, mice and the like – they get washed up and malinger on the shoreline. No sir, best, I'd say, to hang up your swimming trunks for a summer. Maybe more."

Paul had done exactly that. The beach – if such it could be called – seemed to creep a little closer every night, until a shift happened sometime in mid-August. The lake levels dropped a bit, leaving a few inches of oozing exposed mud to define the bank. Here green things flourished, haloed by thick clouds of gnats, though a stand of nascent willow shoots was quickly forcing out all other vegetation. They grew, no doubt, from a blasted willow stump nearby, its long-dead pith revived by the rising water levels. Some seed or spark of life must have lingered in the rot, for its shoots grew rampant, sometimes gaining a half-foot in height a day. Lithe and verdant, feathery leaves hissing against each other with conspiratorial sibilance…their rustling drowned out his long-beloved rhythm of lapping water. Soon they would block out the view of the lake, start to encroach on the cabin.

Paul eyed the willows with displeasure as he resumed splitting wood. Given his druthers he would've cut down the whole cluster, but Diana had fixated on the shoots, even now locked away in her studio poring over a series of charcoal sketches she'd done of them that morning, backlit by the sunrise. A sterile season for her artistically, the usual vistas of rolling farmland, forest, and lake providing little inspiration…. Paul felt glad to see her pick up steam, though he worried local galleries would be disinterested in her latest direction. All these intimate close-ups of invasive bugs and plants, roadside trash, even roadkill – far from the bucolic broad-brushstroke charm of her former work, which always sold by the truckload, going up in innumerable indifferent dens, living rooms, and studies. Paul even noticed one of her paintings in the lobby of the dentist's office on his last visit. He frowned and hacked at the wood, brooding at his wife in her studio.

As if cued by his rumination, Diana emerged into the early dusk, executing a quick yoga stretch. Splattered head-to-toe in paint, the fey look she wore animated an expression otherwise intense and somber. In both hands she clutched charcoal sketches of the willow shoots. Without a word, not even looking to her husband, she approached the shoots on the swollen bank and held up her studies for comparison. Paul paused in his work to watch her, thinking she moved oddly, almost with a sleepwalker's gait.

At last, after long minutes of watching her stand almost motionless, save for a meander of eyes from the renderings to their inspiration, he cleared his throat.

Diana jumped. Literally jumped, so high her feet squelched in the moist sand. One of the studies crumpled in her hand.

"Paul! I wish you wouldn't sneak up on me like that," she said, in a scolding tone.

The Willow Stand

Paul suppressed a frown. He hated that tone. It reminded him of their worst and darkest times, when he'd still been drinking.

"Hardly snuck up on you. Been here chopping wood for the last half-hour." He kept his voice tight, controlled. "You just didn't notice me. I understand I can't hold a candle to those damn willow shoots."

Diana's offended demeanor crumbled at the hurt in his voice. "Oh, Paul," she said, with only a brief glance at the ruined study, "I'm sorry. Of course you didn't sneak up on me. I noticed you there, even. It's just, well, honestly I think I might be a bit dehydrated."

Paul dropped his axe and walked over to her, taking her a bit brusquely in his arms. "Look at you," he said, unable to suppress a grin. "My little paint monkey. What have you been working on in there all day?"

Diana's face clouded. She hesitated before saying, "Nothing. That is to say, nothing I'm ready to show you yet."

"Hmmph. All paintings of those damn willows, is it? You know that would pique my temper."

"Paul!" she laughed, falling deeper into him. He felt her body shudder, then collapse with a small sigh, as if some great tension were exiting it. "Not just the willows. I finished up the bear carcass. And that skinned skunk we found by the mailbox.... Now, don't look at me that way. I know you're worried about me."

Her eyes were pools of faerie-touched hazel, fiery with the bright soul behind them. Paul saw nothing there to cause concern, save perhaps an unaccustomed distance, as though she were peering at him through a magnifying glass, he infinitely small and she infinitely tremendous. Again he thought of his drinking days, and of his grudging reformation (dry a decade come December 1st). Her coolness, however mute and well-concealed; her spectral aloofness, almost as if she – or he – were intangible, barely perceivable. Lately she'd taken to wearing a silver crescent-moon pendant, making her withdrawal seem almost celestial in scope. Paul smiled more broadly as he pondered these things, biting the inside of his cheek.

"I'm only worried about your latest direction. All this death...and those invasive species. Japanese beetles! Who in northern Michigan wants to look at paintings of Japanese beetles eating cherry blossoms?"

Diana's pupils contracted, becoming even more distant. "I'm painting the reality," she said. "Everyone wants an idealized cottage or treeline or lighthouse to hang on their walls. But do you realize, in a few hundred years all of this that's not underwater will be bamboo? It's taking over, Paul, creeping out from decorative gardens to infest the woods. And giant hogweed, right here in Michigan! Flourishing poison ivy and fox grapes due to carbon emissions, whole species migrating or dying off…. What we're seeing is the future, and it amazes me." Here she cut herself short, seeing the sour look on his face.

Paul looked from her to the too-high lake, to the stand of willows sprouting anomalous in the sand. "It frightens me," he almost-didn't say.

"Change frightens all of us. But that's why I have to paint it, Paul. Painting it makes me not afraid of it – makes it all a part of the same picture." Here she reached up, touched his cheek and kissed him tenderly. "I know we feel differently, about so many things. But this is what I need to do."

He kissed her back, enclosing her hand clutching the crumpled study in his. He remembered the words of their marriage counselor, driven into his skull with the subtly of a railroad spike: *She has strong desires. She won't stop wanting what she wants. Either make peace with that, or move on.* "I love you," he said aloud.

"I love you too, Paul." For a moment longer they held each other. Paul winced as a mosquito lit on his neck, but refused to break their embrace. *Of course, it could be carrying Eastern Equine Encephalitis….* He slapped at the bug and blood squelched on his neck, running down to stain his collar.

The Willow Stand

Diana, once again wraithlike, pulled away. "You should go clean yourself up," she said.

He looked at the dark blot of blood on his hand in disbelief. "Yes...I guess I should."

When he came back outside it was twilight, crickets murmuring meditatively from the forest's verge. Diana had returned to her studio and lit the halogen lamps, which always meant a long night. Paul cursed the mosquito for robbing him of her intimacy.

He saw her rough drawings of the willow shoots lying on the ground. Looking up, he perceived by comparison just how much the actual shoots had grown since that morning. *Whiiiiiiish* went their greening fronds as they clustered together and chuckled, dangling in the scummy water. The wind caught up the studies and blew them beyond the treeline, like merry ghosts on a tear.

Paul clenched his teeth and finished chopping wood. Later, he made them both dinner and left a plate out for Diana, should she choose to come to inside.

⌘⌘⌘

"...John, it's just not like her. Diana's in her studio all day and all night. She's still drawing nature.... From memory, I guess. Keeps making sketches of that willow patch; must be using them as guides. What? Oh, I keep busy. Job's mostly just point-and-click these days. Even an old geezer like me can keep up. Getting away from the news cycle was a big part of coming up here, but the internet is everywhere.... It's what she chooses to focus on. Show her a beautiful meadow, and she picks out the one invasive species that will eventually overtake it. You heard of walking carp? Once they get into the Great Lakes they'll grow almost as big as dolphins, she says. Fuck. Sometimes I envy climate change deniers. What? No, I worry about the environment too, but I don't keep it at the forefront of my mind 24/7. Not healthy.

"It's like a morbid fixation. We had a few friends out last weekend, she showed them some of her new work and they were stunned. Maggots crawling on a piece of Tupperware by the roadside, next to a shit-filled diaper! I don't know, something about 'cleansing corruption,' maggots juxtaposed to plastic, which isn't biodegradable…. You could seen right through them they went so pale. Suppose I should be happy she's gotten focused on those damn willows, but it just seems like the latest obsession. What? Yup, I can see 'em right outside my window. It's because the waters are so high…don't know. Not like this before, in all my years up here. The lake's scummy and stagnant, though it never got very hot. And those willows…. I'm letting them grow for now, at least until Diana loses interest. Then it's hack-and-slash, right down to the waterline. They're already over six feet tall! Can't get to the dock… must be that old stump. Thankfully Diana never took to painting it. Think I'll hack it up tomorrow."

⌘⌘⌘

He disposed of the stump – with some difficulty. For her part Diana didn't remark on his labors, which occupied most of next day. Paul at first tried hacking up the thing with his axe, but it proved resilient, the old wood rotten inside but cased in weather-toughened bark. He came at it next with a chainsaw, no doubt disturbing Diana as she sat on a stool by the willow stand, composing more studies. She sketched placidly as he spared no Herculean effort, eventually resorting to gassing up his father's old tractor and pulling the stump up by force, leaving behind a gaping hole ringed by sandy, crumbling verges. Even as Paul jumped off the tractor to inspect his triumph a rushing sound, as of unleashed water, thundered from below, accompanied by a subterranean trembling. Paul swore as a wave of filthy viscous water burped out of the hole. Only then did Diana break from her reverie, coming over to gape at the foulness bubbling up from below.

"Paul, my God! Are you all right?" she asked, coughing as she shielded her nose from the stench.

Paul grit his teeth to keep from retching. "I'm fine," he said in a hollow, nauseous voice. Together they watched as the noxious water

The Willow Stand

leeched back into the ground, draining away with an obscene sucking noise. The willow shoots trembled and twitched their limbs, though no wind blew.

"Well, I'd say you hit the septic system or something. The water's gotten so high – is it possible?"

"No. Septic tank is out by the garage. There shouldn't be anything under there." Even as he spoke Paul remembered something his father once told him about breaking ground on the cabin. How he'd found the shards of a human skull, and a few broken arrow heads....

Diana laid a pale hand on Paul's shoulder, gripping him through his shirt. "Hey! Earth to Paul," she said, not unkindly. "What aren't you telling me?"

"Nothing. Just – that smell reminded me of an open grave." He stared down into the black hole in the sand. For a moment he considered getting a flashlight and shining it in, but felt afraid of what he might see. Clusters of white, root-choked skulls, hanging suspended in the dark.... "I'm sorry. Whew! Feel like one of those fainting Victorian heroines." He jokingly raised a limp wrist to his brow, winning him a rare smile.

"It's all right. Look, should we fill this hole in? I can help."

Her offer stirred him. It was the first sympathetic gesture she'd made towards him in days.

"Thanks. That would be great."

Together they filled up the hole, using sand and gravel shoveled from the shoreline. This meant Paul had to wander among the willow shoots. They snagged his shirt and whipped at his face, or bent over at weird angles to trip him. Diana, of course, had no trouble navigating to the bank and back. Finally the hole was filled, the horrible distant burble of water quelling. Paul made some off-hand comments about going back to Grand Rapids early, closing up for the season. He felt worried, he said, about the cabin's foundations. "Besides, the weather's turning. Whatever summer we might've had is already come and gone."

Scott J. Couturier

His suggestion dispelled their rare moment of camaraderie. "Paul, you know I have to stay," Diana said, drawing away from him, shovel in hand. "I only started on anything worthwhile so late in the season...really, I'm beginning to wonder if my old work has any value at all."

Paul flashed her a hesitant smile. "It does. According to our pocketbook, anyways."

The wrong thing to say. It was always the wrong thing to say.

"Paul, do you have a problem with what I'm working on? Because if you do, you have a problem with me." She spoke sharply, almost stuttering with the force of her emotion.

Paul blanched, bowing his head. "Okay, I admit it. It's unnerving me. You've gotten obsessive about those willows, for one thing. And dragging dead animals back from the road...I just don't get it."

"Obsessive? Is that what you call inspiration?" Her words were flame, lashing from lips flushed dark with anger. "These willows are growing anomalously, because of climate change – that's why you hate them. You hate the things they symbolize. You would hack them down in an instant if I wasn't busy immortalizing them. My 'obsessive' interest keeps them alive."

She knew. Of course she knew. The poetic eloquence he'd fallen for, coupled to her other talents, her *fire*...idiotically, Paul tried to take Diana in his arms. He wanted to propose a compromise. Something like: if she agreed to leave, he would spare the willow stand. For her.

Diana dodged around him, dropped the shovel and went to grab up her canvas and paints.

"I let you spend all day grinding away at that stump – at me. I did my work in spite of you. Figure I'll need to do that even more in future."

"Diana, it's true. I'm not being fair. At the same time, inspiration isn't the same thing as being..." Paul quested for the right word, "mesmerized!" He took a step towards her, took it back. "Please. Let's leave. We don't even have to go back to Grand Rapids. We could hit the road. Up to the UP, the Keewenaw...we can stop for you to sketch

The Willow Stand

roadkill along the way. I'm not kidding," he added at her dubious expression.

Diana sighed, brushing paint-spattered blonde hair from her eyes. Her ponytail hung half-undone, uncharacteristically. "Paul. Please. I'm not angry at you. I just...what I'm working on in there. I can't give up on it now."

"And what are you working on 'in there'? You haven't been showing me your progress, like usual."

"That's because I need space." It was a pun, based on the space mural decorating her studio's side. She hadn't used it in a long time. "I'll show it all to you when I'm ready, okay? Within the week. But we need to stay."

Her plea was hypnotic. Paul felt his throat tighten. "Of course," he heard himself mutter.

As he spoke, a damp spot spread atop the new-filled hole.

⌘⌘⌘

Paul woke up the next morning alone. Diana had slept out in her studio. Stretching, he rose and went downstairs, intent on making coffee. Looking out the cabin's back windows, he was shocked to see the willow stand had grown *two feet* overnight – as if spurred to new vigor by the stump's destruction. Grumbling a curse, Paul decided to start taking daily photographs of the stand to chart its progress. He would send the pictures to John, give him a better idea of what he was dealing with. *Hey – I can make some studies of my own! Wonder if I'll get in trouble for that, too?*

He immediately felt ashamed of his thoughts. He loved Diana. She loved him. So what if she painted terrible, ugly things no one wanted to buy? Admittedly, his own job – working as sales manager for an online distributor of organic sponges – brought in a comfortable living. As he'd said to John, the willows-as-subject-matter should be a relief. She was coping, coping with the world. He was too. They should both cut each other a little slack.

Scott J. Couturier

At any rate, after surviving four miscarriages, alcoholism, and affairs on both our parts, no upstart stand of fucking willow shoots is going to destroy my marriage.

Later that day, Diana went for a walk alone. She came back with two hunks of fresh carrion – a raccoon and a beaver, mown down by passing vehicles. "And there are so few cars out here," she was fond of saying. "People must swerve to hit them *on purpose*."

Paul watched as she sketched the corpses beside the willow stand, then interred them on a hillside near the driveway. She stuck little pieces of driftwood over their graves. A week later, the hill was speckled thick with wooden markers.

⌘⌘⌘

"...she's got to know the way she's behaving reminds me of the bad times in our marriage. What? Yeah, it hasn't gotten any better. If she would just show me her paintings! She said a week, and it's been two. Every day either locked away or out sketching, or wandering the roads – who knows what she'll drag back? Covered in paint when she stalks in at 4 am, tight-lipped, with the craziest look in her eyes. Puts a padlock on the studio, so I'd have to literally break in to see what she's up to. But I haven't insisted on anything. I'm not going to get boxed in and accused of being an asshole, you know, the aggressor in this situation.

"...We were doing okay before coming up here. She was wound up, but we still talked. Now, it's like I'm living with a stranger, a stranger who's getting stranger. She went on again last night about 'high days', more of that New Age pagan baloney she got into a couple years back. You ever heard of Walpurgisnacht? Yup, the 'witches' sabbath.' I said, 'I am the Walpurgisnacht, goo goo g'joob!' I thought it was funny...she didn't.

"Did you get those pictures of the willows? Yup, practically trees now, each trunk near two inches thick. You can see by the time stamps how fast they've grown...what? Well, thanks for agreeing with me. It *feels* invasive. I went and took out the dock this week. Big waste to put it in. The water was sludgy, almost chunky. I couldn't wait to get out, and

The Willow Stand

bleached my waders afterwards. Of course those damn willows snapped at me as I walked under them – yes, they're that tall! John, I feel like I'm being held prisoner here. I've put up with a lot, even went into town a couple times to blow off steam. You know I worked hard over the years to *not* see Diana as crazy, because she never was. I was the crazy one, putting off all kinds of shit my mom did to me onto her. Then, just as I got used to understanding that, she had her breakdown…which I try to never think about.

"Yeah, thanks. I'll send you more pictures 'as they develop' – a better joke before all this digital crap. But hey, without computers we'd both be out of a job, am I right? Ha, okay. Tell Cindy 'hi' for me. We should all do dinner when we get back."

⌘⌘⌘

Paul gulped, steadying himself. "I need to see whatever it is you're painting."

Diana looked up from her poached egg, the wide black circles framing her eyes making her look more alarmed than perhaps she was. "Whatever for, Paul?" she asked, voice cracking despite an effort at nonchalance. She smelled of pond water and turpentine.

Paul cleared his throat. He knew he looked like hell – no sleep last night, the whispering willow-fronds slithering into his head like snakes. "I just need to see," he said, in a voice that broke like hers. "I mean, I know your process is private, but you've always shown me your progress before. It's like," here he paused, teeth biting into his lower lip, "like you're hiding something from me."

He saw her change her mind in a flash. "Of course, if it means that much to you," Diana said, taking a quick sip of her coffee. "Let me finish my egg, and I'll show you some paintings of the willow stand. I know how much you hate it – I didn't figure the fruits of my obsession would interest you."

Scott J. Couturier

As good as her word, she brought in samples after breakfast. A tall, swaying stack of modest-sized canvases: Paul's eyes widened as she laid them out end-to-end.

"I've never seen you paint so many of just one subject," he said, impressed despite himself.

"Well," she said, eyes downcast, "I've had plenty of inspiration."

Paul examined the successive paintings with ever-increasing puzzlement. It wasn't that they depicted anything alarming – in fact, he found some of the renderings downright mundane or sloppy. Her universal subject was the willow stand at various stages of its development. Almost, it was like going through the sequential snapshots he'd gotten into the habit of taking every morning, before she woke up.

"Well, these are pretty straightforward." He said it aloud, immediately regretting it. Diana could get sensitive when he talked about her work that way. However, she wasn't feeling sensitive today; in fact, his comment evoked a smile.

"See? Nothing to be alarmed about. Nothing to hide." She moved forward, as if to gather the paintings back together.

Paul halted her with an outstretched hand, flipping over several of the canvases. "I don't see any dates on these," he said.

"So?"

"You always date your work."

Diana shrugged, turning to fetch a box of orange juice from the refrigerator. "I'm just not feeling particularly worried about linear time these days," she said, popping the box open and taking a swig.

Paul's teeth clacked together. "If that were true, you would've had no trouble going back to Grand Rapids early."

She laughed at him, mockingly (or so it seemed). "Paul," she said, eyeing him with a sense of wry suspicion, "you really look terrible, dear. As if you'd seen a ghost or something. Did I wake you when I came in? Is that what this is about? Or, has something terrible happened? I haven't checked the news." Her voice quickened with worry.

The Willow Stand

Paul shook his head. "No." He stared at the last painting in the sequence, showing the willow stand at its most lush. There were some odd blotches visible between their thickening boles, shadows almost anthropomorphic in definition. The sky in this picture showed darker, storm clouds massing in the backdrop. The surrounding trees were afire with changing leaves, some already stripped bare, but the willows shone an enduring green.

Diana sighed. "Well," she said in an undertone, "at any rate these should sell. Don't you think? 'Willow Stand by Lake Clearwater, No. 23.' Oh, they lap that kind of stuff up."

"Perhaps...except for these shadows, here." He turned the painting around and pointed them out to her. "A bit off-putting, don't you think?"

She laughed again. From mirth to worry to sadness, back to mirth – was she taking her medication? "You're so sensitive, Paul. You've seen how darkness plays in the stand when the moon is just right. Really, I think you're showing an awful dearth of imagination."

She stacked up the paintings and marched outside, still laughing, lower back curved beneath their weight. Paul waited for her to return; instead she set up her easel beneath a brown tarp propped near the willow stand. It was a wet, dreary, rain-spitting day. Diana wore a navy blue poncho, gray earmuffs, and a silver scarf that streamed behind her as she began, resolutely, to sketch.

Paul watched her for a long time, deciding to say nothing of his growing sense of unease. He'd meant to tell her, using it as leverage in a renewed argument for leaving. Now he knew: there would never be an excuse good enough.

⌘⌘⌘

Paul's hatred of the willows festered in his mind like a canker. Eventually, he did talk about it with Diana. It went about as well as he expected.

Diana's eyes flared as he struggled to express his misgivings.

Scott J. Couturier

"Of all the...being afraid of a stand of trees. Really, Paul, and you a woodsman! This is just some ridiculous lie, cooked up to make me go back to town."

He fixed her hot blue eyes with his own: brown, heavy, and tired. "Why would I lie to you? You never used to think I was lying, even at my worst."

"At your worst you became a man of honor. Honest about every drink and affair, expecting me to absorb it all. And I did," she added, shivers running through her voice.

Shit. "Look," Paul said, halfway reaching out with one hand. "Remember what the counselor told us all those years ago, about suspecting each other? We have to learn trust if we're going to save this marriage."

"I thought this marriage was already saved," Diana said, lips moving but almost emitting no sound. "I must have been wrong." She turned to peer out the window at the willow stand, looking back just as Paul's mouth slid open, preparatory to deploying a well trend round of apologies.

"Do you know what the willow symbolizes?" Diana asked. "Female energy, vitality, and rejuvenation. See how fast they grow? And from that desiccated old stump! Nature is full of wonders, Paul. Even in the grip of our human-made crisis it strives to thrive and mutate, to adapt. The world ten-thousand years from now would appear totally alien to human eyes from our era. Yet, all these changes are the result of our hubris! The Anthropocene, a bold new epoch…. Someday the industrial revolution will be viewed for what it is. A blip. An aberration. Just another strata in the geological record, disproportionate in size due to its frenzy of production-and-consumption. Archaeologists will never look back on our works in wonder. They'll be too busy shoveling through endless seams of plastic trash to do more than sigh, or sneer in disgust at our excess."

Defensive non-sequitur. The rambling outburst had precedent, especially in the last few years. Paul gulped, unsure of how to respond.

The Willow Stand

"...the willows," he ventured at last. "I hear them whispering to each other, in words almost *human*. Explain that to me."

Her eyes glittered. "The world is full of mysteries," she said. "They need no explanation."

"So you believe me?"

Diana shrugged, the silver crescent glinting between her narrow clavicles. "Even if I did, I can't leave. Not now, Paul. You promised me."

Had he promised? Paul felt the contents of his mind lurch about like dregs in an old wine skin. "I knew you wouldn't leave," he whispered, "but I had to tell someone."

"Why not call that old AA buddy of yours? Always ready with an ear. Be nice if I wasn't the topic under discussion, for once."

⌘⌘⌘

"...that's what she said. And we're still here, John. Growing colder all the time – I had to get the chimney cleaned out yesterday. Huh? She's got a couple space heaters going out there. One day I thought about unplugging them, saying I tripped over the cord...yeah, it's gotten that bad. I do things in my head I would never do in real life. What? No, haven't touched a bottle. I've still got respect for myself, even if she doesn't.

"Weird dreams lately. In one, I'm wading into the lake, and it's full of dismembered corpses. The stink of blood...never smelled it like that before, except when gutting a deer. Huh? And do what, John? Just leave Diana here? Go knock her over the head with a club, like some caveman? No. I'm standing by her, even if it drives me crazy. Because she's all I have left. Because I love her.

"Tell me about it. Feels like the whole world is ending. More protests.... I told Diana, thinking she'd want to go back and participate, but she barely blinked. Now Detroit's on fire...and what's this about some new, deadlier version of the flu? Christ. Planet Earth is turning into one giant goddamn Petri dish. Yes, I know I sound like my wife. When she's right she's right.

Scott J. Couturier

"Thanks. I'll send you some new pictures of the willow stand. Starting to blossom, just when everything else is turning brown and falling off. It's not natural. But then, what is natural anymore?"

⌘⌘⌘

That evening, Paul saw Diana dancing among the willows.

It was the middle of a cold, moonlit night. He sat staring out the kitchen window, alternately at the willow stand – plump, fuzzy blossoms glowing silver – and at Diana's halogen-lit studio. A strange evening: the tap water came out looking, smelling, and tasting like blood. Little scratching noises sounded in every corner, like the cabin was infested with phantom mice. On Diana's hillside cemetery, will-o-the-wisps bobbed over each makeshift marker, fluorescing rainbow hues. Paul drowsed despite these manifestations, only to jerk violently awake when Diana burst into the darkness stark naked save for the pendant at her breast, moonlight streaming against lily-pale skin spattered with brown paint. He watched with a growing knot in his stomach as she twirled and loped with inhuman grace, moving like a tree bough in a high wind.

After hearing of the protests he'd spent several days packing, hoping his passive-aggressive urgency would somehow transfer to Diana. Instead she ignored him more than ever, rarely leaving her studio to come inside the cabin. Was she eating? Was she drinking? Not his business, apparently. The one time he went to knock on the studio door, Diana cracked it open an inch and peered out with bleary eyes, something like a henna tattoo of a tree visible on her forehead. "Yes?" she'd said, in a ghostly un-voice. Before he could speak a crash had sounded behind her, like an easel tipping over. She slammed the door in his face with a burst of curses.

That afternoon Paul finally caved, went into town and had a drink or two. Or three. He came back hours later, reeking of alcohol, to find Diana still sequestered. Once upon a time he would have gone and hammered on the studio door, kicked it in if need be. Instead, he crawled into bed, hoping to sleep off his illicit drunk without her ever knowing of

The Willow Stand

his slip-up. His thoughts as he fell into uneasy dreaming were a muddied mess: anger and resentment at her, anger and shame at himself, the high water, the willows. Now, risen groggily in the middle of the night, still half-drunk, he beheld Diana dancing in ecstasy beneath a gravid moon, eyes so wide they shone like sapphires in its refracted glow.

To the willows: she clung to them, ran her hands over them lovingly. The thin trees trembled, showering her with a cloud of silver-molten leaves. Diana laughed bawdily, her hair streaming out like a banshee's train, twisting as if alive. Paul ground his teeth together as he saw shadows emerging from the treeline to cavort with her, spectral shapes with curved horns and faun's feet, swollen breasts and thick, tumescent cocks. He heard a distant music, played on reeds: something old stirred in his blood, and almost he went out to join Diana in her revel. Almost he stripped off his pajamas; almost he howled with a weird and foreign sort of joy.

Surely this was all a dream – a terrible, alluring, vexing, awful, seductive dream. He should pinch himself, or go flick the lights on-and-off. Brain racing with fearful excitation, Paul shut his eyes tight, but he could still hear the reedy music, each luscious trill inciting blood to throb in his groin and temples. Was she dancing faster, faster, until she became a wild blur? At last his eyes flew open and he rushed for the door, grabbing up a hank of rope.

⌘⌘⌘

Diana felt the call in her blood. Humming to herself, she ran hands up and down her body, fingers twisting at her erect nipples. After smearing herself with bark-brown paint she left her studio, gasping as the moonlight bathed her. It was cold, bitterly so, yet she'd stripped off her garments without a care. The voices calling from the woods kept her warm, and the dance! – she leapt like a nymph down to the shoreline, laughing with sensual delight. The willow stand loomed over her as she dashed amid its fronds, switches lashing against her naked flesh to leave strips of reddening welter. She laughed at the pain, at the burning

Scott J. Couturier

Hunter's Moon, rampant in a sky full of coiling, racing clouds. Raising her hands, she cried out in worship to the forest, the waters, the stars, the earth, the moon, the clouds, her own inflamed flesh and spirit. Out in the lake something rumbled in the depths, unseen but sensed.

Growing up in Detroit, she once dreamed of 'escaping north.' Learning to paint, focusing on nature as her subject: realizing she could create endless banal repetitions of farmland and winding beach to please a decadent, money-fat clientele. Inoffensive paintings, which of course Paul approved of; he always shied from the dark, even in the pathetic depths of his drunkenness. But all the while her soul yearned. She read things in secret and spoke to the trees, reckoning oracles in the winds of a troubled world. Of course, she could never tell any of this to Paul – just another breakdown, another madwoman in search of an attic. No, no. She wouldn't give him, or anyone, that satisfaction.

Emerald ash-borers. Asian tiger mosquitoes. Garlic mustard, autumn olive, spotted knapweed. Invasive creepers, vines, flowers, microbes, insects, birds, fish, humans. Pervasive microplastics feeding colonies of hybrid bacteria, bamboo forests stretching from the Great Lakes to the Gulf of Mexico. All life, life, life – indefatigable life! Roads eaten up by the green shoots, cars that once mowed down animals rusting into component atoms. Life, life, sweet life. All we are is the mulch of what we will become.

A light shone out over the water. Diana turned towards its source. There was Paul, standing on the cabin's deck framed by the kitchen lamp. He stared at her like a man transfixed, unmoving and silent, face a mask void of expression. Slowly, with a lustful chuckle, she angled her arms towards him, beckoning him to join her.

Paul – if only he knew. About the voices of gods in her head, old and new, speaking in languages of rumbling stone and gnarled root, of spore and shoot and deadfall, punctuated by the *clack-crash* of colliding antlers. *Father Cernunnos! Mother Gaia!* It was all there, in the paintings...Paul would eventually see how completely she had surpassed him. Poor fool, he never even realized it.

The Willow Stand

But was that fair? She hadn't known it either. Only now did she understand.

A roil of cloud passed over the moon. Darkness fell, providing her a chance to vanish, to escape. With a cackle Diana leaped into the woods just as Paul reached the willow stand, panting and calling out her name. He held a length of rope in his hands, intent on tying her up. *Unfortunate mortal*, she thought, leering down from the height of a fire-crowned oak, now a spirit of the forest attaining her natural vantage. *I suppose he'll make a big deal out of this tomorrow at breakfast.* Then, a blast of succulent dark air embraced her, bearing her aloft and away.

Change! How indescribably beautiful it all was.

⌘⌘⌘

"...John? That you? Yeah, I know what time it is. I need to – to tell you what's happened.

"I wasn't going to call the police. I saw how she changed...John, you weren't there. I know it sounds crazy, and you can ring the cops as soon as we hang up, but listen to my story first. Listen to the whole thing, then tell me I'm insane.

"After she ran into the woods I broke open her studio. How? With a goddamn axe, that's how! She'd reinforced the doors with plywood, but I was running on pure adrenaline by that point. What I found inside...remember I told you she showed me some of her paintings? Not dated, and pretty lackluster. Just diversions. In her studio I found dozens of canvases, some of the willow stand – some of other things. She painted the willows at every stage, with dead animals in the foreground, finally rendering them as a black jungle with red eyes peering from the darkness. And these crazy, indescribable landscapes, with horned *things* dancing in circles, eyes aglow from trees with bright pink leaves or stands of mutant bamboo. All of them *were* dated...well, I noticed something strange. I went back to the house and got my pictures of the stand, dated as you know. I compared them to the dates on her paintings. John, she was *making* the willows grow. How I don't know, but her paintings are always a few days ahead, as if predicting – *manifesting* – their growth. Yes, I know how fucking crazy it sounds! You said you'd listen...just listen. I NEED you to listen.

"The willows...they look like that last painting now. I can see things out there, moving among them. So tall they loom over the cabin, blotting out the moon. And that *other* thing. But, I'm ahead of myself. Yeah, I've been drinking, but no time for that now.

"There was a last painting, still wet, leaning in a corner. I turned it over thinking it might hold some clue – somehow, I knew it would. What I saw made me sick to my stomach. Diana had *painted herself naked, impaled on the willows*. How she did it I don't know...anatomy's not her strong point. She'd been getting better with the roadkill, but this was so real I felt like I could reach out and touch her. There she was, naked as a jaybird, willow shoots sticking out from her open mouth. They entered her in various places, her armpits and groin...titled 'At Ease Among The Trees.' Jesus, John. I need another drink.

"Okay, I went back and looked for her. An hour wandering through the woods...several times it seemed like I found her, or was very close. I'd hear her laughter, or something that felt like her hair would brush my cheek. But every time I shone the flashlight – nothing.

"I came back to find hoof prints all around the cabin. She's got horns now: I know that, somehow. Found all these books in her studio. *The Golden Bough*, *The White Goddess*, *Vulgate of Pan*. If I just keep looking for her, I'll find her. Not as she was, John, but as she is now. I'm going out again tonight – no, you can't talk me out of it. I'm going out tonight and I'm not coming back, no matter what I find. The willows...they're leaning over to scratch on the roof. I hear her laughter in every rustle of leaves and moan of wood.

"So that's it. Call the cops if you want, but don't go worrying about me. Change has come, and I can't shy from it anymore. Already a few specks of bark are growing on me. Thanks for being there, John, through

The Willow Stand

all of this...and thanks for understanding. Whatever remains in me that's still a man, I owe to you. But even that must be left behind."

Illustration by Sarah Walker

GreenFingers
by Sarah Walker

The record cover is different than the others. Most of the ones you have seen here are of bands you know, all flashy and well-polished photos gracing the fronts. But this one, it is beat up and worn, torn at the edges. Absentmindedly you stare at its odd design for a few moments. Occult like symbols dance across the borders and in the center is drawn a single tree, its skeleton branches reaching into a black void of a sky, only a few little bright spots indicative of stars. The colors are black, white and a dirty brown, reminding you of the leaves outside, now faded from brilliant orange into black as they decay.

Suddenly, there's an older man next to you. He smells like dirt. He has a filthy quality you don't much like. You step a bit to the side to keep him from touching your shoulder. He leans back in anyway.

"Ah, an unknown classic…"

The man at the counter looks up from his phone and glares at the man talking at you. You hazard a side glance at the creep and see that the man has twigs in his hair. His belly hangs loosely on his plump frame as if he's just lost thirty pounds. He sees that you are looking at him. His face splits open in what you take as a lascivious grin with crooked teeth all greenish yellow. Is that a bit of grass between his incisors?

"Leave the kid alone. I mean it," the counter man says. You feel your face reddening. You don't like being talked to and when men, specifically older men, talk to you, your first impulse is to run and hide.

The man continues, "Are you really ready for that?" and before you can answer, he jumps in. "No, you aren't ready for that…" He tries to take the record from you. Stunned, you keep your grip. You cannot think of what to say.

Greenfingers

"Hey!" Counter man shouts at the man. "Stop harassing my customers. I'll throw you out! I mean it!"

The man suddenly stops. He puts his hands up and backs up a little. "No harm, no foul," he says.

You feel sick to your stomach, but you don't move. You hope it looks like you are being tough when in all truth you are simply terrified. Though away from you now, you can still feel the man staring at you. You keep ignoring him.

Finally, he sniffs loudly and moves further away, glancing once over his shoulder as he goes to another aisle. You turn to see where he has gone, and he catches you looking again.

He winks. You do not want him to meet your eyes, so you glance down. His feet are wrong. Too short, blocky. His pants seem to move of their own accord as if he's wearing something alive underneath. An image of weasels squiggling under the filthy fabric pops into your mind.

Embarrassed, you look away and back at the record. The picture looks different now, greener somehow. An unidentifiable feeling washes over you. Maybe the record is one of those devil-conjuring ones. You have read about such things.

The man is still in the other aisle and when you look again, his hair is longer, his eyebrows so bushy now they almost cover his beady black eyes. He grins again.

Anger rushes into you. Who is he to tell you what to do? Who is he to tell you what you can and cannot buy? It isn't his record.

Men are always doing that to you. It is not enough for them that they try and own your body, now they want to own your mind.

So, you walk up to the counter carrying the odd record and you buy it.

As the man at the counter shoves the record into a plastic bag with "Reggie's Records" written across in bright red block letters, the paper record sleeve makes a dry sound as it is pushed into the bag. The sound feels familiar, like when you are walking through dead grass, and as you

Sarah Walker

pass the money to him, you notice your arms have broken out in gooseflesh.

You don't think much of it. You turn for one last look at the strange man, but you see he has vanished.

A little annoyed you can't rub the purchase in his face, you walk out into the street, an early October gust of air rushing coldly at you as soon as the record store's door is shut behind you, the hydraulic arm pulling it shut quick and efficient. It seems so small compared to the great outside.

The blast of wind dies down quickly though, and it returns to the warm autumn afternoon. You walk, heading to your house. As you walk, you begin to feel excited at the purchase, the strange man at the store forgotten. Maybe it's a collector's item, you think.

Once you arrive home, you stop and wait outside to make sure that your parents are gone. You sneak around the side of your house peeking into the windows to be sure. You let out a held breath when you notice no one is there, thankfully.

You go to the door and open it with the key that is left under the mat.

Your new father often calls your mother stupid for this hiding place, saying that someone, a Satanic cultist perhaps, will break in and kill them all. She does not argue, but she keeps putting the key there, responding, "Yes, of course." Then the horrible silence returns.

Up the stairs you go, all the way to the top of the aging house, the eyes of the multitude of Jesus paintings following you as you try to ignore their stares. The faces of these gods are all the same. They do not have the flaming eyes one would expect of a real god. They feel flat and powerless, made of watercolor and mushy pulped paper.

Your room is the attic. Up here it is colder than the rest of the ancient building because the roof is falling apart. If you look up, you can see the afternoon sky starting to darken through the holes between the slats.

Your new father says that one day, he will insulate your room. But he never does. If truth be told, you know it isn't his fault. He never has the

Greenfingers

money to. At least once the rain starts every year, he puts a new tarp up so that you don't get wet.

Despite this, you like the attic. You've gotten used to seeing your breath at night during the wet winters and hearing the sound of the toads outside. Your parents told you long ago that toads were the Devil's minions, that they speak in a croak because they are warped inside. And though you nod and pretend to agree, secretly you listen to them and hope the Devil is real because those swamp creatures have been more of a friend to you than those dead-eyed saints and alabaster angels watching you from around the house. They are so alien in their perfection. You even asked your mother to at least take them down from the bedroom so they wouldn't watch you while you sleep, but she always refuses.

"You need them for protection," she says. "Especially a girl like you, especially at your age."

It still makes you mad to think of what she says. What is a "girl like me?" You bite your lip. You are used to being angry. They always have something to say to a "girl like you." At this thought, you pinch the meaty part between your thumb and forefinger, forcing your anger out through the brief pain.

You look around the room as you slip off your boots and glance at the picture of Jesus and a lamb that your mother has hung. You often cover it, but the piece of fabric has fallen again and the Savior stares at you, his hand buried deep in the lamb's thick pelt.

It bothers you, so you get up and put the fabric back. You let out a breath and feel better. Up here the walls of wood are your real family; aren't they the ones who really hold you safe against the winter winds? Aren't they always there when the darkness comes, and your parents are nowhere to be seen? You smile when you think of the big oak that grows next to the decrepit structure called home. Is it trying to talk to you when its branches scratch the roof during thunderstorms? Are the scratches secret messages that the tree is sending you? If so, you have yet to parse out what it is trying to say.

Sarah Walker

You take your newest acquisition out and examine the cover again. Now you see there isn't just a tree on the cover. In the shade a shape stands, a shadowy man it would seem. You think back to what you saw in the store. You are certain there wasn't a person there before. How could that be? As you examine it, you begin to imagine it is the man who tried to take the record from you. It looks like him and it is like he has followed you home. You give up thinking about it after a minute when you realize the insanity of where your nervous thoughts are leading you.

You look back at the letters along the edge. They still make no sense; you see with relief. You wish you could read them, though. It feels like if you stare at them long enough, they will become what they should be, the message the world has been trying to convey to you via trees and toads finally decoded. The truth would be finally unbound from its swaddling of lies. You would be able to see, finally. But the symbols remain obscured, and you still do not know what they mean as you walk over to your record player.

It sits on an old and dusty bookshelf. The wood is cracked and, here and there, plastic fake wood stickers are peeling off, revealing the rough plywood beneath. If you look closely, you can see mold growing along the edges of the real wood. You lean in a little and take a breath—it smells like yellow mushrooms in the rain. If you touch it, plumes of amber pollen burst into the air and onto your hands where you let it settle. It is soft and coats your skin in a powdery film.

You glance back at the stereo. The record player is old. It was your grandmother's when she was young in the 1980s. You like that and wish she were still around with her sandalwood scent, but she is dead, having died when you were only six. That was before your mother met your "father." Before your mother "found God".

You frown thinking of your grandmother. Your new father wouldn't let you keep anything of hers. He said it was all "tainted" after the old woman died. He claimed that objects have "magical power" and that the Devil uses those objects to trick humans into worshipping him. Your new

Greenfingers

father never lets you have anything, no jewelry, no nice clothes. He says you must be frugal. That you must stay "pure."

You feel like crying for a moment. This is all you have left of your grandmother and your past, short life before the new father came. At least only your mother knows you have it. If your new father found out, he would make you throw it away, grandmother's stereo or not. Your mother only let you keep it after you found it in an old box your mother had hidden. You promised you would only play Christian music and never let your new father find out. But the truth is, you play anything you can get your hands on. Everything that comes out of the stereo is a homage to her.

You slide the record out of its cover and see the shiny black plastic grooved with sound. The record looks newer than it did in the store. Maybe it is coming back to life, you think. You know trees can do that. So can toads, like that one who was in a rock for over one hundred years, let out alive and kicking when the rock was split in two, you remind yourself.

Carefully you place the record onto the turntable and let the needle settle itself into one of the grooves. As the sound of the needle passes to the speaker, you decide that maybe your new father is right, maybe objects do hold magic. Aren't records a kind of magic? How can a pattern cut into plastic make one hear a song from another time? You know you are listening to ghosts when you play the records.

As you stand there, you feel a delicious feeling of breaking the rules and you grin silently to yourself in expectation.

You walk back to your bed and lay down, the springs in the ancient mattress poking into your thin back. You wait for the sound to take you away, but it does not come, the song is too long in starting. You sit up when you think you still can't hear anything. Has the stereo finally died?

But then, quietly, you realize you can hear a sound. You sit there, mouth half-open, trying to make out what you're hearing. Maybe it is a faint drumbeat? And a buzzing? You strain to hear more, but you can't hear it any better. Now it seems like only silence is pushing through the worn speakers. Maybe you didn't hear anything at all. Maybe you are just hearing your own heart thudding in your ears.

So, you stand and walk over to the speaker, leaning in close, trying to determine if there is even a sound there at all when a man's voice says very clearly:

He's coming.

You almost hit your head as you jump back, the top of the cabinet where the speaker sets is barely avoided when you react to the surprise noise.

You stand for a moment, trying to catch your breath, recalibrating what you think you hear as the buzzing sound increases. Slowly the sound changes and you can tell it's not just buzzing. No, you can hear that now. It is a faint singing, and underneath that singing, a sound like the katydids humming in an August heat. There are definitely words there, but you cannot understand what the voices say. It is in a language you do not recognize.

It feels very familiar.

The sound of the tree's branches on the roof pull your attention away. Usually, the tree only does that when the winds are up and roaring, pushing its branches to dance wildly, but now, though you cannot hear a wind, you can still hear the scraping. It is louder than you have ever heard before. Maybe the old oak is dancing to the music.

Now you can hear scurrying, too; sounds of what must be birds' feet as they scuttle hurriedly across the roof. They click and scrape, and you think you can hear them chirp, but it is hard to tell with all the noise from the tree and the music that keeps growing louder pouring from your grandmother's stereo.

The sound changes suddenly and now you can hear what sounds like a forest. And like a movie being played to your third eye, images of a verdant green world flash into your mind. You try to pull your mind away, back to what you know must be real, your attic room, your lonely

Greenfingers

life, but the music will not be denied. You see the bursting green world as if it opens eagerly before you and not the attic that you know is there... that you hope is there?

This new place in your mind is huge. And it never remains the same. No, it is moving and growing, changing with each millisecond. You can barely keep your head up as it swims with the motion. Even the rocks in the distance are growing, the trees bending as they curl upwards towards an alien sun. And at their base crimson flowers bloom, their faces bright red spots of blood dancing in the summer air.

The music pulls you deeper into this world, and you feel yourself flying forward when up ahead you can see something different. Suddenly you have arrived there, and you see it is a hollow. In the center lies a pile of white branches. You move closer against your will and you realize they are not branches at all. They are bones, a pile of human skeletons draped in jade green mold and lichen that look like lace. You understand suddenly you are in a graveyard of sorts, deep in the hidden wood. Lilies grow off the dead in their pile, their sweet fragrance made ripe with the corpses' decay filling the air. You become terrified.

You use your fear to force yourself back, out of the waking dream where you fall to the floor with the effort it takes to bring you back. You pant and vomit, wondering what is wrong with you. How can you see those images and still be awake?

Does it even matter?

You try and stand, but you are still too dizzy, your head is full, your ears are roaring. You try and stand again, deafened by the roar, but you cannot. You look over at the record player and you can tell the record is still playing, spinning on the turntable. You look up and realize you don't know how long you were dreaming. It must have been longer than you thought as the falling night has painted the room's corners black.

Slowly the nausea fades but now you can feel a fluttering, a tickling. It dances across your ankles and feet, so you look down. Butterflies have appeared out of nowhere. Are you going mad? But then you see no, they haven't appeared out of nowhere. They are crawling out of the wooden slatted floor, their tiny black legs breaking apart the dried wood and popping back the splinters. They were in the womb of wood, you think. They were just waiting to grow. They fly around your crouching form, their wings black and their eyes shining gold. You can hear them speaking to you:

Come with us…come with us…

Now, finally you can stand, and you jump up and back away, watching in horror as where they land, vines begin to grow. You are so stunned you just stop, slack-jawed and wide-eyed and you think you would have just stood there that way for eternity if the vines hadn't begun wrapping your small legs tightly, spirally up your form. You try to pull back, but they have trapped you.

And the music plays on.

Whatever is happening, you think now your new father must have been right. The Devil is in these objects, in the wood, in the toad's voice, in your grandmother's record player. You scream for someone to come and help you.

But it is too late. You realize that now even the walls are growing. You watch as a vine rips through the picture of your parents' god and tears the painting in half as mushrooms pop into existence across the floor, everything becoming coated in living things. Along your bookshelf even the books are growing, more mushrooms springing out of the bookbinding, bits of spore bursting into the air. Frogs and toads are hopping out now, lizards slither across the floor. Yes! Everything is growing!

And with a pollen-thick explosion, the great forest of your mind springs to life in front of you.

Terror grips you as you can hear animals in the mix now, their roars and the padding of their clawed feet. And then, the sound of someone screaming. You look into the jungle to try and see who is making that terrible sound. And then you can see. It is your parents, and you watch

Greenfingers

teary-eyed, laughing and crying as they both vanish under the living green quilt, screaming for their god to help them, screaming for someone to make it stop growing as the foliage forces itself down their soon quieted throats.

And it won't stop growing. It never will and you wonder briefly if the flowers will grow out of their corpses, too.

The room is now completely gone and above you see the sky as it appears, the roof peeling back, letting in the outside. The immense, huge, giant, *outside.*

And you know that the *outside* has always been the victor. Build your houses, build your neighborhoods, build, build, build, little men, you think, now hysterical. Build but nature will take it all away, it will sweep you all into the void with one well-placed tornado or wave or earthquake. It will use your own nature against you, and you will kill each other, infect each other, down and down and down you will go.

You are sobbing now, weeping, and powerless to do anything, when a figure comes out of the greenery. It is the man from the store, but then it is not the man. He changes each second you stare at him. You cannot get a bead on what he really is. At one instant he is leaves and light, the next a horned man, dangerous.

Suddenly he rushes forward, moving so quickly he becomes a smeared painting, traveling through the living jungle from leaf to trunk, to dirt and rock and back up again, he is a living wave until he's standing right. Before. You.

You stare and see that this god's eyes are not flat and painted. No!

You see that this god's eyes are alive with the *outside*, with the flame.

Those raging eyes promise rebirth despite death. He promises a return to the top despite being cast far below, into a deep forty fathoms down. Round and round, up and then down, back up again to crash below.

His eyes are that flower in the corpse that you saw blooming in the dead.

Sarah Walker

And this god's eyes welcome you.
He puts out one blazing burning hand…
Will you take it?

Illustration by Sarah Walker

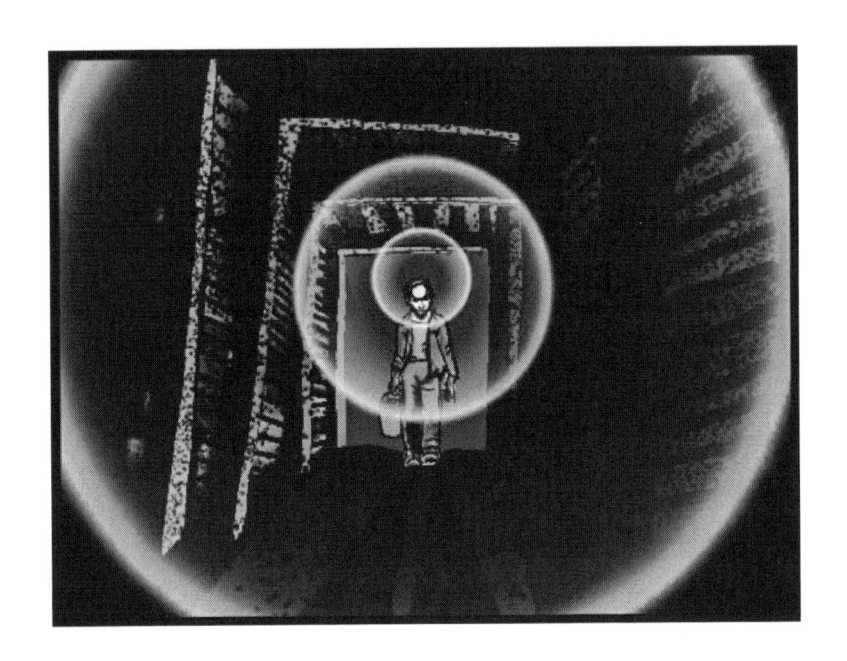

The Blackdamp
by William Tea

The darkness. It shined.

It sounded contradictory, but that didn't make it any less true. The sky above Dale Harley was black as a bible, but also speckled with glinting spheres of pale light. They were like cold, glassy eyes staring back at him from some faraway place. Another world? Maybe a better one.

He'd almost forgotten how many stars the night sky held. Back in Karrasburg, the city lights gave even the blackest gloom a ghostly orange glow that rendered such shimmery pinpricks mostly invisible. Returning home to Strix Township, located out on the farthest, most rural fringes of Calvary County, Pennsylvania, it was like seeing the stars for the first time anew. It was like being a child again.

He didn't like that feeling.

Somewhere beyond the tree line, an owl hooted. Dale turned his eyes away from the sky and back to the door. He held his breath and crossed the threshold. Linoleum-covered floorboards groaned as he entered the kitchen of his youth.

It looked the same. Same furniture. Same wallpaper yellowed and peeling at the corners. Same scorch-marked oven mitts dangling from hooks above the stove. The only thing missing was Dale's mother huddled over a pot, mixing stewed tomatoes into macaroni 'n' cheese while singing along to country music on the radio.

Right now, about 20 miles away in Embersville, the closest town with a hospital, Dale's mother lay in a bed with a half-dozen tubes entangling her, like webbing on a housefly. She might not even be alive if her friend Gloria didn't make it a point to come over every single Sunday. The pair would cut coupons and talk gossip.

The Blackdamp

When he was younger, Dale had dismissed Gloria as a nosy busybody, but he was grateful for her now. Right away, the woman had known something was wrong when Dale's mother failed to answer the door.

Trudging upstairs towards his mother's bedroom, Dale's hand searched his pockets for the matchbox he'd been sure to bring. Its contents rattled, same as the loose metal knob when he opened the door.

The room was startlingly bare.

Dozens of framed pictures still hung on the walls—Dale's parents' wedding, him as a child sitting on his grandfather's lap, a group shot from some family reunion he only half-remembered; although strangely missing was the portrait of Jesus Christ that had once looked down from above the door.

Almost everything else was gone.

For some reason his mother had stripped the mattress of its sheets and blankets. Even the pillows were missing. He checked the end-table drawers and found them empty. Same with the closet and the dressers. The lamp she'd always kept close for late night reading had seemingly vanished.

Dale furrowed his brow but continued his task. He struck a match and watched it burn. It stayed lit all the way down to his fingertips before he blew it out. He struck another and got the same result.

Maybe I'm barking up the wrong tree.

Just to be sure, he wandered in and out of the other second-floor rooms, striking and snuffing matches in each. The house was small, so it didn't take long. There was his mother's bedroom, his own childhood bedroom, a storage closet, and a room his mom had once used for scrapbooking. Strangely, they all had a thin layer of dust covering every surface, as if they'd barely seen anyone pass through in years.

Somehow both relieved and dissatisfied, Dale made his way back down to the first floor. Hoping to sit and think for a minute, he ducked through the door to the living room. That's when the stark emptiness upstairs finally made sense.

For the most part the living room looked unchanged from his youth, right down to the wood-paneled walls, shelves of old photo albums, and outdated cathode TV set. Except...

On a small table beside the couch stood his mother's reading lamp and a stack of ratty secondhand paperbacks. A recliner in the corner held most of his mother's clothes, folded neatly in crooked stacks. The few garments that weren't there were instead draped on wire hangers hooked onto the sides of an old china cabinet. A thick blanket and a raggedy afghan lay strewn across the sofa, while a pillow with an unmistakable head indentation had been shoved up against one of the couch's arms.

On the floor nearby, a long metallic cane rested in a damp, dark circle spilled from a toppled can of Diet Pepsi. A second circle of dried vomit overlapped the first, forming a sickly Venn diagram.

When did she start needing a cane? Dale wondered. *Sure, it's been a while since my last visit, but it hasn't been long enough for me to have missed a development like that. Has it?*

He could only guess that she'd moved herself down to the living room when it became too painful climbing the staircase every day. The rest of the mess told him that this was where Gloria had found her.

He held his breath and kneeled down next to the sofa. He struck a match. It flared to life...

...only for the flame to immediately shrivel and die.

He struck another and got the same result.

Then another. And another.

"Shit," Dale muttered.

The blackdamp.

It was here. Probably came seeping up from the cellar. Odorless. Invisible. Deadly.

The Blackdamp

Suddenly, he couldn't help but notice the alarming quickness of his heartbeat, the strained shallowness of his breaths. His eyes darted across the room. Sure enough, the windows were all sealed tight against the cold autumn winds. Which meant that, with the door closed, there was hardly any ventilation at all.

Head swimming, Dale hurried back outside, eager for fresh air.

It shouldn't be here, he thought. *The house is well outside the fire zone.*

As a child he'd heard stories about the folks who used to live in the north end, how the gas—"blackdamp," the miners called it—came up from the earth and leaked into people's homes. It kept them from lighting candles. It blew out their pilot lights. It gave people headaches, made them see things that weren't there, strangled them in their sleep, and worse.

Eventually, everyone who lived in the affected area had been forced to move. A good chunk of Strix Township had been amputated and abandoned because the soil beneath it was bleeding poison into people's houses.

It was supposed to have been contained. The amputation was supposed to stop the rot.

If Dale was right, though, it meant the fire was spreading.

As he made his way back to his car, something small and furry darted across the lawn. Then came a flash of movement, something diving from the trees on a flurry of feathers. Just like that the little creature was gone, snatched up by a shadow.

Dale couldn't hear the owl's triumphant screeching moments later. Not over the engine of his car.

He did not hear the whimpers of its prey either.

⌘⌘⌘

More than thirty years ago, Dale had sat on his grandfather's lap, listening to the old man's stories while his mother flitted around them like

William Tea

a hummingbird, snapping pictures and whispering how cute the two looked together.

Like his father before him and like his very own brother—God rest his soul—and like Dale's daddy now, Dale's grandfather had worked his whole life as a coal miner. And in all that time, he'd learned just how ancient this old world was.

"Older than you, grampa?" Dale had asked, to which the elder man nodded and laughed.

"People think that outside, in the woods, that's where the old world lives. But I say it's deep down beneath our feet, hibernating in the earth. In the guts. And the farther down we dig, the closer we get to whatever it was that came before us. That's why I'm so proud that me and your daddy and *my* daddy and everybody else around here are miners. We're the ones that do the digging. That's important."

"I thought it was important 'cause of the coal, those rocks mama throws in the furnace. That's what keeps us warm in the winter, right?"

"That's right, Dilly Bar. And that *is* important. But it's also important for us to be down there because, well, y'know that oldness that's down there? That oldness that's older than old and even older than your pop-pop? I think that's where we all came from. It's God, or Mother Nature, or whatever you want to call it. The very heart of this land that gives to us and provides for us. No one knows it better than us mining folk. We hold it with our hands every day. We breathe it in."

"I'll tell you something my brother told me," the old man continued. "That's your grand-uncle, God rest his soul. He was a miner, too."

"Did he get old and retire like you, grampa?"

"Uh, no. He…"

The old man had trailed off, then, coughing and clearing his throat.

"Mining is good work and important work, but it's also dangerous work. There, uh, there was this flood, see. The tunnels got too close to the Muttontoe River. The walls, they got too thin. Water came spilling in. We lost a lot of good miners. A lot of good mines, too. Folks came real

The Blackdamp

close to losing everything before that Andras company swooped in. Most other parts of the state weren't so lucky. Most places stopped mining completely. Sad state of affairs. Anyway, the hell was I talking about?"

"Your brother."

"That's right, your grand-uncle! Now, see, he was many years older than me, and he worked them mines a lot longer and lot deeper than I ever did. And believe you me, he saw some pretty amazing stuff."

"What kinda stuff?"

The old man had squinted his eyes then, before peeking over both his shoulders like he was checking for spies. Then he'd whispered a single word.

"Tommyknockers."

Dale's own eyes had gone wide, even though he hadn't even known what that word meant. The seriousness with which the elder man said it was enough to convey its importance.

"Tommy who?" he'd asked, causing his grandfather to laugh again.

"Tommyknockers. The ghosts of long-lost miners."

Dale's mother groaned.

"Hush. Let me have my fun," he'd said, never taking his gaze off the young boy. "They call them tommyknockers because that's how you know one of thems around. Before you even see them, you hear them far off, in the dark of the drifts, hammering away just like they were still among the living, working hard for their bread."

"Mama's says there's no such thing as ghosts."

"Oh, does she now? Well, my brother seen one. How could he have seen one if they weren't real?"

At this, Dale had looked to his mother for comfort, but her attention had shifted to fiddling with the camera in her hands. It took the boy a long time to figure out what to say next.

"Are they scary ghosts?" he'd finally asked.

William Tea

"Maybe. Maybe not. No one can agree for sure. Some folks say they're here to help us, to protect miners from cave-ins and the like. Other folks think they want to hurt us, to lure miners away from safety with all kinds of tricks and traps that put them in danger. Me? I just know what my brother told me. He said if I ever hear the pounding of a tommyknocker, I'd best get aboveground right away. Because whether they're causing the bad things or trying to warn us, either way bad things happen."

Dale had looked to his mother again. She'd stopped working on her camera and offered her son a weak smile as she cradled the side of her face in one hand.

Dale had smiled back, then suddenly been struck by a thought.

"Grampa, you said tommyknockers used to be miners, right? Do you think your brother maybe became one?"

The elder man hadn't responded. Instead he'd wiped something from his eyes and, after clearing his throat again, suggested a trip to the Dairy Queen.

A few years later, Dale's grandfather died in an Embersville hospice. Dale had barely even recognized him when he saw him at the funeral. The man had been reduced to little more than a skeleton, his skin waxy and unreal.

Cause of death: pneumoconiosis. Or more commonly known to mining folk, black lung.

⌘⌘⌘

I shouldn't have left the house so quick last night, Dale thought.

He should have grabbed his mother's cane and brought it back here to the hospital. He could have brought some of her books, too. If only so she had something from home waiting for her when she finally got better.

"When"? More like "if." I am a journalist, after all. I'm supposed to choose my words carefully. Wouldn't want to imply something is a sure thing when it's not.

The Blackdamp

Dale pushed such thoughts aside and turned back to his phone call. Jazzy Muzak tested his patience as he checked the time again. Sure enough, he'd been on hold for over 15 minutes already, and this was the third time he'd been transferred. The third time, that is, after his first two calls had ended in "accidental" hang-ups.

Maybe he shouldn't have mentioned he was with the press. Then again, if he hadn't then the pencil-pushers at Andras Energy probably wouldn't have had the decency of even *pretending* they weren't giving him the runaround. The handful of times he'd actually gotten through to someone he'd almost immediately been transferred to another department, then another, then another. Either no one in the whole company knew who was actually supposed to be in charge or they were just hoping he'd hang up and go away.

Dale paced the hospital waiting room, alone except for an elderly couple sitting in the far corner, the husband seemingly asleep while his wife paged through out-of-date magazines.

Suddenly, the Muzak stopped and a voice replaced it.

"Hello?"

"Hi," Dale said. "Hello. Yes."

"I am so, so sorry to keep you waiting, Mr. Harley," the voice said. "I'm Angelo Blake, the senior media relations officer for Andras Energy. Before anything, I want to assure you that I am here to help in any way I can. Just to confirm, what organization did you say you work for?"

"I'm with The Citizen Leader."

"Oh, how great. I have a subscription myself."

"Yeah. Listen, I was hoping to talk to someone about the spur of tunnels that runs beneath the northeast section of Strix, specifically the plot of land near the intersection of Harvest and Woodruff."

"May I ask, is this for a newspaper story you're writing or…"

"Ah, yes," Dale said.

His mind searched in vain for something to say that would put the company man at ease. He ended up letting his answer sit there,

236

unexplained. A pregnant pause followed, until Blake seemed to realize that no more details were forthcoming.

"Well, Mr. Harley, I'm afraid I'm not authorized to go into detail about any of Andras Energy's current business operations. If you have more specific questions, I might be able to refer you to someone better suited—"

"What I would like to know," Dale blurted, "is why there's blackdamp seeping into my mother's living room."

He hadn't meant to come out with it so directly, but already Dale could feel his knuckles tightening and his face growing hot. The time for playing nice had passed.

"I'm sorry?" Blake said.

"Blackdamp. Choke-damp. Stythe. Y'know, the shit that's produced by coal oxidation. Like through burning. Like if there was a whole goddamn mine on fire, building up shitloads of gas until there was nowhere else for it go but the surface."

"I'm sorry, I'm not sure I follow, sir. The whole area you described is—"

"Right on top of one of your coal mines."

"Inactive, I was going to say. The drifts in the northeast section are no longer in use."

"No shit. Kind of hard to keep working a tunnel when it's on fire."

"Mr. Harley, are you referring to the coal seam fire of 1989? That's—"

"No, I'm referring to the coal seam fire of right fucking now!"

Dale suddenly realized he was shouting. He glanced in the direction of the elderly couple, only to find the man still asleep and the woman seemingly intent on staring a hole into the ceiling.

"Unless I'm mistaken," Dale said, lowering his voice and slipping out into the hall, "that fire *started* in 1989, but it's still burning underground today, is it not? It didn't go out, did it? I feel like I would've heard about that."

The Blackdamp

"Eh, yes. I mean no," came Blake's frazzled reply. "I mean—God, I shouldn't even be telling you this—the reason our northeastern sector recently closed is because the coal yields there have fallen below a level where profit offsets extraction cost. Management has decided to focus its current efforts on the southern sector instead."

Dale power-walked through the hospital with the phone glued to his ear, catching glimpses of battered bodies languishing in sterile beds.

"As for the fire zone," Blake continued, "that's an isolated problem. It's completely cut off from the rest of our network. There is a 200-foot-wide trench encircling that entire area and much of the drift system has been filled in with noncombustible materials. We would not be *allowed* to do business in Strix Township if the fire weren't safely contained. Teams from both the Appalachian Environmental Commission and the Mine Safety and Health Administration conduct regular visits on-site, as well as inspections of our current operations."

Dale pulled a pen from his pocket and hastily scribbled both organizations' names onto the palm of his hand.

"I would also like to point out," Blake said, "that Andras Energy personally bought out all the residential property in the fire zone and generously paid to rehome all displaced citizens. We here at Andras Energy are totally committed to the safety of our workforce and to the health of our community, and—"

"Oh, shove your corporate PR spiel up your ass," Dale barked, unable to help himself. A passing nurse shot him a dirty look, but he brushed her off.

"You didn't seem too committed to the safety of my dad. Or to the health of my granddad. Or to the health of my fucking mother who, I repeat, has blackdamp *in her home* and is now in critical condition with severe hypoxia and hypercapnia. Do you know what that means? It means her body was so oxygen-deprived that she might have fucking brain damage now."

William Tea

The heavy stairwell door banged against the wall as Dale burst through, coming to a stop in the relative peace and quiet of the fourth-floor landing.

"I am very sorry for your mother's current health crisis," Blake said, "but I can assure you, whatever the cause, it has nothing to do with any mine gas or anything caused by our operations."

He paused briefly.

"That said, I think I speak for everyone at Andras Energy when I extend our most sincere sympathies to you, and to show how much we mean that we would be happy to help take care of any medical costs that might accrue during this—"

There it was. Might as well be a confession. Andras offering to cover his mother's hospital expenses wouldn't be enough to sustain an article, but it was enough to let Dale know he had the scent. Now he just needed to follow it.

"I got to ask," Dale said, "do you guys pay the doctor bills for every random person who ends up in the hospital with some problem *completely unrelated* to coal mining, or just the ones you really like? What, you're afraid I'm going to sue? Y'know, I might. But first I'm going to make sure everyone knows the truth. And then you won't be able to get a job burning hash browns at the Waffle House."

Before Blake could get in another slimy word, Dale hung up in disgust.

He sat down at the bottom of the closest staircase and seethed in silence.

They knew. They fucking knew and they tried to keep a lid on it. And then they tried to buy me off.

He knew he should go back to his mother's room, if only to stay close, hold her hand, maybe provide some kind of anchor to help her find her way out of the darkness. But being cooped up in there with nothing but a hissing ventilator, a beeping EKG, and Seinfeld reruns on the TV made him feel powerless. Hopeless. Trapped.

The Blackdamp

He'd left Strix Township to get away from those feelings. Damned if he'd let them worm their way back inside.

He checked the clock on his phone again. It was almost quitting time. For the local miners, that meant drinking time.

Hell, Dale could use a Yuengling.

⌘⌘⌘

"I'm telling you, dude! Two chicks at the same dance! It was like a fucking Flintstones cartoon or some shit, me running back and forth between both of 'em trying not to let either one get wise! I even used the same condom both times!"

Ian Pitt slapped the tabletop and laughed heartily.

The coaches used to call him "Pitt-Bull" back when he played wide receiver in high school. His grades had always been shit, but his skills on the field made him popular. So, too, did being the only kid in class with a tattoo. Freshman through senior year, he'd had a different girlfriend every semester. Someone—probably Pitt himself—had spread a rumor that he'd even seduced the pretty young substitute who sometimes filled in for AP English.

He and Dale hadn't been close back then, but they'd gotten along well enough and shared a few mutual friends. Two decades later, that was enough to get Pitt reminiscing as if he'd just reunited with a long-lost twin.

That's how it is with these guys who never leave home, Dale thought. *They've got a good thing going at first, but they hold onto it too long. Then one day they wake up with a receding hairline, high cholesterol, and a stool with their name on it at the same dive-bar their dad used to get drunk at. Give a guy like that an excuse to relive his glory days and he'll talk your ear off.*

Dale didn't want to talk about Pitt's glory days, though. He wanted to talk about the man's life now. Specifically, Pitt's job as a miner for Andras Energy. Before the former high school Lothario sauntered in, Dale had tried striking up conversations with two other miners, but his reception had been colder than the beer on tap.

William Tea

"Yeah, those were crazy times," Dale said, forcing a smile that he hoped didn't look *too* fake. "What are you up to these days, though? You said you're working the deep mines, yeah?"

"Deepest of the deep," Pitt said.

"That's cool. Did you go into that right after graduation or what?"

Pitt poured himself a refill from the sweating pitcher on the table.

"I mean, basically, yeah," he said, squinting as if he'd been asked a complicated math question. "My dad was the foreman at the time, so I already had the hook-up. I figured it was just something to do until I found something better, but then I kind of got used to it. It's tough as shit, but I'm a tough dude. How about you?"

"Me? Not much to tell. So, working the mines doesn't worry you?"

"What would I be worried about?"

"I don't know," Dale said. Underneath the table, he pulled a digital tape recorder from his pocket and switched it on.

"Safety issues, I guess. You're all the way down there with literal tons of rock hanging over your head, operating all this heavy machinery in the dark. Seems like a lot of shit could go wrong. Collapses. Explosions. Toxic gas. I mean, there was that big flood that one time…"

"Yeah, but that was, like, before I was even born."

"—and then that fire when we were kids. It's still burning out there in the far north end, isn't it? I hear if you go driving past that way, the air's all hazy with smoke and gas and shit leaking up from cracks in the ground."

Dale raised his mug to his lips with one hand, then grabbed a napkin to wipe away the suds with the other. Pitt didn't seem to notice the recorder beneath the napkin when Dale laid it back down.

"Honestly, dude, I don't think about it too much," Pitt said, leaning back to scratch his neck. For the first time, Dale noticed the crucifix wrist tattoo that had once been the man's calling card had been covered up at some point. In its place now was some kind of bird. An owl, maybe.

The Blackdamp

"I mean, it comes with the job," Pitt continued. "If you ask me, a job without some kind of risk isn't much of a job at all. Like, how you going to call yourself a man if you're not willing to put your life on the line for your family, right? The Pitts have always been tough. I'm not afraid of some burning coal on the other side of town, and I'm not afraid to get my hands dirty either."

Dale took another drink from his mug and swirled the cheap, bitter alcohol in his mouth. He considered his next words very carefully.

"I guess you're right," he said. "I'm probably overthinking it. Especially with how often you have inspectors poking around. I'm sure they take good care of you guys. They must practically live down in those drifts with you."

Pitt cocked an eyebrow.

"What are you talking about?" he asked.

"Well," Dale started, "I heard the Mine Safety and Health Administration and the Appalachian Environmental Commission both have inspection teams come out here pretty regularly to check on things. I know you said you're willing to take the risk, but it must be comforting having these government babysitters, I guess—sorry, I can't think of a better word—uh, y'know, reassuring you that you're not *really* in serious danger."

Pitt burst out laughing again, pounding the floor with his foot like this was the funniest thing he'd ever heard.

"Dude, are you kidding? The MSHA and the AEC don't do shit. They don't take care of us. *We* take care of us. I mean, their so-called 'inspection teams' are just one guy, and they're both the *same* guy. Literally, the same dude reports to both organizations. Got himself a cushy office up in fucking Karrasburg, I think. A guy like that isn't going to make the drive from Karrasburg to Strix on the regular, get me?"

"Well, even still, just because he doesn't make it out here all that often..."

William Tea

"All that often? Try never! Fuck that guy. We don't want him around here and he knows it. I bet you dollars to donuts he just slaps a new date on the same old inspection report every year or whatever. Besides, I think I heard that dude's wife works HR at one of the company's fracking sites. Y'know, natural gas? I wouldn't be surprised if she gets a nice bonus whenever mine inspection time rolls 'round, just to remind hubby to keep his nose out of our fucking business."

"You really think that?"

Pitt rocked back in his chair, pushing its two front legs up off the floor.

"All I'm saying, dude, is I ain't ever seen no inspector down—"

Suddenly, a pair of hands clamped down on Pitt's shoulders. The legs of his chair slammed back down. Hard.

A harsh-looking face leaned in until it was cheek-to-cheek with Pitt. The stranger had a shaved head and a nose like a needle, and a rictus grin that reflected not an ounce of warmth.

"Hi there," he said. "What you kids talking about?"

"Oh h-hey," Pitt stammered. "This is my old friend Dale. Dale, this is Jay Stearne. We're…"

"Co-workers," Stearne said, letting go of Pitt's shoulders. He pulled an extra chair over to the pair's table and sat down, his every movement slow and deliberate. "Professional colleagues. But I didn't ask for introductions. I asked what you two were talking about."

"We were just playing catch-up," Dale interjected. His eyes locked with Stearne's. He could tell the man wanted to intimidate him but decided to deny him the satisfaction of knowing that it was working.

"I'm just telling him, y'know, about my life," Pitt said. "About my job, all that shit."

Stearne kept his eyes trained on Dale.

"So, what about you?" he asked.

Dale shrugged.

The Blackdamp

"What about me?"

"What about *your* life? *Your* job? All that shit."

"He's a local," Pitt interjected.

"Well, I've never seen him before."

"I grew up here," Dale said. "I have an apartment in Karrasburg now, so—"

"So, then you're not a local," Stearne said. "Not anymore."

"Dude, he's not—"

"I really think you ought to shut the fuck up!"

And just like that, Pitt shut the fuck up. Dale couldn't imagine anyone handling the football star like that back in the day.

Stearne turned back to Dale.

"Please," he said. "Go on."

"What do you want to know?"

"What do you do for a living?"

"I'm a writer."

"What do you write?"

"Lots of stuff." He shifted in his seat. "Different things. For The Citizen Leader."

Stearne closed his eyes and shook his head, then looked at Pitt.

"A fucking newspaper reporter. You're a real fucking idiot."

With the man's attention elsewhere, Dale reached for his audio recorder, hoping to slip it back in his pocket before things could go any farther south.

Then things went farther south.

Like a coiled snake, Stearne's arm lunged forward, grabbing the device before Dale could even touch it.

"Audio record time," Stearne said, repeating the words on the screen. "Twenty-three minutes and 57 seconds. Fifty-eight seconds. Fifty-nine. Twenty-four minutes."

William Tea

In one smooth motion, the man turned and launched the recorder at the wall like he was pitching for the Hewers. It exploded against a sign above the bar that cheerfully declared *WE SERVE MINERS, NOT MINORS.*

Every conversation in the building suddenly stopped dead. The only sounds remaining were the mechanical hum of the ice machine behind the bar and Warren Zevon blaring from the jukebox.

No one made a move to help or argue or break things up. They all just watched as Dale angrily jumped to his feet.

Stearne shot up to meet him. A vein thumped in the man's forehead. He cracked his neck.

"Sorry," he said, clicking his tongue. "Butterfingers."

The man was taller and broader than either Dale or his drinking partner. Stearne made the former Pit-Bull look more like a Chihuahua, right down to the nervous shaking.

Still, Dale didn't shy from meeting the man's gaze. For what felt like an eternity but was really not much more than a minute, the two stood face-to-face, unflinching.

"I think I should get going," Dale said finally, barely able to coax the words out through gritted teeth.

"Smart idea. Unless you want the next time your name's in the paper to be when they run your obituary."

Dale had to actively concentrate to get his feet moving. He started towards the exit, then at the last second decided to take a chance.

A job without some kind of risk isn't much of a job at all. Isn't that what Pitt said?

Not taking his eyes off Stearne, Dale circled the fuming man to approach his former classmate. He grasped Pitt's hand and pulled him close for a hug.

"It was good to see you, man," Dale said. "Keep in touch."

Please, Pitt, for once in your life don't be fucking stupid, he thought as he headed towards the exit. *Don't open your hand to look at the business card I just*

The Blackdamp

slipped you. Not in front of Stearne. Just quietly sneak the damned thing into your pocket without a word. I'm begging you.

Forcing himself not to look back, Dale waited for a liquor bottle to come flying at his head any minute, or for Stearne to jump him.

Nothing happened. Instead he stepped outside into the crisp autumn night, zipped his windbreaker shut, and drove back to his motel room in Embersville, anticipating a long night of uneasy sleep.

⌘⌘⌘

As a child, Dale had always held his breath whenever he passed a cemetery. He never really knew why he'd done that. It was as if the knowledge had entered him by osmosis, that this was expected of him.

As a man, he no longer bothered with such rituals, least of all in Strix Township. If he did that here, he'd never breathe again. The whole place was one big graveyard.

Dale's grandfather had only been in the ground a year when he received some new company.

A whole lot of new company.

Dale, still just a boy, had been watching TV when the phone rang. His mother had admonished him as she hurried past. She'd been right to; he should have been doing his homework.

For the rest of his life, he would wish he had been. Because if he'd been doing his homework, he'd have been upstairs in his bedroom. And he wouldn't have seen his strong, optimistic, level-headed mother rendered helpless by something as simple as a phone call.

Even more than what followed, the sight of her in that state had shattered Dale's sense of security for all time. Afterwards, he'd never again look at the world with a child's eyes. Afterwards, he'd never be able to unsee the ugliness of the life that had been built up around him, given to him, planned for him.

For the rest of his days, he would do everything in his power to escape that life.

William Tea

"Mommy?" Dale had asked, trying to contain the panic growing within him. "Mommy, what's wrong?!?"

He'd rushed to her side as her strength had evaporated, leaving her collapsed in a heap, still clutching the telephone while sobbing into the carpet.

At the time, all he could do was wish for his father to come home from work. *He* would know what to do to help Dale's mother. *He* would know what to say, how to fix things, how to return the world to normal. Of that, Dale had been certain.

But his father never did come home from work.

There'd been an accident, some miscommunication that led to the wrong worker putting the wrong bundle of explosives on the wrong wall. One of the drifts suffered a cave-in, and, worse yet, the coal veins had started burning.

It would take the company days before they recovered even half the miners' bodies.

As bad as Dale's grandfather had looked when they buried him, the boy's father must have been worse. The funeral had been strictly closed casket.

Dale's mother wept nonstop through the entire service.

⌘⌘⌘

George Costanza had just made the fatal mistake of asking the Soup Nazi for bread when Dale's phone rang. He didn't recognize the number but picked up anyway.

"Hello?"

"Uh, hey."

It was Pitt.

Well, at least that meant Stearne hadn't torn up his contact card and dumped the man's body in a ditch somewhere.

The Blackdamp

"Sorry about last night," Pitt said, as if reading his mind. "Jay's a good dude, but he's got a hot head sometimes. Especially when it comes to out-of-towners."

"Yeah, well, I'm not an out-of-towner."

"Dude, I know that! It's just, like, Stearne is on this whole townie loyalty trip where he thinks moving means turning your back on your home or something. I don't know, sometimes it makes sense."

Dale rolled his eyes and switched off the television. The black screen reflected an image of his bed-ridden mother back at him. He turned away to look out the window.

Traffic clogged streets for the lunchtime rush. One block over, the city roads bled out into a highway that cleaved through the rolling hills and rust-colored woods separating Embersville from Strix Township. Here, everything felt cramped and dirty. There, the landscape was beautiful and open.

It was easy to forget that beneath the pastoral surface, a blaze closer to Hell than Dale ever wanted to come flickered and flashed through otherwise unlit corridors.

"So, is that why you called," Dale asked, "to tell me I turned my back on my home?"

"Dude, c'mon. I'm calling you because that's clearly what you wanted. What's going on with you? Were you seriously recording me last night? Jay said he thinks you were trying to grill me for info because you want to get the company into trouble and put us all out of work."

"I can't get anybody in trouble if they haven't done anything wrong."

"Don't play games with me, man. Why are you here?"

Dale sighed. The worst part of admitting something to another person was how real that made it. Dale couldn't just keep moving forward on autopilot; he had to slow down long enough to consider everything that had happened so far, and everything that was still to come.

"Fine. You want the truth?" Dale said. "The truth is I'm here because my mom isn't doing too hot right now. She's in Embersville ICU."

"Shit, dude. I'm sorry."

Dale cleared his throat and fought the tingly feeling building up behind his eyes.

"They found her passed out in her living room," he continued, "barely breathing, with dangerously elevated carbon dioxide levels."

"Is she…?"

"I don't know," Dale said, not wanting Pitt to finish his question. "And nobody can tell me what caused it, either. But it got me thinking, you remember the mine fire from '89? Remember how everybody who lived in the fire zone had to move because of the blackdamp coming up from underground?"

"You don't think…? "

"My mom's symptoms are similar to those of someone who's been exposed to blackdamp. And our house is situated right above a mine spur that, coincidentally, Andras Energy recently had to close. I think the '89 fire isn't as well-contained as they say. I think it's been slowly spreading into other drifts and I think Andras is trying to keep it hush-hush. They're sending you guys down there despite knowing how dangerous it is, and the people who live up top are completely oblivious to the poison seeping up from their floorboards."

Pitt didn't reply.

"Listen," Dale said, exasperated, "I'm not trying to put anybody out of work. I'm just trying to figure out the truth. If you know anything that could help, please tell me."

More silence followed. When Pitt's response finally came, it was short and monotone.

"I got to do some thinking. I'll call you later."

Before Dale could say anything else, Pitt was gone.

The Blackdamp

Unsure what else to do, Dale turned back to the television. Pressing the ON button banished his mother's reflection from the empty screen, replacing it with mugging comedians and canned laughter.

Occasionally, Dale forced himself to look over to the bed-ridden body with which he shared the room. It was hard to reconcile the unconscious, unaware, barely even breathing *thing* with the loving, laughing woman who had raised him on her own for most of his life.

That woman had always been smiling, always taking photographs and pasting them in scrapbooks. That woman had instilled in him a love for words, for reading and writing and telling stories. It was the only way he'd learned to make sense of what seemed so often a senseless world. That woman had loved to sing along to the radio, and sometimes even danced.

Picturing that woman struggling to walk, to climb the stairs, to even stand up straight, it was like a blade twisting between Dale's ribcage and heart.

He searched for any sign of that woman in the sunken body next to him, scanning its frozen face for even a faint glimmer or ghost of her vibrancy.

Just one, that's all he needed. Just long enough so that he could thank her for everything she had done and meant to him, and so that he could apologize for abandoning her. He'd never meant to do that, but in his haste to escape Strix Township and the fate that awaited him there—the same fate that had met his father, and his grandfather, and countless other—that's exactly what he'd done.

Try as he might, though, Dale could not detect any hint of his mother lingering in the skin that once housed her soul. And so, she remained unappreciated. And he remained unforgiven.

After a while, the Seinfeld reruns were replaced by a series of infomercials for increasingly absurd kitchen appliances. Dale was dangerously closed to convinced that he really did need a "Vegetti Spiralizer" when, hours after their last conversation, Pitt called back.

William Tea

"How bad do you really want to know the truth?" he asked.

Dale thought long and hard before answering.

He took his mother's hand in his and found her fingers cold and limp. Her skin was almost devoid of color, faded like one of her photographs. He squeezed tightly, wishing she would squeeze back.

She didn't.

"I don't want it," Dale said. "I need it."

This time, Pitt didn't hesitate.

"Midnight. Meet me out at the train crossing near the central mining office, the one that cuts across Midkiff Road. Park out of sight, beyond the tree line if you can. And wear lots of black. If you're not there when I am, you're S.O.L. I ain't doing this again.

⌘⌘⌘

Just as Pitt had instructed, Dale dressed head-to-toe in black. This far from home, his wardrobe was limited, leaving him with a black button-down shirt, black dress slacks, and black faux-leather Oxfords. He looked more like he was going to a funeral than committing a criminal offense.

Pitt, meanwhile, looked every inch a cartoon burglar, wearing a black sweatshirt tucked into tight black pants, with black gloves on his hands, translucent shoe-covers over black sneakers, and a black duffel bag thrown over his shoulder. He even wore a black knit cap like it was the middle of winter. The only thing missing was a little black domino mask.

"Have you done this before?" Dale whispered, trying to resist the urge to use his phone as a flashlight as he stumbled over half-buried roots and jutting, broken stones.

Pitt flashed a knowing smile, perfect white teeth like a crescent moon in the dark.

"Not here," he whispered back. "But me and the guys used to sneak into the amusement park in Miner's Glen sometimes during the off-season. Fun spot to get shitfaced."

Suddenly, he stopped.

The Blackdamp

"Shit, watch out."

Dale froze next to Pitt, just in time to realize they were standing on a ridge overlooking the heart of Andras Energy's mining operations. Below, a great round scar had been gouged into the center of Strix Township. Encircling it, rows of arrow-headed hemlock trees stabbed towards the starry sky in a fruitless attempt to pierce the glittery, cosmic monochrome. The forest itself sparkled in kind with the glassy eyes of owls and other nighttime predators.

It would be a vision of natural beauty if not for the fenced-in crater in the middle, with its square, windowless buildings, jumbles of slanted conveyer belts, and jagged dung-piles of raw coal.

"Be careful," Pitt whispered. "Go slow."

Dale followed the man's careful descent down the steep, dirt-caked hillside. He almost lost his footing at the end but came to a skidding stop next to his companion at the base of a towering chain-link fence. The barrier stretched out as far as he could see in either direction, surrounding the entire property.

"What now?" Dale asked.

Pitt jerked his thumb upward while his other hand reached into the duffel bag.

Dale turned his eyes towards the sky. Loops of blood-hungry barbed wire sat perched atop the fence.

"How the fuck...?"

Before Dale could finish his question, Pitt pulled out a heavy roll of matted green carpet.

"Trust me, dude."

"What about night security?"

"They only keep one guard on duty, and he's set up all the way over by the main entrance. There's a reason I picked this spot. *Trust me.*"

"Are you sure there's no more than that? This is a big place."

William Tea

"Who do they got to keep out? Ain't nobody around for miles that don't already work here or depend on somebody who does. This is the last coal mine left in all of Calvary County. No one wants to see the company do bad, or else we all do bad. Everyone around here is standing on the edge of a knife, man. We're just trying to keep our balance."

With that, Pitt ascended the fence with surprising swiftness. Dale supposed an athletic upbringing and a physically active job had their benefits. His own sedentary lifestyle, meanwhile, left him ill-equipped for breaking and entering.

As his former classmate draped the thick rug over the wire, allowing him to drag his body across unscathed, Dale thought about Pitt's words. He thought about how the people of Strix relied on Andras Energy to keep from falling into ruin. Over the last few days, he'd repeatedly told himself that exposing Andras would surely save lives. But how many other lives might he destroy in the process?

He couldn't worry about that. Not now.

Dale stuck his fingers into the chain link and gracelessly hauled himself up. He hadn't even made it halfway before the feeling went out of his hands. At least the carpet kept the barbed wire from biting.

Dale wobbled when he landed on the other side, knees working overtime not to buckle. He shook his hands to get the blood flowing again, then looked around.

At the opposite end of the complex, he could just barely make out the gawping mouth of the adit, a giant corridor that sloped down into the earth. There, each day, shifts of miners rode tram-like personnel carriers called mantrips down into the sunless innards of Andras's mining operations.

Between here and there stood a labyrinth of trailers and excavation equipment. Hunching down, Pitt led Dale to a squat, single-story building that looked like an intermodal shipping container. A sign over the door read *SITE MANAGER'S OFFICE*.

Dale started towards the door, but Pitt shook his head.

The Blackdamp

"Not that way," he whispered. "Alarm."

Instead, he pointed with his chin towards a rectangular hopper window near the roof. It was just barely big enough for a body to slip through.

Dale was about to ask how Pitt had known the window would be open, but already the former football star was climbing up the HVAC unit towards the makeshift entrance. After he squirmed his way through, he popped his head and chest back out and reached his arms down to Dale.

Even with help, scaling the side of the building was an awkward, painful affair. The only thing that proved more awkward and painful was trying to squeeze his out-of-shape frame through the slender opening. Dale couldn't help but remember Winnie the Pooh, fat with honey and lodged in the entrance of Rabbit's burrow.

With a little stomach-sucking and one ripped sleeve, though, Dale finally made it inside.

"Okay," he said. "Now what?"

Pitt shrugged.

"Dude, you're the bloodhound. Find some confidential files or incriminating memos or some shit."

"What am I supposed to be looking for, a folder with a big red *TOP SECRET* stamp on the front?"

"You said you wanted to get the truth. So, go ahead. Get gettin'!"

Dale sighed. With no other leads, what choice did he have? He sat down at the site manager's desk and start rifling through stacks of papers, looking for something, *anything* that might validate his theory about the tunnels below his mother's house.

While he searched, Pitt kept peeking out the window near the front entrance. Watching out for security, Dale figured.

After several minutes rifling through the desk and a nearby filing cabinet, Dale was just about ready to say to hell with it and steal the manager's entire computer hard drive. Then he heard Pitt mutter something under his breath. A single word. It sounded like, "Finally."

Before Dale knew what was happening, Pitt punched a code into the security keypad and threw open the door.

On the other side stood Stearne. And he wasn't alone.

Pitt stood back as Stearne and several other men streamed into the building and dragged Dale back outside. He struggled to pull himself free, but a sharp blow to the temple was all it took to render him compliant. Even still, Stearne followed the strike with several more, just to drive the point home.

With buzzing lights flickering to life high above, Dale found himself pushed to the dirt as a small mob formed around him. Some of their faces he recognized. They'd been at the bar the night before. Others were total strangers. Aside from a few dressed in security uniforms—*"just one guard," my ass*, Dale thought—their rough countenances and blue-collar clothes told him they were miners.

Dale braced himself for the ensuing pile-on, but to his surprise the men stood still, watching quietly. Only Stearne came forward, pushing the sleeves of his sweatshirt up to reveal a tattoo of an owl on his wrist, exactly the same as Pitt's.

Without a word Stearne pulled Dale up by his collar, only to be met with a punch to the jaw.

Stearne staggered back, but before Dale could capitalize the man was already on him. Dale put his arms up on either side of his head, trying to shield his face while Stearne wailed on his back. A knee to the stomach sent Dale back down to the ground, before a kick to the ribs had him doubled over and drooling blood.

Even still, Dale tried to fight back. With his assailant circling, Dale suddenly lunged out, aiming a jab at the man's crotch. He missed by inches as Stearne jumped back. Pitched forward by his own momentum, Dale caught himself with the same hand he'd tried to attack with.

The Blackdamp

His opponent capitalized with a vicious heel kick that snapped Dale's wrist like kindling.

Stearne backed off while Dale howled and folded over, cradling his injured armed to his chest.

Then another man approached.

This man looked nothing like the others. He wore a business suit and tie, polished shoes, and horn-rimmed glasses. He was clean-shaven, well-dressed, young, and soft. Hardly the look of someone who toiled underground from sunup to sundown.

"It's a pleasure to meet you, Mr. Harley," the man said, his voice bright and friendly.

The man bent down and shook Dale's hand, apparently oblivious to the agony of his fractured wrist. Despite the pain, Dale was mindful enough to notice the owl tattoo that peeked out from under the man's sleeve.

"We spoke on the phone," the man continued. "I'm Angelo Blake. Senior media relations officer."

Blake straightened back up and considered the pitiful sight in front of him for a moment. He shook his head, apparently disappointed, then put his hands on his hips as if he were a teacher lecturing a delinquent student.

"Do you know what it is that lives in the earth, Mr. Harley?"

He pointed to the stars.

No, not to the stars. He's pointing beyond them.

To the black.

"The same thing that lives out there," Blake said. "Darkness and cold. Both of these things were here long before we were, and they will be here long after we're gone. They're older than God. They're older than all the gods. And it is only by their grace, *by their mercy*, that we are allowed to exist at all."

William Tea

Blake stood and approached one of the watching miners with his hand outstretched.

"We're prisoners, Mr. Harley, trapped between the cold darkness in the heavens and the cold darkness in the earth. And so, the shadows give us this."

The man handed Blake a piece of coal. It seemed to have been freshly cleaned, as its surface gleamed like a mirror, turning rays of moonlight into tiny white flashes that juxtaposed against its pitch-black angles.

"They give us little pieces of themselves," he said. "Darkness made solid, so that we may burn it and keep ourselves warm another day."

He bent down beside Dale and pressed the smooth stone into the injured man's hand.

"Feel that? That's—"

Without hesitating, Dale wrapped his fingers around the rock and lashed out at Blake. The man reeled back unscathed while Stearne pounced forward, snatching the hunk of coal away before beating Dale back down into the dirt.

Shaken, Blake stood back up, cleared his throat, and readjusted his tie.

"I'm sorry for what happened to your mother, Mr. Harley, but even shadows get hungry. Sometimes lives are lost. Sometimes they're taken. We know the dangers and we accept them. Just as we accept that some of us might lose people we love. Is that not a small price to pay for all the lives that are *saved*, that are kept under solid roofs and given good food to eat and water to drink, that have the means to pay their bills and stay off the streets?"

Dale tried to answer, tried to tell Blake to go fuck himself, but his throat filled with blood and all he could do was wheeze.

"I assure you, Mr. Harley, we here at Andras Energy are committed to the safety of our workforce and to the health of our community.

257

The Blackdamp

Everything we do, we do for the greater good. And sometimes, the greater good requires..."

Blake paused, as if looking for the right word.

When he found it, he smiled warmly.

"...*sacrifice.*"

Blake turned and walked back into the crowd of miners, stopping only to tell one of them to "get the mantrip ready." Once he was gone, the others moved in, closing in tight around Dale like a noose.

That pile-on he'd been expecting earlier? It finally happened.

As blows rained down, swelling Dale's eyelids and crunching his bones and loosening the teeth from his gums, unconsciousness offered itself up to him.

Gratefully, he accepted it.

⌘⌘⌘

When Dale came to, he almost didn't notice. Very little changed, after all. It was like he was floating in a void, unable to see even own hand right in front of his face. Might as well still be unconscious.

Little by little, though, his mind found footholds through its other senses. The feel of cold grit beneath his aching muscles. The sound of his own tortured breathing. The stink of dank, ancient soil. The metallic taste of his own blood. Eventually, he remembered there was such a thing as "up," and so he tried to get there.

It wasn't easy. His body rebelled.

One of his legs had been shattered even worse than his wrist. It flopped uselessly like a dead fish as he pushed himself up a nearby wall. The surface was near freezing cold, and rough-hewn. It didn't take him long to realize where his attackers had left him.

With his ear against the wall, he could hear a faint popping noise like Rice Krispies in milk. He knew from his grandfather's stories what it was: the sound of tons upon tons of crushing earth pressing down on the mine from above.

William Tea

How far down was he? How far from the surface? How long would it take to get back? And if he did, what would be waiting for him? Violent men with matching owl tattoos? A locked gate? A loaded gun?

That's assuming there even is a way out. For all I know, they collapsed the drift entrance and left me here to die wandering bloody and blind.

He checked his pockets, but they'd taken everything. Phone. Car keys. Even the cheap ballpoint pen he never went anywhere without.

With nothing else left to do, and without any idea he was even going in the right direction, Dale limped forward, sliding along the rock wall that served as his only support.

After a while, he became all too aware of how hard it was getting to breathe and how fast his heart was racing. There was something else, too, a rhythmic pounding sound, like someone hammering at the walls of reality. He couldn't tell if it was the thumping of blood in his veins or the pulsing ache that rocked in his skull. Or something else entirely.

It was impossible to keep track of time. How long had he been pushing forward? Ten minutes? Twenty? Sixty? The black seemed endless

Then, finally, light.

Just a small one at first, far off in the distance. But it gave Dale something to follow. And so, he drifted towards it, a milk-white moth drunk on candle-fire.

Soon enough, that solitary spark was joined by another. Then another. Then another. They multiplied like cells on a microscope slide until there were seemingly thousands. For a moment, he thought he must've made it outside without realizing; what he saw now could only be the starry night sky.

Then he noticed the way the stars seemed to bob and weave. *Maybe*, he thought, *they're fireflies instead*.

But they were neither.

The Blackdamp

Even this weak illumination, so far away, was enough to help Dale's eyes adjust to the previously impenetrable gloom. As they did, he began to make out the telltale shapes of mantrip tracks beneath him and roof-support frames above. He knew there were lightbulbs up there, too. Somewhere. How to reach or activate them, though, was another matter entirely.

He reached his hands out, searching for something to hold onto. The murk was still difficult to navigate, and the wide, empty space did nothing to help him find his bearings. Despite every painful step forward he managed, the distant lights never seemed any less distant. It felt like he was walking on a treadmill, constantly plodding along but getting nowhere.

And it wasn't getting any easier to breathe.

He continued pursuing the lights ahead, until one broke away from the others and seemed to enlarge.

No, he realized after a second. It's not growing bigger. *It's coming closer.*

In time, he recognized the light as a headlamp attached to a miner's helmet.

The light shining in Dale's eyes made it difficult to see the stranger's face. It could very well be one of the same men who'd brutalized him. But it could also be someone else, someone who could help. Dale tried to call out to the stranger, but before he could the man at last wandered close enough for Dale to make out his features. And what he saw then made speech an impossibility.

The stranger's face and limbs were hideously swollen. His skin was unnaturally pale, almost bone-white, save for a dim blue undertone and a patina of grime that clung to every inch. Antique miner's garb drooped from his body, heavy and wet, as if he had jumped into a swimming pool without stripping first. His boots squelched with each step.

Lumbering closer, the man opened his mouth as if to speak, but instead of words only foul, filthy water came out. It tumbled over his chin like a rancid river before splattering into a discolored puddle at his bloated feet.

Dale stumbled backward, tripped over the mantrip tracks, and fell face-first to the floor. He tried to clamber back to his feet, but his injured leg refused to cooperate.

His breathing and heartbeat became even more ragged, but he couldn't tell if it was from blackdamp or fear.

Rolling onto his back and pushing his palms flat on the ground, Dale raised his rear up off the ground and scooted back, trying to keep the misshapen, slop-spewing thing at bay. Another wordless moan spilled yet more reeking fluid from its grotesque face. It poured so much and for long that Dale thought it might never stop.

His arms ached and shook with every inch he lurched back. The splintered bones in his wrist seemed to grind together, the pain so great he feared he might bite through his own tongue. He knew his ravaged body wouldn't be able to sustain these pitiful escape attempts much longer. Between all he'd been through—the tragedy, the violence, the poison in the air—he didn't know how much he had left in him.

Maybe I'm hallucinating, he thought. *Please God, let me be hallucinating.*

If he was, God didn't care.

Another light moved closer.

Like the first, its source was a headlamp. The twin beams crisscrossed in the shadows. Then the first light swept across the newer figure and, once again, Dale saw things he wished he could unsee.

This man, too, was dressed like a miner, but that was where the similarities ended. Where the first stranger stood soaked, this one smoldered. The skin on his face and hands sizzled, ashy and charred, with orangey embers burning beneath the surface like veins of molten ore. Thin ribbons of smoke slithered from flaking, bloodless wounds.

Worst of all, the burning stranger was not alone.

The Blackdamp

Through a third light did not join them, from behind the pair came a sound like coughing. Soon, this other man was out in front of his companions, their lamps bathing him in alabaster light.

Unlike the other two, this man, withered and gaunt with flesh that crackled as he walked, didn't wear miner's gear. Instead, from his slender bones hung a black suit that looked two sizes too big. His tie and shirt collar were speckled with blood stains that multiplied with his every hack and wheeze.

It didn't take Dale long to recognize the dead man's face. He looked much the same as he had at his funeral. Dale half-expected the dead man to address him as "Dilly Bar," just the way he used to.

Tommyknockers.

Some folks say they're here to help us...

Other folks think they want to hurt us...

Dale's grandfather drew closer, flanked on one side by his brother and on the other side by his son.

"Are you here to help me or are you here to hurt me?" Dale whimpered, his voice raspy and raw.

He felt dizzy. He couldn't run away, or walk, or even stand. Not like this. Not even if his legs still supported him. The walls and ceiling of the mine closed in from every angle. Every ounce of the countless tons of earth overhead weighed on his chest. He gasped over and over but struggled to fill his lungs.

"ARE YOU HERE TO HURT ME?"

What started in Dale's throat as a desperate roar came out a shallow, breathless whine.

He curled into a ball and covered his eyes as the three miners towered over him. Cold water sprayed his skin. Hot smoke. Sticky blood.

"Please don't hurt me," he pleaded.

Then he waited for them to do just that.

William Tea

He laid there trembling for a long time, but no assault came. When Dale looked up again, they were just standing there, looking down at him. Burning. Bleeding. Drowning.

Then they parted, and another face emerged from the shadows.

Even with a respirator mask and feeding tube obscuring its lower half, the features were unmistakable.

"Muh-muh-mama?"

No. She can't be here. She's back at the hospital. Alive. She's not like them. She's alive.

Isn't she?

Her hands reached out to him, plaintive, and he saw then the hoses and wires that snaked across her arms and chest, slinking all the way down her polka-dotted hospital gown to the floor, where they stretched alongside mantrip tracks back into the same inky nothingness from which she'd come.

As she stepped closer, he thought for sure those things would pull taut like chains and tug her back into the black, but she continued on unhindered while their length seemed to double. As did their number.

"Puh-please," Dale whimpered.

"No more hurt," his mother cooed, her words barely decipherable with all the plastic strapped to her face and piped down her throat. She knelt down in front of him and took his hand in hers. Her grip was strong and healthy and warm. Behind the mask, her mouth spread into a distorted smile.

Unable to stop himself—or perhaps unwilling—Dale threw his arms around his mother and nestled his head against her breast.

"No more hurt," she said again.

As Dale's eyes filled with tears, the tubes entangling his mother seemed to shudder and change. They became fleshy and alive, and seemed less to be feeding the woman and more to be *filling* her. He could feel them moving like snakes beneath her skin. For the briefest moment, he got the distinct impression that what held him now was not his

The Blackdamp

mother, but something *puppeteering* his mother, wearing her image as if it were a cheap Halloween mask.

He didn't like that thought, though, so he banished it from his mind. He squeezed her tighter, ignoring the unnatural shifting and twisting beneath her flesh.

"I love you," Dale whispered with the final breath that he could muster.

"I love you, too," came her reply.

And that was good enough for him.

In the distant tunnels beyond them, thousands of dead miners switched off their headlamps one by one. Soon, there would be no more stars and no more fireflies.

Now and forever, Strix Township belonged to the cold, cold dark.

Illustration by Sarah Walker

The Untold History of the Grimorium
by Maxwell I. Gold

Over seven-hundred years ago, the first account of that horrid amber God was penned into existence, and to this day it can easily be deemed as one of the most wicked pieces of literature ever written. When Flavius Gauntius, son of Augustus Gauntius, a wealthy and powerful merchant in the city Palermo, first laid eyes on the ruins of an ancient city in the North African desert, the young Sicilian poet knew that it was no mere hallucination, or glint of moonlight off the dusty mountains of sand. There was something even more sinister, something seemingly dead for over fourteen billion years, that had finally been awoken.

He had discovered remains of parchment that were thought to be from the Dead Sea Scrolls, though it told a much different story and the words linked onto the pages carried a much darker tone as if some primitive form of humankind, worshipping some old black gods.

"I do not know how to describe this text if it is appropriate to deem it that. It is so esoterically devastating I was enraptured with its words, drunk on each phrase, but still so horrified at the black hieroglyphs, images of dying neutron stars that filled my thoughts, which bore the most destructive of things and histories of old dead gods which could only be matched by the Necronomicon in dreadfulness or praise."

Flavius had studied in Damascus, surrounded by stories and great mad Arabs and nameless Cyclopean desert cities from beyond conscious thought. In 1253 A.D, the young poet's hunger and obsession drove him to study the dilapidated piece of parchment furiously and with a methodic intent that even terrified his estranged mentor. Soon, dark visions would come to flood his thoughts. Despite some warnings, he wallowed in esoteric writings, talking of an ancient city constructed in titanic size by a species born of some protoplasmic obscenity.

The Untold History of the Grimorium

※ ※ ※

"I saw things beyond my comprehension and the scope of an era. While the city was masked in much of our modern architecture, it was only that. A shadow out of a time, projected onto our Earthly plane for reasons unknown to us and just as quickly as I had walked through the marbled corridors, smelling the alien incense that floated like a toxic haze over voluptuous silk pillows, it disappeared into the night. A ghost city that now haunted my memory like an echo of fourteen billion years long dead." – The Grimorium ca. 1301

※ ※ ※

The Grimorium became a tome of galactic maladies, constructed from the remnant thoughts of a man's dying mind. Contemporaries of his day thought him mad, zealots were more like a gentle wallflower compared to his growing demented state of mind, and even his teacher thought the words spilling out of his mouth were that of some otherworldly daemon. Even Roger Bacon, famed alchemist, upon Gauntius's return to the continent, denied the poet's request to read on such a "profane metallic deity." All record of the text had slowly disappeared from history, and the old poet had, too, become a relic of his own insanity. In the dank cave of Mother Shipton, in the misty years of the middle 15th century, a yellowed piece of freshly inked paper was found. Cosmic narrations of this poor unfortunate continued on.

Even Gilles de Rais, one of the most contemptuous men to exist, trembled at the notions and black speech of the old poet.

"Still, this wanton idle blaspheming would not hinder the will of a soul whose very consciousness was now in gracious servitude to the Nuclear Thing at the edge of time. Let my fury be theirs, so shall It consume all men's fears! Golden furies were once ours and now concealed in flame; but let courage seek no more and lay dead in ash as yellow eyes gawk from the edges of my nightmares."

※ ※ ※

Maxwell J. Bold

Even as the years dragged on, the ashen and deadly aspirations of humanity's dastardly hopes grew too hungry; the words of the Grimorium seemingly lost in the grey, pragmatic spaces of thought. Around 1651, it seemed the dreaded pages of Gauntius's text had resurfaced, coming across the desk of famed political philosopher, Thomas Hobbes. A leviathan of words and phrases, unmatched and unnatural to his fellow man, most cowered in comparison to the man's monstrous intellect. Though, now, forced to bow in submission at the cursed words of an ancient god.

"My mother gave birth to two twins: myself and fear. Though, it seems I was incorrect on the summation of such things. There's something truly evil, arguably unnatural in the world of men that leads me to question that which was unquestionable. Where the foundations of a posteriori truths once gave me ease about the reality in which I rest, now, after my senses had touched, smelled and even tasted the defamed pages, I knew man's truth held no more promise. No more logic."

The years blurred and the rest, as it was, became history including what Hobbes attempted to bury within the pages he wrote. The Grimorium itself drifted back into shadow and static, unworthy of the guise of man's pathetic wanderlust.

Industrialization, the prospects of glittering cities dipped in iron and gold without nature, without fabled gods, soon spread throughout the world like an infection. Wood and wrought were replaced by steel and stone, concrete skeletons looming over deforested plains dripping with wires and woe. Mushroom clouds and molten theories of new gods in the atomic age sought to supplant nature, to remake it, until text of the wandering Sicilian poet graced the eyes of one J. Robert Oppenheimer.

"In the Atomic Age, Man has yet to fully understand the complexities of the natural world, despite our primal urges to control it. It's in our genetic code to attempt to subdue that which is inevitable, and any attempt would otherwise be an exercise in futility. The true Atomic Force, is one I have discovered lying in nature, fourteen billion years in the past."

The Untold History of the Grimorium

※ ※ ※

Man lost his way. The Grimorium was the scythe, there to cut down wiry strands of untamed hopes of a species now coated in plastic and false dreams who'd forgotten where they came from. Forgotten were the ancient gods, fourteen billion years at the edge of time atop a throne of ivory and blood that gave them everything. Man had become ungrateful. It was apparent on that unfortunate day over seven-hundred years ago, when Ad'Naigon, glaring down through a thousand hideous yellow eyes like amber stones, had chosen the poor soul who would be his vessel.

Trapped, screaming across the generations through pages of dried and torn parchment, the dissonant voice of a cursed man wallowed in the shadow of his doom.

Even now, standing on the brink of a new age, a great reckoning, gathered around this pitiful little fire in the woods, you listen to my story. Laughing, snickering, questioning history as it's presented. Confounding the unnatural possibilities how time and space conspired in synchronous harmony to destroy your reality as if it was yours to begin with. You had lost your way. The Grimorium still is the scythe, there to cut down wiry strands of untamed hopes, your species now coated in plastic and false dreams forgetting where they came from. Forgotten were the ancient gods, fourteen billion years at the edge of time atop a throne of ivory and blood that gave them everything. You had become ungrateful.

Illustration by Sarah Walker

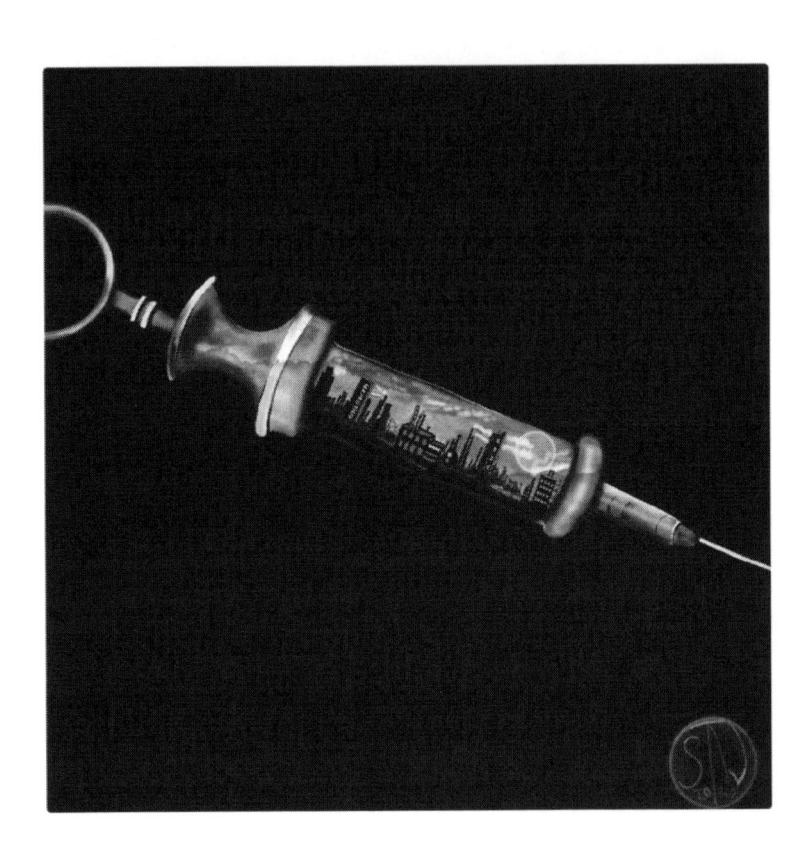

The Mill District
by Maquel A. Jacob

Garbage from the overflowing trash cans the city had not come to pick up in weeks rolled along as the wind pushed it down the deserted street. The concrete structures and sidewalks made everything else look grey. Even the abandoned brick and mortar stores seemed to be have been absorbed by the gloom. Nightfall was still a few hours away, yet the sky had dimmed, the muted sun casting murky shadows.

I walked with my head down, kicking pieces of garbage that lay in my path as I tried to ignore the scenery. It was the same every day. No better; no worse. A constant cycle of hell on Earth. My jeans were no longer blue, crusted with week old dirt. There were holes on the inside of my gym shoes and a few in my t-shirt. The hoodie I'd pilfered off a dead homeless guy was tied around my waist.

I looked up at the ten-foot stone wall that enclosed the district, isolating it from the rest of the city. It was built long before even my parents could remember. No one could explain the reason for it except crime had escalated to the point where city officials had declared the zone not salvageable. The old ones who were there when it happened were long gone.

Deliveries were either airdropped in the center or made under surveillance of armed military guards at the only two gates stationed on opposite ends of the territory. Cops were in short supply and to have them actually show up would be a miracle. Granted, someone calling them first was highly unlikely.

Out in the horizon was the old mill. A steel behemoth that insulted the skyline and made no apologies. At night, terrifying sounds echoed from that area.

The Mill District

Thinking about it made me pick up my pace to the alley I called home. I scratched the track marks on my left arm, the wind grazing across my skin made them itch.

Between an old bake shop and a pizza parlor lay the vast dark littered with bodies huddled under filthy blankets and raggedy single tents. Further in was my tiny space. A green tent with a tarp over it for extra protection. Some of my neighbors were already sitting outside their tents with hot plates going. I reached into mine and brought out the little hibachi grill.

"What's the gossip, guys?" I asked while setting up.

The guy across from me, about the same age, pushed his black, greasy hair from his face to expose his dirty pale skin and brown eyes. The multicolored shawl wrapped around his shoulders was tattered.

"What's up, Doug. Word is someone from the other hood went missing," he said.

"Another one?" The woman who resided a few feet from my neighbor yelled. Her overlarge knit hat covered most of her face and long stringy hair flowed from beneath it. She let out a huff. "Betcha they was snooping around that mill."

"That's just bullshit our parents told us to scare us," my neighbor snorted.

"Oh, yeah?" The woman scooted closer and I could smell her rank odor. "Then what are those noises, huh?" She leaned back. "That mill ain't been running for decades."

"I heard monsters live there," a male voice from the other side of the alley yelled.

"Now, that's just stupid." I leaned back into my tent and pulled out a half pack of hotdogs from my mini cooler. "Monsters aren't real."

"Hey." My neighbor reached over to tap me. "Got any dope?"

The woman's body perked up. I glanced over at her dubiously.

"If I did, it wouldn't be enough to share."

Maquel A. Jacob

"Aw, come on," the guy whined. "You know I got you whenever I have any." I nodded at the woman and my neighbor caught on. "It's cool. Next time."

"Right, right."

The woman slumped in disappointment and went back to tending to her dinner on the hot plate. We ate in silence and chatted until sundown. When the cringing screams filled the air, everyone in the alley packed in for the night. Twenty minutes later, my neighbor tapped on my tent and stuck a hand in. I sighed, pulled a small baggie out of my front pants pocket, and slapped it in his hand.

"You're a good man, Doug."

The hand disappeared and I crawled into my sleeping bag. Only stupid people prowled the streets at night. I got a new glass tube out the shoe box and a spoon, and lighter off the crate I used as a nightstand. I picked a few decent sized rocks from an already open baggie and loaded them into the tube. Using the lighter to heat them up, I waited for the dark grey smoke to make its way down the chamber before taking a drag, inhaling deep. The euphoria crept in.

Sweet mother.

It wasn't the same high as when I used to shoot the stuff, but it did the job. Plus, no more needles. Always trying find clean ones and what not. That shit was a pain in the ass. I drifted off into a drug filled haze, smiling.

⌘⌘⌘

A foghorn assaulted the late afternoon air, blasting the workers' ears and mine. We all turned to its source. The foreman of the cleanup project stood atop what was left of a brick building. His large belly stuck out a few inches from the bottom of his shirt, hanging over his pants.

Nasty. I shook my head in disgust as I removed the hardhat to wipe sweat from my brow.

The Mill District

The foreman switched to a bullhorn. It clicked on loudly creating feedback. Everyone winced, covering their ears.

"Good job today. That's it for now. When we get another gig going, we'll send out another flyer. Your pay is coming in a couple of days."

Lots of groans and cussing. I felt a bit let down, too. I was running low on drugs. Only one baggie left. And I really wanted to hit the showers at the truck stop. Maybe get a new pair of shoes. The clean-up projects were the only jobs paying in the district. The city had sent in a crew to round up residents willing to make the communities better.

No one cared about the community. Pretty much everyone was working to get money for drugs, alcohol, sex, then food.

All us workers dispersed, making sure to give our names to the manager who wrote them on a clipboard. That's how he kept track of who to pay. Can't mess up your money. I went with some other workers to the park that had an old playground. A few transients were hanging out as well. The taco cart was open and already had a line. They were a buck each, fifty cents extra for chicken.

My neighbor came out from the front of the line with six tacos in his hands. He came over to me and joined me on the concrete slab embedded in the ground.

"Got you three of em." He raised them up like he'd won a prize.

"Oh man, thanks. I owe you."

"Nah. We good."

I took the three from him and we ate in silence.

Another man came up to us, taking the last bites of his taco before speaking.

"Hey, you guys wanna score some good shit?"

"What, you sellin?" I asked.

The man waved a hand of him as if knocking away a fly.

"Pfft! Nah! I mean go get it."

"From where?" My neighbor asked between chewing.

"Straight from the source. Dealers, man. They get it first then let the runners do the sale."

"Huh?" My neighbor stared at the man like he was crazy. And rightly so. "Are saying…"

I stopped him and leaned towards the man.

"What the fuck are you on? Have you lost your damn mind?"

"Hey!" The man puffed his skeletal chest out, his ribcage outlined against the thin shirt. "No need for that shit! Tired of the half-cut stuff, is all."

"Dealers come from the direction of that mill. No thanks." My neighbor unwrapped his last taco and took a bite.

"Well, you change your minds, this where you find me." He was about to walk off then stopped. "Name's Rod, by the way." Of course, it is. Then he was off, his long gangly arms swaying behind him as he walked pelvis first.

"What the hell, man?" My neighbor shook his head. "I know we all hard up, running out of money and shit. Pay day is only two days away."

"I'm sure he's cracked or something. Don't worry about it."

I finished my last taco. And glanced out at the old mill.

⌘⌘⌘

Stealing from drug runners is not a smart idea. Even more so for the ones above them, the actual dealers.

Yet, there I was high as kite lying in wait between two dumpsters for my partner, Rod (remember him?), who I'd met less than a month ago, to lure in our prey.

We had both run out of money in the middle of the week a while back and by chance met again in one of the homeless alleyways. Neither of us considered ourselves homeless. It was just a safe place to congregate. I would have preferred running into him at the park. He's a bit scary in an alley at night. After some deliberation on how to resolve our financial woes, we decided to join forces for a snatch and grab operation to score free drugs and reduce depletion of already meager funds.

My neighbor was totally against it. He begged me not to do it. The woman across the way asked if she could have my shit when I disappeared. Ain't that some shit?

Times were getting harder and a fix once a week wasn't cutting it. For Rod and me, alleviating our addiction was top priority. Safety; not too high on the list. We stole from anyone we thought might be holding. No fear of retaliation. I mean, most of them were already high and couldn't give chase anyway. The runners were a little tricky and I thank the stars the both of us could run our asses off and lose them.

So far, the last few jacks had gone well with no one getting hurt.

Now, our prey for tonight: A seemingly young and scrawny dealer. Slight build, denim jacket with the sleeves cut off and a hairless cherub face. We had scoped out our next score's corner all day. He was a high roller who kept tight vigilance on his sector. Because of that, he probably had no reason to believe anyone try to rob him.

Arrogance at its finest. My partner, Rod, determined he was good for the taking.

Huddled against an abandoned building a block away, we watched the guy make transactions, counting the number of baggies we could see in his pockets whenever he pulled one out for a customer.

"If he tries to fight, I think we could take him down easy enough," Rod said.

"Probably new. He can't be more than eighteen," I replied.

"Cool. I'll go around and ask for a score then surprise him."

He nodded towards a dark alley up the street to our right as he reached in his jacket to show me a rubber baton.

"Where the hell did you get that?" I exclaimed.

"Some dudes were beating down a cop. Got it as it rolled away from him."

Maquel A. Jacob

"There was a cop in the district?" I was more fascinated with that story than the crazy, stupid thing we were about to do.

"This should stun him enough for me to drag him. Just don't let him see you 'til I give the signal."

I left him to do his thing while I scurried off into the alley where I contemplated the many cons of this deal. Less than six weeks of trust and I was committed to the deed. As soon as I heard the yells mingled with the grunts of a large animal, I knew something was wrong.

"Somebody help me!" I heard Rod screaming over and over. "Somebody! Please!"

That would do him no good since cries for help were ignored in the district. Plus, there was no one else around this area at night except, well, drug dealers and junkies. And me. Not even the hookers came this far in so close to the mill.

Rod and what I assumed would be the drug dealer came into view, but instead I saw a large creature with grey mottled flesh. A handful of hair sprigs sat upright on the top of its lumpy bulbous head and blood red eyes, absent of whites with tiny black pupils glowed in hunger. Horn-like fangs protruded upwards from the bottom corners of its mouth in a deep arc. It sank its jaws into Rod's shoulder as he struggled, cutting off the screams. Thank god. Only the crunching of flesh and bone echoed in the dark space.

Wedged in my dark crevice, I watched in silence as the thing commenced devouring him, his body finally done twitching as life was torn out. I dared not move, waiting for the creature to finish its meal. My eyes burned from the constant staring, but I couldn't turn away. The monster's thick talons dug into Rod's face and tore open the skull, peeling it away like soft shelled crab. Taking big bites. Cleaning out the cavity in mere seconds. Each bite splashing blood across its face and torso, staining the denim jacket.

The grunts it made reminded me of a movie I saw once with a pig farm that ate people. Bile rose in my esophagus in protest of the scene

The Mill District

before me. Sour chunks of half-digested tacos filled the roof of my mouth, making me gag. In fear, I instantly stifled the sound by clamping one hand tight over my mouth. Less than ten feet away the massive creature turned its head slightly, straining towards my direction. Listening. I hunched further down, an attempt to make myself smaller.

The creature's slimy grey head swiveled back around, the lumps and wrinkles a moving landscape. Its eyes opened wider as the monster took another bite turning the horned fangs into ruby painted bones.

What felt like an eternity later, the thing finally dropped what was left and snorted a small piece of human tissue up its snout. Its body began to morph as it turned, walking away. Grey skin faded to pale flesh, its sparse twigs of hair growing thick and blonde. The red eyes changed to baby blues that glinted in the candescent streetlights. At the edge of the alley entrance the creature was no more, replaced by the unintimidating drug dealer from earlier. He wiped his face with one hand while using the other to brush wet blood across his denim jacket. He frowned at his blood-stained hands and began licking them clean. Dark flecks peppered his hair.

I waited until the footsteps faded before removing my hand to unleash the river of vomit that had backed up. Its force pitched me forward onto hands and knees, my fingers sliding in the mess. Crawling out of my hiding place, I cautiously made my way to the street. The slight chill in the night air felt good against my sweat drenched skin.

Rumors about drug dealers being monsters had spread all over the district, but no one took them seriously, me included. Of course, they murdered people. People getting their arms torn off and stuff I heard every now and then but shrugged off as the price for dumbasses pissing them off. I just never believed in the tall tales.

Until now. Seeing it with my own eyes was like a wakeup call. Or, more like my mind had just been broken. Withdrawal came with a vengeance, knocking me upside the head like a sledgehammer. A single thought took over.

Maquel A. Jacob

I need a fix!

Out of misguided survival instinct, I went back into the alley and took all the money from my dead friend's pockets. Now fifty dollars richer, I set out on my hunt. My buddy, Rod, forgotten, tremors pulsing through me, I went on the prowl in a hazy stupor fueled by need. No more ambushing drug runners this time. Pulling that trick again would be crazy.

I may be a junkie, but not stupid. You're probably thinking otherwise.

Back in familiar territory, I found a drug runner and scored a twenty sac. I headed back to my tent in a daze, not understanding the muffled sounds of my neighbor as he came towards me. His voice cleared up at too high a decibel.

"Doug! Hey, man. You okay?"

I pushed him away and scrambled around in my tent for my tools. With shaky hands, I got the rocks into the tube but couldn't click the lighter. My neighbor helped me out and I finally got a huge puff out.

"What the hell happened? You got vomit and shit all over you."

"Yeah, well…" I took the lighter from him and got the tube smoky again. "Rod's dead." I took another hit and leaned back, letting the high consume me.

"Oh shit!" My neighbor's form was getting fuzzy. "How?"

"Dealer."

The woman across the way came into my fuzzy view.

"Well that was damn stupid. Serves him right."

"Monsters." I managed to get out.

I finally understood why the stone fence was built. That the cleanup project was just there to keep everyone busy and away from the mill. That the mill had monsters who disguised themselves as humans to sell drugs.

Drugs: to keep the residents unaware and primed for hunting.

Illustration by Sarah Walker

Fine and Fancy Arms
by Gordon B. White

My grandma told me that before Great-uncle Harwin passed, Jesus save him, his parsimoniousness was such that he lived at the bottom of the steepest hill in Mosby County so that he wouldn't have to use the extra gas driving home from the mill each night. He would jimmy the engine off when his one headlight hit the crest, downshift the mushroom-gray primer-patched Ford into neutral, and coast the decline to where his red dirt drive began and then in as far towards his home as he could before it rolled to a stop and he walked the rest. The only cent he ever spent on that truck, leaving aside the afternoon he bought it at a bank foreclosure auction on the Mosby Courthouse steps, was when he had Walter Hern in Statesville County jury-rig it so that Harwin could drive despite his double arm prostheses.

The branch of my family tree on which Harwin was but one bud had, for many years, been renowned in Mosby County as water witches. Not every one of them, of course, but more of the boy children could than couldn't hold onto a forked rod of beech or peach, or even apple wood, and dowse out at least some kind of water. Even when Harwin was a small boy—back when he was so apple-cheeked and freckled that his own mother had a coronary when she mistook him for an enormous ladybird coming through the tobacco leaves one bright afternoon—the witching was particularly strong in him. Branches would writhe and whip in his hands, dancing like a chicken in church until, bam, right down into the ground. Sure as spit, there'd be water.

And so, Grandma told me, between the novelty of his round, red cheeks, and the uncanny consistency with which working wells were dug at his direction, young Harwin became quite a cause célèbre. He was ferried all around the Eastern counties in a mule cart to raise water for

Fine and Fancy Arms

the farms from Mosby to Statesville to Dutch to Degram. At age eleven, he was even summoned halfway across the state to the Governor's Mansion for a commendation, whereupon Governor Ledsome himself pinned a little medal with the State Seal on Harwin's lapel and handed him a handsome silver-painted stick while the press bulbs flashed. When Harwin's father found out the photograph was going to run in the city paper the next weekend he drove all the way back out across the state again on Sunday, only to find it had run in the Saturday post and not a copy was left for any price. The loss of that paper haunted Harwin's father, not in the least because it had been the last photograph taken of the boy with his original arms.

What truly happened to Harwin is, as Grandma would say, uncertain. Mosby County, son of sharecropper—there's no immediate reason to assume that Harwin's mangling must have involved foul play. Mowers, tractors, threshers, bailers, harrows, buggies, feral pigs. An eleven-year-old boy could lose his arms on any day that ends in Y, although, Grandma would also grant you, losing both at once was a bit unusual.

But here's what I've heard, when my second cousin has been deep in the mash and decides he wants to tell me the real story. He says that it was a pack of jealous boys from the next farm over, who finally tired of rosy-cheeked Harwin and his silver stick and his little medal getting all the attention. They dragged him to the edge of the thresher's great grinding maw, just to put the fear into him, of course. But a slip, though —or even a push, perhaps—and that was that. Left arm gone just above the elbow; right arm, just below.

I've heard the same story from my second cousin's sister—well, almost the same—but she told it that it was Harwin's father who had grown tired of all the boy's attention. Another version involves the Noonwitch, but even I won't speak of her and her teeth like porcelain spades.

Whatever way it came to pass, beyond his arms, Harwin lost so much blood in the incident that his round, red cheeks drained out like wineskins, leaving the slack and pasty jowls that hang-dogged him for the rest of his life. How he made it to the hospital the next town over was in the back of the hay wagon, the ragged ends of his arms tourniqueted off but still bleeding through the straw until it stuck to his stumps like red and golden feathers. How he made it through the night, well, that was a miracle. When he returned to Mosby County six weeks later, he was wearing welfare issue arm prosthetics—two sizes too big, with rough leather cuffs and rusty hooks. People would see him walking along the side of the road, crestfallen, heavy wood and wire arms dragging in the dirt, hunched like a swayback mule under the weight.

Such indignity, of course, could not be abided. Everyone across the Eastern counties had a story about young Harwin, and so they came together to do him a charity. Donations were collected by the Mount Zion Baptists, the First Free Will Baptists, the Free First Will Baptists, and even the Church of the French Jesus, which bore that unfortunate appellation due, rightly or wrongly, to a perceived metropolitan character imparted by the swept tips on their stained-glass Messiah's otherwise pencil-thin mustache. Regardless, they collected enough to commission little Harwin a set of willow wood arms—light and thin, but beautiful. Willow wood isn't a strong material, the craftsman warned them, but it was the general consensus there wasn't much work Harwin would be doing.

The arms were delivered to the Pastor and they were fine, indeed. However, the church elders couldn't agree on when or how or at which church to present them to Harwin—although they all agreed the French Jesus was out, and even its leaders didn't argue—and so they waited until the Mosby County Fall Fair, at which time they brought Harwin up on the outdoor stage so that all assembled could "give him a hand." The Pastor had been particularly pleased with that little jest and repeated it twice for the crowd.

There, in front of God and everyone from Mosby County—and some from Statesville, Degram, and Dutch, too—they strapped the fine willow wood arms onto the sad, pale boy. The Pastor shook Harwin's

Fine and Fancy Arms

right wooden hand and the boy stared at it as if he couldn't quite understand the thing, while all the while the audience stood beaming at him, waiting for his outpouring of gratitude. My grandma, just a girl then, was there, and she remembered how they waited. And they waited.

Then Harwin's new right hand shot out as if he were waving hello to someone in the wings. The Pastor dodged back as Harwin's left followed, swooping in an arc before crooking at a mad angle. Murmuring, the crowd watched as little Harwin followed some unseen attention, clomping across the boards, new willow arms waving out in front as if pulled by invisible strings that stretched up to great hidden hands in the sky. The Pastor, still waiting for his thanks, followed.

Harwin stumbled down the stage steps and then bowed deeply, arms touching the ground, and the crowd gave a smattering of confused applause, but then he swung back up. In his right willow hand, a small fold of money was pinched between the stiff fingers. The smattering of applause increased accordingly. Patting his pockets, the Pastor descended from the stage and took the clip from Harwin's outstretched prosthetic.

"Why, this is mine," the Pastor cried. "I must have dropped it on the way to the stage, but the boy's arms felt it when we shook and then found it. Truly this is the prosperity of the Lord! Give unto the least of you, and you shall receive."

The assembled county men and women roared, the meaty smacking of their palms a veritable storm. The Pastor took Harwin's still-extended hand and lifted it as if he was declaring the victor of the Annual Sack Race, but Harwin's fine willow arm twisted and jerked, pulling free. With another reeling lurch, arms windmilling, Harwin was out into the grass, then off towards the barns set up for displays of odd-sized livestock and produce. The Pastor and all of the crowd followed a few steps behind, breaths held and waiting.

Harwin stopped momentarily, then tipped over as the hands swung down to a tuft of grass. The left one arose, fingertips pressed like a bird's bill, with a small gold band bit between them. The Pastor stepped forward and, with some effort, pried the discovery loose.

"A ring," he said to the crowd. "Blue stones, set three in a row." He turned it around, peered inside. "An inscription?"

Ms. Maybelline Harp pushed her way to the front. "Does the inside say, *let not the waters rise*? Oh please, Pastor."

He confirmed it did and Maybelline broke into sobs. "That was my mother's ring, and she lost it here at the fair three years ago."

The crowd Amen-ed and Hallelujah-ed, and the Pastor reached once more for Harwin's hand, but warily this time, and with good cause, for the now the boy's willow arms threw themselves back towards the barns and Harwin practically tore off after them. Everyone followed at a run—women had hiked their skirts, gentlemen mopped their brows, the children whooped and hollered—and all the while poor, pale-cheeked, fine-armed Harwin hurtled towards the animal barn where the prize-winning livestock had all been gathered earlier that evening for the ribbon ceremony.

Into the barn he flew, and then stopped. Not everyone in the crowd would fit, of course, and the Pastor had to elbow his way inside. There they all stood waiting, as arms raised before him, fingers spread like he was warming them before an unseen fire, the boy perambulated the enclosure and held those willow hands up to each animal, one by one, just a few inches away from their skin. First, Judd Brumb's award-winning heifer. Then Mrs. Richard Cleave's rabbit, which had earlier been crowned the largest in the counties. Then all of the Lewis Family's Polish chickens, bobbing their tufted feather wigs under the scrutiny. Then to Gaith Mathel's blue-ribbon sow, the tallest and fattest that had been entered in fifteen years. Harwin stopped before the pig.

Holding out his wooden hands, eyes closed in studious concentration, the boy seemed to be reading a kind of magnetic Braille that hovered over the pig. It was clear by now that whatever witching he had employed through the mere dowsing rods was amplified by the replacement of his

Fine and Fancy Arms

natural limbs. Already he had found a dropped billfold, a ring lost for years, and now this. Whatever this was.

Gaith Mathel's pig was a monstrous thing. Pale pink, so fat that its eyes had sunken away, covered from dripping snout to crusty haunch with blonde bristles that held the chaff from the hay bedding. On its flanks, large blue-gray birthmarks marred it like mud that wouldn't wash off.

"Keep that armless bastard away from her!" Gaith called out, pushing towards the front.

But he couldn't get through the wall of attentive bodies; not before Harwin's willow hands once more swooped down and came to rest on the pig's massive flank. At first, it seemed like a muscle tremor, or maybe flatulence, rippled the pig's hide, but as the crowd watched, the blue-gray birthmarks began to move across the skin. They swirled together, coalescing like a movie being projected on the screen of the pig, until they formed a woman's face.

"Oh, thank the Lord!" the face on the pig's side said, and more than one delicate soul in the crowd swooned. "It's dark in here, and I fear my husband has done something terrible!"

Then the face began to scream, and the pig squealed and shat, and the fine willow hands flew down once more, this time arising with a half-digested finger bone from the pile of excrement. The Pastor fainted, and the men in the crowd grabbed Gaith Mathel, and the blue-gray face on the side of the pig kept screaming for a whole day until the police shot the pig dead and had Tom Zicker, the butcher, dig what was left of Gaith Mathel's wife, who was meant to be visiting relatives one state over, out of the sow's intestines. After that evening at the Mosby County Fall Fair, Great-uncle Harwin was once again a cause célèbre.

In the years that followed, dowsing work was steady pay for Harwin. No longer limited to just the Eastern counties, folks from all over the state would pay to have him carted out and waltzed across the fields, waving his arms above their farms to point out where to dig. There was a system,

Dorbon B. White

Grandma said, with respect to how many fingers on which hand were extended times a number based on which of the other hand's fingers were curled plus some other factor, but, well, Grandma would have been the first to tell you she hadn't a head for numbers. The point was that if a digger did the math, he knew exactly how far below the sod the water sat. It was a sight to see, I hear, and Harwin's trips became events, until he was fed proper and put up in every town that needed a well or a pump or just a good show. He filled out as he grew up, although his pale jowls, drained of blood when he lost his arms, remained flaccid throughout his life.

If dowsing water was regular, honest work that kept Harwin's family fed, it was the other sort of witching that put money in his own pockets and made him fat. It began with finding the odd lost watch or heirloom brooch, something he did for the farmers when he was already out at their farms, but there are other people for whom gold and silver are worth more than water. Not infrequently, long black cars were spotted cruising through Mosby County in the evening like gar through the still waters of Cotner's Creek, ferrying young Harwin to and fro on less public errands. Part of his payment was for discretion, I imagine, and so I have only rumors to relay—a wealthy patriarch who passed and the only copy of his will misplaced; a money box blown clear when an outhouse distillery exploded; more than one coot's buried treasure lost after he was too addled to recall where it'd been hid. It was even said that a cabal of mysterious benefactors staked Harwin a few times to go down to Waller's Hollow—Waller's Holler, as it was known back then—for days at a stretch to search the swamp, grid by grid, in pursuit of that fabled cache of Confederate gold. I do not believe he ever found it, but I do believe he was rewarded handsomely for trying.

So it was that in the sixteenth summer of Harwin's life, four years into witching with the willow arms which had by then become dinged and scratched through constant vigorous use, Great-uncle Harwin, flush with pocket money, commissioned himself a pair of fine and fancy arms of his own design. He had them made one each of beech and peach,

Fine and Fancy Arms

inlaid with little strips of ash and ringed by copper bands. They were wondrous, and whether they worked better than the willow ones or just looked it, Harwin's lot continued to improve.

In his sixteenth year, he also bought the family an automobile. In his seventeenth year, he bought them a new house on their own plot of land. In his eighteenth year, early one evening as the first crisp autumn breeze was tugging the first orange leaves from the Mosby County elms, a long black car arrived to summon Harwin once again to the Governor's Mansion. This time, he knew, there was likely no commendation, but the allure of silver that wasn't just a painted stick was too much for him to refuse.

The car arrived at the Mansion sometime between midnight and morning, while it was still dark out and the gas lamps by the gateway bathed everything in an unusual glow. Fall had settled on the Governor's grounds early, and in the moonlight the trees were already red and brown and partially bare, like hands reaching out of the earth. The driver did the roundabout and let Harwin out by the grand entrance where the butler, an elderly manservant with a stiff back and one mustard-yellow eye, was already waiting. Harwin was groggy and his mouth was sticky, having slept fitfully along the ride, but the butler shooed Harwin up the steps to the enormous front doors, which opened as he approached.

"Welcome," said Governor Ledsome. He was a tall man, barrel-chested, with more iron in his mustache than he'd had when Harwin had last been there so many years before, but he wore his age well. Beside him stood his brother, an official of some rank in the Governors cabinet, and the spitting image of his gubernatorial sibling—if the spit had bubbled and slid a bit where it'd been spat.

"You're here to find an ill spirit that has been deviling us," the Governor's brother said. The brother was an older, more bulbous, version of the Governor, and he leaned heavily on two thick hickory canes with silver dogs' heads for handles. His left foot was wrapped in loose bandages, bare toes sticking out and red as coals. He winced at the slightest shift.

Gordon B. White

Harwin shook his head and tried to apologize. Ever since the incident with Gaith Mathel and his pig, Harwin's father had forbade him from witching out spirits and haints. Of course, he didn't mind working Harwin to splinters on the dowsing rounds and would turn a blind eye to the more suspect requests his son fetch a "lost" object, but spirits were the line that could not be crossed. Harwin, eighteen and alone in the Governor's Mansion, meant to hold firm and respect his father's wishes, Jesus love him. He made it five whole minutes until the Governor's brother sighed in evident disgust and, without any negotiation, named a price that dropped Harwin's jaw so low that even his saggy jowls went taut. Harwin and the Governor shook hands, hot flesh and cool peach wood, to seal the deal right there.

Harwin slid off his overcoat with the aid of the mustard-eyed butler and then raised his hands. The grand entrance hall with the marble floor, the baroquely papered walls bedecked with a gallery of governors past, and the deep crimson carpet leading toward the grand staircase was like a great echo chamber. As the Governor and his brother watched, Harwin's shoulders trembled and the wave of sensations rolled across his muscle, into the wood, and down to the tips where the fingers of the beech and peach hands slowly spread out like fiddlehead ferns in the rain. The antennae spread, Harwin began to walk slowly about the hall.

"This presence," the Governor began, "has been with us since we moved in."

"Before even," the brother added, then coughed. "I mean, perhaps."

"We need you to find it," the Governor said. "Find it and contain it."

"And then?" Harwin asked.

The brother groaned. "And then you just leave that to us, boy."

As Harwin went, his arms trembled, shaking like branches in a breeze, although nothing was blowing in that big stuffy house. Harwin checked the hallways and the sitting rooms; the grand stairs and the narrow servants' steps in back; the kitchen, the bedrooms, and the privy, too, his fine and fancy arms out before him, testing the air, and the

Fine and Fancy Arms

Governor and his brother lumbering behind. He even checked in the basement with the cold black candles and the broken salt circle, although that too was empty, and the brothers shooed him out quick. All through the house, however, he could feel the tickle of something lurking just under the surface like a barn rat that got beneath a pie crust.

Everywhere he went in the mansion, Harwin felt the haint's threads as clear as if he'd stepped through a spiderweb and couldn't brush away the sticky filament. He kept walking, spinning, doing the stations with no result, and all the while the two brothers dogged him to harumph and haw. The Governor stood so close that he might as well have been a cape on the boy's shoulders, while the brother hobbled along on his bandaged foot, the two canes always tapping just behind, and the mustard-eyed butler lurked in the shadows. Harwin searched every nook and every corner, but although the sense of a presence never left, the gentle tug it exerted on the fine and fancy arms was always like the river's current on a fishing line—never the trout's bite.

The sun was rising, and the big blanks of the drawing room windows were starting to light, when Harwin, bone-tired and weary from hours on edge, had to surrender. He turned to face the brothers, head hung in disappointment both at his failure and at the prospect of losing the absurd purse he'd been promised. Then the trout bit.

Harwin staggered forward as the arms wrenched him towards the Governor's brother. The man recoiled, but between the swollen foot and the rest of his ailments, couldn't move far or fast. Luckily, Harwin locked his knees like a mule and leaned back, the straps and buckles of his wonderful arms groaning as the limbs groped towards the brother. Whatever presence they had picked up on must have been missed at the first meeting in the foyer, but hours together had strengthened the call.

"Calm yourself," the brother bellowed as he swung one of his silver-handled canes at Harwin, clacking it against the straining arms.

"I'm sorry, sir," Harwin grunted against the effort of keeping them away. "They seem to be pulling towards your, err, foot."

Gordon B. White

In short order, and despite the very profane protestations, the Governor and the mustard-eyed butler got the brother up onto the billiards table, pinned him down by the arms, and peeled the soiled bandages away from his foot. The appendage was enormously engorged and horrendously gouty, the big toe knuckle's tophus bulging like a mouse hiding beneath the tight red skin and all the rest of his little piggies swollen up in crimson sympathy. The brother howled, "Don't you touch me!" but the Governor gave Harwin a look to remind him just whose mansion he was in. Harwin nodded and let go of his efforts to control the arms.

Down the beech wood arm swung and cracked the brother right on the enormous ball of the gout, splitting the skin and bursting it like an egg. The brother screeched and fell backwards, eyes rolled up in his skull by the pain as the beech wood fingers pinched and dug into the chalky, white discharge. Even Harwin had to turn away as they rooted, but then they clacked shut, and he began to pull. Slowly, surely, inch by inch, Harwin prised the haint out of the mess left of the big toe knuckle. It stretched out like dough, the ghastly face of it elongating as Harwin pulled, but then it snapped loose and Harwin fell back, ankles over wooden elbows, the haint in his hands. It squirmed and cussed, but Harwin held it tight, cupped like a lightning bug between his palms.

"Get me a box or a jar!" Harwin shouted from where he sat sprawled on the floor. "Something made of maple or iron or glass. Quick!"

The Governor and the mustard-eyed butler hurried out of the room, leaving the brother splayed out on the billiard table's felt and Harwin clasping the haint in his fine and fancy hands. The brother moaned from where he lay, insensate from the agony of his flayed gouty toe.

"Hey, you," the haint whispered, its voice high and growly from behind Harwin's fingers. Harwin peered in through the tiny gap between his thumbs. The haint looked like a little man in a suit, but with a goat's head with three long horns. It stared directly at Harwin and said, "Let's talk."

Fine and Fancy Arms

A half-hour later, Harwin left the Governor's Mansion with a sack of money and another little tin pin bearing the State Seal. The Governor had taken his brother, only just back from the bliss of unconsciousness, to his room to await a doctor. The brothers took with them a Mason jar, sealed with red wax, and wrapped in butcher paper with the Lord's Prayer written on it which Harwin swore to them would keep the haint contained so long as they never opened it to check. Only the yellow-eyed butler—still in his coattails—saw Harwin back outside and into the long black car.

When Great-uncle Harwin got out of that long black car, he was rich by Mosby County standards. In just a shy of a year, however, he was rich by any standards. His talent for witching out the lost and now the damned, too, had always been strong, but his subsequent success was absolutely prodigious. Lost rings were found buried in boxes of stolen jewelry which, unclaimed, went to Harwin. Just walking to the general store, he couldn't help but trip over a roll of paper money. He even found a small vein of emeralds once while planting tomatoes in his garden.

And what about the other kind of work? Ever since the story spread of Gaith Mathel and the pig witched out by Harwin, people had begged him to plumb out their haints and horribles. Harwin had turned them all down at his father's wishes, but, by coincidence, his father passed away shortly after he returned from the Governor's Mansion. Again—Mosby County, a hard life of sharecropping—there's no reason to assume Harwin's father's death involved foul play or black magic. None at all. Don't even ask.

In any event, after the appropriate period of mourning, Harwin had no more reason to turn those jobs down. The work just kept coming.

Those midnight jobs, however, are stories best saved for a different time. There isn't a family still in Mosby County—and more than a few who aren't—that doesn't have a Harwin story about an uneasy spirit, ghost light, or other apparition which Harwin wrestled down and cast out with his fine and fancy arms. It will suffice to say he earned enough to buy the largest house in Mosby or even Statesville Counties, set on top

Dorton B. White

of Mosby County's highest hill. It had one room for Harwin and his radiant wife, who he brought home from one trip out to the mountains for a particular witching and who kept mostly to herself; one for his frail mother, who had never quite recovered from the heart attack in the field; one for his baby son, Jesus save that boy, too, for that's a tragedy; and enough space left over still for the help and for Harwin to lose track of anything that wasn't strapped onto him.

For a time, too, witching took Mosby and Statesville and Degram and Dutch Counties like a craze. In those years, you couldn't find a tree with a Y-shaped branch left within the county lines such that a whole generation of Mosby County children never learned to shoot a slingshot, and although Grandma wouldn't say it, I think she believed that's why they lost so many boys in the War. Harwin himself, of course, made no small amount of money selling and signing such implements, although his own luck never seemed to rub off.

No, Harwin's new source of luck seemed to reside entirely within those fine and fancy arms. He himself never talked about it, but gossip spread that ever since that night at the Governor's Mansion, Harwin had some extra bit of medicine in there. He was never seen without the arms, of course, but the same wasn't necessarily true vice versa.

Ham Stetelson once said he saw the arms—by themselves, no Harwin—out by the mash still, dancing and pouring tumblers of moonshine over one another, but then Ham would get real quiet when you asked him where this still was. Winnie Jeffs said she saw them walking along the road one moonlit night, crawling on their fingers like spiders with the arms up in the air like meaty tails, but why she was on the road at night, she wouldn't say. Still, the whispers were eventually enough that they got out of Mosby County—Dutch County, too—and must have even made it back to the Governor's Mansion.

It's no secret that in the intervening years the state at large had fallen on tough times. The whole country had, it seemed, but avid readers of the local rags would have known that, on the whole, the Governor and his brother had done far worse. Just for instance, the brother's position as

Fine and Fancy Arms

a chair of a certain agricultural concern had been cut; several of their joint investments came under heavy scrutiny; and one very unfortunate stable fire had killed five prized thoroughbreds, three and a half of which belonged to the Governor. It was, perhaps, no surprise then, when Harwin received a hand-delivered message in a stiff white envelope dropped off by a long black car.

Give it back.

Harwin's little boy's nanny saw it before Harwin tore it up, and that's all she said it said.

Now, I can only speculate—and Grandma would have had my hide for speculating, being just one step up from gossip—but I believe the letter was from the Governor and his brother. I believe they had deduced, or at least they believed they had deduced, that Harwin had taken the haint that night and secreted it away inside of his fine and fancy arms. They would, of course, have been too careful to say so in a letter, but I believe they had long ago brought the haint from the Just Beyond Here to help them accumulate their wealth, and one night it had gotten away from them, hiding first in Governor Ledsome's brother's gouty toe until Harwin had extracted it and then smuggled it out beneath their noses in his wonderful beech and peach wood arms. I also believe the Governor and his brother were too subtle to send a hatchet man with a literal ax to extract it from Harwin, and that whether required by the rules decorum or demonology, I think they wanted the transfer to be willing. They'd invited Harwin into their house to find the haint—and he had—and now it was Harwin's until he chose to hand it over.

Of course, that could just be me rationalizing things, as is my wont.

Whatever the reason, after that missive, Mosby County began to suffer peculiarly under the Governor's attention. A series of draconian regulations applying only to a very specific subset of farms raised taxes by 300% in one year. A local tobacco surcharge bottomed out prices the next. On the third, a state of emergency was declared with respect to the South American Cotton Weevil which, of course, had only been

Gordon B. White

reported in Mosby County, resulting in the cull of the entire crop. The rates for the tenant farmers rose and evictions followed. Landowners signed on with shadowy consortiums whose "development plan" was to let the fields lay fallow until such time as they changed their minds. All of the schools were closed, the hospital in the next county shuttered, too, and somehow even the Church of the French Jesus lost its tax-exempt status with the state.

Through it all, though, Great-uncle Harwin, high on the hill, still prospered. People hired him to find their lost family plots now, looking for any burial goods their kin may have had. He was brought to even the barest clapboard shack to search for hidden treasure. Everyone had a haint they thought was killing their animals or poisoning their wells, though maybe the Governor had men for that, too? The witching craze hit a fever peak and although no one would risk offending Jesus by asking Harwin to bless their rods, they'd still offer him a handful of dimes just to touch them and say, "Good luck."

This was the time, too, when everyone who had even a quarter—never mind a half—a talent for witching started eyeing Harwin's arms, wondering if they, too, might better amplify their aptitude through certain judicious replacements. This, I have determined, is when Waller's Holler—home of the fabled lost Confederate gold—became known as Stump's Hollow. I won't elaborate on the obvious reason.

At this point, Harwin withdrew into his fine and fancy house, with his fine and fancy arms. His wife was pretty and fancy, his baby healthy and fine, but there on that highest hill, he could see Mosby County around him dying. The Governor's grip of taxation and regulation choked it off until the fields were brown. The well-off folks fled, leaving big empty houses with big broken windows. Those too poor to go had given Harwin the last of their cigar box savings from under the floorboard in the hopes he might find a forgotten haul, or some nugget dropped by chance. The line of half-armed men and children left a trail of blood from Stump's Hollow, up the hill, to his front door, all hoping for just a

Fine and Fancy Arms

touch of his fine and fancy luck so that they, too, could strike it just rich enough to survive.

What must it have been like, I ask you now, to have been Great-uncle Harwin, surveying the blighted landscape you'd help create? To know, too, that out of all of this ruin, you—by the luck alone of what was in your arms—would be fine? Would you have given it up willingly? Would you have unstrapped those arms of beech and peach and put them in a box and handed them to the driver of a long black car? Would you have given up your house on the high hill in the hopes the fields would grow again and Judd Brumb, Ham Stetelson, and the Lewis Family with their Polish chickens might all come back?

Or might you have tried to hold on, with your fine and fancy arms? Might you have tried to prepare your baby boy for that fallow world out beyond your windows where the only way to live was witching? What would it have taken, I wonder, for Harwin to press his baby boy's rosy arm still beneath his cool, beech palm? Would he have thought it was a kindness to prepare him for that world while still so young? Could Harwin have asked his wife to wrap his peach wood fingers around a meat cleaver's grip and told the nanny to get the towels ready? Could you?

But, Mosby County, even the son of a rich water witch—there's no reason to assume Harwin's baby boy's passing involved foul play. Whooping cough, croup, cholera, consumption, feral pigs. A baby boy could die on any day ending in Y, especially with the nearest hospital shuttered.

Regardless of how, when it happened, Harwin broke. His wife and his help disappeared that very evening and the curtains were drawn and even the folks down in Stump's Hollow said you could hear the wailing roll down from the house on the hill. It was only Winnie Jeffs, walking down the road in the early morning—coming home from where, she would not say—who saw Harwin standing at the end of his drive, handing an oblong box to someone in the back of a long black car. He was wearing the old welfare issue arm prosthetics he had first been given as a boy, although now two sizes too small, but still with rough leather cuffs and rusty hooks. And that was that—the end of Harwin's witching.

There isn't much left to tell. Harwin sold the big house and moved himself and his mother to the bottom of the hill, into the tiny house where he remained for the rest of his days. The rest of the money he'd saved, and all but a pittance of what earned through the rest of his life, he split amongst the Mount Zion, First Free Will, and Free First Will Baptists to distribute as charity. Over the years, Harwin and Mosby County survived, although neither ever fully recovered. As to what happened to Governor Ledsome, or his brother, or the fine and fancy arms—well, let us say that they died. And let us say it was in some horrible way that would make us all feel better, even if I don't know that that's true.

And as to whether anyone else in my family has the witching, I cannot say. I can tell you only that I sit here before a sheet of paper, wooden pencil in my hand, letting it tell its lies and scratch out truths of its own accord, in the hopes that we might yet find a sense of meaning, or at least what passes for it in the end.

Illustration by Sarah Walker

Her Dark Hymn
by Hayley Arrington

There was a woman in a glen.
She sang of faerie and of fen.
She sang to bright and dark of moon.
She sang a wild, discordant tune.

I heard the song she sang one night.
It made me in the world feel right.
I thought of her I'd ask a boon.
She sang a wild, discordant tune.

She glanced at me as one held dear.
She beckoned as I listened near.
Not ceasing in her dreadful rune,
She sang her wild, discordant tune.

A picture of my heart's best sin
Was formed by glorious, dark hymn.
A bride of Satan I'd be soon,
So sang her wild, discordant tune.

Her melodies brought no dismay.
Dark secrets were hers to convey.
And so I joined in her commune:
We sang a wild, discordant tune.

Illustration by Rai Bryan

Hyenas
by Michael S. Walker

There were two of them: two ugly yellow bitches and they had their snouts down in a trash heap on the eastern edge of the city. Hermela stood in the doorway watching the hyenas with trepidation. She clutched her three-month infant son, Dani, to her breast. The baby had just fed and was lying peacefully in her arms now, cooing, a small trickle of her milk still running down his plump chin.

"I hope they go on their way soon," Hermela whispered, in English, drawing her son in tighter. She truly wished that her husband, Abel, was here right now but he had just gone off to his job as a city street sweeper for the Safety Net Project. He would not be back for five hours or so. She wished that he did not have to work at nights, because the city was a dangerous place, but the small family needed the money in a bad way. The street sweeping job was the first work Abel had been able to obtain in months.

As she watched from the open doorway of the corrugated shack, another larger hyena came and joined the two who were foraging. Suddenly they all were fighting and sniping at each other, baring their razor teeth over some gray treasure that looked to Hermela like a portion of donkey hide. Their high-pitched whines and yips echoed through the shanty town, making Hermela's heart quicken in her chest. Once again, she drew her infant son in tighter. The baby seemed to be contentedly asleep now, oblivious to the melee outside.

She really did wish that the beasts would shut up and move on, and soon. Even though Abel had told her many, many times that she had nothing to fear from the city's small band of hyenas—that the chances of being attacked by a wild dog were much greater—she still feared and hated their frequent appearances in the shanty town. She had heard the

Hyenas

rumors from her best friends, Nyala and Aida, and from many others, how hyenas routinely dug up shallow graves to devour the corpses of the poor. How they were known to bite off the fingers and toes of rough sleepers in Addis Ababa after dark.

And that sometimes…

Hermela looked down at her sleeping son, at his peaceful unblemished brow.

"No …" she whispered, shaking her head. "No."

She retreated into the shack. Quietly as to not disturb Dani. She did not want to look at the ugly trio of hyenas battling right now or think about something unthinkable like THAT…

She carefully placed her sleeping son down in his little white crib. She kissed his small, burnished forehead.

As the hyenas continued to murder outside.

Stop…Our Lord, make it stop…

And then, thankfully, blissfully, it did stop. There was silence. Only the pulsing of crickets in the thick night air. Someone, off in the distance, chanting their nightly prayers to Allah.

The usual, comforting sounds of her city after dusk.

For a long while, Hermela stood over her son's crib, watching him as he slept, continuing to pour love and protection down on his small, naked body. The relative silence outside continued, assuaging her, soothing her, bringing her heart back down from the skittering heights.

God, she hated hyenas. Had since she was a little girl living with her parents in Bishoftu, before she had come to the big city seeking work. Before she had met Abel. Once when she was eight, she had watched a whole pack of the mangy brutes bring down and render an impala, just outside of the town where she sometimes went with her father to gather teff seeds. The incident had left an indelible, fearful impression on her. The way the hyenas had fought over the entrails of the impala. Like demons.

Michael S. Walker

And she hated their ugly features, too. Their bat-like ears. Their coal eyes and woebegone little faces.

Their often-concealed savagery...

Since then, she had often had nightmares about hyenas. How they had brought down that small antelope with quick, orgiastic efficiency. And there was some other, more disturbing dream that Hermela could never quite remember when she awoke. But a dream that also seemed to have the beasts at its center.

Well, that smaller pack was probably gone now, Hermela reasoned, as the truce outside her door continued. They were probably on their way to other trash heaps and spoils. Other battles in the many slums of Addis Ababa...

Yes. Probably. Hopefully. Yes...

Hermela gave her infant son one more loving glance. Then she turned toward the wood stove at the far end of the shack. Soon she should have to get busy cooking—maybe some legume stew or something. For Abel, sweet Abel, when he returned, tired and hungry, from the streets.

She stared at the cracked mirror hanging above the stove, realizing that her breast was still exposed from Dani's recent meal. Quickly she covered herself again with her red cotton tunic.

And then, she noticed through the smeared gaze of the mirror that there was a hyena crouching in the door of the shack. Staring at her with large black quizzical eyes...

Lord, no....

Hermela stood there frozen, her back stiff and straight, gaping at the ugly interloper in the mirror. Wishing it to go away as her heart, once again started to thud in her chest...

But the brute did not go. It just sat there on its haunches, its eyes and snout forming a grim, black mask.

Deliver us from the evil one...

Hyenas

Hermela's first, instinctive thought was to fly to Dani and pick him up once again. But she found—to her horror—that she really could not move her body at all. This was more than some momentary fear. She could have quickly risen above that if there were the slightest chance her son was in danger. No. This was...something else. Something beyond her.

Something...*supernatural*. That was the only word for it. It was as if she was being held there, against her will, by the hyena's sable gaze.

Hermla prided herself on being a no-nonsense, rational woman. She looked down with disdain on the superstitions that many Ethiopians still held fast to as having sway and potency in the world. Her father had been such a type. He had believed, all his life, that the Evil Eye was out there in the world. He had always, his whole life, carried an amulet with him—the kitab—to ward off its effect.

As Hermela stood there, her feet rooted to the dirt floor of the shack, her eyes trying to unlock from those two black holes in the mirror, another hyena came and joined the first interloper. It, too, sat there on its haunches and regarded Hermela with a gaunt, mummy-like face.

Noooooo.

Try as she could, she could not move. She could not even turn to see if Dani was alright in his little crib. One consolation: if the hyenas did make a move into the shack, if they tried to attack her son, the crib itself might prove an obstacle for them. The sides of it sat up rather high and there wasn't too much space between its many slats. Not enough for the beasts to get their heads very far into the bed, probably. Maybe...

And then, once again, Hermela thought of that pack of hyenas, bringing down the impala outside of her home. Hermela would have shuddered if she had even been capable of that.

Dani Dani Dani...

If she could just get to the kerosene lamp on the wooden table in the center of the room, she would probably fling that at the beasts. That might be enough, Hermela thought, to frighten them. Scatter them. Send them scurrying down the night streets of Addis Abbaba.

Why…why could she not move? There was no logical reason for it. No fear that could bring about this complete, steadfast paralysis she was now experiencing.

Suddenly it seemed as if there were hundreds of glowing eyes floating out there in the distance, beyond the environs of the shack. Beyond the two hyena sentinels who still stood in the doorway, as motionless as Hermela herself.

Hundreds of incorporeal beasts. Shadow hyenas…

In her fear and wonderment, a word automatically came to Hermela's frenzied mind.

Bouda.

Her father had actually believed that there were people out there in the world, shapeshifters called Bouda, who could transform themselves into hyenas. And then back again at will. There had been an ironworker in their town that he had been convinced had this power. Another manifestation of the Evil Eye. As a matter of fact, there had been many people in Bishoftu who had believed this. Her father had forbidden her from ever venturing close to this ironworker's hut or playing with any of his children. She had thought such beliefs silly then.

But now…

How was it she could not move? What could it be but the thing she had derided her whole life?

The Evil Eye.

Outside, those weird eyes seemed to continue to float above the two motionless hyenas, turning from black to gold and back…they seemed to multiply as Hermela tried over and over to move, to shout, to do *something, anything.* If only she could reach Dani and protect him. If only Abel would return right now. If only…

A multitude of hyenas, God knows how many, began to bark and wail outside of the shack. It sounded, to Hermela, as if there were

Hyenas

thousands of them now, thousands of them triumphant in the dirt streets.

Surely, someone will come, Hermela thought. *Nyala, Aida…*

And then, to her surprise, someone did come. A man entered the shack. A stranger. Once again, Hermela saw his face in the mirror above the stove. He was, perhaps, the most striking man she had seen in her thirty years. He was very tall—close to two meters or so. Way taller than Abel, her husband. He had a broad, dark face and nose. His flawless skin was almost the same rich color as Yirgacheffe coffee beans, the beans Hermela had picked day after day in her teenage years. He wore a white gold-brocaded dashiki and matching pants.

His eyes were black and as impenetrable as the hyenas that still stood in the doorway.

He seemed to now float into the shack, like some handsome gleaming ghost. Hermela did not know if it were some trick of the cheap mirror, but it looked to her as if he actually *passed through* the hyenas. As if the two dour guards were made of yellow smoke and not flesh and blood and fur.

Hermela's heart spiked once again in her chest. And this time, perhaps not entirely from fear as she gazed at this new intruder.

But this was…what was the word? Hermela struggled to remember, as the man stood behind her appraising her with his coal-black eyes. He was certainly a stranger to her. He was so very striking looking, so handsome. She would have remembered seeing such a man before. In the streets of the shanty town. At the water pump. Or anywhere at all in the capital, for that matter,

The cacophony outside seemed to reach some kind of fever-pitch, as if the pack of hyenas were now tearing each other apart or something. And then, the man raised one gold-brocaded arm and waved it sharply through the thick night air. And all was silent, save for the sound of Hermela's heart beating like drums in her ears. She didn't even hear the sound of crickets now.

Michael S. Walker

She found though, somewhat to her relief, that the man's signal had had the added effect of releasing her from her weird paralysis. She turned to him now, not even thinking of Dani, who she imagined was still sleeping safely in his little crib.

"Who...are you?" Hermela whispered, her voice almost catching in her throat.

As that heartbeat in her ears seemed to take on a palpable shape. Became a word.

*Bouda...Bouda...Bouda...*it sang.

The man took one step closer to her. He smiled at her: a smile as white and as dazzling as his immaculate shirt.

The doorway hyenas were gone now. As if they really had been composed of smoke.

"I am a friend," the man said. His voice was nasal, offsetting. Strange counterpoint to his beautiful features.

Something deep in Hermela's soul, some instinctive murmuring, told her that this was not the case at all. At all...That this man was *not* a friend.

But her heart quickened even more, as he took another step in her direction.

"Hermela..." he said. And another step. "Hermela..."

And then, the sound of his stringent voice saying her name seemed to echo over and over in her ears, seemed to replace the sound of her heart in her ears sounding that archaic word:

Bouda Bouda Bouda

Hermela Hermela Hermela...

The stranger's eyes now began to change from black to gold. And back again to black, rapidly, as he called her name. The same as those ghost hyaenas had earlier...

Hermela Hermela Hermela...

Hyenas

He touched her bare arm. And a single desolate wail ricocheted through the streets outside in the wan orange light, sounding to all the world like some mourner bereft of any earthly hope. The stranger's touch sent a pulse of electricity surging through Hermela's (now) trembling body.

Hermela Hermela Hermela…

And then it seemed as if a whirlwind of those eyes, those gold/black eyes, was scouring her own field of vision. Moving like suns in some time-lapse photography displaying dusk/dawn and then dawn again in seconds. The stranger seemed to fall away from her as those preternatural eyes whirred. The shack itself seemed to fall away. Hermela began to feel an emptiness and then a cloying nausea. She thought she might vomit or even pass out as the phenomenon continued/accelerated. As the beastly eyes dominated totally her own vision.

After what seemed an eternity, Hermela's sight cleared…

Where was she?

Hermela looked around. She was no longer in her house. No longer in the shanty town. No longer in Addis Ababa it appeared.

Where…

Before her was a warka tree, its green and brown branches spread out. It sat there, like some giant mushroom, under a pink, coral-colored sky.

It took Hermela almost a full minute to realize where the stranger's touch had (mysteriously) landed her.

She was home.

Bishoftu…

Well, not exactly Bishoftu. A couple of leagues east of the district where she had lived with her father for close to twenty years. Before she had moved to Addis Ababa and met Abel.

Abel…Hermela could not even summon up her husband's face as she continued to stare at the warka tree, its lush leaves touched now (apparently) by dawn. She knew this particular tree well. Like an old friend. In its shade was a small Orthodox cemetery, its plots marked mostly by Coptic crosses and limestone steles. Many neighbors from her former district had been laid to rest here once-upon-a-time.

Her own mother had been buried here. When Hermela was only two.

Above, and to the right of her, Hermela now heard a sonorous voice.

"A-BA-TA-CHIN HO-YE YE-MET-NOR BE-SEMAI."

Hermela did not even have to look to know who was speaking. (Even though she did look.) It was her own father, chanting The Lord's Prayer —his favorite—in Amharic.

Her own father, who had died nine years earlier during a drought.

And here was another weird thing. Hermela now seemed to be very, very close to the ground. Her movement through time and space had somehow diminished her in size. As she looked over (and up) toward her father's voice, she caught a glimpse of her own body clothed now in some white handspun dress.

Hermela was a child again…

And yes, holding her hand was her own dear father, Abraham, looking younger than she ever remembered him being. His hair not shot through with white. His back not bowed by years of hard labor.

"MEN-GIS-THE, TEM-TA-LIN KIB-RE-HEN, EN-DE-NAI," her father continued to murmur.

Before Hermela could say anything, express her joy at seeing her father alive or her astonishment even at any of this, he abruptly let go of her hand. He let out a sharp cry and from his tunic he now produced that amulet he had carried all his life—that Bible scroll in a little leather pouch meant to be a boon against…

The EVIL EYE.

He held the kitab in front of him now, aiming it toward the tree and the cemetery. Once again, Hermela looked over at the tiny, jagged plot of land.

Hyenas

There were hyenas there. A pack of seven or so, their black snouts down among the crosses and steles.

Her father now ran toward the ugly ghouls, still holding the kitab before him as he ran.

"Bouda!" he shouted at the pack.

In concert—it seemed—the startled beasts looked up, baring their sharp teeth. They snarled at him. She thought, for one terrifying minute, that they were going to attack him.

And then as her father reached the edge of the cemetery they turned and fled. Actually, vanished would be a better word. They all vanished as if they had been made of yellow smoke.

All but one...

And to Hermela's amazement, this sole hyena, the largest in the pack, seemed to rise up. Rise up on its back legs. Seemed to expand as it stood its ground against her dead father.

It became a man...It became a man...

It became the man who had entered her shack...

"Bouda!" her father shouted, brandishing the kitab at this monster.

There could be no mistake. It was him alright. The same handsome broad face. The same cream-colored skin. The same brilliant, gold brocaded tunic.

This was the dream she could never remember. This...

Only, it hadn't been a dream.

The man looked past her father as if he didn't matter at all. Talisman didn't matter at all. His black eyes sought out Hermela's own in the distance. The eyes flashed gold. And then...

As quick as that, Hermela was back in her own shack. The man was gone.

My child!

She turned, rushing towards her child sleeping in its crib, worried something terrible had happened. But she needn't have worried. The child was safe. Hermela reached down to pick up the baby when it opened its eyes.

They were no longer human. They were the color of burnished gold as it stared up at her with a relentless hunger.

And then, it was upon her.

Illustration by Sarah Walker

King O' the Wood
by Can Wiggins

Where do I begin to tell you this story, a story more likely found in a long-hidden book of magic spells? How can anyone do justice to a fairy tale, how does anyone spin gold from straw, turn a pumpkin into a coach, have an adventure in the middle of an ordinary day?

The best thing is to start at the very beginning and go all the way to the very end.

⌘⌘⌘

The King of the Wood stood His ground as He had for years, decades, four score and seven, centuries, eons. He had seen what He believed was the dawn of time itself. But, as nothing in the Wood was as old as He, there was no one to talk to regarding this

⌘⌘⌘

Rowan Blake talked to trees. Specifically, she talked to those trees that made up part of the massive forest that grew on the sprawl of land behind her home. She climbed up to their highest perches and settled down on limbs so wide they reminded her of the benches at Aunt Ma'am's church. She hunkered down and stared at the wood grain, the knots, the imperfections which seemed perfect to her; or, more often than not, she stretched her long thin legs out, resting against a sturdy trunk while she looked as far as her eye could see. She spied the tops of far-off buildings, not visible from the ground. She always pretended she was looking at the next big city down the road but knew what she really saw was not Greenville, but the weathervane on Mr. Porter's barn and the church steeple on Highway 441.

She saw flowers, little specks of color, dotting the ground below. She saw birds' nests, often empty. But sometimes she discovered a clutch of

King O' the Wood

eggs or, once in a great while, a newly hatched baby bird or two, their mouths opening wide if their nests were bumped by a clumsy girl.

Warm breezes rose and fell around her in summer as the sun filtered through the leaves. She smelled the rain as it lashed through the countryside while she holed up in her forest. She didn't mind the rough bark or sticky resins.

And she didn't mind the occasional scare of coming up on a wild thing as she made her way through what was their home. How quiet they all were. How close they could get without giving themselves away. It was like magic.

Not even snakes bothered her, which flummoxed everyone except her brother. Ben told wild stories from around the world about snakes, promising her a trip to the Serpentarium at Edisto Island once he was out of the Air Force.

The last time they visited the forest together, they saw a long gloss of blue-black beauty he told her was an Eastern Indigo.

"You ever see one, you need to follow it," he said. Like Rowan, Ben was tall and lanky, his gray eyes so pale they startled folks meeting him for the first time.

"Why?" she asked.

"If you see the snake, it means the king is nearby."

Rowan knew America didn't have kings. There were presidents and Indian chiefs but no kings. Did Ben mean a real king? Did he mean a fairy tale king? Or did he mean a sign and wonder like Jesus Christ, the King of Kings himself? Her questions were rapid fire, like she had expected this sparring match.

"Overthinking it, Ro—as usual." Ben laughed, but not in a mean way.

She didn't say anything. She didn't want to argue with him on his last day home.

When they left the forest that afternoon, they held hands, keenly aware of the divide that would soon separate them. Ben gave her what

Can Wiggins

he called marching orders, bits and bobs of advice he said would help her while he was away.

"You need to help around the house and garden more. Don't wait for Aunt Ma'am to tell you to pick up, or wash dishes, or set the table. You're not a little kid anymore. And find yourself a real hobby, one you like and can learn from, one you can devote yourself to. Find something outside of yourself that helps you learn about what's inside of yourself."

"You talk like a Boy Scout."

"I am a Boy Scout," he reminded her. "Was, I mean. Oh yeah, and you don't have to go to church to be a good person."

Rowan had already devoted herself to the forest and the inhabitants in its domain. This wasn't hard for the girl as she already spent a lot of time just past the tree line. Just past the tree line was as far as Aunt Ma'am wanted her to go but Rowan always managed to drift into the woods, still close enough to hear Aunt Ma'am call her name but far enough in to lose sight of the house and garden.

She always left tokens of that devotion when she entered the forest. She carried in tiny pieces of sparkly cloth or paper, and sometimes a Mercury dime—real silver, which Granny insisted the spirits liked—shoving her gifts into a small hole on a stump she used as a marker, like Granny had taught her. She chose bright things easily seen, shining in the sunlight.

"A guest always takes a present when they visit," Granny said. "Make sure you take a little something when you visit. Just in case."

Rowan now patted tree trunks with real affection when it was time to leave, "just in case," as she made her way home on what Aunt Ma'am called a pig trail.

"You stay where you can hear me," the woman repeated when they sat down for the last homecooked meal with Ben. "And you always answer me when I call. Okay, baby?"

Aunt Ma'am knew Rowan wasn't going to hear her one day, and then what?

Ring O' the Wood

And Rowan knew Aunt Ma'am had already planted rosemary and mint for protection and invisibility against that day around the corners of the slate gray house as well as in the four corners of her bountiful garden, like Granny had taught. Worry still gnawed at the woman, despite the promises of tried and true old-time root work.

"Bad things are going to happen, no matter how much folks prepare," Granny said once. "You ought to know that by now."

And now, Rowan noticed Aunt Ma'am's expression. Tight like her voice. Like she was holding back. Ben bumped Rowan's shin under the table, shooting her a look that meant business.

She assured Aunt Ma'am she did, she *did* understand her, she said she would do exactly what Aunt Ma'am said. And she meant it when she agreed with Aunt Ma'am. She always meant it when she said these things. Still, it was hard not to slip deeper into the haven the forest provided.

She knew one day she wasn't going to hear Aunt Ma'am and then what?

Ben was gone before she blinked. That last day had gone so fast. Rowan thought about it for a week and wished Granny was still alive.

She wished she had learned everything Granny knew but that would have taken years, which Granny didn't have.

⌘⌘⌘

The very next Saturday, Aunt Ma'am started up. Breakfast was over but the adults slung another cup of coffee down their throats, and Uncle Furman read the morning paper as jazz poured out of the radio he kept in the kitchen.

"Let me tell you why I want you to stay close. A girl disappeared in that forest, baby. You was little and wouldn't remember but it made the news for a while. Somebody said she was walking along the road with a little suitcase and she went in them woods and—that was that."

"What happened?"

Can Wiggins

"Nobody knows. She just disappeared."

Uncle Furman rattled his newspaper. His voice rolled like faraway thunder from behind the sports section. "Some folks think she met a boyfriend and took off for Greenville. Not ever'body likes living out in the country. And her daddy was a shiftless drunk while her mother was a religious nutcase. Don't repeat that, Ro. It's a sad business."

Rowan directed her remarks to the newspaper. "No sir."

Aunt Ma'am wasn't finished.

"That's an old forest, Rowan."

"It's a pristine wilderness," Uncle Furman murmured.

Aunt Ma'am kept going. "It goes for miles and it's been here longer than any of us, believe you me."

"It's an old-growth forest," Uncle Furman said.

"They's lots of places to get lost in, in those woods," Aunt Ma'am said. "They say several people have gone missing in there over the years. Not just unhappy girls. They's no telling what's in there."

"Yessum."

With that piece of business out of the way, they walked outside to the clothesline and hung out the weekly wash, the bleached bedsheets blindingly white. They didn't talk much, listening instead to the faint strains of music floating out from the half-open window. Now and then, they heard Uncle Furman cough.

A plane droned overhead as they finished up. Rowan followed its path, shielding her eyes with a freckled hand.

"You miss Ben?" Aunt Ma'am suddenly asked. A clothespin hung out of the side of her mouth like a cigarette.

"Yessum."

"Well, I do, too. Your Uncle Furman misses him. Nobody to take fishing anymore." Aunt Ma'am took the clothespin from her mouth, dropping it in an apron pocket. "He'll come visit as soon as he's done with that basic training."

King O' the Wood

Rowan figured Ben would be shipped out as soon as he was good to go. She read the newspaper, she watched the news, she heard people talking. There was trouble all over the world now, some of it not that far away. Military was on call all the time.

"Won't be too long," the woman said. "You'll see. He's going to just show up here one day with a bunch of laundry for me to wash and a snow globe from Texas for you."

She winked at Rowan who knew that wasn't likely to happen. But it was nice to think about and she didn't say anything different. She didn't want to sass Aunt Ma'am. Aunt Ma'am and Uncle Furman were good to her and Ben. The fact that Aunt Ma'am remembered how much she liked snow globes was telling.

Rowan's rituals grew more elaborate as that first summer without Ben progressed. By the time August was on the calendar, Rowan was slathering mica-laden sand over her arms and legs. She sparkled like a jewel as she entered the forest, her head crowned with wildflowers and twigs which she carefully removed before leaving the woods on Ma'am's request.

"I don't mind you play-acting like you're a heathen," Aunt Ma'am said. "I just don't want anyone to see you looking like one."

Rowan searched out and read more books about trees and forests around the world, favoring those with botanical prints or illustrations, sometimes taking them into the woods so she could compare what she saw in the books with what she saw in the forest itself. Sometimes she read aloud to the trees and anything else that might be within earshot.

She knew she was different. She didn't understand why she did some of these things any more than she understood why she wore dirt and flowers when she went to the trees—only that it felt right. She liked believing the trees knew what she was telling them, knew she wanted to communicate, knew she loved them and everything around them and that, maybe one day, the forest would speak to her.

And one day, it did, just like Granny told her.

Can Wiggins

She kept an eye out for the Eastern Indigo. That story about the snake leading her to the King was never far from her mind, although she did scoff to herself about herself now and again.

Eleven years old and still believing everything she heard and read. Gullible.

But, like Ben said, myths and legends almost always had one foot in fact.

⌘⌘⌘

One afternoon, deep into the summer, the grownups listened to the radio in the kitchen as Rowan washed and put dishes away. Then, with a reluctant okay from Aunt Ma'am and a nod from Uncle Furman, she ran to the tree line.

They stayed inside the house, the overhead fans on along with the window unit in their bedroom. Usually they sat outside in case she called for them but that had never happened. They decided she had discovered what she could and couldn't do, what was and wasn't safe.

The forest was cool inside, even during the tail end of summer. Its canopy was a shelter from the pervasive heat of late summer in the Deep South. As the wheel of the year turned, it was a different story as leaves came down, carpeting the forest floor with bright colors as well as the possibility of new dangers. But that wasn't for a while yet.

Rowan made her way to her regular marker, the stump just past the tree line. She squatted down to pat the marker before leaving a nickel and a sprig of rosemary, her behind not quite touching the ground, and stopped.

Something was different. She felt the top of the stump where it had been lopped off and disfigured so long ago, her fingertips searching for what her eyes couldn't see. And then she did see.

Runners, green and vibrant, were under and around the old stump. Rowan felt moss, barely there but it *was* there. Her fingertips felt what would soon be a thriving green cover and she stood, thrilled and spooked at the same time by her discovery.

King O' the Wood

"You're alive!" she whispered. "The King is keeping you alive." Even as she said it, she knew how nutty she would sound if anyone heard her. But nobody heard her. Nobody was around.

Something rustled in the greenery nearby and she jumped. Her breath caught in her throat as she followed the sound—a quiet sound. A subtle sound. And then, she saw it.

The Eastern Indigo.

It slid out and away from the leaves of the fallen limbs it wrapped itself in. Its elegant form a single stroke of beauty, the snake raised its sleek head off the ground, opened its mouth, and hissed.

"Take me to the King!" Rowan whispered.

As an answer, it took off, disappearing down a hole that was too small for her to follow.

She stared down the hole. Nothing. But the stump was alive. That was something.

⌘⌘⌘

"You're gonna reach in one of them banks of leaves and get bit one day," Uncle Furman fussed when she came in. Spotting Rowan at the edge of the woods, he often watched from a respectful distance while she busied herself checking on animal nests and dens in deadfalls. He had recently told Ma'am he believed Rowan needed to be given as much freedom as possible. He believed the more freedom Rowan had, the more likely she would listen if she was told no about something.

"You don't know girls," Ma'am answered.

"Sometimes there's snapping turtles in deadfalls, Ro," he said. "Foxes. I've seen bobcats." He paused for emphasis. "*Cop-per-heads.*"

"I know."

"They don't like to be messed with, even if it is an accident. And Lord help you if you wake up a bear."

"No bears," she said.

"There could be," he said.

Can Wiggins

"No bears."

⌘⌘⌘

Saturdays were for errands and the library. Rowan adjusted to the new schedule—one that didn't include Ben—and found she liked it better than the old schedule.

Uncle Furman dropped her off at the library on Saturdays while he tooled around town, running errands. His errands consisted of buying the most groceries for the least money at the Piggly Wiggly every week and getting a haircut once a month. Furman believed in eating well but remained careful how he spent his paycheck.

His grocery list included a treasure trove—chicken, coffee, milk, cream, grits, sausages, collards, green beans, potatoes, canned spinach, Spam, eggs, cornmeal, and bread. There was always a carton of Camels as well as a generous supply of Pepsi and vanilla wafers. Rowan checked every week and noticed he rarely changed anything, although he always bought a turkey for Thanksgiving and a pork roast for Christmas.

He also bought carefully so he could afford any over-the-counter medicines Aunt Ma'am wrote down. Sometimes there were newspapers from other cities, and he brought those back to the house, too. Jammed in with the vittles, mastheads peeked out of the paper bags.

He always tried to bring home the *Charlotte Observer*. Aunt Ma'am had lived in Charlotte years ago and still talked about it with such love and longing that people who heard her often walked away with tears in their eyes.

While Furman handled business, Rowan took a leisurely walk through the library, looking through the books in the kids' section first as she slowly made her way to the adult section where the good stuff was kept. None of the grownups chased her out, least of all the librarian. Miss Clark always helped Rowan look for special books and those were unfailingly in the grownup stacks.

Rowan loved the library. Long ago, it had been a bank, and there was still a sense of very important business being conducted on its premises.

Ring O' the Wood

Wooden floors, polished with an expensive-smelling oil, held still-fine tables with cubbyholes and bankers' lamps. Artwork consisted of people throughout the ages in various settings, all of them reading.

Today was no different than most Saturdays she visited, and Rowan soon approached the desk where the librarian sat, several books open before her.

Rowan dove right in, her voice hushed to an obligatory whisper. "I'm looking for a book about trees, their entire life cycle. What they're like, what they go through, what happens if lightning hits them, do they feel it, do they communicate with other trees in the same forest—are they aware of other lifeforms? Things like that. Can you help me, Miss Clark?"

"Oh, my goodness." Miss Clark looked at Rowan as if it was the first time that she was seeing her. "I almost didn't recognize you. You are getting so tall."

Rowan gave her a tight smile. People she knew and even some she didn't always commented on her looks now—her height, her long legs, her face, her freckles, her coloring, her hair, how skinny she was, how tall she was, how odd she was, how unusual she was.

Miss Clark leaned forward, eager to help. "Well. That *is* a different request from what we usually have. Most folks don't believe anything other than human beings have feelings or a soul or that they think or—" she hesitated and then laughed, a birdlike flutter of a sound. "However, there's a book by someone named Whitlock that you might would like. But it's a very old book. It's in the restricted section upstairs."

Rowan's eyes widened. "Restricted. Like—censored books?"

Miss Clark shook her head. "No. These are books that professors and teachers and writers use in their research. And they aren't allowed to check those books out, either. Some of them are rare. Some are out of print and hard to find. Some are fragile due to their age. And some are considered esoteric and beyond most folks' understanding."

Rowan didn't hesitate. "May I see this particular book, please?"

324

Can Wiggins

Miss Clark did hesitate. "Well, we can go up there, but we can't make this a habit, young lady."

"I won't. Thank you." Rowan followed Miss Clark up the stairs behind the librarian's desk, a formidable affair in and of itself. She wondered how long she would have to wait until she was allowed upstairs on a regular basis.

"This book was written by a man named Absalom Whitlock. A local if I remember correctly."

"Absalom? Like King David's son?" Rowan took this as a sign and wonder, thinking of the wayward Absalom's sad and terrible death, his long thick hair caught up in a tree's branches, as if the tree itself had reached out and trapped him so that his enemies could strike him down.

"Oh. Yes. I hadn't thought of that, but yes. And an odd name, you have to admit."

Rowan nodded. "Absalom is a name like Judas. They were both so wicked nobody uses those names anymore."

"Here we are," Miss Clark whispered. Her blue-black hair shone under the lights. She opened the heavy beveled glass door with a small silver key. The girl wondered what secrets the librarian was privy to as she crossed the threshold into forbidden territory.

⌘⌘⌘

On the way home from town, Uncle Furman announced he was sitting on a quarter tank of gas and he didn't like that. He preferred a full tank when going into the week ahead.

"Going to Reese's?"

"We always give Reese our business. Small. Local. Don't forget that. Give the little guy your money when you can."

Uncle Furman eased the truck onto the pavement, and Reese met him at the pump as Rowan bounced out of the cab, hightailing it into the building. It was bigger on the inside than it looked on the outside, its cement blocks painted pale blue.

King O' the Wood

Besides the gas pumps, Reese ran what he called a store in the building. He kept cold drinks in a vending fridge and two metal racks that held chips and crackers. There was nothing hot, but a standing wood stove placed just inside the door where a cluster of old men sat on ladderback chairs on fall and winter mornings. In summer, they sat outside in the same chairs, lined up like birds on a wire. Old men with nothing to do but sit and gossip.

Behind the counter, there were cigarettes, cigars, pipe tobacco, and snuff. Reese had nailed all the old license plates from every car he had ever owned to the panel beside the smokes. Some went all the way back to 1935.

Rowan wasn't sure how old Reese was. He might have been Uncle Furman's age; he could have been older. He wasn't a smoker, he wasn't a drinker, and he wasn't a churchgoer. He had been at that filling station since the war but sometimes she wondered which war.

Inside, in the cool dark, Rowan wandered up and down the three aisles, checking the goods before hitting the snack stand. She had a little cash—not much, but enough to get her own chips and an extra soda if she wanted one.

A figure stepped out in front of her, trapping her between the wall and the postcards.

Rowan had no idea she was on Hovie Gilstrap's radar. She had seen him at Reese's before, of course. He always dropped in on Saturdays to grab smokes and a six-pack of beer. He didn't tarry and he didn't chat like most folks did.

He made a show of noticing her.

"Well. Look who it is! Little Rowan Blake."

Rowan tried mustering a smile but all she managed was pursed lips.

"Ain't so little anymore, are ya? Is'at right? Huh?"

His voice grated and a malodorous mix of sweat, tobacco and hard times circled him like a vulture. He was stringy, his skin dark and leathery

Can Wiggins

from too much fun in the sun. He reminded Rowan of a piece of beef jerky, one that nobody would ever think about buying, let alone eating.

"Hey Hovie."

"Hey yourself, little Rowan Blake! You sure are getting big—" He hesitated, then made a deal of looking her up and down. "—in all the right places. Yes sirree. You growing up real nice in *all* the right places."

A shadow fell across an already darkening situation, and a hand came from behind Rowan, gently grasping her upper arm.

"Honey," Uncle Furman's voice was in her ear. "You go pick us out some extra snacks for the game."

"Sure." Rowan turned and almost ran out of the aisle. She knew something was happening, something bad and strange, and she heard Furman's voice. He didn't try to keep it down. He didn't care if he embarrassed Hovie Gilstrap or anybody else.

"She's eleven years old, Hovie. E-*leven*. Keep that firmly in mind. And I'm watching you. Just like everybody else. We're all watching you."

A family-sized bag of potato chips in her hands, Rowan turned to watch the exchange. The air hummed and wavered around the men, and she popped a sweat as her breathing hitched.

Hovie tried staring Furman down but couldn't manage the grit it would take. Then he made the mistake of sneering at Furman. A vet who made it home all in one piece. A man who, once home, walked into hell without hesitation to pull two kids out for himself and his wife to raise. A person who said he was a Christian and a Democrat and that should be enough for anyone.

"You need to walk away right now, Gilstrap. While you've still got teeth in your head."

Hovie turned and sauntered out, every man in the place eyeballing his exit. Furman visibly relaxed, then turned and smiled at Rowan as if nothing had happened.

"Did you get those chips, Ro?"

"Yessir."

Ring O' the Wood

"Well, let's pay for 'em and get on home. If we hurry, we'll catch the game from the get-go."

They were home in time for Game 1 of the World Series and Aunt Ma'am's egg salad sandwiches, a tasty treat with plenty of sweet relish. The chips went in the pantry.

⌘⌘⌘

The next weekend, Rowan planned to take off for the deep part of the forest, once and for all. She had found an old, overgrown trail she wanted to follow, sure that it led deeper into the trees. She was itching to see how large the forest was.

"Ro, do not go far. A storm's coming. Tornado weather. We don't get 'em often but we never know. Don't want you carried off right when school's starting," Uncle Furman laughed. She grinned. "Okay."

"We had that big one a few years ago. Tore up Ellis Richards' farm," Aunt Ma'am reminded them.

"She put up a hex sign on her new barn, didn't she?"

Aunt Ma'am laughed. "Lord yes. She did. Like that's going to stop nature."

"Couldn't hurt," Rowan said. The adults looked at her and she added, "If it makes her feel better, it couldn't hurt, could it?"

⌘⌘⌘

Inside the tree line, Rowan bent down and whispered soothing words to the stump which now had tiny mushrooms sprouting from its moss. She patted the stump and watched as the mushrooms seemed to wiggle in response to her touch. She didn't want to make a big deal out of it, but she thought they knew who she was. What she was trying to do.

She placed a little offering on the stump and waited. She didn't want to rush into anything, but she knew she was soon coming up on winter weather and that this would cause a lot of resistance from Aunt Ma'am about going into the woods.

Can Wiggins

She looked past the area she usually stayed in. There was an opening, as if the trees had moved back to allow things to pass through on their way to the deep forest.

She had never noticed this before and wondered if the forest kept people away. And if it did, why? Was the King a real being? A heavenly creature? Was he a monster, a sacred monster?

Rowan heard a telltale rustling sound. She pressed her lips together, taking a deep breath through her nose, standing still and waiting. "You can't rush magic," Granny had told her more than once. "Magic takes care of itself. Mind you do the same."

And there he was. She had read up on the snake and discovered his generic name translated to "lord of the forest" which made sense to her. Sleek and magnificent, he was easily eight feet long and muscular. He lifted his head up again, and again looked directly at her. But when he opened his mouth this time, the hiss was like a song.

And the song was an invitation. He waited for her to follow which she gladly did. She figured she might as well see what she could see, just like the bear who went over that mountain. Nobody was here to stop her—not really—and surely, after all this time, the forest knew she was friendly.

She had read Absalom Whitlock's strange and beautiful life's work. He believed and wrote and taught that trees were sentient creatures, like any living thing. He believed they communicated with each other as well as other lifeforms in the forest. They helped each other grow and thrive and even made room for new trees. He wrote there was a reason ancient peoples had worshipped trees, had buried people in or under them as honored dead or sacrifices, had so many legends and tall tales about them.

She wished she had known Whitlock. Of course, he supposedly broke down, ending up in a mental ward for several years. This was because of unbelievable things he allegedly witnessed in an old-growth forest he himself later admitted were scientifically impossible.

King O' the Wood

Rowan looked around as she kept walking, the forest now spectacular hues of green, from the deepest black greens to pale yellow lime colors, saw thick trunks and saplings. Moss and mushrooms, unrecognizable plants, herbs, birds she didn't know the names of. She checked her watch, a little facepiece with no band, kept in a pocket.

An hour. Impossible. She had just started.

Uncle Furman said he'd never sell this land or parcel it out. She smiled, remembering that. She liked knowing the trees were here before her and would be here after her.

There was something comforting about that. No Sky King god for her. She liked being right here on Earth. To her, Earth *was* Heaven.

⌘⌘⌘

Something heard Rowan as she entered the deep forest. The King heard everything. He had ruled before the land—already inhabited—was discovered by a violent, marauding force from across an ocean.

He knew about oceans. His messengers told Him about them long ago. He stood His ground, landlocked in place, when they returned on the wing from adventures they sang about as He held court. He watched as animals walked through His woods, had been unable to stop much that had happened, had watched when the Sky threw down fire, helpless as others burned, always replacing themselves with newer greener versions of themselves, had felt one of His lesser limbs crack while encased in thick, numbing ice so long ago He wondered if it had been a dream.

And now, He heard the girl. He knew she was near. He had dreamed she would come and here she was. He knew she had seen the snake, had followed the snake with little fear. He would have to do the impossible and He was ready. He had done it before. He would do it again. People like that were very few and very far between. He welcomed her.

⌘⌘⌘

Can Wiggins

Rowan stood as if rooted. She had walked out of the forest and into a meadow with thousands of wildflowers. And standing out against the backdrop of another luxurious tree line stood the King of the Wood.

She froze as she took in the King's scale and magnitude. Rowan wasn't good at guesstimations but knew this tree was at least as big as her house.

"Hello," she said. She sensed His breathing and felt the ground responding, reaching out as He sensed hers.

A sawing sloughing sound, a great bellows, the sound of the void breathing.

She walked right up to Him and opened her arms, leaning against Him. She pressed the palms of her hands into his bark, her fingertips feeling the rough, bumpy grain. She had found Him. He was real.

She slowly walked around Him, taking everything in. Wondering. Questioning. And then, she saw His face.

⌘⌘⌘

After her visit, Rowan wanted a closer look at the grove near the meadow's edge, visible from where she now stood. She wanted a sketch to compare with Whitlock's work.

She spotted a distant thunderhead on the horizon and knew to hurry. The last thing she wanted was trouble with the folks.

Rowan apologized to the meadow's flowers as she picked a few for Aunt Ma'am. The petals shouted with color and she wanted to show them off to Ma'am and Uncle Furman.

Soon enough, she stood among the trees, some of which appeared damaged at first sight. On closer inspection, she realized a couple of them simply had their roots growing above ground. Weird.

Rowan rushed over to study one tree's exposed root system. She felt incredibly lucky, excitement rushing through her stick-thin frame. This looked like the illustration in Whitlock's book but even better because this was the real deal. She smelled the rich earth around the roots and reached out to touch those roots when another scent flooded her nostrils. A stench. A rot.

She knew that smell. Something was dead. It was close enough and strong enough that she looked around for an animal carcass.

Despite herself, Rowan recalled Uncle Furman's warning about bears. A chill slipped down her spine and fanned out, prickling her arms.

She covered her nose and mouth and peered into the maw of the underground before her. A glint of gold. The number 9—faded to near nothing—seemed to float atop a background of dimming red…

A sweater. Near-skeletal hands shot out of the sleeves of that sweater.

A crack of thunder startled her so badly she cried out and sprang to her feet, the spell of what she saw broken as memory and understanding emerged.

Barbara Cooper's red sweater, her birthday number on her new red sweater, loomed in Rowan's mind. Rowan remembered that sweater, remembered how thrilled and proud of that sweater Barbara had been that last day. The last day she was seen, the day she got off the bus, one stop before her regular stop. She wanted a candy bar for her birthday, and she got off the bus in front of Reese Owens's gas station. Her mom gave her the sweater that morning so she could wear it to school.

And now, what had been Barbara looked like a doll, a dried-up doll, a mannikin like in the stores or the movies or the Sears Big Book—

"Hey there."

Rowan shrieked, whirling around.

Hovie Gilstrap stood just inside the tree line, not far away from her and the trees.

"So. Found something, huh?"

Rowan, still numb and sickened over what she had discovered, was mute. She stared at him, trying to understand why he was there, trespassing on private property, and he smirked.

"Cat gotcha tongue?"

Can Wiggins

The sky lit up with the coming storm that now moved over the land. Another sudden and painfully sharp crack of thunder and Rowan jumped as Hovie looked skyward, turning around slowly as if enjoying the show.

"Gonna have us a storm, ain't we?" He turned toward her with a crooked grin. "We definitely gonna have us a party, ain't we? Huh? That right?" He motioned towards the hole in the ground. "Me and her had a party. Didn't last long."

He snickered, then took a step towards her.

Ben had once told her that sometimes the difference between living and dying was as simple as getting away. She took off.

"Jack rabbit, huh?" Hovie hollered. "Well, 'at's awright. I can run, too."

The clouds roiled above the trees. Leaves danced in the wind as the storm looked for a place to land.

"Ain't this some hellacious weather?" Hovie shouted.

He sounded far away but Rowan didn't stop to check. She didn't turn around to see where he was. She knew where he was. He was behind her and that's where she meant to keep him. That's where she meant for him to be when she ran out of the forest, Aunt Ma'am on the porch calling her name.

A hard blow landed, almost knocking her down. She stumbled but didn't fall. She realized Hovie was throwing rocks at her, trying to bring her down like she was an animal that needed to be chased off or worse. She heard the things he was hollering at her, things that were terrible, frightening, crazy. What he was going to do to her and her little lickety split when he caught her. How he was going to eat her lickety split right up, he was going to ruin her for anyone else, he was going to split her lickety wide open.

Another glancing blow on her shoulder drew a roar from the girl as something snapped in her. She shouted an age-old threat at Hovie.

"I'm gonna tell!"

King O' the Wood

That threat was a curse as far as Hovie was concerned. Not swearing and not profanity. A curse. If she told, if she got away and told on him it was as good as a death sentence for him.

"You ain't gonna live long enough to tell, you little bitch!"

And then, the earth itself tilted and Rowan knew everything there was to know about Hovie Gilstrap.

His voice now held the difference between night and day. It held a howling rage that was no longer human. She didn't dare turn for a look. It wasn't Hovie Gilstrap behind her now. It was a monster, and it would turn her to something far worse than stone.

He sounded like he was gaining on her, hitting the ground with long even strides. But Rowan had long limbs herself now. She had grown a lot in a year, in a summer. She was happy of those long legs now.

And as the monster's roar came closer, she knew this was it. Do or die. She got away or she didn't. She believed she could get away. She believed she *would* get away. She knew she had to pace herself, but she still had to outrun this son of a bitch.

She ducked out of the tree line and slammed across the clearing, propelled by a power she hadn't known was there, ready any minute to leave the earth itself, vaulting up into the sky, her legs like pistons, fueled by something she felt but couldn't name.

Where her breath came from, she didn't know. She didn't care. Her lungs were like bellows now, deep and with great reserves. Her jaw slackened, dropped as she remembered Ben's lessons of breathing shallow, even and waiting, waiting till she couldn't wait anymore to flat-out run. Too little too late, she would lose the race. Too much too soon, she would lose the race.

She had to stay just enough ahead, she had to zigzag like the jack rabbit Hovie had called her.

Rowan knew if she was to get away, she had to maintain the lead. A long crack of thunder and lightning bolted overhead.

Can Wiggins

Rain now fell so hard, so fast and so cold she believed this was what getting slashed by a knife felt like.

Hovie bellowed as he gained on her, cursing, and crowing as he stumbled, losing his footing, then springing up again like a weed you can't tear out of your garden.

The sky was the color of an overripe plum, a purple so deep it shone black. Rowan feared being struck by lightning, but she feared the storm chasing her even more.

She kept running, circling around the tree line, as she again burst into the deeper part of the forest.

Rowan almost lost heart when she saw thick tree limbs bending, arcing toward her. A groaning crack echoing through the vale sounded almost human, and she ran right to the King of the Wood, not stopping as her legs took her up and into the tree itself, mighty limbs serving as her stairway.

Hovie saw what Rowan had seen and he stopped, breath caught in his throat, not comprehending what was before him, what he saw. Rowan knew the feeling but doubted he would go beyond that first shock. She knew what he saw. It had almost stopped her in her tracks when she saw it too.

The tree was huge, like something in a fairy tale.

And it had a *face*. As God was witness, the King of the Wood had a face, with a heavy brow, deep-set pockets for eyes, then a nose, and a slash for a mouth below a scarred upper lip.

He saw Rowan climbing up, climbing into the leaves, into the branches and, as he shook off the sights just seen, he tried following her, hollering as he pursued her on territory that was not his. "A'ight, bitch, gonna get you now. Treed you like a coon, didn't I? Huh? That right?"

Hovie Gilstrap reached up and grabbed at branches and leaves, tearing them as he tried to find purchase to pull himself up off the ground and into the tree, just like the girl.

King O' the Wood

"You ain't nothin' but a low-rent pissant!" he hollered. "You don't even know who your daddy is or what he done! Your daddy wun't nothin' but a goddam carny. He killed your white trash mama! Bludgeoned her to death in her kitchen and run off…"

Rowan stopped where she was, what she was doing. Turning, she stared down at Hovie. She was more than angry now. Angry and disgusted and terrified all at once. She had never felt such a mix of emotions. She had never felt such a mix of sensations.

Hovie didn't repeat himself. He didn't dare. The expression on Rowan Blake's face didn't belong to the little girl he was after. That little girl had vanished. This girl—this *lack*—was going to nail him to wherever he landed with now-splintering features.

The branches sprang back, and there was a shearing noise like a silk dress ripping apart. Rowan watched, eyes wide, as Hovie bounced off his perch, landing hard on the soaked ground. Runners, thick and thin, whipped around in the wind, unmoored from the ground and each other. Wind funnels formed, whirling like dervishes, leaves and dirt joining in. And then, the true storm moved in.

Rowan drew a sharp, shaking breath, not of fear but of wonder and ecstatic joy, her eyes wide as she bore witness.

She had been right all along. This was real.

The King of the Wood uprooted himself and moved over the land to mete out justice.

⌘⌘⌘

"What did you see?"

The sheriff was kind, his voice softer than Rowan would have believed. She said she knew he probably saw her as just a big kid, but he said she was a big kid who had managed to outrun a tornado and a murderer after finding a dead girl in the woods.

She found out later that Ma'am had screamed for her from the porch after Furman came out of the woods without her. Furman had picked his

Can Wiggins

wife up and bodily carried her down to the cellar where they waited out the storm. "Otherwise, she'd'a been up in the air herself," he told people later. "That twister was right on top of us."

She found out Ma'am promised all kinds of things to God if He spared her. When Rowan showed up with her story of Hovie Gilstrap and finding Barbara Cooper, Uncle Furman looked almost sick, bright red splotches blooming on his cheeks as he called the sheriff.

"We thought you was a goner, baby." Aunt Ma'am hugged her tight, noticing the bumps and cuts from the debris thrown at Rowan during the storm. She and Furman had already decided not to punish her. What she went through had been plenty, Furman said.

"It's easy to get turned around in there," he told Ma'am.

"However did you get away, baby?" Aunt Ma'am asked.

"A tree. A tree saved me."

⌘⌘⌘

The King of the Wood stood His ground as He had for years, decades, four score and seven, centuries, eons. He had seen what He believed was the dawn of time itself, and He would see the end of it as well.

Illustration by Alan Sessler

Jenny Green-teeth
by Chelsea Arrington

Dear children, dear children, come play in my pond!
Be sailors in search of new lands!
Be fairies and witches with sticks for your wand!
Come children, come give me your hands!

My name's Jenny Green-teeth, I'll take you below
To my home in the swampy green muck.
I'll tell you a tale all good children should know
And give you a penny for luck!

Ignore my green hair as it snakes around you.
Do not fear my slimy black claws.
My hideous pallor of green and of blue
Should not give you more than a pause.

I'll cradle you close in my ghastly thin arms
And sing lovely songs to your bones.
You'll never tire of my elegant charms
Or how my voice cries and moans.

So come to my pond, my sweet darlings dear.
Come wade in the depths of the green.
I see your curled heads, your souls drawing near!
Come to your new mother and queen!

Illustration by Sarah Walker

Of Blood and Flowers
by Chelsea Arrington

The wood was deep and dank and dark.
The wood was wet and damp.

I did not see the darkening sky
As I trod into the depths that day.
The wood held pleasures I had not known.
It smelled of roses and moss.
I walked along the path until
I had to stray away.
Into the depths of darkness I walked;
Into the scent of death.
Into the pathless land I trod, unaware
Of gore or guile.
Into a green web of desire I went;
Into a country of lust.

The wood was deep and dank and dark.
The wood was wet and damp.

A child of woman I was, a woman so rare and strong.
She was a woman of fire and blood.
She gave me her name and her mantle
And set me on the road to Hell.
She sent me with her sweet kiss,
With sickly butterfly vanilla flavors.

Of Blood and Flowers

She set me on the road to Hell
To reprieve her of her past.
She gave me bread, cakes, and ale.
She sent me into the wood.
Upon my head she placed a hood;
Upon my shoulders, a cloak.

The wood was deep and dank and dark.
The wood was wet and damp.

"Do not stray, my little one. Do not wander
In the wood. Beware of man and wolf, my girl.
Do not engage beast or bird.
Speak not to angel, troll, or tree.
Gaze not upon flower
Or pond. For the devil, he lurks
In every heart and waits upon every maid.
He seeks your soul and longs for your flesh
To dance with him below."

She smiled a knowing glance.
She gave a knowing nod.
I thought she loved her daughter that day,
I thought she loved me still.
Yet I, her girl, she gave away,
She sent me unto Hell.
Into the deepest wood I went,
Into the darkest place.

Chelsea Arrington

The wood was deep and dank and dark.
The wood was wet and damp.

Yet, I had no thought of fear,
Despite my mother's words.
I had no thought of wolves or thorns.
The path led me through the dark.
To my mother's mother I walked that day,
To give her my prayers and bread.
To my mother's mother I fled that day,
She, who was my only comfort.

My grandmother held the earth in her hand;
She held the heavens too.
She sang of sweet wonders of life and grief
And gave me her heart's love.
My grandmother sang the love songs of earth.
She sang of the trees and the sky.
She sang of the love of man and God.
She sang of the sea and the wind.
She was the love of my soul.
She was the love of my heart.
She knew the secrets of plant and pain,
Of stars and moon and dreams.
She was the love of my soul.
She was the love of my heart.

The wood was deep and dank and dark.
The wood was wet and damp.

Of Blood and Flowers

Upon that day, I walked to her;
I walked to her from the path.
I heard the song of her soul in my head,
Yet the flowers were much too bright.
The flowers upon the ground,
They also sang a lovely song.
They knew my name and called to me;
They cried out with their scent and beauty.

The wood was deep and dank and dark.
The wood was wet and damp.

I heard the voice of my mother,
Yet knew her to lie and tease.
Her face full of scorn I saw in my mind
And knew that she was blind.
Her youth and beauty were spent,
Squandered on lovers and wine.
My father had used her and left her to bleed,
To bleed and maybe to die.
She did not remember the romance of youth.
She did not speak the language of flowers.
Her dreams were hoary, frost-bitten, and dead.
Tears turned to ash in her eyes.
She could not hear the song of my heart,
The poetry of my childish soul.

At her warnings I scoffed as I ran off the path.
Her commands I waved away.
Who was she, this whore and scold

Chelsea Arrington

To keep me from the deep?
Who was she, who'd seen the world,
To tell me I too could not see?
Her face and fears, I swept away.
I laughed and kicked at the dirt.
She was home. She was not here.
She could not direct my way.

The wood was deep and dank and dark.
The wood was wet and damp.

The sun shone not upon my hands,
Nor upon my brow, nor feet,
But illumined only the flowerets:
The gold and red and violet.
Colors of blood, colors of life:
Colors of the sun and sky ablaze with fire.
I lay my red cloak upon the ground.
It could not shield or mute me.
She wanted to hide me,
To keep my colors dark,
Yet she gave me a scarlet cloak.
A scarlet cloak to hide the child.
A scarlet cloak to mask my glow
In the deep, dark wood.
My hair, a similar hue:
Red and gold, a halo of flame
Upon my head did grow.
Be quiet, and stay upon the path.
Speak not to beast nor man.

Of Blood and Flowers

Keep down your head, avert your gaze.
Do not look into the eyes of flowers.
They will lead you straight to Hell.

Yet, flowers, such a heady scent had they;
Their perfume enticed and seduced.
So, among the profusion of flowers I lay,
Among the bed of flowers.
Upon a bed of licentious flowers I lay
And breathed deep of their rich scent.
My hands were white among the red,
The scarlet, and the crimson.
My hands, as in prayer to some Pagan god;
My hands open to receive.

The wood was deep and dank and dark.
The wood was wet and damp.

The shadows moved, the air was still.
I lay and breathed deep of the wood.
I felt his presence drawing near.
I smelled his musk and power.
He looked down at me and smiled a smile,
A smile of secrets unknown to me.
Man or beast, I knew not which lay upon my body.

My hair filled his hands.
His breath filled my nose.
His golden eyes engulfed my soul.
The hair on his chest was thick and

Chelsea Arrington

Black, carpeting my snow-white breasts.
His voice growled within my ear,
A deep and throaty sound.
Then there was blood and blood and blood;
Then there were scarlet waves.
My eyes saw red, I smelled earthy wine
And felt the darkness of death draw near.
Within my darkness, he planted seeds:
Seeds of crimson flowers.

The wood was deep and dank and dark.
The wood was wet and damp.

When I awoke, the sun shone down
Upon my bed of flowers.
Red rose petals adorned my face,
My hair, my hands, and feet.
Blood red petals adorned my cheeks,
My thighs, my breasts, my wrists.

Along the path I trod that day,
Along the path to granny's.
The sun was bright and dappled
Gold upon the well-worn path.
My grandmother lay dead in her bed.
In a bed of blood she lay. Her thighs were open,
Her eyes were wide, a smile played upon her lips.
Her death in pleasure, pleasure and pain.
She died with secrets in her soul.

Of Blood and Flowers

The wood was deep and dank and dark.
The wood was wet and damp.

My mother, she is a grandmother now
And she lives in the deep, dark wood.
She sings of the moon and the trees and the sea.
She sings of the sky and of God.
She sings the love songs of earth
And waits for my daughter to come
With bread, and cakes, and ale.
She waits in her bed for the blood
Dreams to flow once again.

The wood is deep and dank and dark.
The wood is wet and damp.

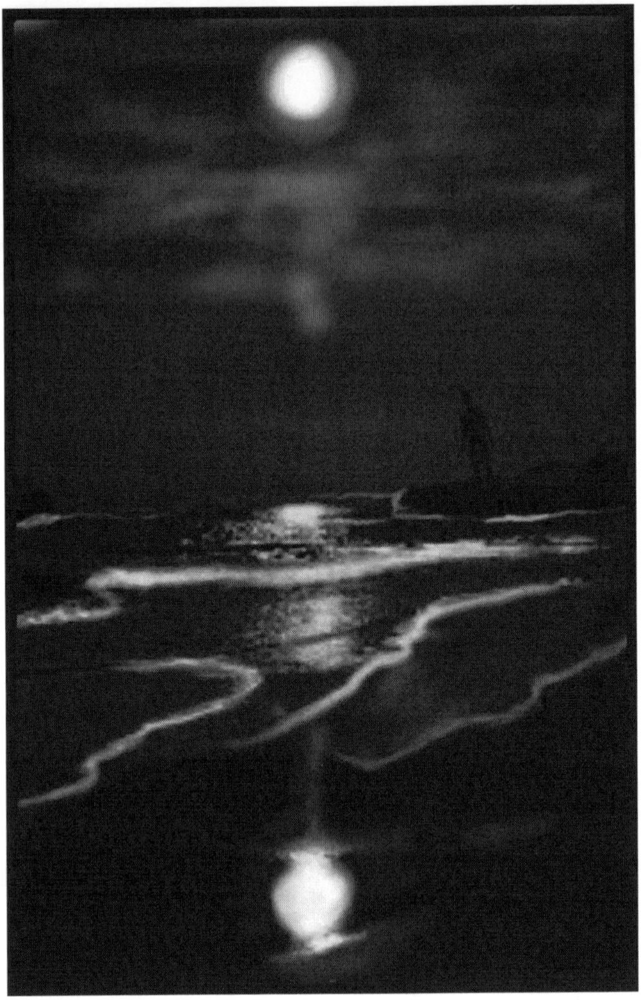

A Slow Remembered Tide
by John Linwood Grant

"I'll leave you here, then," said his wife as she parked the car by the seawall – and he knew that she would, not just for the two weeks whilst he was in the boarding house, but for every day to come. He felt it in the half-hearted kiss, in the tremor of her fingers on his shoulder. He knew, without further discussion, that his retreat to the coast would turn into a series of cream envelopes from solicitors, and awkward phone calls. Their marriage had died quietly, over a long time, without anyone really caring.

He watched her as she slid back behind the steering wheel, and he saw in her only a bundle of indifferent memories which he would no longer share. They had been together for eighteen years, but he could already imagine forgetting her face, her name. Which left the sands, the long sands, and the lead-colored waters of the bay.

There was no certain horizon; the sky bled into the sea, indistinguishable; gulls clustered on the foreshore, a chatter of grey backs, cold yellow eyes. Beyond them, a cormorant perched on a single dark rock which stood out from the sea, a sentinel against the flood.

He recognized it all.

Disturbed by a dog walker farther along the shore, the gulls rose in a dirty cloud, wheeling and shrieking only to settle again fifty yards down. Maybe there was a sea elsewhere which was blue or turquoise, even ultramarine. Here it was slate-colored or brown, muddied with sand, with shreds of old fishing nets and bladderwrack on its flood. He remembered popping the dried bladders, the bubble-wrap of childhood

A Slow Remembered Tide

There should have been something wonderful inside – a pearl, a drop of sea-honey, anything. But there wasn't.

Only stale air, like the alcohol-heavy breath of the dead on his neck…

It took him less than ten minutes along the sands to reach the boarding house – quiet, too much brown paint, and the smell of disinfectant.

"Mr. Mainprize. I have you booked for two weeks, is that right?" The owner jerked her head and clucked to herself as she took his details.

"For now."

He took his bags up to the room. A sink, a bed, one chair. If he added a stove, it would have been the bedsit he stayed in when he fled from this town.

Gulls cried outside the open window, pale post-it notes on grey skies. They were there to tell him that he could never forget.

They were right.

⌘⌘⌘

There had to be a first encounter with someone from his past, and there was, outside the chip shop on Monkgate that evening.

"Chris! Chris Mainprize."

He squinted at the florid face, the torn anorak.

"Uh, hello."

"You remember me – Steve. We had that party, back in eighty-seven, you know, right before you left."

He remembered. Cheap cider on the beach; coast-girls with calf muscles and cheekbones. The party lasted until dawn. By noon he was on the train inland, heading for an anonymous place in an anonymous city.

John Linwood Grant

Christopher let himself be guided into a nearby pub, where bored teenagers played pool, baiting each other. They were him, at sixteen or seventeen. Steve bought a round of drinks and took over a copper-topped table.

"...She married a butcher, of course. Three kids, gone a bit mad now."

Christopher nodded. The alcohol was making tidal movements inside him. Steve Rhodes. That was the name. A friend you left behind more by accident than anything.

Steve paused, licked foam-smeared lips. "Look, Chris, mate, I've got to ask. Are you back to join us, you know, for the--"

"I can't." Quick and sharp. "It's... too much."

The conversation turned, awkwardly, until the glasses were empty. Neither of them mentioned Christopher's father. Old friends had become new strangers.

"It's important," said Steve, as they headed for the pub door. "But you never got that did you?"

I grew up with other worries, he wanted to say, but stayed silent as his once-friend left. The slam of the door was a fist against the side of his head, a heavy boot to his belly.

Other worries.

⌘⌘⌘

Everything at the boarding house was boiled – eggs, ham, cabbage, mince, potatoes. Except the toast. He imagined the landlady's frustration at not being able to boil that as well. She fussed between the two occupied tables at dinner.

The only other guest, a tall woman in a worn tweed skirt-suit, squinted at him over a forkful of mince. He tried to smile, failed.

In his room, he opened the single window, paint flaking off the sash cords. A container ship was crossing the bay, so slow at this distance that

A Slow Remembered Tide

you couldn't be sure it was really moving. There, by the gleam of the moon, was the cormorant on its solitary rock.

He slept and knew nothing until the clink of breakfast plates from below.

The next morning was hard and grey, so whelmed by November dank that it might as well have been raining. The parish church in town held his mother tight in its shadow, the gravestone hardly weathered. He owed her this one visit, the first since the funeral.

"I came back," he said, dropping garage-bought flowers by her head.

She didn't answer.

Twenty years. Twenty years since his father drowned in the long waters which stretched to Norway and beyond. The body came back, torn by rigging and bloated by the sea, but Petty Officer Mainprize was no longer inside. Christopher and his mother knew where he was.

That had been the breaking point.

"I'm leaving this place, mum. I need a life," he told her back then.

And she'd been pleased for him. There wasn't love between them, but there was family, familiarity. She only lasted four years after her husband's death.

Her funeral was a small affair.

"I'm sorry, Christopher." The vicar, ten generations of the coast in him. "She was a good woman. And your father… he was a complicated man."

Complicated? They used that word for someone who had friends and kept down a steady job, yet shouted abuse at his son and hit his wife. A man who could shake your hand and lend you a fiver, then threaten you when he was in his drink, large frame rolling as if he was out there on a heavy sea.

It wasn't complicated, not to Christopher. It was crude and simple. A brute and a bully.

John Linwood Grant

The vicar looked troubled. "There are so many who are lost to us unless we keep the faith. Forgotten, unmourned, or unforgiven. Will you not be coming home… this autumn, I mean? For…"

"No."

And he had kept to that same answer, kept to it throughout a loveless, childless marriage well away from the coast.

He stood over his mother's grave and wept. He could do nothing for her, there in the damp earth. There was always the sea, and its needs…

⌘⌘⌘

The cormorant – a cormorant – kept its watch; three children screamed on the edge of the outgoing tide, observed by bored, shivering parents. Grey waters, grey skies, and a vast fingernail of sand.

"My son is out there," A voice from behind him.

He recognized the tall figure from the boarding house. The Tweed Woman, older than him, carrying the last of her fifties on narrow shoulders. He drew in the sweet rot of seaweed.

"I lost him ten years ago," she added.

He struggled with this sudden intimacy. "A fisherman?"

"Drowned off the point. There are fewer of us who understand each year. So, few to bear so many."

He stared at his shoes, at the mismatched laces. A herring gull examined an empty cigarette packet. The family were packing up, leaving litter across the sands – plastic cups and crisp packets, an unwanted bucket and spade.

Something about the woman made him risk the topic he feared.

"Do you ever… have you felt him, your son?"

"No. But others will have. As long as we keep him, safe with us…"

They had coffee at the only stall on the promenade still open at that time of year.

A Slow Remembered Tide

"The eleventh day of the eleventh month." She was looking at two old men by the stall, red poppies pinned to faded brown overcoats. "It's like an echo, isn't it?"

His blank face drew another laugh from her. His wife Mary had only smiled, carefully. He didn't know women who laughed.

"I'm Christopher."

"Corinne." She took out her purse. "I'll pay for these."

He spilled sugar into the coffee she handed him. "It's not like they would have known. When they signed the Armistice, I mean."

She shrugged. "Perhaps they felt it, rather than knew it."

"Martinmas."

It was the first time he had used the word aloud in decades. One of the old men looked up, frowned, and went back to their conversation.

Christopher drank his coffee quickly, and pleaded other engagements, before he found himself drawn in. He had nothing planned. Buy toothpaste, maybe something for lunch from the supermarket, and a pair of thicker socks…

"Chris, mate."

Steve Rhodes, waiting by the small supermarket in the same torn anorak. He was guarding half a dozen shopping bags.

"Wife's inside. Forgot something." He came closer. "So… are you going to be there, to let them in?"

Christopher was trembling. "I can't cope with it, Steve, I can't…"

Steve drew in a deep breath, then sagged like the forgotten shopping.

Christopher fled.

Lying on his bed, the words were on his lips, passed down from his mother. Auburn and Hartburn. Owthorne, Monkwell and Ravenser Odd. The litany was still there. And the ships, dinghies and fishing cobles, trawlers, and warships. Coal-barges.

John Linwood Grant

To drown on this coast was different. There was always the eleventh day of the eleventh month, and on that day, there were always those like his mother, Steve, Corinne...

Waiting for Martinmas. He'd known about it since he was seven years old, though at first, he knew nothing of what it meant. He recalled his father, vest stained with sweat and spilled beer, lashing out when she tried to take Christopher with her to the shore. He was eleven years old when she tried to have him participate. In the end he accepted chocolate from his father and let his mother go on alone. Threats and treats, as always.

He went down to get a cup of tea. Corinne was in the shabby lounge, eating biscuits.

"So, tomorrow," she said. "I can't imagine you came back here by accident, not at this particular time."

"I had nowhere else to go."

Trying to shift the subject, he babbled. He took his wife, Mary, and laid her out in words. He talked about his failing job in light engineering, and a marriage which no engineer could have fixed, no matter how many tools he had. Unable to stop, he wrung himself dry of anything which mattered except...

"And who did you lose back here?" she asked at the end.

"My father." He was trying not to see tattooed fists and thick, drink loosened lips.

The front door clicked, and the landlady peered into the lounge.

"I bought digestives," she said. "I hope that's all right?"

⌘⌘⌘

At ten the next morning he walked the beach again. The cormorant was absent, but there was wrack from the previous night's tide – the floats from fishing nets, and great brown blades of kelp tugged up by a squall. He wanted to avoid the sad Armistice ceremony at the town Cenotaph, and the annual parade of bedraggled Cubs and Sea Cadets.

A Slow Remembered Tide

Back in town by three, he saw discarded poppies on the streets. With a doner kebab rebelling inside him, he watched buses leave for Hull and York. Their departures told him only that he wasn't on them.

Corinne watched him at dinner that evening, as he moved mince and potatoes around on his plate.

"Alright, he was a bastard," he said to the waiting silence. "My father. He worked the freighters out from Hull – Merchant Navy. Sometimes he was away for a month or more. That wasn't so bad. He came back with money, and then we had it all for a few days – presents and hugs, trips out, whatever we wanted."

She moved her chair nearer. "And after that?"

"He drank. Bought rounds for everyone, a man with a hundred mates while he had the cash. Then the long nights. Waiting for him to get back, lying in the dark and listening to my mother cry as he shoved her around – or hit her." He looked up, angry. "She tried not to cry out too loud, in case it woke me."

"You were always awake, though."

He couldn't express his sullen anger, the poison that lay in his thoughts. He told her of the 'incidents' which ended in the Casualty Department - "She slipped and fell badly, didn't you, old girl?" his father lied. A night when his father gave him a drunken hug and said he loved him – but the next morning, breakfast was on the floor and she was crying in the bathroom.

After his father broke her arm and came close to laying Christopher himself out with a wild swing, his mother had told him the full story of Martinmas, the truths which she had hidden before. That was the year before his father died, before a storm off Denmark pitched George Mainprize into the North Sea for the last time.

"At first I thought her talk was a sort of escape. Her fantasy, a way of pretending there was something more enduring, more important. And when I knew better, when I believed her, I couldn't - I can't – cope with it, with what we are supposed to do, knowing he's out there."

John Linwood Grant

"You need to be kind."

"To him?"

"To yourself. There's whisky in my room. Help yourself to it and try to sleep. I'd join you, but they are waiting."

"I know."

When she left, he was alone with an aching head and a grease spattered tablecloth. He went upstairs. In the half-dark from the landing, his room was the sea. The cry of a night gull, the low throb of waves, the smell of the wide waters. At the open window, he saw lights down on the far beach, a handful of bright dust.

By the bedside lamp – frayed cord and yellowed shade – he read the letter that had come that morning. She must have posted it before she drove him up here. She was at her mother's place in Surrey. She didn't want to be with him again, no blame, simply resignation.

A lone seabird shrieked, and church bells sounded. He knew which church, and why. He knew that his father, the bloody-fisted bastard who had ruined his childhood, would hear them too.

Whisky laced his boots and tugged on his jacket. The front was quiet.

There are fewer of us each year, she had said.

The gathering was far down the shore, by the mouth of Auburn Beck where it ran into the sea. Lost Auburn, a village taken back by the North Sea and held tight to its breast, like it held his father. The beck was a fair walk, and he could get there too late, claim good intentions…

Church bells rang out again, and he picked up his pace, heart pounding. Once there would have been torches of tar, and ship's lanterns on poles – now mostly flashlights and mobile phones lit the water's edge, though some bore oil lamps.

It wasn't as large a gathering as he'd expected. Less than thirty. The last celebrants of something older than the town itself.

He edged closer. A burning torch sputtered and flared, held by a tall figure standing ankle-deep in the water…

"Corinne!" he shouted.

A Slow Remembered Tide

She turned, as did the man nearest her. The clergyman seemed little older that at their last meeting – perhaps a slight sinking of the cheeks, but nothing that challenged his strength or resolve.

A flashlight shone in his face, making him blink. When his vision cleared, Steve was there, only a few yards away. The man's face struggled between relief and doubt.

"Are you..."

"I'm here," said Christopher.

"So you are," said Corinne, handing him her torch, a length of wood with one end a mass of twisted rope and pitch. The smoky flame created more shadows than there should have been.

"The tide comes," said the vicar. "We have this day, or none, until another year passes."

Men and women stood with their boots soaking up the saltwater, a cold wind on their faces as they faced the sea.

"Auburn and Hartburn. Owthorne, Monkwell and Ravenser Odd." The vicar, reciting as if he were tolling off the names of saints. "Lost but remembered."

"Great Colden and Ringborough," called another.

"Newsham and Turmarr." Corinne's voice, followed by the names of ships, so many ships. Dutchmen floundering on the sands; trawlers driven onto the rocks.

"The St Ninian, the Falmouth..." That last one lost to a U-boat off Hornsea. The recitation grew, and Christopher found himself adding those he could remember from his mother's list.

"This is The Time, our last harvest of the year." An old man spoke up, his voice cracking, and Christopher recognized him as one of the men from the coffee stall. He was still wearing his poppy. "Winter comes, and we would not leave them out there, alone. Let them join us, let them rest within us and by our hearths. We bring them in, we offer them remembrance."

John Linwood Grant

The man bared one arm and cut into the wrinkled flesh with a small knife. There was little blood. He shook his arm over the incoming tide, letting the water take it.

"Others forget; we do not."

Christopher saw other around him do the same, and hesitated, but Corinne was there, holding out a thin blade.

"For the Old Hallows," she said.

"For the Old Hallows." He took the knife and cut into his arm, wincing; she led him closer to the water, so that the dark red drops were shared with the sea.

The listing of lost settlements and ships was over, the heart of Martinmas begun. The names of men, women and children were spoken over the tide, people calling them out, at first in turn, then together in a jumble of voices. He shivered, listening to the litany of the dead. There were gulls above, echoing the names in their cries.

"We bring you in," the vicar called out. "We are refuge and remembrance. We are here, before the year's turning. A haven for the drowned."

Christopher felt it, then - the pale host of fishermen, tangled in nets, torn by propellers, and the strong swimmers who found riptides which were stronger. Small children lost in two inches of water; ploughmen who dared the low cliffs too close to a storm. Those who took lifeboats out, and never returned; sailors who barely felt the splinter that pierced them or fell under the rattle of machine gun fire. And the hopeless souls, those who flew from cliff-tops to free themselves… so many, so very many.

"We call you back for another year and we are here to hold you, who are not lost whilst we remain." Four or five of the celebrants spoke as one. "We bring you to the land, that we may carry you all of our days."

The whispers had become voices, counterpoints to the names cried out by the living. The dead came with flashes of silver, borne on the

A Slow Remembered Tide

flanks of fish. They closed on the celebrants in the writhing of the kelp beds, their loneliness forgotten.

"We bring you to the land, that we may carry you all of our days," Christopher repeated.

His body shuddered with memories which were not his, offering shelter to those who had passed. Some were angry, some shrouded in solitude, but there was no threat. The momentary pain of welcoming them was nothing, for each of them sought only remembrance.

The gulls urged them in, the lost and drowned, and Martinmas held Christopher in its grip. He called out a dozen names - he knew them from his mother, from the gravestones which surrounded her. He echoed them from others' lips, crying out the name of Corinne's son as well. A man in the water fell to his knees, sobbing, his arms outstretched; Steve and his wife were the far side of the vicar, swaying with the impact of what came.

There was one more name, inescapable. A man who only Christopher could truly remember.

In the torch's flare he saw the black rock standing proud of the waves, a cormorant waiting, sinuous neck in motion. Corinne gripped his free hand.

His father was in the myriad voices, only one of the many hundreds being drawn from the cold, uncaring waters. Once he had hated his father; now he could hold him, safe, and let the passing year judge them both...

"George Mainprize," he murmured, and his throat tightened. "Dad!"

⌘⌘⌘

And there were beasts in the water, all manner of silvered fish, and the deep pools of seals' eyes were witnesses to the drowned.

And Auburn had its Martinmas.

Illustration by Alan Sessler

Witch Woman
by Hayley Arrington

A witch woman on a wolf did ride in the gloaming.
They followed the moon over three hills
Till they reached the place of ash and oak, in their roaming.

With her staff, the witch woman stirred the air to foaming.
All boiled and roiled and gave her the chills.
A witch woman on a wolf did ride in the gloaming.

Diurnal creatures of the forest began homing.
They were called thence by her dusk-filled thrills,
Till they reached the place of ash and oak in their roaming.

The wolf called to his brothers and sisters, all howling,
Feeling blood quicken from all their kills.
A witch woman on a wolf did ride in the gloaming

And she saw spirits enter that woodland, all yowling.
All nature harkened to her wild will
Till they reached the place of ash and oak in their roaming,

And with wild limbs they danced her sylvan spell to forming.
No longer could her magic stand still:
A witch woman on a wolf did ride in the gloaming
Till they reached the place of ash and oak in their roaming

A very special thank you to our Kickstarter Contributors

Lars Sveen
Lars Backstrom
Charles Wilkins
Jason Smith
Bob Riordan

Printed in Great Britain
by Amazon